4,80

"THIS ISN'T PART OF THE SCENE."

Simon brought Blyth's fingertips to his lips, and her hand jerked. "No?" he asked.

"No."

His grasp made her thumb move against his mouth, his teeth, his lips. "Shall I stop?"

"Y-yes."

He looked up, the tip of his tongue still grazing her skin. Her cheeks were flushed; her eyes were heavy and bright. "And if I don't?"

"I'll make a fuss."

"Will you?" His arm slid about her waist. He had to be closer, had to feel her near to him. "Will you, indeed?"

Her mouth was close to his, so close that he felt her breath as she spoke, felt it as his own. "Yes."

"I don't believe you, princess." He lowered her hand, though he didn't release it, and was gratified to feel her fingers cling to his.

"You'll not make a fuss over me," he said, and lowered his head. . . .

◁ W9-AOS-979

WONDERFUL LOVE STORIES

☐ **SECRET NIGHTS by Anita Mills.** Elise Rand had once been humiliated by her father's attempt to arrange a marriage for her with London's most brilliant and ambitious criminal lawyer, Patrick Hamilton. Hamilton wanted her, but as a mistress, not a wife. Now she was committed to a desperate act—giving her body to Hamilton if he would defend her father in a scandalous case of murder.

(404815—$4.99)

☐ **A LIGHT FOR MY LOVE by Alexis Harrington.** Determined to make the beautiful China Sullivan forget the lonely hellion he'd once been, Jake Chastaine must make her see the new man he'd become. But even as love begins to heal the wounds of the past, Jake must battle a new obstacle—a danger that threatens to destroy all they hold dear.

(405013—$4.99)

☐ **IN A PIRATE'S ARMS by Mary Kingsley.** They call him the Raven. His pirate ship swoops down on English frigates in tropical seas and he takes what he wishes. Taken captive while accompanying her beautiful sister on a voyage to London, spinster Rebecca Talbot is stunned when the handsome buccaneer winks at her and presses her wrist to his lips. She daringly offers to be the Raven's mistress if he will keep her sister safe.

(406443—$5.50)

*Prices slightly higher in Canada

Buy them at your local bookstore or use this convenient coupon for ordering.

PENGUIN USA
P.O. Box 999 — Dept. #17109
Bergenfield, New Jersey 07621

Please send me the books I have checked above.
I am enclosing $_____ (please add $2.00 to cover postage and handling). Send check or money order (no cash or C.O.D.'s) or charge by Mastercard or VISA (with a $15.00 minimum). Prices and numbers are subject to change without notice.

Card #_____ Exp. Date _____
Signature_____
Name_____
Address_____
City _____ State _____ Zip Code _____

For faster service when ordering by credit card call **1-800-253-6476**

Allow a minimum of 4-6 weeks for delivery. This offer is subject to change without notice.

Masquerade

by

Mary Kingsley

A TOPAZ BOOK

TOPAZ
Published by the Penguin Group
Penguin Books USA Inc., 375 Hudson Street,
New York, New York 10014, U.S.A.
Penguin Books Ltd, 27 Wrights Lane,
London W8 5TZ, England
Penguin Books Australia Ltd, Ringwood,
Victoria, Australia
Penguin Books Canada Ltd, 10 Alcorn Avenue,
Toronto, Ontario, Canada M4V 3B2
Penguin Books (N.Z.) Ltd, 182–190 Wairau Road,
Auckland 10, New Zealand

Penguin Books Ltd, Registered Offices:
Harmondsworth, Middlesex, England

First published by Topaz, an imprint of Dutton Signet,
a division of Penguin Books USA Inc.

First Printing, September, 1997
10 9 8 7 6 5 4 3 2

Copyright © Mary Kruger, 1997
All rights reserved

 REGISTERED TRADEMARK—MARCA REGISTRADA

Printed in Canada

Without limiting the rights under copyright reserved above, no part of this
publication may be reproduced, stored in or introduced into a retrieval
system, or transmitted, in any form, or by any means (electronic, mechanical,
photocopying, recording, or otherwise), without the prior written permission of both the copyright owner and the above publisher of this book.

BOOKS ARE AVAILABLE AT QUANTITY DISCOUNTS WHEN USED TO PROMOTE PROD-
UCTS OR SERVICES. FOR INFORMATION PLEASE WRITE TO PREMIUM MARKETING DIVI-
SION, PENGUIN BOOKS USA INC., 375 HUDSON STREET, NEW YORK, NEW YORK 10014.

If you purchased this book without a cover you should be aware that this
book is stolen property. It was reported as "unsold and destroyed" to the
publisher and neither the author nor the publisher has received any payment for this "stripped book."

To my nephews,
Scott, Mark, and Jay Kruger,
who have added so much richness
and joy to my life,
from Aunty Mary.

Chapter 1

It was a fine day to die.

Standing in the tumbrel as it trundled along London's roughly paved streets, Simon Woodley swayed to keep his balance, inside and out. London was enjoying an uncommonly fine summer's day, he thought detachedly, studying the crisp blue sky that arched overhead, dotted here and there with billowy fair-weather clouds. For weeks, months, he had languished in Newgate without a sign of the sky. Now it seemed as if that patch of blue would be the last thing he'd ever see.

For the tenth time he tested the bonds holding his wrists behind his back; for the tenth time they held firm, testimony to his jailor's thoroughness. Oh, they weren't about to let him go, not him. He was an itinerant actor, found standing over the body of a respectable Canterbury merchant, a bloody knife in his hand. The trial had been swift, the judgment final: death by hanging. Simon grimaced at the thought, swallowing against a persistent lump in his throat. He'd thought little of death; at eight and twenty, why should he? But when he had considered it he'd seen himself elderly, able at last to play the fine Shakespearean roles youth denied him, Prospero or Macbeth or even Lear. There were also those who thought he'd meet his end at the hands of a jealous husband, but . . . ah, well. If he had loved not wisely, at least he had loved well. He regretted now that he hadn't done so more often.

Oxford Street was becoming more congested as the procession neared Tyburn. There were other tumbrels behind his, for hanging days were held only eight times a year, a cause for public holiday. Behind the tumbrels rolled hearses, black as night, and the mourning wagons. The condemned had had their final service in Newgate chapel, in an enclosure that contained a symbolic coffin; the procession had stopped at St. Giles to give the convicted their traditional last drop of beer, before facing the last drop of the gallows. In the distance tolled the deep, doleful bell of St. Sepulchre's Church; ahead there was nothing but the scaffold.

Assuming a pose of cool indifference, face blank, shoulders relaxed, Simon surveyed the crowd that lined both sides of the street. Looked like his death would draw more of an audience than his appearances onstage ever had. The crowd was a motley collection of urchins and streetwalkers and respectable tradesmen, all come for the spectacle of a public hanging of a vile murderer. Him. And though he'd committed many a sin in his life, he was certain he didn't deserve this.

Deep in the crowd, which was pressed close against a rickety half-timbered building and huddled under the overhanging eaves, walked a woman. There was nothing remarkable about her that he could see; she was dressed in a gown of some greenish stuff, with a laced bodice and a white shift beneath, and a neat cap hiding her hair. Young, though, if he was any judge, and passably shapely, yet that wasn't what was so unusual about her. In this crowd of leering, jeering, taunting spectators, she was the only one not watching him.

The tumbrel had slowed to a crawl, its progress impeded by the press of people. From the corner of his eye he could see scaffolding in the distance, and he turned his head sharply, watching the woman as she made her slow progress against the crowd. Anything to keep from thinking of what lay ahead; anything to stay upright, strong, shoulders braced, as if nothing much mattered. And the woman intrigued him, because no matter how much the crowd yelled, no matter how she was pushed or jostled, she simply would not look at him.

Turn your head, he commanded silently, staring at her, turning on the full force of his will and his charm, as he did when he faced an audience across the footlights. It was power, to hold the emotions of an audience in sway, to make them sigh or laugh or gasp. Occasionally, though, there would be one person who wasn't convinced, one person who would sit back, arms crossed, daring him. Daring Simon to make him believe that the words he spoke were real and not the product of a skilled playwright. *They* were his challenge, those people; they were the ones he played to, and when he saw the dawning belief in their eyes, when he knew he'd won them over, he felt joyous, powerful, able to do anything. He wanted to see that look now on her face, to know that she believed in the role he played so hard. He wanted it to be the last thing he remembered when the noose was slung around his neck.

The tumbrel came to an abrupt, jolting stop, and Simon lost his balance. Unable to catch himself, because of his bound hands, he pitched forward, stumbling to his knee. " 'Ere, now, wot you think yer doin'?" Craddock, his guard, demanded, and grabbed Simon's arm, jerking him roughly to his feet. "You'll not escape us. Not with that"—he nodded—"awaitin' you."

He wouldn't look. Simon knew if he did, he'd be lost. But he'd been caught off guard, forcibly reminded that he was a prisoner, and as he straightened up he saw it. The scaffold, with its stairs leading up. The gallows. And, finally, the gibbet, from which hung a new hempen rope, tied in the intricate coils of a noose. For him. The knowledge slammed into his gut, and in that moment his pose, his poise, deserted him. In that moment, the woman in green, caught in the midst of the crowd, looked up.

Ah, but she had a face like a flower, eyes blue as the sky and features as delicate and precise as a cameo. She was his salvation, something to distract him from the horrors ahead. Strands of hair escaped in wispy curls about her cheeks and trembled against her lips, full and pink and parted. In dismay? He didn't know. He knew only that she was seeing what everyone else in the crowd saw, a convicted felon, a desperate murderer, about to meet his Maker. And that, God help him, was not how he cared to be remembered.

It wasn't easy. Not with the image of the gibbet swaying before him, not with the thought of the long walk up the staircase and the short drop into eternity. Difficult, but he'd played to hostile crowds before. Slowly he gathered the remnants of his role about him: legs outspread in a wide, confident stance; shoulders braced and broad; and his head up, with just the faintest hint of a disdainful, mocking smile upon his lips. By God, he'd done it, he almost felt that way again, brave, defiant, and because of that, because the woman continued to stare, her eyes wide and distressed and startled, he did something quite in character with his role. He winked at her.

She wasn't going to look. Blythe Marden kept her eyes determinedly ahead and her shoulders hunched, turned away from the spectacle unfolding to her left. A hanging. The thought made her shudder, and yet the crowd about her was in holiday mood, as if a man's death were something to be celebrated. They chattered and laughed, hoisting children to their shoulders to gain a better view, carrying baskets of food and jugs of ale, quite as if they were going on a picnic. And all the time the tumbrel trundled slowly on, the man it carried standing tall and straight and proud, scornful of the racket going on about him. He was a convicted murderer, that Blythe knew, and so probably deserved to die; but even so, she would not shame him by staring at him like some exhibition in a zoo.

A man pushed ahead of her, treading heavily on her foot, and she pulled back, wincing. Not a word from him, of apology or even acknowledgment, as he went on, adding his shouts to the cacophony aimed at the condemned man. Blythe pressed harder against the wall of the crumbling old Tudor building, though she was already close to it, and wished herself anywhere but here. Anything would be preferable: listening to Mrs. Wicket, her employer, harangue her about the lack of morals in today's young people, of which she herself was apparently a shining example. Administering one of the noxious potions that Mrs. Wicket insisted would ease her palpitating, excitable, and, in Blythe's opinion, healthy heart. Even, God help her, she thought, shuddering with distaste, rubbing Mrs. Wicket's swollen, bunion-laden feet. Instead, she was out in this ravening mob, trying to reach the apothecary's to obtain yet another potion Mrs. Wicket had heard of, and which Blythe, doctor's child that she was, knew would do absolutely no good. Not that Mrs. Wicket would listen to her. Blythe was only her companion, and so her opinions were of no value.

Yet another man stepped in front of her, blocking her way, and at the same moment an exultant roar went up from the crowd. Involuntarily Blythe looked up, and her breath caught in her throat. The tumbrel carrying the condemned man had come to a stop, its progress halted by the sea of humanity flowing about it. Inside the tumbrel the man who had held himself so proudly was being hauled to his feet. He was staring at her. For just a moment Blythe saw across the distance separating them something she would never have expected: stark, heart-rending fear. It rose up within her, too, cutting off her breath, choking her, as the reality of what this man faced struck her. He was about to die, and he knew it.

Then it was past, that look, as if it had never happened. Unable now to keep from staring, she watched as he drew himself together again: braced his legs in a confident stance, threw back his shoulders, raised his head. But he was young, she saw in surprise, surely not much beyond her own years, and, really, rather handsome. The loose stained shirt and breeches torn at the knees could not disguise a body built tall and broad. Though his pallor spoke of weeks without sunshine, prison had not broken him. He stood at ease, a man with tawny hair clubbed back and tied with a ribbon, a man who would be comfortable whether with a king or among rabble. A man who was, she knew, deathly afraid, though she doubted anyone else in the crowd saw it. He had courage and pride, and that he was going to his death seemed suddenly a monumental crime.

"Murderer! Now you'll know what it feels like!" someone yelled in the crowd near Blythe, and she blinked. She'd forgotten. He'd killed a man in cold blood, stabbing him again and again until he was past death, and all for money. A sordid crime, and why Blythe had felt any sympathy for him, she didn't know. Suddenly ashamed of the compassion that had swamped her earlier, she began to turn, and at that moment the man in the tumbrel did something truly astonishing. He winked at her.

For a moment Blythe stood rooted to the spot, while hot waves of shame washed over her. He'd seen her staring, no better than anyone else in the crowd, and how had he reacted? With courage and humor and—how dare he?—flirtatiousness. Well! He was shameless. Doubtless he deserved all that was coming to him. She'd not waste a moment's more thought on him.

Blythe turned sharply away, her gaze set on her destination at last, the apothecary shop at the next corner. She would not—would not!—look back at the man in the tumbrel, trundling along again as the soldiers forcibly cleared a path, though she could feel the almost magnetic pull of his gaze. Of all the people here today, why had he chosen her? Helpless, she turned back, in time to see the tumbrel pulling ahead and the crowd closing in behind. His eyes met hers over the bobbing heads of the people separating them, and then the crowd swallowed him up, hiding him from view. He was gone, and for the life of her Blythe didn't know why she felt so bereft.

*   *   *

She was gone from his view, shielded by the ravenous crowd. Simon tightened his lips and raised his head, not caring anymore. The farce would end in a few moments. There was no longer any need to play his role. Around him people jeered and yelled, but he paid them no heed. The gibbet was ahead, looming ever closer and closer, and how he'd come to this pass, he didn't know. He only knew he was not a murderer, no matter how the circumstances appeared.

The tumbrel lurched to a stop. Unprepared, Simon stumbled forward a step, and the crowd roared approval. Instantly he straightened. Well, and hadn't he faced hostile audiences before? Provincial louts who jeered at plays they didn't understand; young fellows on the town who came prepared with overripe tomatoes and worse, should the performance not meet their expectations. Usually Simon defied them all, fueled by their scorn and his own stubborn pride into giving a performance that won them all over. He would not do differently now.

And so he assumed his role again, holding his head high, a cool little smile upon his face. Never show your fear, he'd been told long ago when first he trod the boards, and he'd be damned if he'd show it now. Besides, he thought, his smile turning ironic, he'd always wanted to play London.

" 'Ere, you, time to face wot's comin' to you," a voice said roughly, and a hand grabbed at his arm, jerking him off balance. The crowd roared again, and Simon pulled his arm free.

"You needn't drag me, my good sir," he said, his voice cold. "I know what comes next."

"Oh, you does, do you?" Craddock cackled, grabbing Simon's arm again. "Well, you just watch yourself, 'cause I ain't goin' to let the likes o' you escape. 'Ere, it's the scaffold for you. Hung good and proper, you'll be."

Better to be well hung. The errant flash of gallows humor caught him by surprise, turning his haughty sneer into a smirk. The smirk lasted as he was dragged from the tumbrel onto the uneven cobblestone paving

of the street. Beyond he could just see the fresh green
of Hyde Park and the market gardens that marked
London's western end, peaceful in contrast to the pan-
demonium surrounding him. The crowd pressed closer,
unimpeded by tumbrel or guard, their yells harsh and
their breath foul upon Simon's face. Their cheers were
joined by those of the well-to-do, who had paid good
money to sit in specially constructed stands. Why this
glee at his hanging? Who was he to them?

A clicking noise, of metal on metal, caught his attention as he was pulled through the crowd to the
small clearing surrounding the scaffolding's stairs. Still,
Simon would have paid it no mind had not a hand
suddenly caught at his sleeve. "Alms for the blind," a
voice whined, and, startled, Simon looked down at the
beggar. He was a sight, his hair dirty and disordered,
his face thick with many days' grime, and his rough
clothing torn and faded and patched. In his outstretched hand was a tin cup, clattering with a few
sparse pennies. The gray eyes turned up to Simon
seemed milky, sightless, and very, very familiar. With
a jolt, Simon recognized the beggar. It was his uncle
Harry.

"I have no alms, old man," he said, his mind racing
furiously. To see his uncle here was not surprising;
Harry had never deserted him before. But in the guise
of a blind beggar? Hope rose unbidden within Simon.
Something was going on.

"Bless you for your kindness, my son," Harry said.
"Friends will watch over you."

" 'Ere, you, get away," Craddock said, shoving past
Harry. Simon let himself be pulled along, forgetting
his self-appointed role. Friends watched over him? He
raised his head, scanning the crowd, and would have
stopped in surprise had Craddock not continued to
pull at him. By God, that was young Henrietta over
there, dressed as a youth, as usual, because of her
height. And the foul-mouthed harridan who screamed
at him as he passed—good God, Aunt Bess! She and
Harry were the leaders of the theatrical troupe of
which Simon was a member; Henrietta was their

daughter. That meant the others must be close by, as well. Something was going on, indeed.

The clearing at the base of the scaffold was at last reached. Soldiers stood at the ready, muskets held across their chests, bayonets fixed, watching both the crowd and the prisoner. More soldiers stood to the side, beating a steady tattoo on their drums. Still more were on the platform, along with the executioner, his face shrouded by an ominous black hood, and a priest of some sort. Simon flicked a cursory glance at the priest and then returned his gaze. By all that was holy, the priest was Ian, his good friend and fellow actor.

He stumbled up the stairs, muscles tensed, not with fear of what was to come, but in anticipation. He had no idea what Harry had planned, but there was a part in it for him somewhere, aside from victim of the gallows. When the time came for him to play his role, he would be ready.

He was at the top of the stairs now. All about him was a sea of humanity, and he could find no familiar faces in the jeering, jostling crowd. Yet he had no doubt they were there. The thought gave him strength as he was shoved forward, onto the trapdoor that opened onto eternity. "Do you have any sins you wish to confess, my son?" Ian said, in mellifluous tones, coming forward with a Bible clasped in his hands.

"Many, vicar," Simon said, lowering his head. "What's afoot?" he added in the quick, piercing stage whisper he'd learned as a child.

"The rewards of the just. Be ready, my son." Ian straightened as the executioner came forward. "Have you any last words?"

The noose settled about Simon's neck as heavily as a steel collar. "Only that I wish you and yours good fortune, Vicar."

"God will provide." Ian stepped back. The executioner placed a hood over Simon's head. Simon swallowed, his Adam's apple working convulsively, and Ian could almost smell his fear. Simon was brave, but at a time like this, when it was just a man and his Maker, what must he be thinking of? Worse was that he was innocent of the crime; of that Ian was certain. It was why he and the other actors had launched this rescue attempt. Pray God it would work, or Ian knew he himself would suffer the punishments of the damned.

From the base of the scaffold, drums beat out a sudden tattoo. The executioner laid his hand on the lever to open the trapdoor, and a deep, expectant hush fell over the crowd. It was at that moment that an impressive array of produce began to fly up from the crowd: Rotten lettuces and cabbage, old potatoes and last year's apples hit executioner and soldiers alike, with an overripe tomato landing with a glorious splat in the middle of the executioner's hood. He staggered back, and though his grip on the lever loosened, he managed to pull it, just enough for the trapdoor to unlatch. Simon's feet slipped on the suddenly slanting surface; the noose settled tightly about his throat, and he began a desperate dance, trying to regain his footing.

As he struggled, there was a sudden blue flash from the base of the scaffold. Ian had been expecting it, but even so his eyes were dazzled for a moment. Still, in the confusion no one noticed him jump forward. A quick slash of his knife, and the noose was cut free. With Simon's weight now fully on it, the trapdoor opened. "Go with God, my son," Ian murmured, as Simon, still bound, still blinded, fell through the trapdoor. It quickly banged shut from below. Ian's job was nearly done.

He rubbed his eyes, as if he had been dazzled, too. "Look!" he yelled, pointing toward the crowd. "He's getting away."

Only a few of the soldiers heeded him, but that was enough. They jumped off the platform, and others quickly followed. Good. With all the confusion, Simon's whereabouts just might still be unknown. And it was time, Ian thought, to make his own departure. "Exit, stage right," he muttered, and slipped down the scaffold's stairs.

*   *   *

Simon fell through space, legs flailing in panic, and was caught by hands holding his arms, his shoulders. He struggled, but then the hood was pulled off his head and he saw his captor. "Uncle Harry!" he gasped.

"Quietly, lad." Harry's voice was urgent as he cut the bonds that held Simon's wrists. "We haven't much time."

"Uncle—my God. Where are we?" he asked, stupidly, for events had happened too quickly for him to comprehend them.

"Under the scaffold. Phinney and Henrietta are creating a distraction. Phinney's made up to look like you, by the way. Let's get that off you." Harry pulled the noose over Simon's head. "Bess, the paint—"

"Yes, Harry," Aunt Bess said placidly, quickly stroking lines across Simon's forehead. Charcoal, Simon realized, and at last guessed what they were doing.

"Who planned this?" he demanded, shrugging into the rusty black coat Harry held out.

"Quietly, lad. Henrietta did. Girl's got a good head on her shoulders."

"Some powder for your hair," Bess said, reaching up to untie the ribbon that held his queue. "There! You look quite the old man now, with that gray hair."

"And you'll need this." Harry thrust a cane into Simon's hand. "Aye, you look the part, but remember, lad, looking's only part of it."

Simon grinned. "I remember," he said, and grasped the walking stick, bending over it. He knew the disguise was crude; he knew that the illusions of the stage were usually all too apparent when seen up close. His family was risking their very freedom to gain him his, however. He could not but fall into their scheme. "How would an old man think, feel—"

"Exactly. I taught you well. Now. There's no time to lose. There's a cart waiting at Hyde Park Corner. Ordinary farmer's cart, you know the thing. Old Gaffer's driving it."

"I'll make for it. And you?" Simon said, sobering.

"We'll take care of ourselves, lad." Harry's voice was gruff as he pushed Simon out through a loose board from the dubious haven under the platform. "Go with God, lad."

"You, too, uncle. Aunt." Simon gazed at them, the only real parents he had ever known, and then turned, slipping into the milling, tumultuous crowd. He was free. He was also still in danger.

No one noticed Simon; they were too involved in their own survival. What had been chaos only a few moments before had intensified into something close to a riot. Close by, two men were brawling, throwing punches with more enthusiasm than accuracy, while a woman pummeled one of them on the back, screeching at the top of her lungs. More men fought in another mad tangle of arms and legs, while in the distance Simon could hear musket shots. Most people seemed intent on escaping the square, pushing and jostling each other, so that few made any progress, and more than one pickpocket plied his trade with zest. It was, in short, the best opportunity Simon would have for escape.

Shoulders hunched, muttering as if he were a crazed old man, Simon raised his walking stick, prodding a backside here, a leg there. Men swung around at this fresh indignity, but fell back when they saw him, old and obviously infirm. In most circumstances, Simon knew, the artificiality of his disguise would be obvious. The charcoal lines on his brow, the gray powder in his hair, would never pass close inspection. Today, however, no one challenged him; nor did anyone applaud, though it was the performance of his life.

Ian was gone from the scaffold, Simon noted as he pushed and shoved and prodded his way across Tyburn Lane. Nor was Henrietta anywhere to be seen, or any of the other actors Simon was certain had been here. He was on his own, but that was just as well. His family had endangered themselves enough for him. Now he had to gain his freedom and thus justify all they had done.

Musket shots sounded again, closer this time, and

the people nearest him scattered in panic, nearly knocking Simon over. Somehow he stood his ground, glaring at the soldier who stood only a few feet away, musket leveled. "Shooting helpless old men now, sonny?" he said in a voice that cracked and quavered, and the musket lowered, the soldier turning as bright a red as his uniform. He was very young, Simon noted, little more than a boy.

"Sorry, old man," the soldier stammered. "Go on your way."

"What is the world coming to?" Simon muttered, turning. The crowd was thinning, and the pedestrian walkway was just on the other side of the chain-and-post barrier. Once he reached it he could blend into the crowd, and slip down the street to Hyde Park Corner. Only a few people stood between him and freedom. Unfortunately they were soldiers, apparently returning from trying to find him; worse, one was Craddock. Cursing to himself, Simon abruptly changed direction, plunging into traffic to cross Oxford Street, though it was the opposite of where he wanted to go. He'd have to take a more devious route to his destination and hope that Old Gaffer was still there. Still hunched over the walking stick, he shuffled along, muttering, not looking at anyone. Ahead was a quiet side street, nearly empty; once he reached it, he would be safe. Ten feet, then nine, then—

" 'Ere, you!" a voice yelled. "Yes, you, old man!"

"Eh?" Simon turned his head, squinting. Bloody hell. The soldiers were coming toward him, Craddock leading them.

"For God's sake, Craddock," one of the soldiers said, "what's this old bugger got to do with anything?"

"Mayhap he saw somethin'," Craddock said.

"Him? Look at 'im. Likely blind as a bat and deaf, to boot."

"Eh?" Simon cupped a hand behind his ear. *Run*, his instincts screamed, every inch of him quivering with the need to escape. Only by great discipline did he hold still. If he ran, he would only attract attention.

The soldiers were laughing. "Run along, old man," one of them called. "Don't get into any trouble."

"Eh?" Simon said again, but he began hobbling away, leaning heavily on the walking stick. "What is this world coming to, soldiers stopping them what's minding their own business—"

A man blundered up before him. Startled, Simon straightened, pulling himself up to his full height. "Bloody 'ell!" Craddock yelled. "Hey, you! Stop, I say. Woodley!"

Simon's reaction was involuntary. At the sound of his name he turned, realizing a moment too late what he'd done. "Hell," he exclaimed, and gave up his pose, gave in to the voice inside that screamed louder and louder. *Run!*

"It's 'im!" Craddock yelled again. "Stop! Stop, I say, in the name of the king—"

"Ready weapons!" someone else yelled, and a musket shot rang out. And Simon, feeling a sudden, sharp pain, realized he'd been hit.

"Things are finally settling down, miss," the apothecary said, looking out onto Oxford Street through the heavy glass windows of his shop. "Looks like they've got the carts heading back to Newgate at last. Won't be any hanging today, until they catch that Newgate saint who escaped." He turned away from the window. "It might be safe for you to go. There aren't as many people now."

"Good." Blythe jumped lightly down from the high stool. It had been a frightening hour, waiting out the riot that had erupted when, so they'd heard, the killer who was to be hanged had disappeared from the scaffold in a flash of light. The spectators had scattered in all directions, making the apothecary take up station at the front of his shop, truncheon in hand, against anyone who dared intrude. It appeared now, though, that the danger had passed. "Mrs. Wicket will be furious as it is that I haven't returned with her potion." She and the apothecary exchanged quick, conspiratorial smiles. Mrs. Wicket might have been

one of his best customers, but he knew as well as
Blythe that her complaints were mostly imaginary. "I
hope she doesn't turn me off after this."

"If she does, miss, you'd have no trouble getting
another position, I'd be bound," he said, smiling
warmly at her.

Blythe paused very briefly in the act of straightening
her mobcap. Good heavens, was the apothecary flirting with her? Well, she'd dealt with this kind of trouble before. A woman alone in London learned to
protect herself quickly. "Thank you," she said frostily,
and sailed past him, head held high. "Good day."

"Good day, miss," he stammered behind her as she
gently, but quite firmly, closed the door.

Blythe wasted no time, but quickly set off along
Orchard Street, away from the remaining tatters of
the crowd and toward the quiet of Portman Square.
It was madness to have ventured onto Oxford Street
this morning, but things had now settled down. She
allowed herself a smile as she walked. It was pleasant
to have a man flirt with her, she admitted, even if she
did have to discourage that kind of thing. Even if the
apothecary, a widower, was well known to be on the
catch for a wife to care for his six children and help
out in the shop. Blythe shuddered. She longed for a
home, a family of her own, sometimes with an intensity that scared her. But she had already spent most
of her life in service to others. If she ever married, it
would be because she was wanted for her, herself.
And that, she thought gloomily as she turned into
Portman Square, was not likely to happen.

The square was deserted, with an eerie calm over-
laying the scene. The fine houses had a closed-up look,
partly because their owners had repaired to their
country estates for the summer, but also because of
the events of the last hours. People would be safe
inside, away from escaped killers and roaming soldiers
alike. Not a person moved, not a bird sang in the
trees, and in the unnatural hush some remnant of danger remained. Alert, aware, Blythe quickened her
steps, wanting now only to reach Mrs. Wicket's, and

safety. She'd had quite enough excitement for one
day, she was thinking as she passed a fine townhouse,
when there was a quick scuffling noise from an alleyway, followed by a flash of movement. Before she
could react, her arm was caught in a strong grip.

"Don't scream. I'll not harm you," a low masculine
voice said, and, startled, Blythe looked up at a face
she'd glimpsed only briefly but would never forget. It
was the man in the tumbrel, the killer who had somehow escaped the scaffold. She was now his prisoner.

Chapter 2

Blythe froze, her limbs turning to jelly, her heart pounding arrhythmically. She couldn't help it. In times of danger, when other people might scream or struggle, she went still, mute, frozen into silence. It shamed her, this weakness, and yet it was how she'd always reacted to danger. "Please," she managed to croak out.

"I promise I'll not harm you," he said again. "If you'll just play along."

Blythe forced herself to look at him. His skin was shiny and pale, his hair disordered. He looked different than he had in the tumbrel, older, but in a grotesque way. "Whatever is that on your face?" she asked in a reasonable tone, feeling as if she had split into two people. Outside she must appear normal; inside she quaked, watching the goings-on with fear and a strange detachment.

He grimaced. "Charcoal. Come, princess. We'll walk a bit and then I'll let you go. If you play along."

"An odd word. Play."

"Ah, but all the world's a stage." He smiled, but his grip on her arm hadn't relaxed. Nor had his gaze, vigilant and ever moving, searching for danger. "We are all merely players, Miss—"

"Good gracious, are you an actor?" she burst out.

It surprised a laugh from him. "As it happens, madam, yes. And is that worse than being gallows bait?"

Blythe flinched, an involuntary action, and tried to pull her arm free. "Please let me go. I'll not tell anyone I saw you, if you'll let me go."

"I can't, princess." He sounded genuinely regretful. "They're looking for a man alone, you see. But a man and a woman together, that's different."

"I won't go with you." Blythe surprised herself by stopping still. Her first panic had worn off, to be replaced by a deeper fear. If she gave in to this man without a struggle, what might happen to her?

"No, princess?" His voice was soft. "I'd hate to have to hurt you, but . . ."

The words hung there. "But you would."

He sighed, shrugged, an elaborate lifting of his shoulders. "One does what one must. I'd much prefer"—he tugged at her arm—"that you walk with me and talk to me. 'Tis too long since I've heard a woman's voice."

"Talk!" Blythe stared at him as he dragged her along the slate walk. She wondered if any of the people in the neat brick townhouses that fronted the square were watching, witnessing what was happening to her. "Of what should we talk?"

"Of anything, princess." He smiled, and she saw that his teeth were surprisingly white and even, his eyes unexpectedly bright. "Of the flowers in that garden, or London in the springtime. Of the color of the sky. In Newgate," he said, softly, "I thought I'd never see the sky again."

Blythe glanced up involuntarily as she stumbled alongside him, seeing to her surprise that the sky overhead was deep blue. She hadn't noticed earlier, so intent had she been on her errand. Nor had it mattered. "How long were you in prison?"

"Too long." He glanced quickly at her. "I didn't do it, you know."

She nodded. "Of course not."

His eyebrow rose. "You believe me?"

"No. But 'tis what I'd expect you to say. Of course, you'll do what you have to, to keep me from escaping."

"I see." His mouth was a thin, grim slash in his face. "I won't make you tolerate me for long. Just until—damnation!"

Blythe glanced along the street they had just turned

into and saw what had caught his attention. "Soldiers," she said in relief.

"Yes, damn their eyes." His grip on her arm tightened, and without any warning he dragged her aside, down some stairs into the service entrance of a nearby house. This time she did let out a noise, a squeak of surprise, and his hand quickly covered her mouth.

She froze again, her limbs going limp as he continued to drag her, into a hollow formed by the house's front stairs and stoop. "Hush, now, and all will be well," he whispered.

All would be well? The words penetrated Blythe's haze of terror. Why, he must think her quite the fool if he expected her to believe that. A man such as he, prone to violence, could have only one end in mind for her. He couldn't leave her alive, a witness to his escape.

Oddly enough, the thought cleared the last vestige of fear from her mind, leaving in its place a clear, crystal calm in which her every sense was heightened. She was aware of the man holding her, of her back to his chest, of the masculine heat and smell of him, so different from what she was familiar with. She heard, as if there were thousands of them, the soldiers' footsteps; she felt her captor's muscles tense as the soldiers approached. And she could see, absurdly, that beyond the stone of the stairs, it was indeed a fine day. Too fine a day to die.

The footsteps neared; her captor's hand tightened on her face, and it was too much. Squirming, she twisted her head away, and his hand followed, giving her the opportunity she sought. Acting on instinct, she bit down hard on his thumb.

He let out a muffled exclamation of surprise and pain, and yet his grip tightened. "Do that again and I'll strangle you," he whispered harshly in her ear, and beyond the stairs one of the soldiers stopped, his feet scuffing the pavement.

"Did you hear that?" the soldier said. "Thought I heard someone yell."

"Spread out," a voice commanded tersely, and the

sound of booted feet running echoed loudly in the service entrance. "D'ye see anything?"

"Nothing, Captain," a voice came from some paces away. "Haven't seen hide nor hair of no one on this street."

"He's here someplace." The captain's voice was grim. "He was seen heading toward the square."

More echoing sounds as the footsteps returned. "All's quiet, sir."

"Damme. He's here. If I have to, I'll search every house. . . ."

"D'you want me to start, Captain?" someone asked after a moment.

"What? No. No. No need to alarm anyone. You're right, no sign of him here. So why are you hangin' about?" he said, his voice suddenly loud. "Move out!"

The footsteps marched away. Behind Blythe her captor let out his breath, though his muscles were still tight. "If I take my hand away, will you promise not to scream?" he said, his voice low.

Blythe nodded, and a moment later the pressure was gone from her face. She took her first free breath in what felt like hours, gathering herself, and his hand slammed over her mouth again.

"You promised you wouldn't scream," he said, and at that Blythe sank her teeth into his thumb again. "Ow!" He pulled back. "Now what did you go and do that for?"

"I was not going to scream," Blythe said, with as much dignity as possible, considering she was sprawled back against a strange man's chest. "A lady does not go against her word."

"A lady, are you?"

She turned her head sharply. There was no trace of a smile on his face, though she'd heard the amusement in his voice. An actor. That meant he was capable of putting on any pose he desired. "And you, sir, are hardly a gentleman."

He clapped his hand to his heart. "Madam, you wound me."

"Oh, pish," Blythe muttered, and began to scramble away.

"No." He caught her back, and this time she fell against him, her chest to his chest, their faces much too close, and, as for their lower limbs—well! It was a situation not to be borne. "It occurs to me that we have not been properly introduced," he said, and this time the smile reached his face. "I am Simon Woodley, madam. At your service."

"If you are truly at my service, Mr. Woodley, then you will let me go," she hissed.

"No. I'm sorry." He seemed genuinely regretful. "Not quite yet, Miss . . ."

Blythe stared at him stonily. "What do you plan to do with me, sir?"

"Nothing so very much." Something sparked in his eyes. "But as I am a convicted murderer, I daresay I can think of something."

"I'll scream!"

His eyebrow arched. "After giving your word?"

Blythe glanced away, biting her lip. They both knew she couldn't fight him. "Please let me go."

"Not quite yet." Gripping her arm, he set her aside and got stiffly to his feet, grimacing as he looked down at himself. "Well. This costume was none too clean before, so I suppose a little more dirt won't hurt it. But as for you . . ."

"What about me?" Blythe asked, eyeing him suspiciously.

"Much too clean." And before she could protest, his large, hard hands were rubbing dirt on her cheeks. "Much too proper"—pulling off her mobcap—"and much too neat."

"Stop it!" she cried, as he tugged at the ribbon that bound her hair. It fell in a heavy curtain about her shoulders, more nuisance than anything else, and she pushed it back. He pulled it forward again, tangling his fingers in it and disordering it further.

"Oh, please—"

"There." He stepped back a pace, regarding her with satisfaction, his grip still tight on her arm. If he intended to rub dirt on her clothing, then she really would scream. The full skirt and laced bodice of dark green wool, worn over a linen shift, weren't beautiful, but she had few clothes. And she didn't want him touching her body. "I don't suppose you'd lower your shift to your shoulders—"

"Touch that, sir, and you'll pay!"

"Will I?" He stepped back, his eyebrow arched again. She wondered irrelevantly how he did that. "Some spirit at last? Good."

"Good?" she protested as he stepped cautiously out of the service entrance. "There is nothing good about the situation, sir."

"I don't agree." His teeth flashed in a smile. "We're alive. What could be better? Do you know any drinking songs?"

"What? I should say not."

"I was afraid of that. Very well, then, I'll have to carry you. Metaphorically," he explained at her startled look, as he pulled her out onto the street. "No soldiers, but I'll not assume we're safe yet. Now. You needn't do anything. Just play along." And with that he slung an arm around her shoulders, leaned heavily upon her, and began a slow, weaving, and apparently drunken progress down the street. "Pretend to be supporting me."

"I don't have to pretend, you oaf!"

"Heavy, am I? My apologies." There wasn't a trace of remorse in his voice. "Don't worry, it won't be for long," he said, and launched into a loud, off-key song. " 'Oh, McKinley is dead and McKinley don't know it.' "

"Hush! People will look."

"That's the idea, dearie. 'McKinley is dead and McKinley don't know it.' "

"I am not your dearie."

Simon swayed toward her. " 'They're both of them dead and they're lyin' in bed,' " he bellowed. "Then tell me your name."

"Oh, very well. Blythe Marden."

"There, Miss Marden, and was that so difficult?"

"If I am found out to be with you, my reputation will be ruined," she hissed.

He had the nerve to laugh at that. "My apologies, Miss Marden, but there's more than reputation at stake here. Except for my acting abilities."

"Which are atrocious."

"Now you wound me, Miss Marden." He leaned a bit harder on her, and she staggered. "Are those soldiers up ahead?"

Blythe glanced up. Just ahead was Oxford Street, with its throngs of people, offering a hope of safety. And, indeed, soldiers. "I believe so," she said with grim satisfaction, "and when they see me with you—"

"They will think you helped in my escape, and then what will happen?" His voice was almost gentle. "Don't stare at me so. I know you're innocent, but will they?"

"I will tell them, sir!"

"Looking as you do?" He clicked his teeth. "Not quite the thing, Miss Marden."

"Oooh! Because you—you—"

"Precisely," he said, and launched into song again. " 'And neither one knows that the other one's dead.' "

The soldiers, now only a few feet distant, glanced up, coming instantly to attention. With their muskets held across their chests, they were threatening, menacing. And not just toward the felon who held her captive. Toward her, as well. Blythe's heart sank. Under other circumstances the soldiers would be a welcome sight. Now, though, she knew what they were seeing: two apparently inebriated people making an erratic progress along a quiet, peaceful street. If they recognized her companion as the escaped criminal, would they think her his accomplice?

"What do we do?" she whispered.

"Just play along. It will be fine. And a good day to ye, my foine sirs!" Simon's voice boomed out. "And would ye be after havin' a wee drop on ye?"

One of the soldiers sniggered, until a look from the captain stopped him. "You, there," he barked. "What is your name?"

"Me name, sir? Sure, and it's Seamus O'Reilly, late of Dublin. Ah, me, is there not a drop to be found about here?"

The soldier sniggered again. This time the captain ignored him. "What is your purpose here?"

"Me purpose? Why, came to see the hangin', 'tis sure I did. Foine day for it."

"And a fine thing it is when you let the gallows bait escape," Blythe said in a shrill, nasal voice she hardly recognized as her own. She was aware of the start of surprise that ran through Simon. "A fine thing when you've come for a bit of a lark, like, and it don't 'appen. I've got a mind to complain to someone, I do."

Several of the soldiers were openly smiling now, and the captain had relaxed his stance. "Believe me, madam, no one regrets today's events more than I."

"Well, and such fine talk. Ye're a true gent, sir, that ye are," Blythe said, and lowered an eyelid in an exaggerated wink.

The soldiers laughed, and Simon suddenly leaned more heavily upon her, making her stumble. "Oh, go along," the captain said, the corners of his mouth twitching, as if he held back a smile. "Before we take you in for being a public nuisance."

"Thank'ee sirs, thank'ee kindly," Simon said. "Sure, and we'll be on our way."

"True gents, ye are," Blythe added, tossing them another glance over her shoulder, and then they were past, plunging into the traffic of Oxford Street. Surely he would let her go now.

He didn't. Somehow they managed to avoid the carts and drays and hackneys that seemed to proceed at a mad dash; somehow he managed to keep her close to him, away from anyone who could lend aid. Blythe tugged away, turning toward a soberly dressed gentleman as they reached the other side of the street, and Simon leaned more heavily upon her, making her stumble. "Don't even try," he said in a low voice.

"But you're safe now." The crowd was behind them now as they hurried along North Audley Street, as quiet as Portman Square had been. "Surely you can let me go."

"Not yet. Where did you learn to act?"

"I never did." That sense of being two people overwhelmed her again. "I don't know what came over me."

"You could have a career on the stage if you decided to stop being—what is it you are?' Someone's good wife?"

"No. I am a companion to an elderly woman."

"You?" He looked down at her, and something sparked in his eyes, as if he were truly seeing her for the first time. "A waste, princess."

Blythe could feel herself flushing. "Where are you taking me?"

"Just to Hyde Park Corner."

"Why?"

"I expect to meet friends there. And once I'm away, you may tell everyone how I held you captive. If"—he grinned—"they'll believe you after that performance."

Blythe's lips thinned. "None of this was by my choice, sir."

"But a fine companion in crime you've been, madam."

She cast him a look as they continued along the street, passing more neat townhouses of yellow and red brick, and the occasional fine home of the gentry. "Are you never serious?"

"Life is too short to be serious, princess."

"Life is too short not to be. Haven't you any goals, any ambitions—"

"Lord help me, don't, princess. Don't lecture me."

"But how can you live like this, outside the law—heaven knows what you do to survive—and how can you live with yourself, knowing what you've done?"

Simon's mouth tightened in a grim line. "I didn't do what they said I did."

"No? And I suppose they hang innocent men?"

"Sometimes," he said, and his voice and eyes were so sincere that her breath caught. Why, he might very well be innocent, at that—but he was an actor, she reminded herself. It would be foolish to believe him. "We turn here for Tyburn Lane, and then Hyde Park Corner. Just a few more feet, princess, and you'll be free."

"Why do you call me that?"

"What?"

"Princess."

He considered her for a moment, and she saw for the first time that his eyes were not merely brown, but had golden flecks in their depths. "It suits you."

"Ha." It wasn't quite a laugh. "No one in my life has ever thought so."

"Then that is a shame, princess, and someone should do something about it. Have you a sweetheart?"

"I hardly think that's any of your concern. Who is it you're looking for?"

"Ah, then you haven't. Another shame. And I'm looking for a farm cart, with an old man driving."

"Where?"

They turned onto Tyburn Lane, the double row of walnut trees that lined Hyde Park at its eastern boundary shading them with leaves just turning the rich emerald of summer. "At the corner, they said, but—damnation." He stopped abruptly, jolting her off her feet for a moment, so that she swayed against him. "Where in hell is Gaffer?"

"Who?"

"Never mind. The less you know, the better."

"There's no cart here," she pointed out. There were other conveyances along the road, of course: fine phaetons and town coaches; the mail coach from Reading, rattling by with the horn blowing; there were people on foot and on horseback. What was not there was a farm cart with an old man driving it.

"Damn. He probably had to move on." Simon straightened, releasing her at last, and she rolled her shoulders in relief. "I'll have to go on my own."

"Thank heavens for that!"

"And you'll have to come with me."

Blythe, edging away, was stopped by his grip on her arm. "No!"

"Yes," he said, and began walking east, away from the park, dragging her behind him. "You're my best chance of escape."

"I won't go!" she protested, scurrying to catch up with his long-limbed strides. "They'll remember me, you said that yourself—"

"Can't be helped."

"I won't go." Blythe set her feet, resisting the tug of his hand. "I just won't."

"Won't you?" He turned, and his voice was deadly soft, his eyes alight with an emotion she couldn't recognize. "Have you forgotten who I am, then, madam? A foul murderer."

Blythe swallowed around a lump in her throat. "No. But I'll not go, all the same." She straightened, and where she found her courage, she never knew. "Even if you do kill me."

"Kill you?" he said, and, surprisingly, laughed. "Ah, but then, sweeting, I lose my safe conduct, do I not? No, you're safe for now, but for all that, you're coming with me." And with that he turned and began walking again, dragging her along Constitution Hill.

"I'll scream."

"*Tch.* After giving your word?"

"Everyone knows women have no sense of honor," she said, and dug in her heels again. "Help! This man, he's—"

"Damnation!" Simon exclaimed, catching her to him, though she struggled. And before she could protest, his mouth slammed down on hers.

Chapter 3

The kiss fell on Blythe's mouth, opened in readiness for another scream. She found herself locked in his arms, held tight against his chest, and though she struggled, tried to turn her head, it was to no avail. His lips sucked hungrily at hers, his tongue—good heavens, what was he doing with his tongue? She recoiled at the touch of it against hers, and yet something jolted to life within her. Warmth uncurled in a slow stream, low in her belly, and her arms, as if with a will of their own, wrapped themselves about his waist. God help her, she was kissing him back, and she couldn't seem to stop.

It was Simon who broke the kiss, pulling back and regarding her with eyes dark and unreadable. "Well, princess," he said finally. "Someone's taught you how to kiss."

"What? I never—"

"Too late now, princess." He grinned. "But I'll keep your secret."

"There's no secret to keep—"

"No? Who will believe you did not willingly kiss me? Not with"—he gestured toward the street—"all these witnesses."

She glared at him. "It was a trick. So I'd have no choice but to go along with you."

"Of course it was." He dragged her along. "I do not usually accost women in the street. Even when"—he glanced at her, his eyes glinting—"they kiss as you do, princess."

"Stop calling me that."

"Mmm. Yes. This charade's wearing thin." He

stopped abruptly, and she stumbled. "You're right. They'll be looking for both of us as we are now. You look like a harridan."

"Oooh! And whose fault is that?"

"If I restore you to propriety, madam, will you accompany me?"

"Being rid of you will restore me to propriety."

To her surprise, he chuckled. "I don't think so, sweeting. But we can do something about how you look. Have you a kerchief?"

"Yes, but—"

"Wipe off your face," he commanded. "And put your hair back up in this." From inside his shirt he produced her mobcap, the linen wrinkled and crumpled. Blythe snatched at it, glad to have some semblance of normality returned to her on a day when all was topsy-turvy, though the cap carried with it his scent. Not much, just a hint, but enough to disconcert her. "Useful to have props."

She looked up at him as she finished stuffing her hair, as neatly as possible under the circumstances, into her cap. "Props?"

"Your cap." He nodded toward her hair. "My cane—but I had to discard that. Ah, well." He caught her arm again, pulling her closer against him. "I shall just have to lean on you, daughter."

"Daughter!" Blythe stared at him in disbelief as, hunching over, he seemed to age thirty years before her eyes. He leaned upon her quite convincingly, too, making her almost stagger as she walked, reluctantly, beside him. "You are a thorough rogue. Why is it you haven't been hanged before now?"

"Luck," he said, and though his face was set in the querulous lines of infirm old age, laughter lilted in his voice. "How is it you are not married?"

"I hardly think that's any of your affair."

"Come, princess." He turned his head, allowing, for just a moment, a youthful grin to penetrate his disguise. "I think we know each other well enough by now to converse politely. After all, we are partners in crime."

Blythe stared stonily ahead. The bulk of Bucking-
ham House, in its fresh green garden, rose at her side.
With each step she was farther from her home, and
safety. "Where are you taking me?"

She thought she heard him sigh. "Just across the
river," he said, his voice thin and reedy again as they
encountered passersby. "You are my safe conduct
pass. I am an aged man, in the seventh age of life.
Who would suspect me and my daughter?"

"Your hostage, you mean." She paused. "You won't
let me go," she blurted out.

"Of course I will, princess." He looked at her slantwise. "Why wouldn't I?"

"Because you know I'll tell everyone where you
went."

"Ah, but princess, d'you think they'd believe you?
For it's willingly you come with me. Or so it appears."

"But I'm not—"

"Likely they'll take you in, too, for helping me. I've
made a mull of it," he mused. "Well, I'll make it
right, somehow."

"I doubt it. Please." She hated the pleading in her
voice, hated the weakness. "I'll not tell anyone about
you if you'll just let me go."

"I'm sorry, princess," he said, sounding genuinely
regretful. "I need you to help me out of London. But
I'll make a bargain with you."

"What good will that do me?"

"If you'll help me escape London, I'll let you go.
And," he went on, as she opened her mouth, "in such
a way that no one will suspect you."

The look she gave him was suspicious. "How will
you do that?"

"Well . . . I don't suppose you have any rope, do
you, princess?"

"Rope? No. What in the world for?"

"I'd tie you up. Not tight, of course, but—"

"You would, wouldn't you?"

"Think, princess. 'Twill make you appear more my
captive." His eyes twinkled. "Good props are always
handy."

"We're not in a play," she retorted. "God help us, you're enjoying this, aren't you?"

"I'm alive, princess." His voice was soft. " 'Tis more than I expected from this day."

Blythe glanced quickly at him, but his face, so mobile, was wiped clean of expression. She couldn't trust him, of course. Keep up her end of the bargain, help him escape, and who knew what he would do? He was an escaped murderer, a criminal with no scruples, and he'd use her as he wished. If she didn't go along, however, what was likely to happen? At the very least, she'd be hurt. He was desperate; he'd have to do something to keep her from calling attention to him. And he was right: The longer she stayed with him, the less likely it was that anyone would believe her. Oh, she was in a dreadful coil, and what she was to do about it, she didn't know.

Simon's brow was cold with sweat as he staggered along, glad of his captive's arm to lean on. Damn, but his leg hurt. Though a quick inspection had shown that the musket ball had only creased his skin, it had bled profusely and now, covered by a rag torn from his shirt, blazed with pain. The only good thing about the wound was that it was high on his leg, where the dark cloth of his breeches wouldn't show the blood. Unless he started bleeding again. And if he did, thereby giving away his identity, no use of props would save him.

"There's a crowd ahead," Blythe said. "What shall we do?"

They were on St. George Street, which, by the size of the crowd ahead, led to Westminster Bridge; to their right rose the Gothic towers of Westminster Abbey. Simon paused a moment, thinking. Damn, if only he'd time to powder his brows, as well. He'd have to make do with facial expressions to simulate age. "We'll turn here," he decided, swinging her into a wide grassy area leading to the north entrance of the abbey, heading toward the river. There lay his best chance of escape.

"You'll be caught."

"Not yet." He injected confidence and strength into his voice. If she knew how he really felt, how scared he was, she'd escape from him in a minute, and that wouldn't do. He truly did need her, at least until he was out of London. And, to be honest, she was turning into an intriguing companion. Quarrelsome, maybe, but a blessing. At least, he'd thought so when he'd seen her walking in Portman Square. Under the stairs where they'd hid from the soldiers, with her close against him, he had concentrated only on escape. Only when he'd pulled off her cap had he suddenly thought differently

Sweet Jesus, he was a desperate convict, but he was also a man, and any man would be affected, tempted, by Miss Blythe Marden when she let her hair down. Without her cap, her honey-colored hair tumbled past her shoulders, making her appear at once younger, prettier, more vulnerable. More striking yet was the streak of paler hair arching back from her brow like a thunderbolt, an unusual and arresting feature. Pity such hair had to be covered, he thought, looking at her slantwise and seeing her pale face, her tight lips. Pity, when she was so unexpectedly attractive and alluring, and not just because he had been months without a woman. Skilled as he was at disguise, aware of the impact even a small change could have, he knew well that that pale streak of hair would make her far more memorable to the soldiers that chased him. He wondered if she realized that, and the power it gave her. He devoutly hoped not. It would be good to end this day with a whole skin.

Blythe shifted under the heavy weight of his arm. "How much farther?"

He looked up from under his brows. "Just until we're over the bridge. Then I'll let you go."

"Pish."

"Do you doubt me, princess?"

"Huh. After these past hours?"

"Now, you wound me, you do. Have I actually hurt you?"

"You've abducted me! And—"

"Hush, princess, not so loud," he said, as a man passing by glanced at them. "We're nearly there." Already he could smell the river, the mingled odors of fish and tar, and other, less wholesome things, for the Thames was the sewer of London as well as its water supply. Though he could not see it for the maze of old buildings that pressed closed together along the waterfront, still he had no doubt that they were near the crossing. "To the Rubicon, it is," he muttered.

"What?"

"Nothing to worry yourself about, daughter."

"No. You're the one should be worried. If I scream—"

"Then I'll have to kill you, won't I?"

His voice was so matter-of-fact that Blythe faltered. "With people as witnesses?"

"Aye, but I'm a condemned murderer already. What is one more death on my conscience?"

Blythe swallowed hard. There was a glint in his eye that warned her not to pursue the subject, a dangerous glitter of desperation and recklessness. So far he'd not hurt her, and in truth she didn't think he would. He was an actor, after all, and could be playing a part. But he was, as well, a murderer. She would do well to remember that, and do as he commanded. Once away from London, perhaps she could escape. "What would you have me do?"

"Act properly submissive, as a daughter should," he said promptly, the glint in his eyes deepening. "If that is not too difficult for you."

"I'll have you know I'm a very proper daughter."

"Are you, now? And do you always speak to your father as you do to me?"

"But you're not—oh, never mind," she said, exasperated. "Very well, I'll be a proper daughter. Though you are a most improper father."

His arm twitched. "I hope not." His face was oddly grim as he looked up. Their faltering progress had brought them to an intersection thronged with people and carts and other conveyances with disgruntled drivers. "Ah. Westminster Bridge."

Westminster. Blythe repeated the name to herself. She'd seen little of London since arriving to become Mrs. Wicket's companion, having stayed more or less in Marylebone. She would have to remember the route she took now, when he finally let her go. If he let her go. "There's a crowd."

"I expected it. Can you see the bridge, daughter?"

"What?" Blythe peered ahead, and through the crowd she could just see a massive stone railing. "Yes."

"I am an old man, and frail. I need you for support, and when I talk I don't always make sense. Tell me what you see."

"People." Blythe frowned. "A great many, heading to the bridge, but slowly. I wonder—ah!"

"What?"

"There are soldiers on the bridge." Her voice dropped involuntarily. "I can't see how many, but there are at least three and they're at this end."

"A barricade. I might have known." His voice sounded grim. "Are any of them familiar?"

"I don't know—no, I don't think so."

"Well, that's something at least."

"You're surely not going to try to cross here?"

"All the bridges will be barricaded, daughter, and the others are across the city. Nothing to do but to see it through," he said, as he pulled her forward into the mass of humanity waiting to cross. "Mind your part, now."

"Yes, Mr.—Father."

He grinned quickly, no more than a flash of teeth. "Oh, a dutiful daughter. What's all this crowd, then?" he said, raising his voice in the complaining, thin tones of infirm old age.

A man ahead of them turned, his glance amused. "Soldiers, old man. Stopping everyone who wants to cross."

"Soldiers? Stopping a man from traveling in his own country?" Simon's voice trembled with indignation and weakness. "Something should be done, I say!"

"There's an escaped murderer loose. Haven't you heard?"

"A murderer!" Blythe exclaimed, injecting the proper notes of horror and fear into her voice. It wasn't hard. "Father, did you hear that?"

"What is this world coming to?" he muttered, pressing down on her arm as they staggered forward a few steps. "Murderers running around loose, while soldiers stop innocent people. I tell you, daughter, this is a wicked world."

"Yes, Father. I wish we'd never left Tunbridge."

He peered up at her. "Eh?"

"Tunbridge Wells, Father. Do you not remember? His mind isn't what it once was," she explained in a low voice to the man ahead of her, who watched them with amusement. "To think he was once one of the finest preachers in the south of England—"

Simon choked. "My hearing's still good, missy, don't you forget that."

"Yes, you old fool," she muttered.

"Eh?"

"Of course, Father." Her voice was clearer now, and she exchanged glances with the other man. Odd, but what she was doing felt natural, right. She had that strange sense of disassociation again, that feeling that she was standing outside herself watching; that sense of wonder as from somewhere inside she found the proper words and actions. Never had she done such a thing before today—or had she? She frowned as they neared the approach to the bridge. Yes, she'd played the dutiful daughter before, and if the stakes hadn't been quite so high as they were now, still it had been important.

"Mind your step, Father." She reached out to help him onto the bridge and felt his large, cool hand close over hers. For a moment she was aware only of the contact, the touch of his skin, soft from his confinement, and yet hard as only a man's hand could be. Large, and very strong. She had no doubt he could wreak mayhem upon her with those hands, with violence. Or caresses.

Blythe stumbled, and this time it was Simon who saved her, though he staggered, too. "Mind your step, daughter," he scolded. "You'll land us in the river."

"I'm sorry, Father. The soldiers are just ahead," she added in a lower voice.

"How many?"

"Three—no, four. Three regulars, and an officer."

"And the barricade?"

"They've got a cart across to block the way, and they're questioning people as they come near."

Simon nodded. "As I expected. You'll have to answer their questions."

"Me! But there are two of us."

"I'm a senile old fool. You'll handle it."

"But what will I tell them? Where we are going, where we've been—"

"Think of something. Quickly, now. We're almost there."

Blythe bit her lip. Only a few people stood before her and the crude barricade. Two soldiers barred the way, while the officer frowned menacingly at the people he questioned. At the other end of the cart another soldier stood, musket held ready, as traffic entered the city. Leaning against the solid stone railing of the bridge was yet another man, watching the proceedings with a detached and yet curious air. He was a most stylish figure in a dark blue frock coat edged with braid, with an embroidered waistcoat and a fine fall of lace at his throat. He appeared harmless, a spectator only, Blythe thought, until her gaze met his. His eyes were hard, cold, glittering, making her look quickly away, a chill chasing through her in spite of the day's warmth. Her world was all topsy-turvy when she felt more menace from a curious stranger than from the escaped criminal beside her.

"You, there!" the soldier barked as Simon, tugging on her arm, shuffled forward. "Halt!"

"Father!" Blythe exclaimed, grabbing Simon's arm to hold him back. "Father, wait."

"Eh?" He squinted up at her, hand cupped to his ear in a parody of deafness. Oh, this was terrible. He'd left her to get them out of this mess. "What's that you say?"

"We have to stop," she said, enunciating clearly, and at the same time more aware than she had ever been of her accent, pure Kent. "Father, please. There's some problem."

"Problem?" Simon's lids drifted shut. *"Anno domini, veni, vidi, vici,"* he muttered.

" 'Ere, what's that he's saying?" the soldier asked, musket held across his chest. "Sounds foreign."

"He's praying," Blythe improvised, hoping that that was indeed the effect Simon intended. "He's—"

"Is there a problem here?" the officer said from behind the soldier.

"Ave Maria, gratia plena," Simon muttered.

"My father's upset," Blythe put in, nearly choking. It was one thing to try to fool the soldier with schoolboy Latin, but officers were traditionally upper-class. This man might very well recognize Simon's doggerel for what it was. "My father prays when he's upset, and—"

"Name?" the officer barked.

"Er—Sally Smythe. With a *y*, not an *i*."

"And his?" A jerk of the thumb toward Simon.

"Hieronymous," she blurted out, and felt Simon's arm jerk. "The Reverend Hieronymous Smythe."

"Reverend, eh?" The officer peered down at Simon, eyes narrowed. "Where's his collar, then?"

"He doesn't always wear it. In truth, sir"—Blythe's voice lowered—"he's not quite right in the head."

"Eh?" Simon squawked. "What is that you say?"

"I said you have trouble hearing, Father."

"Eh?" He twisted his head, hand to his ear. "Nothing wrong with my hearing."

"Only if you shout," she muttered.

"Eh?"

"What is afoot, sir?" She looked directly up at the officer, deliberately batting her eyes. "I heard something about an escaped prisoner."

"That is our problem," the captain said loftily. "Were you in town to see the hangings?"

"Goodness, no! We spent the day at Mr. Poole's in St. Margaret Street. He is a retired minister, like my father."

"And he'll vouch for you?"

"Of course he will, and his daughter and house-keeper, as well!" Blythe let indignation creep into her voice. "Do I look as if I consort with criminals?"

"Where are you from?"

"Tunbridge Wells."

The officer's glance was sharp. "You've a ways to go, then."

"We will be staying with relatives in Lambeth. The, ah—"

"Smythes?" the officer put in.

"Certainly not! My dear mother's family. They are Ramsbottoms," she added proudly.

Beside her Simon jerked again. "Ramsbottom?" the officer said, his eyes narrowed.

"An old family, sir, goes back to the *Domesday Book*. Wool, you know. There are those who say"—she leaned forward—"that my mother married below herself."

"And where is your mother?"

"Gone these past five years, and Father hasn't been himself since." She shook her head, casting a sorrowful glance at the man who leaned against her, lips silently moving and gaze blank. "He is all I have now."

"Er, yes." The officer was frowning, and Blythe wondered if he had believed a thing she said. "I think—"

"Please, sir, may we pass? My father is not strong and I fear for what will happen if he's made to stand much longer."

The officer waved his hand in dismissal. "Yes, yes, go on. Shall I summon a hackney for you?"

"Oh, no, 'tisn't far, and I fear we cannot afford it. But I do thank you for your kindness. Good day to you, sir."

"Good day," the officer said absently, his attention now on the crowd behind Blythe and Simon. They were beyond the barricade, onto the bridge. Free. Almost.

"You're an accomplished little liar," Simon said through the side of his mouth.

"Father, such a thing to say! Someone is watching us," she went on, her voice low, urgent.

Simon's steps immediately faltered, and she staggered under his weight. "A soldier?"

"No. There's a man nearby, watching everyone—there, he's looked away."

"Who is he?"

"I don't know, but there's something about his eyes." She shuddered. "He scares me more than the soldiers."

"Likely no one of importance." He twisted his head to look at her. "Hieronymous? Ramsbottom?"

"The officer didn't believe Smythe, even with a *y*," she retorted. "And what of you, spouting Latin?"

"Ramsbottom," he mused. "So now I know what you think of me."

"If you didn't already."

"Careful, princess. I've not let you go yet."

Blythe stepped from the bridge onto solid ground at last. They were out of the city. "When will you?"

"Soon." He continued to limp along beside her, as if he really were infirm. "When we're well away from the bridge."

"But—"

"Think, princess. If the soldiers see you coming back without me, they'll be suspicious. And they'll remember you. They'll remember those names."

"Then I'll return by another route."

"You'll have to." From his cramped, hunched position Simon peered ahead. Compared to London, Lambeth was rural, with the great Tudor bulk of Lambeth Palace rising to their right, and fields surrounding them. He was more exposed than he had been within London's crowded streets, and yet he felt safer already. Lord knew he'd never expected things to turn out as they had. He'd be better traveling alone; he'd make faster time. But until he was certain he was away from danger, he needed the woman upon whose arm he leaned. The strain of the day showed on her face. What would happen when it came time to part, he could not say. She was a danger to him, though perhaps not in the way he'd first thought.

The golden light of early evening surrounded them as they emerged at last from the village into the countryside, their shadows falling long before them. "The sun will set soon. If I'm to be back in London before nightfall, I'd best go."

Simon glanced back along the dusty road and, seeing no one paying them heed, straightened at last. "If you have a place to go to."

"Of course I do. I told you, I've a position as companion—"

"And you've been away all day."

"I'll manage that, thank you."

"By telling who I am, and where I am?"

Blythe looked up at him. No longer slouching, he now loomed over her in the gathering dusk. He had released her, and yet he was near, a threatening reminder of all she'd done this day. "You're not going to let me go," she said.

Simon stretched, his arms flung out, back bent until it cracked. "Ah, that feels good. I might, princess. If . . ."

"If?"

"You give me your word you'll not tell about me."

"My word! How will I explain about myself, else?"

"You'll think of something. Quite a liar, you are, when you've a mind for it."

"I'll have you know, sir, that I am an honest woman."

"Mm-hm. But if you tell of what happened today, your reputation will be in shreds, will it not?"

"I—" Blythe closed her mouth. On that end, he was right. Her reputation was likely in ruins already. "That's a chance I'll have to take, sir, for I do intend to tell everything that happened to me. Including that you forced me to cross the London Bridge."

"Westiminster," he corrected automatically, and then grinned at her, eyes gleaming. "London Bridge?"

"Yes, and you mentioned heading south, did you not?"

"Mayhaps I did." A smile spread slowly upon his face. "An honest woman you may be, princess, but you've a talent for storytelling."

"A good enough talent?"

"What do you mean?"

She faced him steadily. "Will you let me go?"

"Princess, I would never have hurt you."

Her eyes widened. "But—"

"I had chances enough to do so, did I not?"

"But there were people around, and—"

"I am not a murderer, Blythe."

Blythe clamped her lips shut and looked away. Murderer or not, he was right. For all the time she had been in his company, he could have harmed her, and he hadn't. Perhaps she had known, deep down, that he wouldn't. "Then I am free to go?"

"You always were, princess. But I thank you for your help." He bowed low, sweeping off an imaginary hat with a flourish. "Now leave, so you'll not see where I go."

She had never been in danger. If she had tried, she could have left him. "Ooh! I should proclaim to the world just who and where you are."

"But you won't, princess." He grinned. "Not after giving your word."

"I haven't."

"You will."

Blythe paused. "Oh, very well. I won't reveal where you are."

"Good lass. And may I say, 'tis been a pleasure sharing the road with you." He reached for her hand, catching it before she could pull back. "It has been an honor knowing you, madam," he murmured, and pressed his lips to her palm. They were warm, firm, and dry, and their touch sent an odd tingling sensation through her arm, making her jerk away.

"I cannot say the same," she retorted, and turned

on her heel, stalking away. She was free! She could hardly credit it, but he'd let her go. Free, and she could go on with her life as if today's bizarre incidents had never happened. Letting herself relax for the first time in hours, she glanced back, certain that her captor would be well out of sight. Instead, he stood watching her, lips twisted in what might have been a smile, before turning away. And then, with a sudden loud grunt, he toppled to the ground.

Chapter 4

Blythe stood irresolute, looking first one way, toward freedom, and then back at Simon. It was a ploy, of course, to make her return to him. It had to be. Still, as she watched him struggle to his feet, old habits urged her back. She had a training of sorts in medicine. If he was hurt, she had to help him.

Simon, still on one knee, looked up at that moment and gestured impatiently for her to go. Again she looked back toward London, and then, with a little sigh, set her shoulders and trudged toward him. "Are you hurt?"

"Bloody hell," he said through clenched teeth, finally getting to his feet. "I told you to go."

"Are you hurt?"

"Not to signify, no." He turned, took a step, and promptly stumbled. All of Blythe's healing instincts rose up. She rushed toward him, propping her shoulder under his arm. This was no trick. Good an actor though he was, surely even he couldn't fake the way his skin, sheeny with sweat, had gone ashen.

"Not to signify," she mocked, staggering under his weight. "Why, you can hardly stand."

" 'Tis my problem." His voice was clipped. "I told you to go. I'll travel light on my own."

"Doubtless, but I suspect you won't get very far. Is it your leg?"

The glance he gave her was full of suspicion. "Yes, but 'tis not serious. The musket ball—"

"You were shot!"

"—only broke the skin."

"Were you shot?" she demanded, wrapping her arm

about his waist and guiding him to the low stone wall that edged the road. "By whom, and where?"

Simon took another step, grimacing. "By a soldier near Tyburn."

"Not that kind of where, silly. Here. Sit on this wall. Whew!" She stood back as he half collapsed, half sat on the wall. He was a big man, tall and broad. Before, when he'd leaned on her, still he'd managed to carry his own weight. Not this time, though. That made her wonder how he had ever managed to get through London, with all its soldiers and good citizens chasing him, and he injured. For the first time she felt a reluctant admiration for him. "Where on your person?"

He looked up at her and, in spite of the strain creasing his face, actually managed a smile. "On my thigh, princess, in back and high up." The smile widened to a grin. "Rather an intimate place."

She would not blush. "I see." She nodded, taking refuge in briskness. "Well, get over behind the wall and let's have a look at it."

He gaped at her. "What?"

"I said I'll take a look at it."

"But—" For the first time since she'd met him he appeared at a loss for words, staring at her with jaw dropped. "Madam, I shall offend your modesty."

"You won't be the first man I've seen naked," she said shortly, and swung herself over the wall. "Here, I'll help you. Mind your step. It's dry here, but uneven."

Simon didn't move, but continued to stare. "What did you say?"

"I assure you, Mr. Woodley, yours will not be the first bare bottom I've seen. Now, are you coming or will I have to drag you?"

Her bluntness had the desired effect; it sent color rushing into his face, making her bite her lips to hold back a grin. For once, she had the upper hand. "Madam, your help will not be required."

"Nonsense. You won't get two steps without me."

"I'll manage. You don't realize—"

"What I'm talking about? But I assure you, I do,"

she said, relenting. "My foster father is a doctor. I've helped him since I was quite small."

Simon ran a hand over his face, and she could sense his weariness, his confusion. "Why are you doing this?"

"Heaven knows. But if I wanted to harm you, all I would have to do now is run to a house and tell them who and where you are."

"Bloody hell. You would, at that."

"Mayhap. Are you coming?" She thrust her head forward, but her voice had softened. "There's really no one else, you know."

"Bloody hell," he said again, staring at her, and swung his legs over the wall.

"Careful." She bent to him. "Here, lean on me."

"Like hell I will—hell!" he exclaimed, as he put his weight on his injured leg and it promptly collapsed beneath him.

"Tch." Again she wrapped her arm about his waist. "Such language, and this from a man who's played Shakespeare."

"Shakespeare used his share of curses. There's a scene in *Henry V* where Queen Catherine is talking to her maid—" He broke off to stare at her. "How do you know that?"

"Near Green Park, you mentioned the seven ages of man."

"So I did." He lurched again. "Where are you taking me?"

"Away from the road. What, do you fear I'll hurt you?"

"You, hurt me? I am a known murderer, remember?"

"I haven't forgotten. What scene is that?"

"What? Oh. *Henry V.*" The smile she had already learned to distrust spread across his face. "In Act Five. Catherine is about to meet Henry and she is asking her maid about, ah, relations."

"Relations?"

"Marital relations."

"Oh." She would not blush. She would not.

"Though not in so many words," he chattered on.

"The scene is French, but I suspect people of the time knew what Shakespeare was saying. Actually, the word he used was—"

"Never mind," she said hastily. "I think I'd rather not know."

"*Tch*. And you a doctor's daughter, who's seen her share of naked men?"

"If I let you go, you'll fall," Blythe said pleasantly, though her color was high. "I don't think you'd enjoy it."

"No, but you would, wouldn't you?"

"Actually, this is a likely enough place." She stopped so quickly that he stumbled again. Only by grabbing at her did he stay upright. She batted his hands away. "Mr. Woodley, please! We haven't the time for that."

"I wasn't—"

"The trees will shield us from the road, and I smell water nearby. And there's a fallen tree for you to sit upon." Far more gently than Simon had expected, she bent, letting him slump onto the log. "I'd rather there was more space, but I fear you're too heavy for me to support for much longer."

"I didn't ask you to," he said grumpily, drawing his good leg up. " 'Tis cool. We shall light a fire."

"Mm, no, I think not. Anyone chasing you will see the smoke."

"I'd think you'd want that."

"After I've gone to so much trouble to get you here?" She glared at him, hands on hips. "You are really a most uncooperative patient."

"And you are a most contrary woman."

"So I've been told. Now"—she knelt beside him— "take off your breeches."

"Just like that?" He smiled again. "Don't you wish to talk first, princess, or touch—"

"You may mock me all you want, Mr. Woodley, but I am the only person who can help you." By dint of sheer will she kept her gaze steady on him. "Will you take off your breeches, or will I have to cut them off you?"

"Bloody hell," he muttered, turning away. "Who the hell named you Blythe?"

"My parents. Well, sir?"

"They were sadly mistaken as to your character. Bloody hell," he said again, and reluctantly began to unbutton his breeches.

Blythe glanced away, not quite as self-assured as she would have Simon think. It was true she'd helped her father tend to the ill, but the men she'd seen had mostly been old, and their private parts discreetly draped. Never had she been allowed to minister to a young man who was otherwise in the prime of health. She would not leave him, however. She could not leave anyone who was injured, no matter what he'd done. Her father's training had been instilled in her too deeply.

Beside her Simon was wriggling, struggling to get out of his breeches without actually having to stand. His face was averted, and it struck her for the first time that he found this as embarrassing as she did. The thought made her hide a smile. "Do you need help?"

"No," he bit off, and, flinging his breeches aside, settled back on the log clad only in his shirt, legs stretched out, face stony. "Do what you will, princess."

There was no wound that she could see. There were instead two solid columns of flesh, ropy with muscles in spite of his long confinement, and dusted liberally with hair. She swallowed, lifted her chin, and met his gaze, faintly mocking. "Well? Where is it?"

Simon could think of several replies to that, all ribald, but he held his tongue. Sweet Jesus, but he'd never been in quite this situation before. True enough it was that there were many ladies who'd been glad when he'd shed his breeches. Blythe was different. It wasn't lust that motivated her, though why she wanted to help him, he didn't know. He suspected, however, that behind her brisk tone and abrupt manner she was distinctly unnerved. She was, as he'd already guessed, as capable an actress as he'd ever seen.

"In back," he said finally, and twisted onto his side, hoping fervently that his shirt covered his backside, as well as other vital parts. Because, sweet Jesus, she was having an effect on him he hadn't anticipated.

"Hmm." Blythe frowned as she bent over. "It's long, but not very deep."

"As deep as you want."

"I beg your pardon?"

"Nothing."

"Hmm. Well, it'll need cleaning. Did it bleed much?"

"Like the devil. Are you going for water—bloody hell!" he hissed, as something cold and wet and fiery splashed on his leg. He twisted to look at her where she knelt, apparently unflappable as she put the stopper into a small dark bottle. "What in hell is that?"

"A potion Mrs. Wicket sent me to obtain," she said, setting the bottle down. "By the smell of it, it contains a good bit of alcohol."

"Bloody hell. Let me have a drink, then. Come on," he said when she hesitated. "I'll need it for the pain."

"It might help, at that," she conceded, handing him the bottle. "Please turn again. There. My father often used whiskey to clean wounds," she went on in an impersonal tone. "I don't know why that works better than plain water, but it does. The wound shouldn't suppurate."

"Small comfort," he muttered, taking a swig from the bottle. The potion, whatever it was, was dark and bitter, but Blythe was right. It did contain a good bit of alcohol.

"Indeed, when you're on the road. Hmm."

He twisted around again. "I don't like the sound of that."

"What? Oh. I was just wondering if I should just take some stitches—"

"No!" He jerked away. "I mean, that won't be necessary."

"Perhaps you're right."

"Are you done?"

"No, I'll have to apply a bandage. I wish I had some comfrey to put on it, though. Turn your back, please."

"What?"

"Turn your back." She stared at him, her firm little chin outthrust, looking resolute and dauntless and far too pretty for his peace of mind. In the fading light, the streak in her hair shone molten silver. "Where do you expect I'll find a bandage?"

He turned away, grinning to himself at the sound of cloth tearing. "Why, princess, will you use your petticoat on me? I didn't think you cared."

"I don't," she retorted, and he turned in time to see her skirts settle to the ground again. Pity. He'd have liked to have seen her legs. "Will you sit still so I can bandage you?"

"Is that your petticoat? Well, Miss Marden," he said, now the one to be amused, and saw color sweep into her face. "Red flannel?"

" 'Tis practical," she said, first placing a pad on the wound and then tying the piece of cloth around his leg, tighter than he thought necessary. "There, that should hold. You may get dressed now."

Simon scrambled for his breeches as she rose and turned away from him. Now that the ordeal was over, now that his leg had been attended to and he was safe—safe!—from hanging, his normal good humor was returning. Mrs. Wicket's potion probably helped, he conceded. "You're a fine nurse, princess."

"Yes, well." She turned back, and though her face appeared composed, her gaze would not meet his. "The thing to watch for now is fever. Do you think you have one?"

"I don't know." Painful though it was, he stood, hands on hips, grinning at her, hugely enjoying her discomfiture. "Mayhaps you should see for yourself?"

The look she cast him was suspicious. He struggled to keep his face bland and innocent as she sidled up to him, placing her hand on his forehead. "A touch warm, but 'tis to be expected," she declared, snatching her hand away as if burned. "If it gets worse, you'll need to brew tea from white yarrow."

"Princess, I wouldn't know white yarrow from white pine." He watched her as she straightened her mobcap, dusted down her skirts. "Mayhap I need more nursing."

She glanced briefly at him and turned away. "You'll do fine."

"Wait!" The urgency in his voice surprised him and made her turn back toward him. "Where are you going?"

She raised her shoulders and let out a long sigh, the very picture of long-suffering exasperation. He wondered if she realized how skilled an actress she was. "Home, of course, since you no longer hold me captive."

"There's something you don't realize, princess," he said softly, and advanced upon her until his hand was braced on a tree near her head.

To Blythe's credit, she didn't shy away, but kept her gaze steady, though he saw her swallow before speaking. "What?"

" 'Tis dark." His voice was husky. "How do you plan to return to London?"

"It's not dark yet," she protested, but, glancing around, she saw that the shadows had lengthened considerably. " 'Tis only because we're in a wood."

"Mayhaps. Nevertheless, night is coming on."

His gaze was intent, but she forced herself to meet it. "Then I must go while I can. Or do you still keep me captive?"

"No, princess. But I worry for your safety, walking through London alone at night."

That startled a laugh from her. "My safety! When you are the one who's put me at risk? No." She whirled around, freeing herself from that dark, penetrating gaze at last. "I'll not stay. I'll find an inn or some such—"

"Looking as you do? And have you any money, princess?"

"Some." She put up her chin. "All I need do is tell them I was abducted—"

"And that you bandaged my wound, helping me to escape. It isn't that easy, princess."

"Stop calling me that!" She set her lips. Damn him, she thought, relishing the unaccustomed curse. He was right. Traveling on darkened roads would not be safe for her, a woman alone, and might only raise suspicion against her. And she was an accomplice to his escape. Involuntary at first, true, but no one had forced her to clean and bandage his wound. That would be harder to explain. "I'll find someone to take me in—"

"And arrest you. And me."

"You *should* be arrested!" She spun to face him. "What would you have me do?"

"Stay with me."

She gaped at him. "Oh, no," she said, backing away. "You'll not use me that way."

"Princess, I'm too tired," he said bluntly. "Believe me, I have no intention of making advances to you."

"Then why do you want me to stay?"

"Because I got you into this." His lips tucked back. "Because you were going about your life and I've gone and turned everything topsy-turvy. Because"— his voice softened—"I'll worry about you."

He sounded sincere, she had to give him that. Looked it, too, standing there with his shoulders slouched and his hands tucked into his breeches pockets, looking at her with lowered head, like a little boy expecting a scolding. "Well, I can't help that, can I?"

"You could, if you stayed."

"How will I ever explain being away at night to Mrs. Wicket?"

"How will you explain this day?" he countered, and she bit her lips. "I don't think you've much choice, princess."

She glanced away. Through the branches she could see that the sky had darkened. Night was almost upon her. She could take the risk, of course, chance her safety and return to her employer's house, but what would she meet with there? She could never explain her actions to Mrs. Wicket, who'd likely turn her off without a reference. Like it or not, she had no place to go. "Where will you stay?" she asked finally.

"Do you mean, where will we stay, princess?"

She sighed. "Yes, I suppose I do."

"Don't worry so." He reached out to touch her

hand, and she jerked it away. "Things will turn out right. I'll see to it."

"Oh? Then do you plan to return to London with me tomorrow and tell everyone you held me captive?"

"No. That generous, I am not. But the people where I am going will be able to help—"

"You've a destination?"

He looked away. "I'm a strolling player, princess. I know people everywhere."

Blythe frowned, suspicious of his answer. He had been too confident of himself all day, too sure. He had a plan, whether he would share it with her or not. "Come to think of it, how did you escape?"

"You helped me," he said promptly.

"That's not what I meant, and you know it."

"Aye. But 'tis best you don't know any more. If anyone questions you, you won't be able to tell them a thing."

Blythe set her lips in a straight line. "If they'll believe me." How strange to think that, in the eyes of the law, she was guilty of aiding a criminal. That he had threatened her with dire harm would not absolve her completely. "Simon," she said, speaking his name for the first time and turning to gaze directly at him. "All those things you said today—you wouldn't really have hurt me, would you?"

He held her gaze, his eyes dark, inscrutable. " 'Tis true I am a condemned murderer."

"Who has had plenty of opportunity to do me harm." She let the silence lengthen. "Well?"

Simon stared at her a moment longer and then turned away, running a hand over his hair. "No," he said, so quietly it was almost a whisper. "I wouldn't have hurt you."

She nodded. Somehow she'd known that, deep in her being, for quite some time. "Well." Her tone was brisk. "We should be finding a place to sleep, and perhaps scavenge for something to eat. Berries, anyway, and perhaps some roots."

He grimaced. "Hardly tasty fare."

"No, but the best we'll do for tonight. Unless you would care to go to an inn?"

"No. I'm afraid 'tis the open air for us. Come, princess—"

"One thing more." She held back from the hand he held out. "If you so much as touch me tonight, I will be sure to feed you psyllium seeds. Unsoaked psyllium seeds."

"Why?"

"I'm not sure you want to know."

"Try me."

"Only if you wish to have an extremely upset stomach."

He stared at her for a moment and then put back his head, giving a shout of laughter. "I believe you would, at that."

"I would." She nodded. "Consider yourself warned, sir."

"I do." He was still grinning. "Madam, you have my word. Difficult though it is to resist the temptation you pose, I will strive to do so."

"Oh, go on with you," she muttered, and pushed past him. "Well? Are you coming?"

"Aye, princess." He slung a companionable arm about her shoulder, removing it only when she gave him a distinctly cold glare. "Let us find a barn, or at least a hayrick. That way we'll be warm."

"Very well." Blythe nodded, falling into step beside him, watching her footing in the failing light. It was the best they could do for tonight, after a most extraordinary day. But she did not trust Mr. Simon Woodley. Oh, no. She would not, she resolved, sleep a wink tonight.

Two tiny, beady eyes were staring her in the face. Blythe gazed at them in incomprehension for a moment and then jerked up onto her elbows, completely startled out of sleep. "What in the—"

"Breakfast," Simon said cheerfully, rising from his crouch beside her. "Fresh-caught trout."

Blythe sat up, pushing her hair out of her eyes and

feeling at a distinct disadvantage. "Where did it come from?"

"From the stream. Wouldn't happen to have a knife on you, would you?"

"No." Blythe knelt clumsily in the pile of hay. "Why?"

"To clean the fish, of course. Ah, never mind, we'll make do." He squinted off into the distance. "In fact, I know where we can do well."

"Wait." She pushed at her hair again. "I—how is your leg?"

"Better, madam," he said, and to her astonishment made her a sweeping bow. "You are a most admirable doctor. Mayhap you'd like to see for yourself?"

Blythe felt the color sweeping up into her face. "I probably should, yes. Where are you going?"

He turned. "Don't worry, princess. I'll be back soon." And with that he plunged into the woods edging the field where they'd spent the night, he in his hayrick, she in hers. He'd kept his word, hadn't come next or near her. Not that she would have been able to do anything about it. A fine guard she'd turned out to be, falling asleep as she had. Anyone might have crept up on her.

The thought made her rise in clumsy haste, brushing bits of hay from her clothes. No, she was alone. She breathed in relief at that. No farmer worked this field this morning, and that was a good thing. What would happen were she to be seen with Simon was not to be considered.

Where had he gone, anyway? Frowning, Blythe walked toward the brook, not so very far from where she had cleaned and bandaged his wound. After washing her face and tidying up a bit, she looked around her, seeing her surroundings more clearly than she had last evening. Fully country; one wouldn't even know London was nearby. Return there she would, however, this morning, though she didn't know how she could possibly explain her absence.

In the distance a dog barked suddenly, angrily, fierce tones warning off an intruder, faintly at first and then louder. Blythe heard a crashing in the under-brush, and her breath caught. Had the pursuit reached this far? But as the sounds came closer they were joined by a cheerful whistling, making her relax. It was only Simon. Only! As if it were better to be found by a convict than by the law.

Annoyed with herself, Blythe stepped back from the brook, reaching the woody path in time to encounter Simon ambling along with hands tucked in pockets as if he hadn't a care in the world. It infuriated her; the fact that he had somehow managed to club his hair neatly back so that he looked presentable, if disreputable, angered her all the more. "Must you make such noise?" she hissed. "You'll have everyone in the county upon us."

"Why, princess." A smile spread on his face. "I didn't think you cared."

"For you, I don't." She flounced around, preceding him back to their campsite. "But I would like to get through this day with a whole skin."

"This way, princess." He caught her arm, leading her toward the brook again, though to a different spot. "I've a fire going."

She shook her arm free. "Fire?"

"Aye, and a few potatoes I don't think will be missed."

"Where did you go?" she asked suspiciously, dropping down onto the ground near the small, well-banked fire. Buried in its embers were, indeed, pota-toes, and suddenly she was hungrier than she could ever remember being.

"Best you not know. Though you must have noticed the barn last night. No?" From his pocket he pulled out a knife, its blade rusty and pitted, and began to clean the fish. "I paid my first, ah, visit to it earlier and remembered seeing this knife. Don't think it will be missed, either."

Blythe pulled her legs up under her. "And do you often resort to stealing?"

"Only when I have to, princess. I've been told it leads to much worse things," he said, and winked.

Blythe's lips tucked back. He was despicable, really, whistling as he cleaned and cut the fish with surprising skill for a man who made his living on the stage. He was also far more appealing than she cared to admit. Though his shirt was stained, he wore it as if it were cloth of gold; though clearly he needed a shave, the stubble added interesting shadows and angles to his cheeks, pale from his incarceration. And he faced whatever was coming with a smile, which was more than she could say for herself. "You seem used to this."

"Used to it?" He'd taken up a stick and was now systematically sharpening the point. "Here, put the fish on this and hold it in the fire," he said, handing her the stick. "Not used to it, precisely, but an actor's lot is a precarious one. There have been times we've had to live off the land."

"We?"

"Yes, my—" He shook his head. "No, the less you know about them, the better. Excuse me." This as his stomach gave a loud growl. "I think 'tis time to eat."

Blythe's stomach growled as well. She hoped he hadn't noticed. "Do you think the fish is done?"

"Looks it. Come, we'll have a veritable feast, milady."

He changed his personality as easily as his accent, Blythe noted, and yet she had to admit that the meal he'd prepared was a feast indeed. They broke their fast with the trout and the potatoes, plucked hot from the fire. Blythe burned her fingers once or twice, but she didn't care. Never had trout tasted so wonderful; never had a simple potato seemed such lavish fare, even without butter or cream. Better than dining at a fine inn, she thought, and knew she'd remember this meal for a long, long time.

In the distance the dog barked again. This time Blythe paid it no heed. "Where do you go after this?" she asked.

"Wherever the wind takes me," he said, though she was not fooled by his breezy casualness. "And you? Back to London, I suppose."

Blythe surprised herself by heaving a great sigh. Of course she would return to London, preferable as it was to camping out in a field. Yet she didn't want to.

Not yet, at least. "Yes, I've really no place else to go, though I doubt Mrs. Wicket will take me back."

The dog barked again, faintly. "What will you tell her?" Simon asked, finishing off the last potato and lounging back with the air of a man replete and well satisfied with life.

"The truth." Blythe busied herself with gathering up the debris of their meal. "Though I doubt she'll believe me."

"Not an understanding woman?"

"No, not very. Likely I'll have to look for other employment."

"Yet you mentioned family."

Blythe looked up, wary. "Yes, well?"

"Are they in London, too?"

"No."

If her curt answer bothered him, he didn't show it. "Why not go back to them, then?"

"Only if I have to. I—"

"Wait." He was holding his hand up, posture suddenly upright, face alert. "Listen to that barking."

"It sounds like the farmer's dog you bothered before."

"Yes—no!" He bolted to his feet. "Bloody hell!"

"What is it?" Blythe asked, alarmed but not moving.

"They've set dogs on us, that's what they've done. Come on." Grabbing her arm, he dragged her unceremoniously to her feet. "We've got to get out of here."

"But—"

"There's no time! Come on," he said again, and this time tugged at her harder, so that, off balance, she had no choice but to follow. She could hear the dogs now, a deep baying sound, such as hounds made when on the hunt. But hunting season was in winter, and what would be their prey now? She glanced back over her shoulder as she and Simon broke free of the trees, and she saw them, the dogs, coming on across the field as the tide. Behind them were men on horseback, garbed in red. Soldiers, she realized, and, hesitating no longer, pounded along behind Simon. The soldiers had found them.

Chapter 5

"This way," Simon rasped, pulling Blythe back into the trees that edged the meadow. If they stayed in open country, they would be lost. The dogs would outchase them. In the woods they had more of a chance of escape, slim though it was. "Bloody hell."

"How—" Blythe's breath came in sobbing gasps. "How did they find us?"

"I don't know, but we left enough of a trail once we left the road."

"Simon, the brook—"

"Yes, I know, but let's lead them on a little farther before we take to it."

"But why? The water will hide our scent."

"Aye, but we need a place to hide." His lungs burned like the devil, from the exercise after months of confinement; the wound on his thigh had broken open, judging by the wetness he felt trickling down his leg, and yet he felt a strange, fierce elation. He was alive! This time yesterday he'd expected to be hanged, and yet here he was, having feasted on good, plain fare, and holding the hand of a woman whom, though not conventionally pretty, though past the first blush of youth, he was finding more and more appealing. Alive, aye, and he'd best take steps to stay that way.

Abruptly Simon swerved from the path. Blythe, her hand tight in his, followed him unprotestingly into the undergrowth and down a steep bank that had them slipping and clawing for footing. At the bottom was the brook. He plunged in, gasping aloud as the icy water hit his legs. Sweet Jesus, but that was a shock!

"This way," he urged, pulling her along the stream bed. Blythe followed, stumbling behind him when he clambered onto the opposite bank. "And now this."

"What?" This as he plunged them into the brook again, retracing their steps. Blythe was panting for breath, her skirts, heavy with water, clinging to her legs and slowing her progress. "But that's going back where we were."

"They won't expect it. Besides, I spotted a good hiding place this morning, just in case."

"Then we could have gone directly there?"

"Shh! They're almost close enough to hear. We don't want to give ourselves away."

"Where is it?"

"Not far. That willow, ahead. If we duck under the leaves—there!"

Silvery green fronds hit Blythe's face, immersing her in a new world, an emerald world with sunlight filtering through the softly moving branches. The weeping willow hung out over the brook, its leaves hanging down, dancing upon the surface of the water. It was not a perfect hiding place, but perhaps, if they were very still, they would not be caught.

Simon's arm snaked about her waist, pulling her back against him, hard. "Not a word," he said, very low in her ear, and she nodded, though her breath was labored and she was certain he could hear the pounding of her heart. Sound carried strangely in the woods. The dogs seemed now close, now distant. Mixed with their baying were the voices of men cursing and the clattering of muskets. Their pursuers had had to leave their mounts behind and continue the chase on foot. That, at least, was encouraging.

"Over here!" someone yelled, much too close by, and she flinched. Simon's other arm came about her, holding her almost protectively. "They went into the brook, here. . . . Damn!"

"What is the problem?" This voice sounded cultured, almost bored.

"The hounds have lost the scent."

"They can't have got far. We'll cross."

"But—"

"Upon my soul, sirrah, move!" The voice was angry now. "There's no place for them to hide; they had to get to land at some point. Now move!"

"Yes, sir. Move out!"

"Sir!" Another voice, more distant. "The hounds have the scent again!"

"Good." The cultured voice again. "We'll get them."

There was much splashing and stamping as the men crossed the brook, taking what seemed to Blythe to be a very long time. Were there that many in pursuit? She pressed back against Simon. He squeezed her waist encouragingly, and suddenly, in spite of the icy water, in spite of her fear, she felt a strange warmth spreading through her. Senses heightened by the fight for survival, she felt his hand as a burning brand, sinking into her flesh and marking her as his. His chest at her back was remarkably solid and remarkably broad, and his soft breath stirred her hair as his masculine scent stirred her senses. She was aware of him as she had never before been aware of any man, and he nothing but a convict.

"Damn, damn, damn." The cultured voice again, closer, coming from across the bank, very soft, and somehow all the more menacing for it. "Damn the dogs for losing the scent."

"For the Lord's sake, my hounds can't work miracles. If the pair of them went through the water—"

"Quiet!" There was a strange slashing sound, followed by a thud and a grunt. "I'll take no excuses from you. Where do you think you are going?"

"I'll not put up with your abuse, and neither will my hounds," the man called back.

"Damn your eyes, get back here. You've been well paid—"

"You can go to the devil, sir."

"I'll see you there first!" the cultured voice yelled, but even to Blythe's ears his rage sounded impotent. In the distance she could hear men talking, followed by more splashing, as they presumably crossed the brook again. Blythe's muscles loosened in relief, and then stiffened. Through the fronds of the willow tree on the far bank she could see first a pair of highly polished boots, dripping with water and mud; the tails of a blue coat edged with braid; and then, as the man continued to move, his head. His hair, unpowdered, was clubbed back in a queue; his eyes were narrowed, and his lips were full and red. Blythe involuntarily shrank back against Simon's chest. It was the man who had watched them yesterday on Westminster Bridge, and now he was staring directly at them.

He had to see them. Blythe, helpless, caught, stared back, seeing eyes that were a peculiar golden color, like a cat's. Like a cat ready to pounce, and she and Simon were the prey.

"Damn. We've lost them." The man shook one leg, frowned down at his boots, and turned. "They'll pay," he said, striding away.

It was a trap, Blythe thought. It had to be. She twisted to look at Simon. He shook his head. Closing her eyes, she let her head drop back against his shoulder, relishing the solid feel of it. She would not have been able to get through this predicament without him. But then, without him, she wouldn't have been in any danger.

"I think they're gone," Simon said very softly after a time, when the sounds of tramping feet and men's voices raised in argument had ceased, when the noises of the woods had returned to the normal chatter of birds and squirrels and other small animals.

Blythe sagged, feeling her muscles go weak from the release of tension, becoming aware, as if for the first time, of the icy water lapping about her waist. "I'm cold."

"I'm not surprised, princess." Simon rubbed his hands up and down her arms, and then moved, at last. Yet still she felt his warmth and solid strength at her back, a tactile memory. "Come. We'll catch our deaths standing here."

"He really is gone, isn't he?" she chattered, grasping Simon's hand and letting him pull her through the willow fronds onto the bank. "I thought, when he stared right at us—"

"We were in shadow." Simon gestured back at the willow arching over the stream, and Blythe realized for the first time how effective a hiding place it had been. "He couldn't see us."

She glanced up at him. "You don't sound the least concerned."

He shrugged. "Why should I? He's gone. And we, sweeting, are alive," he said. And, catching her about the waist, he swung her around and planted a quick, hard kiss on her lips.

Blythe stood rooted to the spot, hand to her mouth, as Simon, apparently without a care in the world, strode along the bank of the stream. Good heavens, why had he done that? She could still feel the imprint of his lips on hers, still taste him, smell him—and he was walking away, the wretch. Chilled from the water, she shivered, and yet her face felt strangely warm, her limbs weak and restless. Shock, she thought on one level of her mind, and wondered why she hadn't succumbed to it before.

Simon turned. "Coming?" he called.

"No," she said, but her paralysis was broken. She walked toward him, wringing her skirt as she went. "I'm going back to London."

Simon shook his head, his face serious. "You can't, princess."

"Of course I can." She looked up from her task. "Because of the way I look, you mean? The sun will dry me eventually—"

"No, sweeting," he interrupted, his voice oddly gentle. "Because they're looking for you now, too."

She stared at him. "No."

"Didn't you hear that man, whoever he is? He was looking for more than one person."

"Don't you know who he is?" she exclaimed, diverted for the moment from her own predicament.

"No." He frowned. "Should I?"

"Simon, he was on Westminster Bridge when we crossed. I thought he paid us particular attention."

"Bloody hell. Then he'd recognize you. I'm sorry, sweeting." His fingers touched her cheek and then dropped, leaving heat behind like a brand. "I never meant to get you into such a mess."

"Do you mean—are you saying that I'm being hunted, too?"

"I fear so. I'm sorry," he said again. "But somehow he saw through our masquerade yesterday, and he'd recognize you if he saw you again." His face was stark, almost bleak. "You're in danger, Blythe. You can't go back to London."

Dazed, Blythe dropped to the ground, her wet skirts puddling about her. "But do you think he knows who I am?"

"If he figured out yesterday who I was and where we went, yes. What do you think your employer did when you didn't come home?"

"Raised holy hell—I mean, a fuss." Blythe shook her head. Oh, yes, Mrs. Wicket would have indeed made a fuss, not because of any concerns about Blythe's safety, but because of the disruption to her own comfort. Within hours the entire neighborhood must have known that Blythe had disappeared, and . . . "The soldiers will remember me," she said dully.

Simon crouched before her. "I fear so, sweeting. You're a memorable person."

She gaped at him and shook her head. "Then what am I to do?"

"I don't think you have any choice," he murmured. "You can't go back to London."

"Do you mean just run away? I couldn't."

"Why not?" he argued. "What is your alternative, Blythe? Gaol? You'll not like that, I assure you. And if they think you helped me willingly, what do you think they'll do to you?"

"I don't know."

"Don't you? Blythe." He grasped her hands. "Women have been hanged in the past."

She jerked back. "They wouldn't!"

"They might. And 'twould be on my soul." He gazed at her. "I don't want that, sweeting."

"You're already a murderer."

He grimaced. "So people say," he said, and rose. "So. What are you going to do?"

"I don't know." She stared hopelessly ahead. "I suppose I could go home."

"You've family?"

"Yes, but I don't want to go back like this."

"They'll look for you there, too."

Blythe shrugged. "Maybe not."

"And your family, knowing what you've done—will they take you in?"

This time her answer was slower in coming. "Yes. But I'm expected to make my way in the world. If I go home, I'll just be a burden. 'Tis a small village. Everyone will know who I am and what I've done."

"Bloody hell." Simon stalked a few paces away, staring down into the rushing water. This was all his doing. If he hadn't grabbed her yesterday, she'd be going on with her life now. Because he had, however, she had no place to go. "You'll have to come with me."

"Why?"

He turned. "Because there are people where I'm going who will help you."

"You know where you're going, then? I thought—"

"Bloody hell," he said again, and let out his breath. "Of course I know where I'm going. I wouldn't have told you, though, if things hadn't happened as they did." He grimaced. "I'm sorry."

"So you keep saying. Not that it changes anything." She rose at last, and though her legs appeared shaky, her hands, brushing down her skirts, were brisk. "Shall we be on our way, then?"

"What?"

"We should go. Or would you prefer to wait until the soldiers return?"

Simon stared at her, this young woman whose life he had disrupted, and who yet stood before him calm, resolute. By God, but she had courage. She was quite a woman. There was not another he knew who would have come through the day's ordeal as she had. No wonder, then, that he had kissed her.

The memory of that quick, impulsive kiss made him want to squirm. He'd kissed her only because of the sheer joy of being alive, of having survived the present danger. That was all it was, and yet his body remembered, in precise detail, how she had felt pressed close to him in the water, her bottom nestled against him, her breasts warm and soft and round just above his arm. By God, it was a good thing the water had been so cold, or he might have disgraced himself. Strange, because she wasn't his usual type. The women he favored had, like him, too strong a sense of self-preservation to get into such a mess. A mess he had to help her escape.

"All right, then." He held his hand out to her. She hesitated, surprising him; after the day's events he felt almost as if he'd been intimate with her. But then she clasped his hand, her own surprisingly strong and callused, in a friendly grip. A surge of well-being went through him, strange under the circumstances, and yet too powerful to deny. "Let's be off," he said, and they set off to face whatever adventures the road held for them.

Honoria, the Viscountess Stanton, held out a languid hand from the satin chaise longue where she lay ensconced among pillows of lavender brocade. "Tell me he's dead, my love," she purred.

Quentin Heywood stepped farther into the room, glancing toward the dressing room. His coat of emerald brocade struck a blaze of color against the pastel femininity of the room. "Is your maid not here?"

"Clothilde? Bah. She's a foolish one, and she speaks little English. You've little to fear, my love. Come, tell me everything. I was surprised you weren't here last evening."

"I had, er, rather pressing business to attend to." Quentin ambled across the room to look out a window, seeing through the wavy glass a garden blooming with flowers in all shades of purple, from a lilac so

pale it was nearly white to midnight-dark violets. Surrounding the garden were high brick walls, making it
an exquisite oasis in the midst of the city. Since the
viscount was quite serious about tending to his estate,
he was often away from his wife, who preferred London. That perquisite had been left to Quentin, and a
dangerous one it was. If the viscount ever learned exactly what his wife was up to, there would be trouble.
Not for Honoria, of course; she'd manage to slip out
of it somehow. Quentin wouldn't be so lucky. If the
truth got out, it would be his neck stretching at the
end of a hangman's noose.

"Tell me." Honoria's voice held a tiny note of impatience, though its huskiness hadn't abated. "Did the
actor die at peace with his God, pleading his innocence? Oh, I know no one would believe him," she
went on, as Quentin turned from the window. "But
did he dance at the end of the rope as I've heard
they do?"

"My God!" Quentin burst out. "You sound as if
you're enjoying this."

"But I am, my sweet, I am. Two enemies disposed
of, and so neatly, too."

"One."

It appeared to take a moment for that to penetrate.
Honoria turned her head, her pale blue eyes blinking.
"I don't think I understand you."

"The actor escaped."

She didn't react as he'd expected. He'd expected
temper, shouting, perhaps physical violence. Instead,
she lounged back, her face the inscrutable mask that
served her so well at card tables and gambling hells.
"I know."

He turned his head sharply. "How?"

"Really, Quentin, think you so little of me? I had
the news yesterday. How could you have let him
escape?"

Quentin leaned back in the window embrasure,
smiling a little, knowing his apparent lack of temper
would only infuriate her further. Good. So far he had
been the only one in any danger in this escapade. Let

her suffer for a while. "It wasn't exactly by choice, my love." From his pocket he produced a knife and began paring his nails, staring at them intently. "Apparently he had some help. The priest who was to attend his last moments has also disappeared."

Honoria was out of bed, stomping about the room, her wrapper of lavender silk floating about her. "What of the soldiers?"

"Caught up with him and then lost him."

"Oh?" She halted in front of him. "And what," she said, jabbing the tip of her finger into his chest, "of you?"

"God, you're magnificent when you're angry," he said, and caught her to him for a long, ravaging kiss. Her hands clawed at his neck; but then, they often did. He bore the scars of their lovemaking proudly.

She tossed her head when he released her. "You cannot get around me so easily," she said, but her cheeks were flushed, her eyes bright. "Do you mean to tell me you did nothing?"

"Of course not." He leaned back again, crossing his arms over his chest. His not touching her would anger her all the more. It was rare that he had the upper hand with her. He rather enjoyed it. "Woodley left London with a woman. I don't know who she is yet, possibly one of the other players. They crossed Westminster Bridge—I saw them myself, though I didn't realize it—and headed east. After much searching, I ascertained that they had camped in a field near Shooter's Hill, and today I hired hounds and men to go after them."

"And?"

This was the part he dreaded telling. "They escaped."

Once again Honoria surprised him, looking up at him with narrowed eyes. "That rather puts a crimp on things," she said mildly.

"I'm confident I can find them again—"

"Are you?" Her voice flicked out like a lash, and Quentin's unease grew. Honoria enraged was entertaining. Quiet and sharp, though, she was dangerous. "I sometimes wonder what use you are to me, Quentin."

He bent his gaze upon her. "You know quite well."

"What, that?" Her hand flicked sharply toward his private parts, making him flinch, and she gave a little laugh. "Any man can give me that, Quentin, so do not delude yourself as to your value to me."

"Except that I know what really happened in Canterbury," he said quietly.

"And so do I!" She whirled around, her wrapper swirling, her mass of raven-dark hair caressing her cheeks, her shoulders. She had the face and voice of an angel, and the morals of a strumpet. "So do I." Her voice lowered. "So do not think to threaten me with that, Quentin. All I need do is go to the magistrate and lay information against you—"

"And implicate yourself?" His smile was slow, lazy, hiding his icy trickle of panic. "I don't think so, my sweet."

"Ah, but I was here, Quentin." She tossed her head again. "And so was the viscount. Who will believe you?"

Quentin glanced out the window, arms still crossed on chest, thinking, thinking. It was Honoria who had planned this venture; Honoria, who had reason to set the train of events into action. It was he, however, who had taken all the risks, he who had arranged for things to happen as they had, he who had bribed gaolers and guards and magistrates alike. He whose face would be remembered. He who would suffer the consequences. Unless he used his one lever against her.

He glanced at her quickly, to see her regarding him with mockery and triumph. Almost he blurted out what he knew, the evidence that would damn her most completely, and then bit his tongue. Later. Such precious information should not be squandered. "Then it seems, my sweet, that we need each other. I because of what you can do to me, and you because of what I can do for you."

Honoria's eyes narrowed to slits. "What you have done for me so far is to let the actor slip free."

"But not for long, my love. Not for long. I'll find him." Uncoiling his arms, he straightened and began, slowly, to stalk her. "And when I do, I'll take care of him for you. That I promise."

"You have not done overwell to date, Quentin."

"No?" He stopped before her, and his hand rested lightly on her throat, fingers and thumb caressing the soft skin. "But who else can you turn to, my sweet? Who else can you trust not to tell your secrets? You need me," he went on, as alarm flickered in her eyes. "We are in this together, my love."

"Do not fail me next time, Quentin," she murmured, reaching her arms around his neck. "I want the actor dead."

"He will be caught and hanged, I promise you."

Honoria tipped her head back, laughing huskily. "I love it when you talk to me like that," she said, and, pressing her breasts against him, pulled his head down for a long, hard kiss. Satisfactory, thought Quentin, sweeping her into his arms, carrying her across the room, and dumping her onto the feather mattress. There she lay, legs sprawled, eyes bright, as he pulled at the buttons of his breeches. The viscountess was his again. And only he knew the true power he held over her. Satisfactory, indeed.

Chapter 6

Night was drawing on. Blythe trudged along beside Simon, no longer quite aware of her surroundings, no longer sure of what she was doing. Had someone told her two days ago that she would be traveling with an actor turned fugitive, she would have laughed in disbelief. She was doomed to a dull life, always at someone's beck and call, while other people had adventures she could only read about. Now everything had changed. Adventure, however, was proving to be a lot less comfortable than she had expected.

"We'll stop soon," Simon said, the first words either had spoken in some time. It had been a long, weary day, spent tramping along the verge of the road, seeing only occasional glimpses of a fine house on a hill, its towers rising high into the sky; or of the Thames, not far distant. Any sign of pursuit sent them diving into the nearby woods, leaving them bruised and scratched. Because of Blythe's knowledge of plants and Simon's skill in slipping into other people's gardens and barns, they had not gone hungry. Neither, though, had they had a satisfying meal. Now they faced another night sleeping in the rough. She was mad to have done this, mad to have come along. It would have been far better to return to London and face the consequences. Too late now.

"Do you know where we are?" she asked, hearing heavy weariness in her voice.

"Yes. Near Dartford, I think. I've been on this road seldom; we're not usually on the Kent circuit. But if I'm right . . . Do you trust me?"

She stared up at him. "No."

"No?" He clapped his hand to his heart. "Madam, I am wounded."

"Would you please cease your tomfoolery? I'm tired and hungry and—"

"I know." His voice was suddenly gentle. "It's been a hard day. But 'tis nearly over."

"Another night sleeping in the woods," she muttered.

"Maybe not." He caught her arm as the sound of hooves came to them, and pulled her into the shelter of the trees. A moment later, a lone horseman passed them without so much as a glance. "If I'm right, there's an inn just ahead."

"For all the good that will do us. Or do you plan to go up to the innkeeper and ask nicely for rooms?"

"Something like that. It happens I know this innkeeper."

"Did you meet in Newgate?"

"Unfair, princess. No, he once trod the boards, until he married and his wife decided she wanted a different life. For some reason, she didn't find acting secure enough." He grinned. "A good lesson, that, not to marry. Only takes away one's freedom."

"And who would have you?"

"More than you think, princess."

"Not me."

He shrugged. "You've not been asked."

Blythe drew in her breath and then let it out slowly. Foolish to feel insulted, slighted, even, by his comment. A relationship between them of any sort was clearly out of the question. "If it's known that the innkeeper was once an actor, the soldiers might search the inn."

He looked down at her, and his face softened. "Mayhap, but 'tis a chance I think we should take. I could use a good meal."

"And a real bed," she said involuntarily, and then bit her lip, anticipating his retort.

"Aye. Though sleeping rough doesn't bother me overmuch. Mayhaps our innkeeper will also be able to tell me which theatrical troupes are about."

Blythe looked up sharply, surprised that he hadn't made some joke about a bedmate. "Surely you're not going on the stage again! 'Tis the first place they'd look for you."

"Why, princess. You sound concerned."

Blythe's lips firmed into a thin line. "I'm not."

"No?" Simon clasped his hand to his heart. "But you wound me, princess. Dare I hope you care?"

"Oh, for heaven's sake," she muttered, and pulled her arm from his, striding a few paces ahead. "It matters not to me if you're taken again, on the road or at an inn or on a stage!"

"No, I supposed it doesn't." He sounded good-humored enough as he caught up with her and took her arm again. "But think, princess. What better place for me to hide than with other actors? 'Twill be the last place anyone will think to look. Unless" he bent a stern look at her—"you tell someone."

"Who would I tell?" she said wearily, stumbling as he came to a sudden halt. "I'd rather it not be known that I've spent time in your company. Why are we stopping?"

"The inn's ahead," he muttered, pulling her into the undergrowth again as the rumble of carriage wheels reached them. "And busy, by the sounds of it."

Blythe dropped to her knees, tired beyond words. "What is the name of this inn?"

Simon was peering out through the branches at the road, swirling with dust from the passing carriage, a post chaise. "The Tabard," he said absently.

"Surely not!"

He glanced down at her. "Why not?"

"But surely that is long gone? Are we really on the road to Canterbury?"

"How do you know—oh. *The Canterbury Tales.*" A strange smile flickered across his face and was gone, leaving his features grim, hard. When he looked so, Blythe could easily believe him to be a cold-blooded killer. "Yes, as it happens, though this isn't the original inn. The owner once played the innkeeper in a production of *The Canterbury Tales,* which is why I imagine he chose the name."

"Oh. Still, 'tis fascinating, to think of the history of this road."

"Yes. I was always partial to the Miller's Tale."

She could feel her color rising. "You would be."

"Oh?" He glanced at her again, grinning. "You're familiar with it, then?"

"Only enough to know 'tis vulgar. Are we going to sit here all night?"

"No." He straightened. "Best thing is for me to go first."

"But if you're recognized—"

"Best stop saying such things, princess, or I really will think you care."

"Hmph." She sniffed. "It really makes no difference to me if you're caught, except they'll likely think I helped you."

"Which is why you'll stay here."

"Alone?"

"Yes, alone," he said impatiently. "I shall have to seek out the innkeeper privately, and 'twould be best if you're not there."

"So." She rose. "Now that I've outlived my usefulness, you'll leave me behind, like one of your props—"

"I'm not discarding you, princess." He put his hands on her shoulders. "I'll reserve us a room and then come back for you."

She looked up at him uncertainly. Though a moment before she had felt irrational terror that he would leave her, now she wished only to break free. His hands were hard, heavy, warm, and that warmth spread through her. Odd. "You promise?"

"Yes, princess." Very much to her surprise, he dropped a quick, hard kiss on her mouth. "Stay hidden," he commanded, and set off.

Her knees suddenly weak, certainly from hunger and exhaustion, Blythe sank to the ground again. The gloom was deepening under the trees, and about her she could hear the rustlings of small animals and insects, creatures of the night. It was a reassuring sound, one she'd missed in the city, and as she realized that, a strange feeling of calm and well-being fell over her. She had hated London. She could admit that now, with her bridges burned behind her. If the mad events of the days past accomplished nothing else, they had freed her from what now seemed like dismal servitude. Why, she had been as much a prisoner as Simon had.

She was mulling over that astonishing revelation when twigs crackled in the underbrush. She froze. If it was Simon, he would call to her, but this person stayed quiet. Into her mind flashed a memory of that morning, when she and Simon had huddled together in the stream, and of the man who pursued them. It would be best if Simon was caught, she knew that. Not yet, though. Please God, not yet.

"Miss?" a voice said, very small, very tentative. "Are you there?"

"Yes. Who is it?" Blythe said, surprised to hear her voice crack, so relieved was she. Not this morning's pursuer, but a boy.

"Me, miss. From the inn." The branches pushed back, and a boy, dressed in neat shirt and breeches, stood there, his hair tangled, his eyes curious. "Mr. Porter said as to how I'm to come for you. I'm Ben, Miss."

Blythe scrambled to her feet. "Mr. Porter?"

"He that runs the inn, miss. No, not that way. This way. We cross the road and go by the back. And quiet-like," he chattered. "Soldiers have already been here once today."

Blythe nodded, slipping across the road behind the boy and into the trees on the other side. Somehow he'd managed to find a path, faint in the dusk. "I'm glad you know your way."

"Yes. Is it true you escaped the hangman, miss?"

"Me! Heavens, no."

"Shh, miss! As I said. Quiet-like."

"Then don't ask such foolish questions."

"Sorry, miss." Ben's voice dropped. "Me mam said

I ever did talk too much, but Mr. Porter, he don't mind. Thinks I should go on the stage, he does."

"All the world's a stage," Blythe muttered.

"Excuse me, miss?"

"Nothing." Blythe held her peace in spite of Ben's chatter, as, leaving the trees, they reached first a kitchen garden, lush and green even in the twilight, and then an uneven brick path. Before them reared the inn, bigger than she'd imagined; taller and more rambling, with its half-timbered wings and outbuildings. And old, so old it could very well be the original Tabard, she thought, and then reproved herself for her fancies. This was not a pleasure jaunt she was on, but something far more serious.

A door opened as Blythe and Ben approached the inn, and a hand reached out to grab Ben's arm, dragging him in. "There, Master Ben, and didn't I tell you to cease your prattling?" a voice scolded. "Let the poor miss come in." The speaker put her other arm about Blythe's shoulders, pulling her against a massive and comforting bosom. "I'm Mrs. Porter, and there, do you not say who you are. Better that way. Then I can't tell what I don't know, can I? But I'll wager you're exhausted."

"It's been a wearying day," Blythe agreed, blinking. Mrs. Porter had drawn her through a dark passageway, and now she stood in a wide kitchen, its flagstone floor clean and polished, the fire in the wide hearth glowing with embers. A trestle table was set with the remains of what must once have been a fine joint of beef, bowls of potatoes, and several pewter tankards. Blythe was suddenly very hungry, and very tired, indeed. "I do thank you for taking us in. I'm sorry to be such trouble—"

"Indeed, 'tis no trouble, not for Harry and Bess's boy. Sit you down, now, and I'll just pour you a nice cup of tea to have with your supper."

Blythe slid onto a bench at the table. "Harry and Bess? Who are they?"

"Why, Simon's uncle and aunt, of course." Mrs. Porter set down a pewter dish brimming with carved ham, potatoes, and new peas. "But there, you knew that, o' course."

"Actually, no." Blythe looked up. "Did Simon not tell you how we met?"

"Why, no. Should he have?"

"The rogue," Blythe muttered. "He got me into this and he's not making any effort to get me out."

"It doesn't matter, lamb, I know that you both need help. And you'll be safe here. Now, I'll stop my prattling so you can eat."

"Thank you." Blythe bent her head to the meal, sighing with pleasure over fresh food served hot and cooked well. Such things as she had always before taken for granted: a roof over her head, regular meals, a reputation . . . and stifling duties pressed upon her by an uncaring, selfish employer, along with the dreary knowledge of her place in life. The past days had held more than one revelation.

There was a footstep in the passage, and Simon came into the kitchen, ducking his head to miss the lintel. His hair was wet and tousled, his face scraped free of beard, and he wore a clean shirt, loose and flowing and yet somehow defining itself over strong, etched muscles. Good heavens. He was beautiful. Until this moment she'd not realized it.

"Made it safely, princess?" he said, sitting on the bench across from her and reaching for one of the tankards.

"Yes." Blythe fixed her attention on her supper, fighting the urge to look at him. Just to look. "Do they know why we're here?"

"Aye. Though they don't know everything about you."

At that Blythe did look up, and instantly regretted it. Without his beard Simon looked younger, more approachable, not at all the dangerous rogue she knew him to be. "Yes, so I noticed. I can't imagine what they think of me."

"They know you've helped me, and that's all that matters." Draining the tankard, he leaned back. "Ah, that was good. Theater people take you as you are."

"And what we are is an escaped felon and his captive."

"No, princess." He shook his head. "They know the truth—"

"I've the attic room ready," a man said, stepping into the room. "A job it was, too, to do it quiet-like. Lots of folks on the road tonight."

"We appreciate it, Josiah," Simon said gravely.

The man grunted, looking at Blythe measuringly. "This is your companion?"

"Aye. Thank you." This to the kitchen maid who had set a fresh tankard before him. "I'm not sure, but I think she's the makings of a fine actress."

"Really." Josiah Porter assessed Blythe differently. "Going to join a troupe, are you?"

"Good heavens, no," Blythe said. Something about Porter's gaze disturbed her, though she didn't know quite what. "I'm going home." If they would take her back.

"Likely the soldiers will look for you there."

"What else can I do?" she cried. "And we don't know that they know who I am."

"Yet."

"There, master Simon, stop teasing the poor lass," Mrs. Porter exclaimed, bustling over to Blythe and putting an arm about her again. "Likely she'd had as hard a day as you, and not a complaint from her, either. So just leave her be. You must be tired," she said to Blythe, who looked up at her.

"Yes, I am, rather."

"Then come with me." Mrs. Porter tugged at her arm. "There's a room waiting for you."

"Thank you," Blythe said, and, after throwing Simon a look, followed Mrs. Porter up the narrow back stairs.

Josiah stood in the middle of the kitchen, legs braced apart, hand stroking his chin, looking at the stairs. "Can you trust her?"

"I don't know," Simon answered shortly.

"You know women, my boy." Josiah straddled the bench Blythe had just left. "Not a one of them can keep their tongues still. What happens when she returns to this village of hers?"

"As long as she doesn't know where I'm going, I'll be all right."

There was silence for a moment. "Where are you going?" Josiah asked finally.

"On a pilgrimage."

"What?"

Simon speared a morsel of roast beef with the end of his knife. The question Josiah had asked about Blythe was pertinent. Yet, though he'd known the Porters for years, he wondered if he could trust them. "To find the truth."

"You speak in riddles, Simon. If I knew your plans, I could help you. Get word to people, find someone to smuggle you out of the country—"

"I didn't do it," Simon interrupted, his face still. "I'm no murderer."

"Come, lad, I know that," Josiah exclaimed, his voice just a bit too hearty. "Would I let you stay if I thought so? Why, I'd fear you'd murder us in our beds!"

"Brave of you." Simon rose, and though he smiled, his muscles felt tight, stiff. So this was how it was to be, with every chance-met person, with everyone he'd known. No one believed him. Which made his need to find the truth more urgent than before. "I'll not trouble you long, Josiah, and I do thank you for letting us stay."

"Glad to do it." Josiah stood with balled fists on his hips, the very picture of a jolly innkeeper. "Mind, now, you'll have to leave early if no one's to remark you. 'Twill be hard enough to keep you a secret."

"Don't worry. I won't bring any danger onto you. Good night," he added, before Josiah, mouth agape, could answer, and headed up the back stairs himself.

The attic room was nothing more than its name implied, a tiny garret tucked up under the eaves, with a ceiling so low that Simon had to duck his head to keep from hitting it. Damn lucky they'd been to get this, he thought, quietly opening the door. Porter'd been none too happy about taking them in. Thank God this little room was usually used for storage or by the maids, so that the guests weren't likely to know of it.

He wasn't surprised to see Blythe already tucked into bed, staring at him wide-eyed from beneath the covers pulled up to her nose. "That cold, princess?" he said, smiling, sitting on the edge of the bed to pull off his shoes.

"No."

"What, no maidenly protests? No demands to know what I'm doing here?"

"No."

He looked at her then. Her hair was tucked up under her mobcap again and, except for a few tendrils of honey-hued hair, all he could see were huge eyes, blue and as unfathomable as the sea. "You knew we'd be sharing this room."

"Yes."

"All right, then," he said, and, rising, began to pull off his shirt.

Blythe scuttled up to the headboard, pulling the counterpane higher. "Surely you're not—we aren't sharing the bed."

Simon let his arms drop, sighing. "Of course not, princess," he said, and if there was mockery in his tone, it was leveled as much at himself as at her. "I wouldn't dare presume such a thing."

"Rogue," she muttered.

He sighed again, gustily. "Insults. And here I am, doing the right thing."

"My apologies."

He reached again for the hem of his shirt. "Mm-hm."

"Could you please not do that?"

He paused. "What?"

"Please leave your shirt on."

"Princess—"

"Please."

"Oh, hell," he said, and let his arms drop. It was

late. He was too tired to argue. "Will you at least let me have a pillow?"

Blythe's arm snaked out from under the covers as she picked up one of the pillows and handed it to him. A bare arm, he noted in sudden fascination, pale and slim and rounded. His heart started thudding. What was she wearing under that all-concealing counterpane? "Thank you." He spoke with admirable calmness, considering the sudden surge of heat through his body. "And a quilt?"

"There's one in the blanket chest."

"Ah." Simon pried open the lid of the carved oak chest at the foot of the bed. "So there is. Well." He settled on the floor, the quilt wrapped around him. "Better accommodations than I've had lately. Good night, princess," he said, and blew out the taper, plunging the tiny room into darkness.

"Good night," Blythe managed to get out through a very dry throat, and settled against the pillow. The mattress was lumpy and smelled musty, but she was too tired to care. Tired, and yet restless, as the day's events continued to play in her mind. She hadn't missed the way the innkeeper had looked at her this evening. Nor had she missed Simon's wince as he'd settled on the floor. He was doing remarkably well, but his leg had to be paining him.

"Simon?" she said tentatively.

She was greeted by silence. "What?" he said finally, his voice thick.

"Do you think we can trust Mr. Porter?"

The quilt rustled. "Go to sleep, princess, and don't worry about it."

"How well do you know him?"

"Well enough to know he wouldn't betray a fellow actor."

"But he's not an actor anymore."

"Princess, sometimes you talk too much."

"Do I? Funny, no one's ever said that to me before."

"Huh." The quilt rustled again. "Go to sleep, Blythe. Tomorrow's likely to be as tiring as today."

"All right." She turned on her side, facing him, though in the darkness she couldn't see him. "Good night."

"Good night."

In the darkness Simon let out a long breath, stirring reluctant pity within her. He must be exhausted. The day had been long and hard, and he was injured. And she couldn't sleep. "Simon?"

"God," he groaned. "Now what?"

"Is your leg paining you?"

"It wasn't."

"I'm sorry."

"Go to sleep, Blythe."

"Would you be more comfortable in the bed? I don't mean sharing it," she said hastily, horrified at herself for what she'd suggested. "I'd take the floor."

"Will it shut you up?"

"Yes."

"Oh, very well." More rustling sounds, followed by a groan. A moment later he fell onto the mattress next to her, arms outflung and heavy across her body. "There. Is that better, princess?"

"No! How am I to climb out, you—you oaf!" she exclaimed, pushing ineffectually at his shoulder. "Get off me. You're heavy."

"Not a complaint I've often had from women."

"Ooh!" Blythe worked her arm free and sat up. She was trapped between him and the wall. To leave the bed she would have to climb over him. The thought was frightening in its appeal. "Why I ever suggested this—"

"Yes, why did you, princess? Surely it's not because you desire"—his voice lowered—"my body?"

In spite of herself, Blythe choked back a laugh. Though she'd never seen a melodrama, he sounded much as she imagined a stage villain would. "Oaf. I asked you from the kindness of my heart, but if you persist in teasing me I shall push you out."

"I don't doubt it." He settled himself just a little distance from her, and she could suddenly breathe again. "I won't touch you, princess," he said gruffly. "You've my word on that."

"Oh, your word."

"Yes." He yawned. "This is more comfortable than the floor."

"Or the ground."

Simon chuckled. "You're a trouper, Blythe," he said, and as fast as that his breathing evened out.

"Simon?" she whispered. Her only answer was a snore. Well, what had she expected? she wondered, composing herself to sleep. After all, she certainly wouldn't want him in her bed under normal circumstances. It was only because he was hurt and tired. No more. And what, she wondered as sleep overtook her at last, was a trouper?

She fell into a sweet dream, one she'd had from time to time since childhood. She was standing outside a cottage, its features blurry, and beside her was a man, equally indistinct. All she knew was that his arm was about her waist and he loved her. Before them frolicked children, a whole litter of them, her sons and daughters. A family. Joy filled her. What more could she want? She belonged at last, with children to care for and a good, stable man by her side, a man who wouldn't leave. A man who loved her.

A man who was getting bold, as his hand slid from her waist to her breast, claiming it possessively. Goodness, this had never been part of her dream before! She should wake herself up. But what a sweet part it was, as his fingers toyed with her nipple, sending a shaft of pleasure through her. She turned in her husband's arms, and, just like that, he disappeared, something else that had never happened before. Yet she wasn't alone. Blythe blinked several times, disoriented to find herself in darkness when she'd stood in a sunlit clearing; confused as to why she was lying down; and wondering, as if she were dreaming all this, why she still felt a man's solid hand on her breast.

With a start, she jerked fully awake, aware and conscious of where she was, and who was beside her. "Simon!" She pulled back, but his other arm held her fast against his broad, warm chest. "Oh, let me go," she gasped, pushing against him, and at that moment he let out a sound that was half groan, half snore. Blythe went still. The dratted man was asleep.

"Simon," she whispered again, and again got no response. His arm lay heavy about her waist, his hand still fondled her, sending shafts of sweet sensation through her, and still he snored. Drat the man, he wouldn't wake up. She would have to extricate herself from this predicament as best she could.

Carefully she reached up and encircled his wrist with her fingers, easing his hand from her breast. He groaned again and, before she could move, rolled over, so that she was on her back, with him, large and heavy, half atop her. She gasped as his knee bent and his thigh pressed between hers, his body hair rough against her skin and sending prickles and shivers through her. And something was prodding her in the stomach, something hard and stiff. Whatever was he poking her with—oh! She went absolutely still, knowing she should move, yet held there by curiosity, and something more. So *that* was what a man felt like. She'd wondered. Oh, it wouldn't do, their lying together like this, and she should move, but . . . not yet. Simon still slept, unaware of her except as a woman in his bed, while longing filled her. A product of her dream, of course, in which she loved and was loved. She could never feel anything for this man. Even if he wasn't a criminal, he was a strolling player, a traveling man. Never would he stay in one place, establishing the family and life she so desperately wanted.

"Simon," she said, louder this time, pushing hard on his shoulder, and he grunted. "You oaf, get off me."

"Uh," he grunted again, and went still, with a tension in his muscles that told her he was awake. After a moment, he raised his head. "Ah, my sweet princess."

She punched his shoulder. "Get off me. I'm not your sweet anything."

"You're wrong," he said, and, bending his head, captured her lips.

She struggled. Of course. She was a virgin and

wished to stay that way, thank you. Oh, but it was
sweet, being kissed as she'd never imagined, even in
her dreams, his lips firm and warm and wet. Treacherous weakness stole through her limbs, making her
struggles feeble, less frantic. "Stop it," she gasped,
when his mouth left hers to—yes, he was actually nib-
bling at her ear, and though she didn't know why, she
knew it couldn't go on. "You have to stop."

"Not yet," he muttered, and brought his mouth to
hers again, hot, wet, and very, very persuasive. Against
the sensation of his firm, masculine lips moving against
hers, Blythe was suddenly lost. Closing her eyes, to the
room and to propriety, she gave herself up to his kiss.

Chapter 7

Abruptly Simon pulled back. "What are you doing?" he grated.

"What am I doing?" Blythe shot up in the bed, cold reality brutally replacing the hot sensations of a moment before. "I didn't start this."

"You invited me into your bed—"

"You conceited oaf!"

"Hell." He sat up, and in the dimness all she could see was his back, broad in his white shirt. "Do you know how long it's been since I've had a woman?"

"That's not my fault," she retorted, stung by the accusation in his voice.

"No, but, by God, it's your fault I'm in this bed—what the devil are you doing here, anyway?"

"What am I . . ." Her mouth dropped open, and her fingers involuntarily loosened on the covers she held to her breast. "As I recall, I didn't have much choice."

Silence lay heavy in the room. "No, you didn't, did you?" he said finally, and turned his head. "I'm sorry, princess. I didn't mean to get you in such a coil, truly."

"Then why did you take me?"

"I would have grabbed anyone who came along. It happened to be you."

For some reason, that hurt. "And tonight?" she asked, throat dry.

"Hell." He glanced at her. "Tonight was—" he began, and broke off at the sound of a soft scratching at the door. "What the devil is that?"

Blythe went still beside him, muscles tensed. Danger. "Don't answer."

The scratching came again. "I have to," he said, swinging his legs out of bed and tucking his shirt into his breeches.

"Simon, if it's someone looking for you—"

"Why, princess. Do you really care so?"

"No. I do not wish to be caught like this, with you."

"Of course not." The mattress dipped as he knelt on it, placing a swift, hard kiss on her lips. "Stay there," he said, and slipped across to the door. There he stood for a moment, head tilted, listening. "Who's there?"

"It's me," a voice said in reply. "Ben, the stableboy. I got somethin' important to tell you."

Simon glanced back at Blythe, and then opened the door. The figure that flitted in, holding a guttering candle, was small and thin and tousle-headed, and familiar. Blythe relaxed. Not a threat, though at the look Ben gave her she was glad she had not taken off her shift. "What is it?"

"You Mr. Simon?"

"Who told you who I am, boy?"

"Mrs. Porter." Ben stood squarely, though his eyes didn't quite meet Simon's. "You got to get out of here, you and the lady."

Simon again looked back at Blythe. Danger. She couldn't move. "Why?"

"There's someone here after yer. Mr. Porter's goin' to bring him up, but Mrs. Porter, she sent me first."

"The devil!" Simon exclaimed. "Blythe, best you stay here—"

"To be captured? Oh, no." Abruptly her paralysis vanished. She flew off the bed, hastily pulling on her clothes. "I'm coming with you."

"The hell you are—"

"There's no time!" Ben hissed, tugging at Simon's arm. "If I'm seen here I'll be in a deal of trouble. Yer gotta come, sir. Now."

"The devil," Simon said again, frowning as Blythe reached his side. They fell silent as Ben blew out the candle, plunging them into darkness. The door creaked as Simon opened it and peered out onto the landing. "No one there."

"Yet. They're comin' up the front," Ben said, and at that moment the sounds of footfalls reached them, distant but clear. More than one man was coming after them.

"Then we'll go down the back. I won't forget this, Ben."

"Jest yer go now, so's I don't get in no trouble."

"Hide," Blythe advised, as Simon pulled at her arm, leading her back down the staircase she'd climbed earlier.

With no candle to guide them, they felt their way along the rough plaster and board walls, stepping carefully onto treads worn hollow by years of use. Another landing, and another, and the inn remained quiet, dark, no one stirring at their passing. Blythe was just beginning to breathe a little more normally, thinking that perhaps they might make it, when from above there came a sudden pounding. "Woodley!" a voice hissed, sounding so close that she jumped, catching at Simon's arm. It was only as he grabbed her to him that she realized they were still alone on the stairs.

"Woodley," the voice came again, louder this time, and she recognized it as that of the innkeeper. By some echo, noise from above traveled down the stairwell to them. Which meant that any noise they made might well travel upward.

"Very quietly, now," Simon said, his breath tickling her neck. So he knew their danger, too. Slowly they continued down, one careful step at a time, placing their feet just so and hoping no creaking board would betray them. Around the curve there was a faint glow. The kitchen fireplace, Blythe realized. They were almost there.

Far above, a door crashed open, and feet pounded on the bare wooden floor. "They're gone!" a different voice cried.

No time for subterfuge now, or quiet, as feet hammered on the stairs behind them. Their absence had been discovered, and if they didn't hurry, their pres-

ence soon would be, also. "Fly!" Simon gasped, and
pulled at her arm.

Into the kitchen, cavernous in the dim light from
the fire's embers. A curse from Simon as he stumbled,
tripping on a dog sleeping on the hearth; the dog at
once set up a howling protest at being awakened. The
sounds above grew louder, more urgent, and Simon
tugged at her hand, pulling her to the door. They had
to run, they had to flee—

"This way!" a woman hissed from the shadows,
thrusting out a hand, and Blythe gave a little shriek.
"Be quiet, they'll hear you. Here." Dark emptiness
yawned up before her and she paused, only to be
pushed forward by firm, determined hands. Before she
quite knew what was happening, she was swallowed
up by the darkness of what was apparently a storage
bin, Simon beside her, and a door was quietly shut
behind them.

"What—" she began, dazed.

"Hush." Simon caught her against him, so close that
she could feel the tension in every muscle of his body.
"Be quiet."

"They'll catch us—"

"Be quiet!" This as the sound of pounding feet grew
louder, closer, accompanied by shouts and curses.

"Oh, Mr. Porter," a woman said on the other side
of the door, voice trembling. "Did you see them? I
fear I couldn't stop them."

"Where did they go?" Porter demanded.

"Out there. Oh, Mr. Porter, I never had such a scare
as when that man came out at me! How could you
take him in, and he a murderer?"

"Out the back?" Porter interrupted.

"Yes, the dog's after them," she said, and indeed,
in the distance they could hear a dog barking. Blythe
turned a questioning face up to Simon, as if he could
see her, and felt his arm tighten about her waist.

"I'll have something to say to you about this,
woman," Porter growled. "They're out back someplace. Can't be far."

"They had best not be," another voice said, and

Blythe froze. She had heard that voice only once before, but she would never forget it. It was the man who had faced them across the stream that morning and vowed their capture.

"Would I lead you wrong, sir? Come, follow me and we will catch them," Porter said. The din grew louder as the pursuers—how many Blythe could only guess—trooped through the kitchen, and then faded. And then it was only a distant sound. An eerie silence fell, broken only by the cries and complaints of the lodgers above.

The door abruptly opened. "Quickly, before they return," Mrs. Porter said. "They're following Yorick, but that won't last long."

"Yorick?" Blythe said, blinking a little at the light.

"The dog. Where is he leading them?" Simon asked, smiling a little, as if nothing untoward had occurred. Only his muscles, still tight and hard, betrayed the strain he must be feeling.

"After a fish I dragged out earlier." Mrs. Porter's sturdy, competent hands pushed them toward the door. "Come, now, there's no time to waste."

"You knew this would happen?"

"I thought it might. I know my husband."

"I shouldn't have trusted him. Why are you doing this?"

"Never mind that—oh, if you must know, I knew your mother. Now, go!" she hissed, then pushed them out the door and closed it behind them.

"Mr. Porter betrayed you?" Blythe said, dazed by the speed of the recent events.

"So it seems." His voice was grim as he led her by the hand into the woods behind the inn. "What of you? This is a perfect chance for you."

"If you let me go."

"I didn't force you to come with me."

"Not this time, no."

He held back a tree branch so that it wouldn't hit her in the face. "And why is that, I wonder? You could be well rid of me by now."

"I don't know why! What are we doing here?"

"Hiding," he said shortly. "They'll be back."

"But they'll look for us."

"Not here. They'll think us well away by now." He glanced at her, his face shadowed. "There's a fallen tree over there. You might as well sit on it, be comfortable."

"Thank you so much," Blythe said icily, but she sank down onto the log with distinct relief, taking the chance to straighten her bodice and pull on her mobcap. So much had happened in the past hours that her head was spinning. "When we get out of here—"

"Hush." He held up his hand. "Do you hear that?"

Blythe frowned. Faint in the distance she could hear the sound of voices. "What is it?"

"I think they're returning." He stood perfectly still as the sounds of a dog barking and of men's voices came closer. Not a very long search, Blythe thought, clasping her arms around her knees to still her shivers. Or did their pursuers know they'd not got far?

"This dog of yours is worthless." The voice was icy, aristocratic. In spite of herself Blythe leaned forward, trying to peer through the leaves at the speaker. Why was he following them? What had they ever done to him, that he pursued them so relentlessly? "To lose the scent like that."

"Yorick's not a hunting dog," Porter snapped. "It isn't his fault they got away."

"Is it not? Well, then." The voice was silky. Dangerous. "It must be yours, then."

"Someone warned them."

"Oh? Have you a traitor in your house?"

"If I do, I'll soon find out. Yorick!" He gave a sharp whistle. "Back here, now."

Yorick barked, much too close. Blythe realized with horror that the dog was at the edge of the woods. He must smell them, and in a moment he would come in among the trees, exposing them.

"Yorick! Damn dog." Porter's rumble was very close. "Can't think what's got into you. Come on. And stop whining." Yorick yelped, the sound of his paws scrabbling in the dirt echoing behind Porter's heavy tread. Blythe let out a breath she hadn't known she was holding. Disaster had been so very near. "Tomorrow we'll search for any sign."

"Tomorrow they'll be gone, and I've nothing but a pair of ruined breeches to show for the night," the cool, smooth voice said. "I shall hold you responsible for that."

"Who was it that let Woodley escape in the first place?" Porter answered, and with that the inn's door banged shut. Blythe and Simon were alone, save for the rustlings of small animals and the occasional chirp of a cricket.

Simon was the first to move, rolling his shoulders as he turned toward her. "Alas, poor Yorick."

Blythe blinked. "What?"

"I knew him well. But who is that after me?"

"I'm sure I don't know." Now that the danger was past, at least for the moment, Blythe was aware of how tired she was, down to her soul. "I am not the escaped criminal."

"As you are with me, I don't think that distinction will account for much." He held out his hand to help her up. She ignored it, standing without aid, though she swayed with tiredness. There was nothing she wanted more than her hard, narrow bed in her tiny room in London.

"Where are we going?" she asked, falling in beside him.

"Away from here. If we can make progress tonight, we can rest during the day, when the hunt will be the fiercest."

"I can't," she protested, stopping. "I just . . . can't."

He turned toward her, began to speak, and then stopped. The light was dim, but she thought perhaps his face was softening. "Tomorrow we go our separate ways," he said. "Have you a place to go?"

"Yes, where I used to live, in—"

"Don't tell me." He held up his hand. "If they capture me I won't be able to tell them where you are."

"Oh." She stared at him. "You'll let me go tomorrow?"

"I'd let you go now, if I thought you could walk without falling," he said as she stumbled on a tree root and was saved from a fall only by his hand catching her arm. "Best thing for us now is to get some sleep."

How her life had changed, Blythe thought, tramping along beside him, trying to watch for obstacles in her path and to avoid bumbling into trees. She still half thought she might wake up and find this had all been a dream. A nightmare, more like. It was nearly over, though. Tomorrow she would be free, away from a criminal who was too attractive for her own good. Which was something he must never know.

There was nothing for it. She could not return to London, nor to the inn. Sighing, she squared her shoulders. She would simply have to resign herself to another cold, miserable night of sleeping outdoors.

Morning came damp and cheerless. Blythe had had quite enough of adventure. From where she was, trudging along the edge of a lonely, empty road, with anything worth seeing hidden by fog, adventure was vastly overrated. The heroines in the novels she'd read surreptitiously never seemed to notice mundane things such as wet feet and tangled hair, let alone more private problems; there were no privies in the woods. And she was hungry. Since the meal at the inn the evening before, she and Simon had had nothing to eat, nor did food appear to be a likely prospect anytime soon. She wished passionately now that she had never left the shelter of Mrs. Wicket's house or, more especially, her village. Even marriage to the widowed apothecary with his six children was beginning to look appealing.

"There's a crossroads ahead," Simon said, at last breaking the silence. "We'll part ways there."

Blythe looked dully up at him. "How do you know that?"

"Because of where you're going—you did say south?—and where I have to go."

"The coast is south, too," she said, as if she actually still wished for his company.

He shrugged. "I'll find means of leaving the country. 'Tis the only thing I can do, I suppose."

Blythe glanced at him, suspicious of his whining tone. He looked miserable enough, however, just as she suspected she did. Under such circumstances a bit of self-pity wasn't unwarranted. "I hope you're not caught," she burst out.

He looked at her slantwise. "Why is that, princess?"

"Heaven knows." Already she regretted her words. "Any right-thinking person would want to see you hanged."

"Then it must follow that you are not a right-thinking person."

"I'll have you know—"

"Will you be all right?"

The gentleness of his voice stopped her in mid-tirade. "Of course I will. Why?"

He glanced away. "It might be difficult for you, where you're going."

"I don't expect it to be easy. They'll wonder why I've returned, and—"

"And they'll probably know you've been with me the last two days."

Her mouth dropped open. "Surely not!"

"I'm a wanted man, princess, and you helped me to escape. Do you not think they know who you are by now?"

"But I've lived a blameless life."

His lips tightened. "Do you think that matters? Once people believe you're guilty, nothing you say changes matters."

Blythe began to answer and then stopped. Perhaps that was true for him. Not only had he been convicted, but he was an actor, a notoriously immoral profession. In the village of her birth, however, she doubted people would judge her the same way. "I think—" she began, just as his hand sliced down, gesturing her to silence. "What is it?"

"A carriage."

"I hear it." From the road behind, she could just hear the rumble of wheels. "It sounds distant yet."

"Fog plays tricks with sound," he said tersely, as the noise suddenly grew louder. "Into the trees! Now!"

Hiding had become so ingrained a part of her that Blythe didn't question him, but dove into the underbrush by the side of the road, grimacing only a little as a branch hit her in the face. Simon was close behind her, throwing himself down onto his stomach and peering out through the grass. So far this morning there'd been no sign of pursuit, but it was too much to hope their luck would last.

The sound faded again, and then Blythe could suddenly hear the horses' snorting and breathing and the wheels creaking—so close, it seemed the carriage was atop them. She clapped her hands over her ears and ducked her head, not certain why this traveler scared her more than others. Simon threw an arm over her shoulders, pulling her to his side, and she cowered against him gratefully. Only one small part of her brain was detached enough, calm enough to remark on the absurdity of her reaction.

Beside her Simon let out an exclamation, and suddenly he was up, bounding out of the trees onto the road. "Simon!" she gasped. "What are you doing—"

"Hey!" Simon was waving his arms at the carriage, close enough now for Blythe to see that it was an old black traveling coach, a crest apparently having been painted out on the door. It was followed by an odd-looking cart. Long and tall, it was enclosed at the top, and the sides were painted red and blue, with bits of gilt flaking off here and there. The carriage was drawn by a pair of knock-kneed, sway-backed, mismatched horses, and the driver was an old man, thin, hunched over, with greasy long hair falling unkempt past his shoulders. At sight of Simon he pulled hard on the reins, and the horses, tired nags that they were, stopped so fast that the cart jolted. "McNally!" Simon shouted as the driver jumped down from the box, running forward to grab the man around the shoulders and pummeling his back. "A sight for sore eyes, you are!"

"Joseph, what is it? Simon!" Another old man, this one bearded and portly, jumped out of the carriage, beaming. "I say! I was hoping we'd run into you."

Simon laughed, looking suddenly years younger. "And what role are you playing, my old graybeard?"

The portly man chuckled, reached up his hand to his face, and, to Blythe's astonishment, pulled off his beard. Why, he was in disguise. Who were these people?

"We'd heard you might be on this road," the man was saying, slinging his arm about Simon's shoulders, though he was shorter. "Caused a commotion at the Tabard, I understand."

"Porter is not the friend I thought him." Simon's mouth was momentarily a grim slash. "And you?"

"On the circuit, of course, going from theater to theater, and looking for you. Harry bid me to."

"My uncle? Is he well?"

"Not that Harry." The man chuckled. "The young 'un. Henrietta got a tongue on her, that one. Should've heard what she had to say to Old Gaffer when she learned you'd never met up with him."

"There'll be time to discuss this later," the driver said. "No telling who else is on the road."

"Yes. Get in, my boy, and we'll see you're safe—"

"I'm not alone," Simon interrupted, and the two men looked at each other.

"We'd heard that," the portly man said, frowning. "And just what is the story there?"

"You're not my father, Giles, so don't think to lecture me," Simon retorted, and swung toward the woods. "Blythe? Come out, princess. We're among friends."

"Maybe to you," Blythe muttered, cautiously clambering to her feet. She wasn't certain she'd be any safer among a company of actors than she was with one alone.

The three men watched her as she stumbled through the brush to the road, and though Simon was smiling,

the others were not. For people who made their livings
emoting, their faces were remarkably still.

Simon came forward, holding out his hand. "The
best of good fortune, princess," he said, taking
Blythe's arm and leading her to the others. "We've
been found by a troupe of actors. Not quite as good
as the Woodleys, of course—"

"We haven't all day," the driver interrupted. Up
close Blythe could see that he was much younger than
he'd at first appeared. "Not if we're to reach Rochester by evening."

"I won't keep you." Blythe managed to keep her
voice calm. "If you would just drop me at the next
crossroads—"

"As if we would!" The portly man interrupted, and
she realized for the first time that his appearance of
age was also fraudulent. Below his graying hair his
brow was unlined, his eyes sharp. "After what Wood-
head here has put you through, you deserve better
than that. No, my dear, we'll take you to safety." He
took her elbow in what was apparently meant to be a
courtly gesture, though his hand squeezed a little
harder than necessary. "Allow me to introduce myself.
I am Giles Rowley, esteemed player and manager of
the Rowley Theatrical Troupe. You should know," he
went on in a confidential tone, leading her to the
coach, "that not all players are the arrant rogues our
Simon is."

"I am glad to hear that," Blythe stammered out,
looking from one to the other. Giles was smiling, and
even the driver was nodding politely at her. It was
very odd. After two days on the road with an escaped
convict, here she was conversing as if she were in a
drawing room. Madness. "Our driver, this redoubtable
old man—"

"McNally," the driver interrupted, and briefly swept
the wig from his head, revealing startlingly red hair.
"If we don't get started, Giles, no tellin' what will
happen."

"Those disguises can't have fooled Porter," Simon
said, walking by Blythe's side to the back of the cart.

"He doesn't know we're using them, does he?" Giles replied, opening the door of the carriage. "In with you, my dear. My wife is just inside, so you've naught to worry about."

"Thank you." Blythe clambered into the carriage. It was a moment before her eyes adjusted enough to see a very young woman pressed up against the carriage wall, her eyes huge. What on earth had she gotten herself into now?

"My wife, Phoebe," Giles said, climbing in behind her and slipping his arm about the girl's shoulders. "We've some members of the troupe in the prop wagon. The rest are on shank's mare."

"Walking?" Blythe said, though she didn't know why she was so surprised. Hadn't she herself walked the distance from London, twenty-two miles by the last milestone?

"Aye. You'll meet them later." He smiled down at his wife. "Phoebe tends to be shy."

"A pleasure to meet you," Blythe murmured. The girl shrank closer to Giles. Not how she expected an actress to behave.

Simon plopped down on the seat beside her, his breath coming out in a whoosh. "We made it, princess." He grinned at her. "We're safe."

Blythe smiled back with great effort. Safe? Perhaps for the moment. But who were these people she'd fallen in with? And what was going to happen to her next?

"Once was bad enough." Honoria gazed out the window, her hair dark as the night sky. "Twice? Far worse. But thrice, Quentin?" She turned, and though her face was calm, her knuckles clutching the fine golden brocade drapery were white. "Thrice you had him within your grasp, and thrice he escaped. It is inexcusable."

Quentin bowed slightly. The drawing room of Stanton House was brilliantly lit by candles, dozens of them in sconces and candelabras. Their glow shone on the polished cherry side table and reflected in the pier glass hanging over the mantel. "I have no excuse," he said frankly. "He has proven to be a devilish slippery character."

"Do not think to charm your way out of this, Quentin. I am quite vexed." The skirts of her taffeta gown rustled and swayed as she paced to a chair. Even in anger she sat gracefully, head erect, back straight, a beautiful, passionate woman, except for her eyes. They had taken on the hue of her gown and were pale lavender ice, regarding him with no expression whatsoever. Somehow that was more threatening than if she'd glared. "I thought you were competent, Quentin." Her gaze flicked down over his loins, and than back up. "I find I have been sadly mistaken."

Quentin stiffened, stung by the lash of that look. The rogue was proving to be more resourceful than they'd expected, and with more allies, but to say so would sound weak, puling. He would not grovel before her with excuses. Instead, he turned away. "Then I suggest, my lady, that you find someone else to do your dirty work. I wash my hands of this affair."

"But you were glad enough to take my blood money," she shot back, and Quentin stopped just shy of the door. Something in her voice, a tone he'd rarely heard, held him. Could she be afraid? "Oh, come back, you idiot."

Quentin turned, leaning a shoulder negligently against the carved paneling and casually straightening the frothy white lace at his wrist. He wore midnight-blue velvet tonight, with white satin breeches and a waistcoat liberally embroidered with silver thread. Quentin enjoyed fine clothes. So far during this escapade he had ruined a pair of expensive boots and some breeches. Someone would pay for that. "Such compliments you pay me, my lady."

"Quentin, I am growing extremely vexed with you."

"My apologies, my lady," he said, still toneless.

"I don't want your apologies!" She was on her feet now, her eyes alight with anger, hands on her hips and bosom jutting forward. He eyed it with frank fascination as she stalked toward him. "I want you to do what you promised."

He let himself ogle her for another moment before raising his eyes to hers. "And what is that, my lady?"

"That you will take care of the upstart," she hissed.

Quentin reached into his waistcoat pocket for his enameled snuffbox. Opening it one-handed in a seemingly careless gesture, he took a pinch of snuff, while Honoria glared at him, arms crossed over her chest. Honoria angry was far easier to handle than when she was cold, dispassionate. Either way, however, she was dangerous. And that only added spice to their relations. "I don't imagine he considers himself an upstart." He placed the snuff on the back on his hand and inhaled. "Ah, very good," he said, once he sneezed. "A fine blend. I must commend the tobacconist when next I see him."

"I care not about your tobacco—"

"I don't believe he has any idea of who he is." Quentin's gaze sharpened. "It might be best to leave him in peace."

"I shall have no peace while I know he walks this earth! He is a danger, Quentin. Not only to me, but to you, too. Must I constantly remind you of that?"

Quentin leaned his head back. "I believe he is heading for the coast, to leave the country. He is no threat, my love."

"He had best not be." She stepped abruptly forward. At the same moment he felt something press against his groin. Her eyes met his, and a chill of fear skittered down his spine. Oh, they blazed, those magnificent violet eyes, with cold fire and a calculating rage that was far more frightening than any tantrum could be. "Or you'll suffer. That I promise."

The pressure against his groin increased, and he felt a quick shaft of pain. He would not look down, would not give her the satisfaction; but in spite of himself his head bent. Her small white hand held a shiny, bejeweled, and very sharp dagger. "Would you damage that which has given you such pleasure, Honoria?" he said, voice trembling in spite of himself.

"This? Why, Quentin, darling, what makes you think this is so special?" She twisted the knife and then, as he recoiled, stepped back, teeth bared in a fierce grin. "But since it seems to mean so much to you, I shall spare it. This time."

Damn, but it was hot in the room. There were beads of perspiration on his forehead, and his velvet coat felt heavy. "Thank you for your kindness, my lady."

"Do not thank me yet." She paced away, her posture straight, regal. "Find him. Find him and kill him, or it will go ill with you."

Quentin's lips thinned. Just moments ago he'd had the upper hand, or so he'd thought. His gaze flicked to the knife again. Now it seemed she'd been in control all along. "I'll find him," he said through stiff lips, his mind racing through all his possible courses of action. He could do as she bid, of course. He could leave the country himself; he had no kin, no property worth fighting for, though Lord knew where he'd go. Or he could do something else altogether, something to benefit himself. "I shall take care of him, my lady," he said, and, giving her a sweeping bow, walked out of the room.

Chapter 8

The Rowley Theatrical Troupe entered into Rochester
with great fanfare and a procession, consisting of
members of the troupe, colorfully arrayed, led by a
child beating a drum. Conspicuous in the carriage
were Giles, smiling benevolently upon the spectators,
and his wife; slumped below window level was Simon,
with Blythe close against him. He was her captor and
her . . . what? For the life of her, she didn't know
anymore what she felt about him.

She raised her head. His gaze met hers and held,
steady, serious. It came flooding back to her then, all
that had happened the evening before at the Tabard
Inn. That kiss. Mercy, that kiss! Color flooded into
her cheeks with the return of the memories. She was
not naive. She knew that it was possible to be carried
away by passion, though she herself never before had
been. Nor had she ever expected to be, and certainly
not with this man. Not even though his eyes were
warm, knowing; his lips softened, parted; his head
bent. Helplessly she gazed at him. They were not
alone, and their lives were in peril. Yet, if he were to
kiss her again, she would not, for the life of her, be
able to pull away.

"Good." Giles nodded approvingly at the spectators. "We've managed to attract an audience. That
should bring them in. And with so obvious an entrance, no one should suspect you're here."

"Good," Simon said quietly. Though he hadn't actually moved, Blythe sensed his withdrawal from her, in
the tension of his muscles, in the tone of his voice.
And thank heavens for that. She wriggled on the seat,

putting as much space between her and Simon as possible. To have kissed him once was folly, something she didn't intend to repeat. If he thought she would, that she was awaiting his kisses at any time, he'd soon learn differently. She was not about to take up with an actor, let alone with an escaped convict.

"We're to be two weeks here," Giles said, stretching, his arm coming down on Phoebe's shoulder. She shied a bit, but then relaxed, moving closer to him. "And here my lovely bride will make her debut as Lady Macbeth."

"The Scottish play? An interesting choice," Simon said. "I wish you well in the role, Mrs. Rowley."

Phoebe murmured something inaudible, her head lowered, and Giles beamed. "She will delight us all. And you, Simon? Do you join us?"

"No. We will be leaving you here."

"It's true, then?" Giles's gaze was sharp. "You're for the coast."

Simon shrugged, that half-smile that Blythe found both infuriating and enticing upon his face. "Who knows?"

Giles nodded. "Best if you don't tell us. And you, lass, you've a place to go?"

Blythe sat primly, properly, hands folded in her lap. "Yes, thank you."

"A pity. No, not that you have a home, of course. Doubtless after the past days your home will be a welcome sight. But that voice, lass. Ah, what an actress you would make."

Simon made a noise suspiciously like a snort. Well! He needn't find the idea quite so amusing, though it was, of course, ridiculous. "I thank you, sir, but I think I'm best suited elsewhere."

"I am not so sure, but—ah, well, it is your choice, of course. We stop at the Royal Theater." He turned to Simon, suddenly all business. "We've only a few hours to rehearse. Pity your face is so well-known, Simon. We could use your talent."

Simon lifted a shoulder in a negligent shrug. "Another time, perhaps."

"If we are lucky." Giles rose as the carriage jolted to a halt, and opened the door. "And here we are, at the Royal. It's a bit shabby." He frowned. "Looks to have come down in the world since last we were here. But don't worry, my sweet." He smiled down at Phoebe. "The place will shine tonight for you. And you will shine in it."

Phoebe ducked her head, and Blythe felt a stab of pity for her, so obviously out of place in this environment. As was Blythe. The sooner she set off for home, the happier she would be, she told herself resolutely.

Ignoring Simon's hand, she stood up, peering cautiously out of the carriage. All she could see was a high, drab brick wall, pierced by windows but with only one door. "The back of the theater," Simon explained, standing beside her. "The part actors are most familiar with."

"I wouldn't know."

"I realize that, but . . ." He shot her a look. "Have you never seen a play, then?"

She kept her eyes focused ahead, watching Giles escort Phoebe into the theater. "No, never." And though she would like to, this was neither the time nor the place for it.

"Ah, a shame. If things were different I would play Hamlet for you. Or perhaps"—he grinned—"Romeo."

"Or perhaps the part of a condemned man, in which you would do very well."

He jumped to the ground, holding his arms out to her. She ignored him, clambering carefully down by herself. "Enemies to the end, I see."

"Of course. How could we be other?"

"Indeed." Simon edged closer. "However, I suspect I shall miss you, Miss Marden."

"The feeling is not returned, Mr. Woodley."

"Quickly, now." McNally was before them, frowning. "Get inside. The fewer see you, the better."

Blythe pulled back from the hand he had put on her arm. "But I thought I'd go—"

"You will." Simon took her other arm, and so she

was propelled to the narrow wooden staircase that led to the stage door. "But as I have caused you no end of inconvenience these past days, I would like to arrange transport for you."

She glanced at him, startled, and then looked away. Oh, what a performer he was. Now that he was among friends, he was pretending to be kind. Why, he had even managed to make his eyes look regretful. A most skilled actor, indeed. "Thank you," she said coolly.

"The least I can do. And Blythe . . ." He put his hand on her arm as they stepped just inside the theater, making her stop.

"What?"

"About last night . . ."

"What about last night?"

"Ah . . . nothing. Forget it," he muttered, turning away.

"I assure you, I have," she said to his back, and had the satisfaction of seeing his shoulders stiffen.

"Come, Miss Marden." Giles was taking her elbow, with Phoebe still on his other side. "We will find you a place to wait while McNally goes for a chaise."

"You must be hungry," Phoebe said, so softly that Blythe had to strain to hear her.

"I am, rather," Blythe admitted.

"We'll go to the green room. Someone will find something for you."

"Thank you." So this was what a theater looked like, she thought, glancing around. At least the back of one, a maze of narrow passageways, some of which sloped, and stairs that rose into the darkness above. An open door to her right disclosed a large room, where tables were set with mirrors, and several of the ladies of the troupe were already settling with their baggage and their babies. It was dark, drab, workaday. Not what she had expected, and yet somehow she wasn't surprised. After the events of the last days, she didn't think anything could surprise her anymore.

"Here, sit down." Giles threw another door open. It led into a room decorated much as a drawing room would be, with sofas and chairs placed on a fraying rug and pictures dotting the peeling plastered walls. On the far wall hung an enormous gilt-framed pier glass. All the furniture showed considerable signs of use, but Blythe sank into a carved oak chair gratefully. Her concept of comfort had changed in the last few days. Giles frowned and turned away. "And you, master Simon, had best stay out of sight. None of my troupe'll betray you, but I can't vouch for the locals."

Simon shook his head. "I won't stay, Giles. I'm not going to put you in any kind of danger."

"No talk of that, now," Giles said quickly. "Sit down and we'll find you something to eat. Then you can decide what to do. Come, my love." He smiled down at Phoebe. "Let us see if this stage is adequate for your talent." They went out and the door closed behind them, leaving Simon and Blythe alone for the first time since they'd met the traveling troupe.

Blythe felt her color abruptly rising again as the memory of last night struck her. As if he were thinking the same thing, Simon sprang up from the chair and paced the floor. "I can't stay here. 'Tis not safe for anyone," he said.

Blythe leaned her head back against the chair. "Why is this called the green room? The walls are yellow."

"Tradition. Green is a lucky color for the stage." He stopped before a badly executed landscape, frowning. "Likely I'll never be in a green room again."

Drowsiness was fast overtaking Blythe, in spite of her hunger. "What are you going to do?"

He turned, hands tucked into his breeches pockets. "It's best you not know."

She straightened. "Aren't you heading for the coast?"

"I can't tell—" he began, just as the door from the corridor crashed open. Instantly he dropped into a crouch, hands extended before him, wary and ready, shielding Blythe from whoever had come in.

"Oh, Simon, my dear boy," said a musical voice in deep contralto. "Do I still frighten you so?"

Simon straightened, looking just a bit sheepish.

Blythe looked from him to the woman who stood there smiling. Had he been protecting himself, or her? "Katherine." He took the woman's hand in his and brought it to his lips. "As lovely as ever, I see."

"Flatterer. And what have you brought us now, Simon? An addition to our troupe? Though I warn you, we've enough ingenues at the moment—"

"I'm not staying," Blythe put in quickly, annoyed as the woman took Simon's arm and subjected Blythe to a comprehensive scrutiny. Blythe flushed. She knew she looked disheveled, but who was this woman to pass judgment on her? And what was she to Simon? "And I'm no actress."

"No ingenue, either," Katherine said, matter-of-fact and yet not unkind. "Just as well. I've enough challengers vying for my roles."

"No one can hold a candle to you, Kate," Simon said, and Blythe felt again that annoyance. Jealousy? Surely not.

"Dear boy." Katherine patted Simon's cheek absently and chose a chair across the room, sitting with a swirl of skirts that would do a queen proud and that made Blythe's fingers clench. Though she must have arrived with the others, she yet managed to appear pristine and composed, in a full-skirted gown of sky-blue muslin, with a white petticoat beneath, and not a strand of her chestnut hair, piled atop her head, out of place. Nor did her face bear any traces of theatrical makeup. Not quite the painted lady of Blythe's imaginings. "You would do, you know, even if you're not suitable for the ingenue roles."

"Me?" Blythe said in surprise.

"Yes, you."

"But I'm not an actress."

"Stand up," Katherine commanded, and to her own surprise, Blythe did so. "Mmm. She has presence, don't you agree, Simon?"

Simon glanced over at Blythe. "I suppose she does."

"Nevertheless, I am not an actress," Blythe insisted, annoyed by his too-ready agreement.

"But you could be. You would not play the lead,

not yet, but with time and training, perhaps you'd do. And with that hair you'd be striking on the stage."

Blythe's hand flew to her hair. There was nothing, she knew, the least bit striking about her. "I thank you for your kind words, but—"

". . . and that's put the devil in it," Giles said, walking into the room, a sheaf of papers in his hands. "Kate, what are you doing here?"

Katherine lifted an imperious brow. "I was curious."

"I told you not to—well, the damage is done, and in more ways than one. Joseph found you transport, Miss Marden."

Blythe's gaze went to Simon. He held it for just a moment and then looked away. "Did he?" she said, wondering why the news didn't make her happier.

"Yes. But there's a problem." He handed some of the papers to Simon, some to Blythe. "Soldiers are in town, posting these."

"Bloody hell," Simon muttered. "Well, I know I'm a wanted man. This doesn't make much difference."

Blythe glanced down and saw, at the top of the piece of foolscap in her hands, dark letters proclaiming the word WANTED. If these were being circulated everywhere, what chance would Simon have of escape? "Perhaps if you wear a disguise," she said.

"Bloody hell," Simon said again, with more heat this time, throwing the papers down. "What are they about?"

"Do you see where your foolishness has led, boy?" Giles said. "Bad enough the law's after you, but to bring it down on an innocent is a disgrace."

"But we knew the soldiers were searching," Blythe said. "This only confirms it."

Simon's eyes held regret. "Can you read, Blythe?"

"Yes, of course I can read."

"Then read the rest of it."

She frowned at him, but then dropped her eyes to the page again. Underneath the heading, "Wanted," in letters only slightly smaller, was a name she hadn't expected to see. Her own.

Chapter 9

"This can't be right," Blythe said, staring uncomprehendingly at the poster. "I've done nothing wrong."

"I'm sorry, princess." Simon stood before her, hands tucked into his pockets. "I never meant to involve you so."

"But you have, so what do you plan to do about it?" Giles broke in.

Blythe looked up. Giles looked grim. Even Katherine, poster in hand, looked grim. "But it's not that bad," Blythe protested. "If I go home—"

"Where you're known, and where they're sure to search for you," Simon interrupted, crouching before her and placing his hands on the arms of the chair so that his eyes were level with hers. "I'm sorry, Blythe. It looks like you're as much a fugitive as I."

"I can't be!" Blythe slapped at his hand, pushing it away, and stood up so fast he nearly toppled over. "I've done nothing wrong, nothing! It wasn't my fault that you came along when you did—"

He got to his feet, his hand hovering uncertainly near her shoulder. This was indeed his fault. "I know, princess, and I'm sorry. If I could change things, I—"

"You wouldn't." She said it calmly, looking at him over her shoulder. "You'd do the same thing. You would take me captive and drag me across half of England to save yourself. That's all you care about."

He didn't flinch at that, though her words were like lashes on his already sore conscience. "I'm sorry, princess," he said again. "I can't change what's done."

"What are you going to do, boy?" Giles asked heavily.

Simon turned to him, all his plans, all his hopes to clear his name fading. He had lost any right to them when he had dragged an innocent into his escape. "We'll go to the coast," he said, squaring his shoulders. "There'll be some way for us to get out of the country."

"But I don't want to go!" Blythe wailed.

"I know. But what else can you do, princess? If you go to family or friends you're sure to be caught, and what good will that do you? And they'll use you to get to me."

She stared at him. "That's what this is about, isn't it? Not whether I'm safe, but whether you are."

Hell. For once in his life he was trying to do the right thing, and it was being tossed back in his face. "Blythe, I—"

"You're both overlooking something," Giles said. "The ports will be watched to prevent your escape."

Simon shrugged. "That's a chance we'll have to take."

"Silly boy, you haven't learned a thing, have you?" Katherine scolded. She had crossed the room and now stood beside Blythe, an arm about her shoulders. "Perhaps you deserve to be taken, but this innocent doesn't."

He nodded in wry acknowledgment. Perhaps he did deserve it. "I can't think of what else to do."

"The answer is obvious, is it not? Hide."

"Ha!" His laugh was mirthless. "Where?"

Katherine caught Giles's gaze. "In plain sight."

Giles nodded. "In the last place anyone would think to look for you."

"In . . ." Simon's voice trailed off as their meaning penetrated. "You're saying—"

"Stay with us, you and Miss Marden. We'll find something for you to do, and a place to stay—"

"I can't stay here!" Blythe exclaimed, sounding so horrified that they turned to look at her. Her eyes were huge, her face pale, the very picture of fear, making Simon long to go to her. But he didn't. He'd done her enough harm. "I can't."

"Why not, princess?" he said mildly.

"Because I—because you're—well, you're actors."

Giles and Katherine gazed at her politely, as if waiting for her to go on. "I see," Simon said. "You have so little trust in yourself that you fear we'll corrupt you."

"Yes. No! Of course not. But I can't stay here." She swallowed hard, and for the first time since he'd met her, her eyes shone as if she were about to cry. "I don't belong here."

"No, you don't," Katherine said, to Simon's surprise. "You deserve better. But if you'll think about it, dear, you'll see it makes sense."

"We've been searched and questioned already," Giles said. "They'll not bother us again."

"We can't put you in danger in such a way," Simon put in, though in truth he thought it a good plan. They were right, of course. The soldiers would be at all the ports, especially since he had taken care to hint that he planned to leave the country. And it was bad enough he'd dragged Blythe into his affairs, without exposing her either to arrest or life in a foreign country.

"What's life without a little danger?" Giles clapped Simon on the shoulder. "You'll stay."

"Yes." Simon nodded. If he stayed with the Rowley troupe, he would be able to pursue his goal of clearing his name. Blythe would still be with him as well, though he didn't know why that should matter so. What was important was that for once he give her a choice. Even if there really was no choice. "I know I will. I can't speak for Miss Marden."

All heads swiveled to Blythe. She was staring at them, biting her lower lip, furrowing her brow. He wanted to pull her close and kiss the frown away. Especially since he'd put it there. "It's the best thing, princess."

Blythe looked from one to the other, and then her shoulders sagged. "I suppose it is," she murmured, and, swaying, put her hands to her face.

Simon stepped forward, but Katherine was quicker,

laying her arm across Blythe's shoulders. "There, little one. You're tired and hungry and nothing seems right when you're like that. Everything will look better once you're rested."

"I hope so." Blythe had regained her composure and was gazing at Simon, clearly, steadily. For the first time, though, he could not read what was in that gaze. She had learned to shutter herself away. That he might be the cause was bitter knowledge.

"Come." Katherine turned, her arm still about Blythe's shoulders. "We'll find a place for you to stay."

"Who knows, princess?" Simon said, goaded somehow, frightened by the sight of her walking away. "We might even make an actress out of you."

"Mercy!" The wide-eyed look she threw him over her shoulder went some way toward restoring his good humor. "As if I would be one of—"

"Careful," he taunted, hands on hips. "Remember where you are."

"So far, sir, the most dangerous person I've met is you," she retorted.

Giles let out a laugh. "She's got you there, boy. Now leave her alone. You've enough troubles of your own. Oh, and Kate, a moment, please? We need to discuss this afternoon's rehearsal."

Katherine smiled reassuringly at Blythe and then stepped away to speak with Giles. That left Blythe and Simon alone, avoiding each others' eyes, at a loss for words. Simon didn't know why he should feel this way, so tongue-tied and awkward. She was no great beauty, no polished lady of the theater. Just a chance-met companion, whom he had abducted, and who, last evening, had been surprisingly warm and enticing in his arms.

"I think you'll be comfortable," he began.

"They seem nice," Blythe said at the same moment. "I'm sorry. You were saying?"

"No. You speak first."

"Thank you. Your friends seem nice."

"For actors?" His mouth twisted. "Of course, you

haven't had a shining example of our trade to study, have you?"

"No, not quite," she said dryly, her head tilted to the side. "I never know when you are serious and when you are playing a role."

"Then that is to my advantage, is it not?" He raised his head, lips firming. What he was about to say would hurt her. "Last night at the inn, before we were interrupted—"

"Please." She held out her hand. "Let us not talk of that."

"After today, we won't. But last night . . . you clearly expected me to play the rogue."

All color leeched from her face. "I beg your pardon?"

"I believe you understand me. You are right. Sometimes I do play a role."

Blythe jerked back. "What are you saying?"

Simon's hand reached out, and he pulled it back. Better this way, to make a clean break. "Last night meant nothing."

Blythe's eyes were opaque. "I see."

"Do you, princess?" he said, taunting her, taunting himself.

"Oh, yes. And if that was acting last night"—she took a deep breath—"you need to practice more." With that she turned, striding out of the green room, and he let her go. But it was harder than he had ever expected it would be.

"Well, and a fine mess you've made of things," a voice said behind Simon, and he turned to see McNally, leaning against the wall. "Why'd you drag the girl into it?"

"I had to." Simon slipped out a door, hoping McNally wouldn't follow. It had been so long since he'd been in a theater—since before his arrest—and breathing the air was like coming home. A few steps here, and he could see onto the stage, quiet, bare. It drew him, called to him, making him walk faster, through the wings made up of sliding scenery, onto the stage at last. Before him the auditorium echoed in its emptiness, the rows of backless benches worn and polished from the thousands of people who had sat there over the years. In the boxes that ringed the auditorium, velvet curtains hung heavy with dust and age. Altogether it was dull, workaday, and yet Simon knew that when the great chandelier overhead was lit tonight, the auditorium would be transformed into a place of magic, demanding the very best of him. Which was certainly not something he'd given to anyone lately, least of all Blythe.

He shifted from one foot to another, looking high above the stage, where various ropes and catwalks and ladders hung, for access to the scenery needed to set the stage. Lord, what was wrong with him? For the image that had flashed into his mind, of a temptress with honey hair streaked with gold, was not that of the Blythe who had tramped beside him for the last days. It was of the woman who had lain, soft and melting, in his arms last evening at the Tabard Inn.

"I had to," he said again, though McNally, who had followed him, had said nothing. He'd had to hold her, had to kiss her, and if they hadn't been interrupted, he would have had to make her his own, and to hell with the consequences. "The soldiers were after me and I needed help escaping."

McNally dragged an empty crate onto the stage, the sound grating and loud. "So you dragged her into it."

"You're not my father, McNally."

McNally appeared to mull that over. "No, lad, I'm not, but someone needs to set you straight about this. You've ruined that girl's life."

"What am I supposed to do, marry her?"

"No, that would be the worst thing you could do."

"Am I such a bad catch?" Simon demanded.

"Ordinarily, maybe not. But now? There's a price on your head, lad, and don't you forget it."

The silence was thick and heavy. "You think I did it, don't you?"

McNally turned his head and spat. "I don't know."

"Hell." Simon spun around, hands balled into fists.

If even old friends doubted him, what chance had he with anyone else?

"Think of how it looks," McNally went on calmly. "You'd had business with Miller—that was common knowledge—and reason to dislike him." He pursed his lips. "Is it true you had an affair with his wife?"

"No," Simon said wearily. "I barely knew her, and I had enough to deal with, with. . . ."

"Aye, lad, I know," McNally said after a moment. "With Laura."

Simon nodded, his heart aching, as always it did when he thought of Laura. And her child. "But it only made me look worse. I don't know how that rumor started. There's something strange about it, though." He turned. "It was her knife."

"Eh? What's that?"

"When I found Miller. It was her knife." He shoved his hands into his pockets. "She said at the trial that it had been stolen from her. A pretty little thing, a jeweled dagger from the Orient. Brass and glass, really. Miller imported such things, you know. And she carried it with her always."

"Except she claimed it was stolen."

"Yes."

"She could be the one who did for him, then," McNally said.

"She could be."

"Sweet Jesus, boy, then you need to prove it."

"Maybe. I don't know." Simon turned to face McNally. "When she came in and found us—him— she seemed genuinely shocked. I think I would have known were she acting." He paused. "And there's the matter of the money bag found in my room."

"Miller's."

"Yes. Damned odd, wasn't it? That I'd have his money lying about like that? You'd think I wanted to be caught."

"Then you didn't take it?"

"Of course I didn't take it."

"Then how did it get into your room?"

"That is what I need to find out." He turned. "Will you help me?"

McNally frowned. "How?"

"This troupe travels near to Canterbury."

"Sweet Jesus, boy, you're not thinkin' of going back there!" McNally hissed.

"I have to. Someone killed Miller and then arranged it so it looked as if I did it. Stage-managed it, as it were." His smile was grim. "If I weren't familiar with the stage, I wouldn't see it. But I do see it. Well?" He stared at McNally. "Will you help me?"

McNally frowned. "I don't know how—but, aye, lad, I will. Though I warn you, it won't be easy."

"I don't expect it to be." Simon took his first deep breath in what felt like hours. If McNally didn't believe in Simon's innocence, at least he would help in trying to prove it. Mayhaps that was the best he could expect of anyone. "The answer's there. In Canterbury."

"Mayhap." McNally nodded, rising from the crate. "Come, lad. You look dead tired, and it'll do no one any good if you're discovered here. I'll show you where you're to sleep."

"I'd welcome that," Simon said, turning and clapping his hand on McNally's shoulder. It would be good to sleep. And maybe, just maybe, he'd manage to forget about Blythe, and those few magic moments last night when he'd held her. Maybe, but he doubted it.

Blythe awoke the following morning feeling better than she thought anyone in her situation had a right to. Sitting up, she glanced around the lodging room that she shared with Katherine, and shook her head, feeling her hair fall heavy and soft down her back. Clean. She was clean, for what felt like the first time in weeks, and though she had slept on a pallet on the floor, still she had been indoors. In the buttery warm sun streaming through the thick-paned window, matters seemed better than they had yesterday. She still knew little about the people who had taken her in, except that they'd given her shelter, with no questions asked, and would help her get home. She'd done nothing wrong. Nothing. If she could just reach her village, where she was known, she could prove that and clear her name. And she would never have to be bothered with Simon Woodley again.

She glanced over at the bed, which Katherine shared with her dresser, apparently a common occurrence. Apparently, too, they were used to traveling rough; both had commented favorably on the room, small though it was. Once Blythe was settled, Katherine had turned intensely pragmatic. There was a play to be performed that evening. Nothing must be allowed to interfere with that.

Last night Blythe had been only too glad to stay within, away from curious eyes and the fear of being recognized. The morning sun, however, made that fear look slight. She had much too much energy to stay indoors. She was used to working, to being busy. Lord knew what she could find to do in a theater, but surely she'd be helpful somewhere.

She dressed in a skirt and bodice borrowed from another actress, grateful to have clean clothing again, and bundled her hair up under her cap. Thus attired, and with a breakfast of bread and cheese inside her, she set off for the theater. No one in Rochester knew her. The chances she would be recognized were slight.

Still, she looked carefully around as she stepped out the door into a lane. Their lodgings were above a draper's shop and thus were near the center of the city. Since she had been hidden during their arrival, she had had no chance to see her surroundings. Now, as she walked along, she looked with interest at the square medieval keep brooding over the river, with the cathedral in its shadow. Eventually she came to the theater, turning into the alley beside it and finding the stage door. Inside, she plunged into the dusky darkness and blinked to adjust her eyes to the dimness. "Eh, what are you doing here, lass?" a voice said. "Thought you were safe in your room at your lodging."

"I was." She smiled, recognizing McNally, sitting on

a tall stool near the door, though he didn't return the smile. "I was also terribly bored."

"Giles won't like it," McNally predicted darkly. "Not if you bring soldiers down upon us."

"If I had stayed in the room all day the landlord would be bound to be curious," she said, suddenly cool. "Since I am supposed to be with this troupe, then I should be at the theater, should I not? And I imagine," she went on, pressing her most telling argument, "that Mr. Woodley is here."

The corner of his mouth tightened. "That he is, but 'tis different for him."

"Why? Isn't he as much a target for the soldiers as I, if not more?"

"Aye, but he belongs here, miss, for all that. You're a lady. This is no place for you."

That made her smile. "Lately that doesn't seem to matter. Since I am here, I might as well make myself useful."

McNally raised a hand in defeat. "All right. Just don't get in the way."

"I'll try not to," she said, and slipped into the green room. Through another door she could hear voices, rising and falling in the measured cadences of what probably was a play. Shakespeare, she realized, and, slipping between two partitions, looked out upon the stage.

Blythe had never been in a theater before. Her family hadn't had the money to go to performances, and her employer had considered it immoral. Blythe didn't know what she had expected to see, but the workaday scene before her was not it. The stage floor was dusty; the proscenium curtain was faded, with some of the nap worn off the velvet. Beyond the edge of the stage, long backless benches, presumably for the audience, marched away into the distance. A huge chandelier hung above, its candles unlit, and on the stage itself were grouped people in various poses. In one corner a woman Blythe had yet to meet paced back and forth, frowning at a sheaf of paper and muttering to herself. The main group, consisting of several men led by

Giles, were at center stage, declaiming lines, gesturing, and then stopping, sometimes trying a different motion, sometimes, it seemed, simply to argue. And, at the very back of the stage, sitting on a crate, was Phoebe, looking alone and forlorn.

Blythe's heart went out to her. She always had had a soft spot for the misfits, the lonely ones, and she had never met someone so out of place in her surroundings as Phoebe. Except, she thought ruefully, glancing around, herself. Letting her breath out and squaring her shoulders, she made herself stride across the stage.

"What are they doing?" she asked, pulling another crate close to Phoebe and sitting down.

Phoebe jumped, looking both dazed and startled. "Who? Oh. Mr. Rowley, my husband, and the others? They're blocking a scene."

Blythe frowned. "What does that mean?"

"It means they're deciding where everyone should stand and when they move."

"Oh." Blythe watched the actors for a moment, not particularly enlightened. "What happens next?"

"They'll block the next scene." Phoebe sank her chin into her hands, like a child. "That's when they'll need me."

Blythe glanced at her in surprise. "Are you in this play?"

Phoebe blinked. "Of course."

"Mercy." She remembered that yesterday Giles had spoken of Phoebe's role. "Have you played in *Macbeth* before?"

"Shh!" Phoebe's hand shot out and caught Blythe's arm in a surprisingly strong grasp. "Please do not speak so loudly."

"Why not?"

" 'Tis not safe." She glanced nervously about the stage. " 'Tis bad luck to speak of the Scottish play, bad luck to perform it. I argued with Mr. Rowley about it, but he would have us do it."

"Oh," Blythe said, thoroughly mystified. "Excuse

me for saying this, but I can't imagine you as Lady Macbeth."

"Nor can I. I have told Mr. Rowley that I am not right for it, but he would have it that I am." She let out a gusty sigh. "He pats my shoulder and tells me I'll be fine."

Blythe shifted her crate a little closer. "Is there anything I can do to help?" she asked, prompted more by the forlorn note in Phoebe's voice than by any desire to act.

"I need someone to help me run lines," Phoebe said gloomily.

"Run lines?"

"Yes. I've a scene which I can never get right. If someone would read the other part for me I can practice my lines. Pray they'll be correct."

"Oh." Blythe stared at her blankly. Running lines. Well, there was nothing else to do. "Could I do it?"

Phoebe looked up at her. "Would you?"

"Yes."

"Oh, wonderful!" For a moment Phoebe's face glowed, filled with an animation Blythe hadn't thought she possessed. "Here. She thrust a grimy sheaf of papers at Blythe. " 'Tis the lengths for your part."

Blythe frowned at the papers. What in the world was she doing? She'd never playacted in her life. "Where?"

"At the beginning." Phoebe sounded impatient. "Duncan's line."

"Oh. All right," she said, and read the line.

Phoebe replied, her voice suddenly a low, deep hiss overlaid with honey. Blythe stared at her, until Phoebe nudged her with an elbow. "Go on, 'tis your line."

"What? Oh." Blythe looked back at the script and stammered out the next line, her mind reeling. Not only did Phoebe sound different, but she looked different, too: taller, somehow, and older, her eyes like slits, yet with a hint of voluptuous femininity to her mouth. Blythe had never seen the like. How had Phoebe transformed herself so?

"No, no." Phoebe frowned, herself again. "You are

a king. You want to sound confident. Assured. Try it again."

"What?"

"Speak the line again," Phoebe said impatiently. "But this time believe in it. I can't act with you if you don't."

She was in a madhouse, Blythe thought. One actor pacing and talking to himself, several others arguing about where they should stand while speaking words someone else had written. Bedlam. Did Phoebe really expect her to become part of it? Blythe shrugged, cleared her throat, and made a conscious effort to lower her voice, like a man's. "I'll try," she said, and spoke the line again.

Phoebe clapped her hands together, once. "Much better! Go on."

Blythe shook her head in disbelief, looking at the script and silently reading the next line. *Read it as if you believe it. Very well,* she thought, and spoke it aloud.

Phoebe replied quickly, assuredly, very much a lady, the illusion so real that Blythe found herself replying in kind. Back and forth they went, Lady Macbeth becoming smoother and yet, at the same time, sharper. Duncan was confident, assured. He was not stupid, Blythe thought; just merely unaware of what Lady Macbeth and her husband had planned for him. He would stand tall, brace his arm just so, hold his head high, proud but not disdainful, and gracious to his subjects. No woman, not even one so powerful as Lady Macbeth, would put him out of countenance.

Phoebe spoke her last line. Blythe scanned the paper. She could take another part, if Phoebe wanted her to—

The sound of clapping made Blythe raise her head. The people who earlier had been rehearsing were now arrayed on the stage, applauding. Blythe took in a deep breath, disconcerted at being so summarily returned to her surroundings. She was not in a cold, ominous castle in Scotland, but rather a dim, dusty theater in a provincial English town. Strange how real it had felt. "You did that very well," she told Phoebe.

"Did I?" Phoebe looked up at her husband. "Giles, was it all right?"

"Very much so." Giles patted her shoulder. "I knew you'd do well. Have you ever been on the stage?"

Blythe glanced behind her, thinking he was talking to somebody else. "Me?" she said, surprise making her voice rise. "No, of course not."

"Mmm." Giles frowned, and then held his hand out to Phoebe. "Come, wife. We need you for the next scene."

"I was really all right?" Phoebe asked, looking up at Giles as he led her away. Blythe missed his answer, given in a low rumble, but she couldn't avoid seeing the quick, affectionate hug he gave Phoebe. She looked quickly away, eyes prickling in the most absurd manner. Odd, but on this stage filled with people, she suddenly felt very alone.

"That was good, princess," Simon said quietly, sitting on the box Phoebe had just left. "An interesting interpretation."

"How does she do it?" Blythe turned to him, sadness forgotten. "She's such a plain little thing, but I really believed she was Lady Macbeth. She even seemed taller."

"Phoebe? Yes, she's talented." He studied her, eyes cool, assessing, so that she had to glance away. "Would you go over a scene with me?"

That brought her gaze back. "You're surely not going onstage."

"With people hunting me? No." His smile was wry. "But I'd like to keep my hand in."

"Hmph." Blythe hunched over, elbows on her knees. "If you ask me, you've been playing a role all along."

"Not always." His voice was suddenly serious. "Will you run lines with me?"

She raised her hand to brush some hair away from her face and realized with surprise that she was trembling. "I'm tired," she said, startled. "And all I did was read a few words."

"Princess, there are people who would sell their souls to read so well."

"I beg your pardon?"

"Just one scene, princess."

"Well . . . maybe. From the Scottish play?"

He laughed. "You learn quickly. No, I was thinking of something else." His gaze settled on her lips. "A love scene."

If that was supposed to discommode her, it didn't work. He didn't have to know that his look, his words, had made an odd flame leap to life in the pit of her belly; she was adept at covering her emotions. "I didn't think villains had love scenes."

Simon laughed again. "Not usually, no. Is that how you would cast me, then? As the villain of the piece?"

" 'Tis what you are." She glanced away, uncomfortable under that warm, probing look. "Aren't you?"

"Aren't I what?"

She looked up then. She had to know. She had to. "Did you kill that man?"

Chapter 10

Simon gazed at her, the eyes that a moment ago had been laughing, warm, now shuttered. "What do you think?" he said finally.

"I don't know." She bit her lower lip. "You're an actor. You could tell me anything you wanted, and how would I know?"

"You don't know me," he said, his voice low, fierce. "If you did you'd know I'd never—ah, hell." He got up, shoving his hands in his breeches pockets. Fleetingly she reached out her hand, and then pulled it back. Surely he didn't need comforting. "Someday you'll know me." He looked down at her, his gaze so penetrating that, for the life of her, she could not look away. "You'll know me, and then you'll know—ah, hell. It matters not."

"Simon," she called as he strode away.

He looked back at her when she didn't go on, his expression remote. "Were you going to say something, princess?"

"No," Blythe said finally, looking away, realizing as if for the first time that they weren't alone on the stage, though no one appeared to pay them any heed. "No, I—"

"I thought not," he said, and turned on his heel, leaving her behind.

Blythe opened her mouth to call him back yet again, and then slowly, almost reluctantly, turned away. What would she say to him? She didn't believe him to be innocent. Surely, he wouldn't have been convicted, else. And yet . . . and yet there was this niggling doubt in her mind that she simply couldn't ignore. She had known him for only a few days. It seemed much longer, but that was because they had been together so much of the time, and under intense circumstances. That was where the doubt lay. In that time, despite his reputation, despite his threats, he had not once hurt her. The only thing he had done was kiss her—and then tell her it meant nothing.

Blythe spun about, needing to move, wanting to do something, just so she wouldn't have to think, and found herself in the green room. Best not to think about that kiss; best not to admit that, had they not been interrupted, she might have let him continue kissing her, as well as doing much, much more. Lowering thought. Best not to remember that moment in his arms, or to think that very likely to him it really had meant nothing. What that said about her, she didn't want to think.

"You are in my chair," a frosty voice said, and Blythe looked up to see Odette.

"I beg your pardon?"

"You are in my seat! Get up at once."

Blythe leaned back. Odette was all she'd always imagined an actress to be: voluptuous, with a painted face and hennaed hair, and eyes that were hard. Last night when they'd met in the room they shared, Odette had looked Blythe over, sniffed, and then turned away. "Why should I?"

"You stupid, green girl. You don't know a thing, do you? That chair, there"—she stabbed a finger toward the oak armchair—"is Giles's. The one next it is Mrs. Rowley's. And this one is mine."

"Odette." Katherine had come into the room without their noticing. "Miss Marden is unfamiliar with the theater. Do apologize to her."

Odette spun around, fists bunched, and then the fight seemed to go out of her. "Yes, madam." She turned back to Blythe. "I'm sorry you're so ignorant."

"Odette—"

" 'Tis no bother, Katherine." Blythe rose, her lips twitching as the absurdity of the scene struck her. "I do beg your pardon, ma'am." This to Odette, with a little bow. "I won't make this mistake again."

"See that you don't," Odette snapped, and whirled away, swishing her skirts of sea-green silk.

"This is a very strange place," Blythe murmured.

"Theater people tend to hold on to whatever is theirs. Come." Katherine took her arm and led her across the room. "We shall sit here, on these quite uncomfortable chairs, and talk. You look troubled. Is there anything I can do?"

Blythe sank her chin into her hands, much as Phoebe had earlier, as thoughts of her predicament returned. "I don't think there's anything anyone can do," she said gloomily.

Katherine clicked her teeth. "Men. They can be so difficult."

"Men?" Blythe looked up. "Why do you say that?"

"It's all over your face. You and Simon—"

"Simon isn't bothering me."

"No?" Katherine smiled. "What is, then?"

"I have lost my position in London." Blythe bent down a finger. "I cannot go home." Another finger. "I have spent the last few days in the company of a convicted murderer, and now I find myself traveling with a troupe of strolling players! I am sorry, you have all been very nice to me, but—"

"But you judge very harshly, Blythe," Katherine said, and though her voice was gentle, it was underlaid with steel. "You do not know us."

"No." Blythe sank her head deeper into her hands, more wretched than ever. In the space of ten minutes she had managed to offend Simon, which shouldn't bother her, and Katherine, which did. "I am sorry. You have all been kind to me. But when I think of what this will do to my reputation—"

"I think your reputation is already gone, little one. It was gone when you went with Simon."

"I had no choice! And I have no choice now."

"But you do."

Blythe looked up as Katherine rose. "What?"

"You can feel sorry for yourself, or you can do

something about it." Katherine tossed a shawl about her shoulders. "I am returning to our rooms. Do you wish to come along?"

"I . . . no." Blythe looked away. She had been feeling sorry for herself, but wasn't she entitled? She, after all, was not the villain of the affair. "Thank you."

Katherine nodded. "Think about what I've said," she added, and strode gracefully away.

Blythe was staring after her when a figure loomed before her. Startled, she looked up to see Giles. "Yes. Phoebe is right. You'll do," he said briefly.

She blinked. "I beg your pardon?"

"Weren't you listening? You're needed."

"For what?" she asked, half in protest, as Giles took her arm and hauled her to her feet.

"A small role. A breeches part. I take it you've never played a breeches part?"

Blythe dug in her heels, to no avail. "I've never played any part. Would you please—"

"Stand here." He stopped abruptly, behind the small group of people gathered on the stage. "And don't talk."

"But what—"

"Quiet. We need to rehearse. Back to the beginning of the scene."

A man Blythe had not previously met glanced up from his script, his gaze traveling leisurely over her. "You're not the right height, but I suppose that doesn't matter," he said.

Blythe wanted to back away, so tactile was his leer, except that Giles frowned at her. He was somehow far more fierce than she'd ever expected he could be, intent and serious. Did all these people have so many hidden sides? "For what?"

"The trouble will be making anyone believe she's a boy."

"Leave her be, Lester," Giles scolded. "This is her first breeches part. Now, as I was saying, Scene Two—"

"No." This time Blythe did step back. Katherine was right. She could feel sorry for herself, or she could take control of her life again. "I am not a statue, sir, to be moved about willy-nilly," she said, staring at Giles, who continued to frown. Behind her, she heard murmurs of surprise and speculation. "I do not know what I am doing here, nor do I know what a breeches part is. I believe I've been patient over the past days, but this is the outside of enough. Unless I am informed of what you wish of me—no, unless you ask me—I will have conniptions. And I assure you, sir, that will not be pretty."

Dead silence fell on the stage, unbroken by so much as a whisper or the rustle of movement. Giles stared unblinkingly at her, and then, to her utter astonishment, put back his head and let out a roar of laughter. "You'll do, indeed!" he exclaimed, striding across the stage and catching her up in an embrace that left her breathless. "Phoebe, my love, you were right." He beamed at his wife, sitting in the shadows. "She will indeed do."

"But you need to explain things to her, Giles," Phoebe said hesitantly. "You do tend to bully people into things."

"So I do." He set Blythe down, eyes twinkling. "Miss Marden, my apologies," he said, sweeping low in a bow. "I forgot that you are not used to our ways. I do most humbly beg your pardon."

"Granted, sir." His spirit was infectious. Blythe found herself dropping into a curtsy. "Pray explain to me what you wish me to do, and I may—may, mind you—do so."

"Simon chose a good one." Giles grinned at her. "We need a spear carrier—someone to stand here during this scene. There are no lines. All you need do is hold a spear and keep still. Like this." He demonstrated, standing as if holding a long pole stiffly by his side. "A breeches part is a role played by a woman wearing men's clothes."

"And a drag part is a man wearing women's clothes," Lester put in.

Blythe glanced from one to the other. "Oh."

"So what say you? Will you do it?"

"Yes," she said, before she could stop herself. What was her alternative? Only self-pity.

"Good, good." Giles clapped her on the shoulder, making her stagger. "There, stand there, just like that. Places, everyone!" He turned, clapping his hands. "Act one."

She was going to be in a play on the stage. She was going to stand here, in full view of hundreds of people, and pretend to be a soldier. It was terrifying. It was also exciting. Certainly nothing remotely like this had ever happened to her before. Perhaps adventure wasn't so bad, after all.

Simon slipped quietly onto a bench in the auditorium, dim with the drapes pulled across the windows, and leaned forward, watching the rehearsal. Lud, but he'd missed this, the arguments about blocking and stage directions, the chaos of rehearsing several scenes at once, the very smell and sound and feel of the theater. It stung that Blythe had implied that she couldn't trust him because of his profession, all the more so because there was a kernel of truth to it. All his life he had been playing a role, though not the one she suspected. It was sometimes hard to know where that role left off and the real Simon began. It was harder to discover if the real man still existed. He thought so, but after the events of the past months, even he had his doubts.

Up on the stage Giles had dragged Blythe forward, and she, with her customary lack of caution, was having none of it. Simon's mouth tucked back in a smile. He hadn't had a moment's peace in several days; let someone else deal with her for a time. Lud, but if he'd had any idea what she was like when he'd abducted her, he'd have chosen someone different. On the other hand, would a properly retiring and genteel young lady have helped him to escape the various traps laid for him? He doubted it. He doubted also that anyone so fainthearted would have come so willingly into his arms at the inn. For willing she had been, if not at first, and the memory of it was enough to make him wish to groan.

Shifting on his bench, he forced himself to pay heed to the events on stage, to ignore the events happening in his body. The dispute had been settled, apparently to everyone's satisfaction. The rehearsal now proceeded admirably, with Blythe standing stiff in the background, one hand raised, as if supporting a spear. Not as easy as it looked, to remain still while others declaimed their lines, not to fidget with boredom or yawn or blink. She had talent; that he'd seen from the earlier reading she'd given with Phoebe. Now it seemed she had the discipline as well.

Frowning a little, he set his arms on his knees. He'd taken her life away from her, there was no denying that. Mayhaps, though, he had given her another one, one she would not ordinarily have chosen, but which might suit her. He hoped so. He felt guilty enough about what he had done to her, necessary though it had seemed at the time. And then there was that kiss. . . .

He still didn't know quite what to think about that. True, he'd apologized to her and promised it would never be repeated, but he doubted he could keep the promise. He'd startled himself as much as her by suggesting playing a love scene this morning. Part of it had been flirtatiousness, the way he always bantered with actresses. That part had expected flirting in return. Part of him, though, had been serious, and that was frightening. He must never forget who he was, what he was, what he had to do. He had no time for an entanglement with anyone, let alone someone so prickly as Blythe. Ah, but it wasn't prickly she'd felt in his arms. She'd been warm and soft and sweet, all woman, yielding and giving at once. And though he had tasted innocence in her kisses, still her response promised a great deal. For some other lucky man, though. Not for him.

It did no good repining, he thought, and rose. On the stage Blythe's eyelashes flickered as she noticed him, but not by any other movement did she break her part. She wasn't tall, but put her in a soldier's uniform and she'd be a creditable spear carrier. He'd let her hold his spear anytime she wanted.

He gave an involuntary bark of laughter. On the stage Giles turned, face questioning. "Is there a problem?" he asked mildly.

Simon knew that tone. "No." Fist to his mouth, he simulated coughing. "Clearing my throat. My apologies for disturbing you."

"Mmph. We're done for now. Miss Marden, you'll do. Find Mrs. Staples and have her give you a uniform. And you"—he shot a glance at Simon—"should probably be somewhere else."

Simon straightened, his mouth grim. In hiding, Giles meant, and he had a point. If Simon were discovered it would go hard with the entire company, not just with himself. Bedamned, though, if he would confine himself to the old barn outside of town where many of the troupe were staying, when the taste of freedom was so intoxicating. "You are quite right, sir." Placing a hand on the edge of the stage, he vaulted himself up. "And so should Miss Marden, or do you really believe it's a good idea to put her in front of an audience?"

"Hide in plain sight." Giles grinned at him. "Go along, now, and take her with you. Help her find Mrs. Staples."

Blythe, standing at the back of the stage and tucking hair into her mobcap, looked up, eyes wide and startled. "I can manage, I'm sure."

"I'd be happy to," Simon interrupted, and held his arm out. "Well, princess?"

Blythe looked at his arm for a moment and then nodded curtly, turning away and walking offstage. Ah, well, what had he expected? Still, it was as much a treat to walk behind her down the corridor as at her side, to watch her skirts twitching back and forth with the sway of her hips. A quite seductive sway, though he doubted she realized it. "You did well, princess."

"Oh?" She quickened her step. "Then why did you laugh?"

"Not at you, I assure you."

"No?" She stopped, turning. "Why, then?"

"At myself," he said ruefully. "At wanting what I can't have."

"Oh." She glanced away. "Mr. Woodley, this morning I may have said some things—"

"Blythe." He held up his hand. "Don't. If anyone should apologize, 'tis I."

"You? Why?"

"For presuming too much. I forgot that you are not a part of this world."

Her eyes narrowed, and she spun around, skirts flouncing. "You needn't talk to me as if I were a child."

"I wasn't," he protested, following her. Now what had he said?

"I may not have had any choice but to come with you, but I am not some helpless miss." She stopped, glaring at him with fists upon her hips. "I'll thank you to remember that."

He nodded gravely, though the sight of her flushed cheeks and outthrust chest was vastly diverting. Oh, yes, she was very much a woman. "I doubt I'll forget that, princess."

"And that's another thing. Must you call me by that silly name?"

He shrugged. "It suits you. Why are you snapping at me?"

Her mouth opened and then closed again. "I don't know," she admitted. "I am sorry."

" 'Tis of no moment. Come." He stepped forward, taking her elbow. "Let us find Mrs. Staples."

"Simon." She didn't move, and he looked down at her. "Did I—that is, do you think—should I be onstage?"

" 'Tis an easy role, princess. You did well."

Her cheeks went pink. "Thank you, but that's not what I meant. What if someone recognizes me?"

"Not likely, after Mrs. Staples is done with you." He opened a door set into the corridor. "The ladies' dressing room," he said, politely averting his eyes. "Mrs. Staples is in the back."

"Oh." Blythe glanced into the room, a confusion of women in various stages of dress and undress, some speaking lines or applying makeup while looking at themselves in a small mirror, others tending to their babies. At the back of the room a stout matron bent to pin a hem on a gown, while on a table were scattered garments of various sizes and hues. "I . . . then I suppose we'll talk later."

"I suppose we will." He nodded, stepping away from the door. "Break a leg tonight," he added, and walked away, leaving Blythe to stare after him in stunned surprise. Why ever would he want her to suffer such a thing? For the life of her, she would never understand him.

By that evening, Blythe was wishing heartily that she had indeed broken her leg, or that some other dine disaster had befallen her, to keep her from having to go out onto the stage. She could not think why it had seemed so good an idea this morning, such a lark. But then, she had always longed for adventure, and look where that had got her.

"A most fetching outfit," a voice whispered in her ear, and she closed her eyes. Simon. Of course he would be here to taunt her.

"Go away," she hissed, looking out from the wings onto the stage. She was on next scene, McNally had told her, as if she didn't know. She had been dreading this moment all evening.

"I'm serious." Simon's hand rested on her shoulder, and she turned to see him grinning at her. "At least from behind."

The look she gave him would have frozen a lesser man; he only smiled. She knew quite well how she looked, dressed as she was as a soldier, in white breeches and red coat. The breeches were extremely immodest, disclosing the lower part of her body. The heavy coat fortunately afforded her some protection, while the powdered wig, though itchy, helped conceal her identity. Her reputation had already suffered a devastating blow. If it was learned she'd been onstage, she would never recover. And Simon seemed to find the whole thing amusing! "Would you please go away? You are bothering me."

"You're scared."

"No."

"You are." He stepped back, appraising her. "You're pale and sweating. You're not going to cast up your accounts, are you?"

She rounded on him. "I'm not such a poor honey that I'll make myself ill over this! And if I have to go out there to prove it to you, I will."

His smile had broadened into a grin. "Break a leg," he said again, and gave her a push. "You're on."

Blythe stumbled onto the stage, her knees suddenly weak, feeling as if she were indeed about to be sick. Oh, mercy, what had she got herself into? She was no actress, and yet here she was, about to stand upon the stage for an entire scene. She couldn't do it. She couldn't go out there and face the audience she knew waited beyond the edge of the stage, rumbling, ravening. Waiting to devour her. She couldn't.

"Come on, lass." Thomas, who was taking the part of the other soldier, caught her elbow. "We're on."

She had no time to protest. Thomas dragged her a few feet before she recovered herself. Striding next to him, she was only slightly out of breath, and trembled only from head to toe. Walk forward, turn to the left five paces, face ahead with musket by her side, rather than a spear. Stand absolutely still, and let the actors, the real actors, play out their roles, while she and Thomas stood there, bits of human scenery. A soldier at his post would stand at attention, she thought, holding herself stiffly, her sweaty grip keeping the musket upright. He would not move, unless the people he guarded were threatened. And since that didn't happen in this scene, all Blythe had to do was stand in one place.

All at once she relaxed. Phoebe was well away, speaking her lines as if she truly believed them. No

one, on the stage or in the audience, was paying
Blythe the slightest heed. Her breath came easier; her
knees unlocked, and the buzzing in her head faded.
Why, this wasn't so difficult after all. Whyever had
she been so frightened?

No longer tense, she could at last appreciate where
she was. Above her, the vast chandelier, candles
aglow, spread bright if uneven light onto the stage.
Beyond the footlights the first rows of the pit were
similarly illumined, and it was here that her fascinated
gaze rested. The theater was crowded, with people of
all ages and sizes and descriptions. Respectable ma-
trons sat in tightly pressed rows, against prosperous
merchants. A group of well-dressed young men, lounging back as best they could and trying to look bored,
mingled with shabbily dressed, wide-eyed people,
tradesmen or farmers, perhaps in the theater for the
first time. The gentry clustered in the boxes that
ringed the auditorium, their finery of silks and satins
stunning; their manners, as they conversed with each
other throughout the play, leaving much to be desired.
Row upon row the people stretched, those in the back
lit by chandeliers similar to the one on the stage. They
were all different, yet all the same. They all applauded
certain speeches or hissed when they were displeased.
And Phoebe, no longer a timid, plain girl but instead
very much Lady Macbeth, was holding them all
spellbound.

Blythe's gaze drifted back, stopped briefly on the
stage, and then settled again on the audience. Who
were they, these people? What had brought them to
the theater tonight? That scholarly-looking old gentleman there was nodding his head in appreciation, while
a matron of uncertain age couldn't seem to take her
eyes off Lester, resplendent in a doublet of midnight
blue. Beside her a man in a coat of brilliant emerald
brocade and powdered periwig sat very still, arms
crossed. He was the only one Blythe could see who
looked remotely bored. Strange he'd be here, then,
unless he had another reason. Mayhaps he was meeting someone, one of the actresses. He certainly

seemed alert, his deep-set, oddly light eyes peering at the stage as if trying to penetrate beyond the wings, beyond the words and the poses to the people within. Strange, for what would he find? Only some very ordinary actors, and one companion masquerading as a soldier. Certainly not a fugitive from justice—

Blythe's grip on the musket slipped, and the stock clattered onto the stage. Several of the cast sent her sharp looks, but the audience appeared unaware. Thank heavens. Oh, thank heavens. For, unless she was wrong, the man in the green brocade coat, the watcher who seemed bored yet was alert, was someone she knew. She knew his face from her nightmares, where he chased her continually, over a bridge, through a stream. But she knew him from more than dreams. He was the man who had hunted her and Simon from the first, and he was here. Oh, mercy. They'd been found out.

Chapter 11

Blythe's first impulse was to run. What held her there she never afterward knew; it might have been the trembling in her legs or Phoebe's stern glance. Certainly she did realize, if belatedly, that running from the stage would only draw attention to herself. And so she stood very still, gripping the stage musket as if her very life depended upon it, as if it were a real weapon and not a cobbled-together bit of wood and iron and paint. She did not break her role. She had never been on the stage before and likely never would be again, but somehow she was very proud of herself for the amount of poise she maintained. She stayed in character.

The scene came at last to an end, and with it, the act. The curtain fell, shielding her from the audience. Phoebe was suddenly herself again; Giles very much the manager, directing the changing of scenery and the placement of people on the stage. Blythe's part was done. She was no longer a soldier, but a frightened and bewildered young woman. Where was Simon? Oh, she had to warn him. Into the wings, past the actors who would go on next; through the narrow corridor, bustling with people; into the green room, smiling briefly as someone complimented her on her debut. She scanned the room. If she didn't find him soon, he was likely to walk into danger.

"You all right, miss?" McNally said by her side, and she started. "You're all pale-like."

"Am I?" She glanced around again. "Shouldn't you be on the stage, if you're the prompter?"

"I had Robbie take over. What's amiss, lass?"

She turned to him. If anyone could help, McNally could. "I have to find Simon," she said in a low voice. "Do you know where he is?"

"Around and about, I'd imagine. Nervous at being onstage, eh?"

"No," she said, remembering her earlier fear with distant surprise. The threat of going onstage was as nothing to the threat she faced now. "Can you find him?"

McNally frowned. "Probably. Is summat wrong?"

"More than summat." With that same sense of distance she heard herself mimicking his accent precisely, and saw his mouth purse in surprise. "Someone who has been chasing us is in the audience, and—"

"Where?" he interrupted.

"Does it matter? Simon needs to be warned, and he'll need a safe way to leave the theater."

"Aye, it matters, lass. At the interval he might come back here," McNally, said, waving his hand about.

Blythe followed his gesture, frowning, and realized for the first time that she didn't know many of the people in the green room. "Why? Who are all these people?"

"Civilians. People not in the theater," he said at her look of confusion. "Men lookin' for a lady love."

She felt her face growing warm. "Oh."

"Our man might come here. If I know who he is I can post someone to keep him away."

Blythe nodded, wondering again at the loyalty that ran so strong among the troupe. "Front row, center. He has pale eyes and full lips and he's wearing a coat of green brocade. You might see him from the wings."

"I'll look," McNally said tersely, and slipped off toward the stage.

Blythe bit her lips. McNally was competent, and she'd no doubt he'd keep the pursuer away, but in the meantime Simon was in danger. Not that she should care, she thought crossly, threading her way through the crowd to the green room door. The sooner he was caught, the sooner she could go on with her life.

The door to the corridor opened just as Blythe

reached it. She stepped back, but not in time; of a sudden her view was filled by a broad, and familiar, masculine chest. Her hands came up of their own volition to steady herself, settled on warm, crumpled homespun covering firm muscles, and couldn't seem to pull away. His hands caught her arms. "Easy, there," he said, grinning. "You're in a tizzy."

"Please unhand me," she said, as haughty as could be, her worry lost in rising annoyance. Must he stand so close to her, so that she could feel his warmth against her skin, hear the quick rasp of his breathing?

"Gladly, princess." He stepped back, grinning. "Wouldn't want people to think I prefer boys."

"What?" she said blankly, and followed his gaze, long, meaningful, over her body. With a jolt she remembered she was still in costume.

"Not that you don't look fetching," he went on, smile widening. "What is it, princess? Do I scare you so much?"

"Yes. No. It doesn't matter." Oh, yes, he scared her, but not in the way he meant. "Oh, will you please stop talking nonsense?" she exclaimed, and stepped out into the hall, catching his hand and dragging him behind her. The corridor was nearly deserted, giving them a measure of privacy, and yet at any moment they might find themselves confronting their pursuer. "You're in danger."

"So I've noticed."

"I'm serious! We've trouble," she said, and quickly told him all that had occurred in the past moments. Simon's face grew still, but his hands gripping her arms betrayed his emotion.

"Hell," he said when she finished. "Then he saw you—"

"You needn't worry I'll betray you," she retorted, stung. "Else why would I warn you?"

"I didn't mean it that way, princess. Well?" This to McNally, as he approached them from the stage.

"He's there." McNally's voice was terse. "I marked him, and I'll know him if he comes back here."

"Never mind that. We must get Miss Marden away."

"Aye, and you, too, lad, or have you forgotten 'tis your neck they want to stretch?"

" 'Tis why he wants me gone," Blythe said bitterly. "Well, sir, I cannot go. I have another scene yet."

Simon swore, briefly, colorfully. "To hell with the scene. To hell with the play. You're getting out of here—"

"If it were you, wouldn't you go on?" she challenged, hands on her hips. "Wouldn't you?"

"You're not me, princess. And don't you think our friend will recognize you?"

"If he had, he'd be back here already. Please, make him go," she said, turning to McNally. "I've the scene, and even if I didn't, there's no time for me to change out of costume."

"Aye, you've the right of it, lass." McNally nodded. "You've a good head on your shoulders."

Simon swore again. "What she's suggesting is suicide."

Blythe put up her chin. "Hide in plain sight," she said.

Simon blinked, and in that moment she knew she'd won. The performance she'd just given far surpassed what she had earlier done on the stage, but she took little satisfaction from it. She didn't want to go out there again, didn't want to stand still and stiff, a waiting target, but she would. Simon needed time to escape, and she would give it to him. The thought of his being caught was somehow more than she could bear. "Hell, princess—"

Blythe started. Mercy, what was she thinking? "I should be onstage," she said, and, turning, fled from him.

Exhilaration buoyed her as she fidgeted in the wings, grabbing the prop musket from where she'd left it. This was adventure of the highest order, and for the first time she was excited. All she had to do was play her part and then slip back to the room she shared with Katherine. Dressed as she was, she doubted the pursuer would recognize her, and Simon would be able to escape. All in all, a good night's work.

She was still feeling buoyant when her cue came. She stepped onto the stage, marching stiffly, musket propped against her shoulder. Why had this scared her so earlier? All she need do was stand still. Not so terribly hard or frightening. Not like saying lines. In place at last, she set her musket down and stood to attention, her eyes, now accustomed to the glare of the chandelier, automatically scanning the audience and settling on the front row. It took a moment for her brain to register what she saw. Their pursuer was gone.

She gasped, earning a quick, irate frown from Giles, who was well into a speech. Dear God. While she and Simon had argued, their pursuer had disappeared. He could simply have left the theater, but she doubted it. Even now he could be on his way to summon soldiers or to come backstage and make the arrest himself. And here she was, onstage, a perfect target.

The scene seemed to drag on forever. Terror kept her in place, while at the same time her jangled nerves urged her to flee, to hide. If she was not found, then she could not tell where Simon was. But, again, she knew that if she bolted she would only draw unwanted attention to herself. She was well and truly stuck.

The scene came to an end at last. Mechanically she turned along with Thomas, shouldered her musket, and marched offstage, aware as never before of peoples' gazes on her. Of *his* gaze on her, though he was no longer there. Only when she had reached the relative safety of the wings did she let herself so much as breathe. This particular nightmare was over. Shoulders sagging, she stepped into the green room, and stiffened. Across the room stood a man clad in green brocade. Though his back was to her, she recognized the arrogant tilt of his head. He was, unmistakably, the man who had been pursuing her and Simon.

"You did well," Phoebe said almost shyly, and Blythe started. "I'm sorry, I did not mean to startle you. But you did do so well. I almost believed you were a soldier."

Blythe passed a hand over her eyes. As if her performance mattered. "All I did was stand there."

"But that is not easy! I must get back, I've another scene," Phoebe said, and slipped away. Blythe barely noticed. All her attention was focused on that one man, chatting idly with Odette. He was here for her. She could only hope Simon had got safely away.

As if he felt the intensity of her gaze, the man turned, and Blythe abruptly realized that she was as much a target here, in the green room, as she had been onstage. She had to move. Yet, if she did, he would know instantly who she was, wouldn't he? Eyes narrowing, she glanced quickly at Thomas. No one would mistake her for a man, she was too short and slight, but perhaps she could mimic a boy. Angle her head, just so, a confident, almost swaggering tilt to her chin. Brace her shoulders, stand with legs apart. She was a young lad, immensely proud of his achievements on the stage. She had better be. Her life depended upon it.

With a longer stride than usual, she swaggered through the room, winking at Odette, who looked startled, and grabbed a bottle of wine from the table to take a swig. It choked her going down, but she managed not to cough, not to betray that this was an act—and in any event, how likely was a boy to be an experienced drinker?

The man's gaze, hooded, apparently disinterested, was on Blythe as she made her progress through the room. She forced herself to keep her pose, made her shoulders swing a bit more, kept her hips as still as possible. Then Odette laughed, a trill of sound that rang artificial to Blythe, and he looked away, frowning. Blythe picked up her pace, aware that he was there, expecting at any moment to feel his hand on her shoulder—but then she was at the door, and through into the corridor, with no evidence of pursuit. She was safe. Safe! Twice she had faced the enemy, and twice he hadn't realized. Giddy with the same exhilaration that had filled her earlier, she gave a little skip, turned—and, once again, walked full into Simon's chest.

"What are you doing here?" she hissed, frantically grabbing at his shirt and not caring what he thought. "He's in there! If he comes out and sees you—"

"Hush!" Simon clamped his hand over her mouth. Blythe stared up at him, too startled to struggle. "We've no time for this. We must be away."

Blythe wrenched her face free. "But—"

"No buts," he said, and slammed his mouth down on hers. For a moment she forgot everything, who she was, what he had done, the peril in which they stood. All she was aware of were his lips against hers, hard, questing, not at all tentative, but at the same time not coercive. When at last he released her she stared up at him, openmouthed, too stunned to speak or move or even talk.

"Good." Simon wrapped his arm around her, hustling her away from the door. "Now that you're quiet, we may leave."

The outrageousness of that statement startled her into speech. "As if I'm the one keeping us here! Oh, Simon, you could have been safely on your way—"

"Not without you, princess." Simon swung the stage door open and pulled her outside into the cool, damp night. "Up with you."

"What—where—"

"Into this cart." He boosted her up. Now that her eyes were more accustomed to the darkness, she could see that a farm cart of some kind stood in the alleyway just outside the theater, a strange sight at night, but at least a hiding place. Oh, why was he doing this? she wondered, scrambling forward in the hay-scattered cart, searching for a cover of some kind. Why was he endangering himself so?

The cart rocked as Simon dropped down beside her. "My apologies, princess. All right, McNally, we're ready."

"For what?" she asked, just as a load of hay fell on her face and arms. Struggling, sputtering, she came up for air in time to see something more hurtling down upon her. A blanket, she realized, feeling the wool rough against her cheek, and none too clean, by the smell of it. "If this blanket is verminous, Simon Woodley, I shall never forgive you."

Simon snorted with laughter. "Trust you to think of that, princess."

"Men never think of the practical things," she grumbled, though her heart wasn't in it. His arms were wrapped about her, strong, hard, protective, and under her ear she could hear the comforting, steady beat of his heart.

"I thought of one thing, and it's well for you I did."

His breath stirred her hair. It sent little shivers down her spine, a rather pleasant sensation. "What is that?"

"If our pursuer, whoever he is, recognized you, he would have arrested you."

She shuddered. "Yes, I know."

"And you would have told where I was."

Blythe went still, and then, as best she could, raised her head, though she couldn't see him. "Is that truly what you think?"

"I fear so, Blythe."

"But I would not," she said, her voice dull. Foolish of her to think he'd come back simply because he cared for her safety. Of course his own neck was paramount to him. And if that was so, what was she doing lying in his arms? She wrenched away from him, turning onto her side, pressing her lips together hard against unwanted tears. "Although I don't know why you'd believe me."

"You'd do it to save yourself, princess." Simon made his voice matter-of-fact, though every part of him yearned to turn and take her into his arms again, to hold her, to . . . what? Earlier this evening he had known he could not escape if she was not safe, and so had insisted on going back for her. He could understand that. He was not a cad, after all, and it was his fault she was in this mess. But what he had felt just now, when she had nestled against him, soft and warm in her gratitude—oh, sweet Jesus. He wanted her.

Were he someone else, he would turn and kiss her senseless, but he was who he was. She was not for him.

The silence had lengthened, until it was as smothering as the air. "You'll have to come to the barn," he said.

It took Blythe a moment to answer. "The barn?"

"Aye. Where some of us are staying."

"But I've rooms in town—"

"And if you return there in costume you'll attract attention. 'Tis best you not be seen just now."

"Oh." Silence again. "Who are you, Simon?"

That made him raise up on his elbow, as if he could see her. "What do you mean?"

"I—no, I don't know what I mean. Pray don't regard it."

"I shan't." He consigned himself to the torture of lying beside her again, arm over his eyes. Had she but known, that question had haunted him all his life, and it was partly what kept him from turning to her. Who was he?

"Who is he?" Quentin asked, as the green room door closed behind the young soldier who had swaggered so boldly across the room. Something familiar about him, something about the eyes, yet Quentin couldn't place where he'd seen him.

"You are interested in him instead of me, m'sieur?" the actress beside him purred, walking her fingers up his arm. Quentin shuddered with unwanted response, at the same time that he assessed her coolly. Young, passably pretty, with hair that had been hennaed and showed dark roots. Darkness in her eyes, too, eyes that were hard for one so young. He knew better than to get involved with such as her. He also knew she was exactly what he needed. And her hair did go well with his emerald-green coat. "You prefer boys, perhaps?"

Quentin let his gaze drop lower, openly ogling her breasts, displayed in the low-cut gown of blue satin. "To you, Odette? Of course not. I merely wondered, he's such an arrogant young cock."

Odette's laugh was surprisingly merry. "Shows what you know. I mean, m'sieur," she said, picking up her accent again, "that you are an amusing man."

"Oh? And what did I say that was *très amusant*?"

Uncertainty flickered in her eyes for just a moment. "Do you really believe that was a boy, m'sieur?"

"What?" He fixed his gaze on her, hard, probing. "Do you mean it wasn't?"

"No." Odette's smile broadened. "She is a *jeune fille*—actually, a not so young *fille*—who has just joined the company. I do not know why, we have enough women to play the roles. She cannot even act. And"—she chuckled, low, malicious—"if she can disguise herself as a boy, she is no beauty, no?"

"Probably not." He let himself smile, though his mind raced. "Who is she?"

"Now you make me jealous." Odette's hand snaked about his arm. "Am I not enough for you, m'sieur?"

"You're enough for any man, Odette," he said, keeping his smile in place. He knew why the soldier had seemed familiar. If she was who he thought, he'd seen her before, on Westminster Bridge, accompanying an apparently old and senile man. His deduction had been right. What better place for an actor to hide, as he had surmised, than among a theatrical troupe?

Slowly, he cautioned himself. Carefully. He'd lost his prey too many times already because of too-hasty preparations. He wouldn't make that mistake again; he had time enough. Time to set a trap, time to make up to Odette, so that his presence among the troupe would be accepted. Time to put out bait, perhaps, in the form of that shapely little soldier. This time he would make no mistake. Woodley would not escape him again.

Chapter 12

"Haven't seen hide nor hair of the fellow since that day at the theater," McNally remarked as he sat beside Simon. The life of a traveling theatrical troupe was not easy. While the top players stayed in a reasonably comfortable inn and the lower ranks in lodgings, many were housed in an old barn just outside of Rochester. Cheek by jowl they lived together, in usually amiable closeness, male and female alike. Simon, sitting on a bale of hay and watching some of the players rehearse, had seen worse lodgings; barnstorming was common among the smaller theatrical troupes. At least there was a roof over his head.

"Does anyone know who he is?" Simon asked, chewing on a piece of straw. He was deceptively relaxed, his back against the wall of the barn, one knee bent up with his arms dangling upon it. In reality his gaze flickered everywhere, from the loft above that provided sleeping quarters, to the hay-strewn floor, to the open door. Three days he had been in hiding, and he didn't like it.

"No, and likely no one will, unless he shows up again. Odette still insists she doesn't remember him, no matter what Miss Marden says. If you ask me"—McNally hawked and spat—"our man likely didn't make her a generous enough offer."

Simon nodded. He'd seen Odette's type before, women who went on the stage not so much for love of the theater, but because they were in search of a man to keep them in luxury. Not like Blythe. His gaze sharpened as he looked across the barn where she sat with Phoebe, helping her with lines. Blythe had an

undeniable presence upon the stage, and she didn't
even know it. If someone told her, she would be horrified. She was a good woman, and good women did
not tread the boards.

Simon shifted, uncomfortable with that line of
thought. Always, always it came back to what he had
done to her, in taking her from her secure life in London. Though she had settled in easily enough with the
troupe, this life wasn't meant for her. She was meant
to have a husband and home and babies. That thought
made him shift again. Babies were the last thing he
wanted to give to any woman.

"She's good," McNally said quietly, following Simon's gaze.

"Phoebe? Of course she is."

"Aye. But I was thinking of Miss Marden." He
scratched his chin. "Giles is thinking of giving her a
part."

That made Simon look at him. "He can't. If she's
recognized—"

"Aye, 'tis a risk, but if she takes a breeches part,
with just a few lines, she'll be all right."

"No," Simon said. "I won't allow it."

"Oh, won't you?" McNally's eyebrows rose. "I
don't think it's your decision, lad."

Simon gritted his teeth. "Hell, I've done enough to
ruin her life."

"Then stay out of it. Let the lass make her own
choices."

"This choice could get us both arrested."

"Concerned for your own skin, are you?"

"No." He paused. "Not entirely."

"Huh." Silence fell. "You fancy her."

"No."

"Aye, I've seen how you look at her," McNally
went on, ignoring Simon's curtness. "You could do
worse. She's comely enough. Good hair"—he squinted
assessingly—"face isn't remarkable, but it's sweet.
And a good enough figure." He grinned. "Saw that
when she dressed as a soldier."

"McNally, if you keep on like this, I shall be forced to ram your teeth down your throat."

McNally grinned, not a whit abashed. "No offense meant, lad. I think she fancies you, too."

Simon reared back. "Bloody hell! I hope not."

"Now, why would you say that? An attractive woman who has eyes for you—"

"And whose life I've ruined."

McNally glanced back across the barn. Phoebe had risen and was acting out the gestures that went along with her lines, so immersed in her role that she was transformed. So, to a lesser extent, was Blythe, her face intent and serious. "Mayhap not." He hopped down from the bale. "Mayhap you want to ask her before you decide that."

"Hell," Simon muttered again, restless, wanting to be up and about. Still, he stayed sitting, quiet except for his fingertips drumming on his knee. McNally was right. He did fancy Blythe. But with his life in such a shambles, how could he possibly act on his feelings?

With a sudden excess of energy, he pushed himself off the bale of hay, intent only on escape. He was bored with confinement. Under the circumstances it was no wonder Blythe attracted him so. Any woman would, just now.

A hand caught at his arm. "No, my boy, that's not the place for you," Giles said amiably, pulling Simon back just as he reached the barn door. "Not unless you want your neck stretched."

"Hell." Simon rounded on him, all the frustrations of the past days bubbling up. "I'm tired of people telling me what to do. I'll go where I damn well please."

Giles regarded him for a moment. "So be it," he said, and turned. "By the by. I need someone to help me work out a fencing scene." He looked back over his shoulder. "Care to try?"

Simon glanced at the door. Outside was glorious spring, the sun amazingly bright, the grass vivid emerald dotted with daisies and dandelions. He hated being caged like this. "All right," he growled, and turned on his heel, following Giles.

In a corner of the barn away from the other players, the two men picked up painted wooden swords and stood facing each other. Dueling scenes had to be planned out carefully. Each feint, each thrust and parry had to be performed just so, to make the duel look realistic without anyone getting hurt. Simon had played one or two such scenes, though he'd never handled a real sword in a real fight; Giles, many more. "What play is this for?" Simon asked, holding his prop sword up, as if in salute.

"*Innocence Avenged.* A melodrama of the worst sort, but I think audiences will enjoy it. We play it tomorrow night. I'll start, here. A lunge you don't expect."

"And I'll parry," Simon said, holding his sword at an angle. There was a crack of wood as the two swords came together. "What part are you?"

"The villain. Neat footwork there, boy. If there wasn't a price on your head you could go on with this."

"You learn to be quick in prison." This time Simon lunged, catching the other man on the arm.

Giles held up his hand, stopping the fight. "No." He stepped back, frowning. "I expect you to pink me, boy, but not yet. The villain is menacing and powerful."

"And I?"

"You are the young hero, fighting against all odds to save the heroine."

"The villain sounds more fun."

"Oh, doubtless. There, that's better." Giles's sword weaved through the air in a flurry of thrusts. "Step back, no, like you're almost falling. I want you to appear overmatched."

"I'm taller than you are," Simon scoffed.

"That doesn't matter," a voice said behind them. Startled, Simon turned to see Blythe sitting cross-legged on the floor, chin propped on her hand. " 'Tis more important to be nimble and agile."

Simon passed his arm across his forehead. It was

hot in the barn for such exertion. "How would you know?"

"You're doing it wrong, you know," she went on as if he hadn't spoken, looking at Giles. "With that grip an opponent could knock your sword away, and then where would you be?"

"How should I hold it, then?" Giles asked, smiling.

"Like this." Blythe rose gracefully and took the prop sword from Giles's hand. "Your fingers here, along the side, your thumb there, on top. Do you feel the difference?"

"Yes, it feels more secure." Giles frowned down at her as he wiped his own forehead. "And are you an expert at swordplay, missy?"

"Yes, as it happens, I am."

Both men stared at her. "That's a whisker if ever I heard one," Simon snorted.

"Oh, but 'tis true. Mr. Rowley?" She held out her hand. Giles grinned at Simon, bowed, and gave her the sword, hilt first. Her other hand held her skirts in a bunch, displaying a pair of ankles that, clad even as they were in heavy cotton stockings, were enticing. "Six years of working with a fencing master must have taught me something. *En garde,*" she said, and launched herself at Simon with such a flurry of movement that within a moment his sword clattered to the floor.

Giles's laugh broke the stunned silence that followed. "Never before saw you bested in swordplay, boy."

" 'Tis not something that happens often," Simon retorted, bending to retrieve his sword. "Not with most women."

"Have you fenced with women before, then?" Blythe asked.

"I'm known as a swordsman." Simon grinned at her and had the satisfaction of seeing her frown uncertainly. She had no idea of his real meaning. "Have you fenced with men?"

"Often," she said seriously, leaning on the sword. "Would you like me to help with this scene?"

"Go ahead, missy." Giles dropped down onto the floor, grinning. "Woodley can use the exercise."

"But he won't be in the play."

"I'll learn watching you." Giles waved his hand as Blythe stared at him. Her skirts were still tucked up; strands of hair were coming loose from under her cap, pale, shining honey. "Go on."

Blythe paused, and then, shrugging, turned back to Simon. "If you don't mind?"

He bowed. "Lay on, Macduff."

"Not good, to quote the Scottish play," Giles called.

"But appropriate. It refers to a sword fight," Simon explained to Blythe. "Shall we lay on, then?"

Blythe frowned, as if she suspected that he was teasing her, and raised her sword in salute. "Very well. We start so, knees bent, head high."

"I know that much."

"Now." She frowned and glanced over at Giles. "Is anyone supposed to be hurt?"

"Aye." Giles grinned, obviously enjoying himself hugely. "I die at the end. And a great scene it is."

"I'm sure," she murmured, quite seriously. "It will work better if you appear to be well matched. That is, the hero shouldn't win too easily."

"I'd not let him."

"So. The villain—what is his name?"

"Sir Adrian."

"Sir Adrian would make the first move, of course."

"Why?" Simon asked, at once intrigued by her manner, composed and brisk, and annoyed at being ignored.

"Because he's the villain, of course."

"But the hero—name?" he barked at Giles.

"Lucien."

"Good God. Very well. Lucien is fighting for the honor of his one true love. Why wouldn't he attack first?"

"Heroes don't start fights."

"No, but they finish them," he said, taking the villain's role and lunging forward. His sword should have caught her on the shoulder. Instead she bent her arm in a move so subtle it was barely noticeable, and the two swords scraped together, some of the paint flaking off Simon's. Before he could quite recover, she had disengaged, and, whirling about, struck him lightly on the arm.

"There. First blood." Her smile was smug. "Mind your feet, Simon."

"To hell with my feet," he growled, lunging again.

"Oh, well," she murmured, and again whirled away. Caught off balance, Simon stumbled forward, managing only by luck not to fall. "Balance is important," she went on, sounding like a teacher.

Simon straightened, studying her thoughtfully. Careful, now. He could lose his temper at being bested by a mere woman, could strike out again and overwhelm her with sheer force. Anger, however, had got him into more than one predicament in the past. There were other ways. "One must be quick on one's feet," Blythe continued.

Simon made another ironic bow, conceding the opening moves of the encounter to her. "One must, with blades," he agreed. "And with other things, as well."

Giles snorted; Blythe merely frowned. "I am nearly out of patience with you, Simon. Shall we do this or not?"

He studied her, his earlier double entendres suddenly a sword raised against him. "I believe we shall," he said finally, and as he did so felt a shroud of darkness lift from him, a burden he hadn't known he carried. Blythe was light and life; his future was clouded, but he needed her. He hated to admit it, but he needed her.

"Well, then." Blythe's tone was brisk; of course she was unaware of the great revelation that had just visited him. "Shall we begin?"

He nodded, serious now, all thoughts of teasing gone. For this was more than mere swordplay, theatrical or otherwise. Not that he would admit it to anyone else. *"En garde,"* he said quietly, raising his sword in salute, though the real duel between them had begun long ago.

Blythe raised her sword, nodding. "A good touch. A civilized villain is much more dangerous."

Simon lunged. "You're not familiar with the theater, princess, so how would you know that?"

Blythe danced away yet again. "I read. That's not bad for a first attack. And—"

"And if you're the hero, you aren't going to stand back and let me take the offensive. Not if you're fighting for your woman."

"Let Blythe be the villain," Giles said unexpectedly.

Simon dropped his sword and bent to retrieve it. "Why?"

Giles grinned. "So I can use what she does, of course. I like being a civilized villain."

"Of course," Simon muttered.

"Then I attack first," Blythe said, springing forward with a lunge that Simon barely parried with his sword.

"And I press a counterattack." Simon's face was serious as he lunged in return, moving the stick in a great thrust that Blythe knocked away with her own weapon. Wood clacked against wood and then slid apart, leaving them both just a bit breathless.

Blythe danced back and then settled, feet planted, sword held up defensively. "But I am not going to let you in," she said, and pressed forward, the stick weaving in a series of feints and lunges that Simon was hard-pressed to counter. Step by step he lost ground, using the sword for defense only, easing back, biding his time. For the hero was destined to win this fight, no matter how well trained his adversary might be. He was fighting for his lady.

Blythe's sword suddenly slid across his upper arm, rasping against the homespun. "She's pinked you," Giles said quietly. "We'll have to watch that."

Blythe paused, holding up her hand. "Do you use real swords onstage?"

"Have to. The audience'll spot fakes. We can paint wood silver, you see, but we can't make it sound like metal. Or look like it, neither."

"The tips are blunted, of course," Simon added.

"Regardless." Blythe frowned. "Someone could get hurt."

"Which is why we rehearse the scenes carefully." Giles waved his hand. "Carry on."

" 'Tis only a play," Simon said, and suddenly pressed forward. Blythe parried, but with effort; he was fighting for something, and that lent intensity to his efforts. It mattered. The hero had to win this battle.

But the enemy would not, of course, yield easily. Blythe took advantage of a brief opening in his attack to slide her sword forward, catching him on his other arm. "Number two," she gasped, her breath rough from exertion, "and I'll press my advantage."

Simon gave way again, using his sword defensively. "You mean the villain will."

"Yes. Now, if you hold your sword at a bit of an angle, like this, it should look realistic but not hurt anyone."

"But I will win," Simon said softly. Thrust and pull back; thrust and pull back. His size and strength were beginning to tell, in spite of his long confinement. Blythe was obviously tiring. No longer did she attack, but instead parried each blow, stepping back, back. The hero had to win or all was lost, Simon thought, and with one mighty effort thrust forward. Wood cracked against wood; Blythe's arm gave way and then, unexpectedly, held firm. With an odd screeching sound the two swords clashed, sliding upward and joining Simon and Blythe in an odd embrace, upraised blades intertwined, wrists and forearms pressed together, the skirts of her frock brushing against his legs, and her breasts just resting against his chest.

For a long, long moment neither one moved. Blythe's face, upturned, close, so close, was flushed from the exercise, her breath coming fast and her chest rising and falling quickly. Simon's heart had speeded up, and he was aware of dampness on his forehead and sweat trickling down his back. There was also a sensation that had nothing to do with his recent activity and everything to do with his rampaging thoughts. His groin was throbbing.

"Bravo," Giles said, breaking the silence, and throughout the barn there was scattered applause. Simon glanced about; for just a moment he had forgotten his audience. "And brava." Giles put his arm around Blythe's shoulders, pulling her away, and Simon was forced at last to withdraw. "Though I fear that in performance I shall have to let myself be killed, alas."

"Yes." Blythe sounded dazed as she looked back at Simon, her eyes huge. "Yes, I—I forgot this was for the play."

"Seemed real," Giles agreed. "Just the effect we want."

It was real, Simon thought, more real than Giles could know. He raised his word in salute. "A worthy adversary," he said, bowing low. "I would duel with you at any time."

"Thank you, sir." Blythe dropped into a brief curtsy, apparently taking his words at face value. Though what he had meant, even he wasn't certain. "But now—oh! I promised I would help Mrs. Staples with costumes this morning. Pray excuse me," she said, and slipped from Giles's loose embrace, dropping the sword and scurrying across the barn. Though more than one player stopped her with compliments and praise, Blythe barely slowed, until at last she reached the door and disappeared outside. With her gone, Simon could suddenly breathe again, was again aware of the clatter and confusion of rehearsal, and of Giles regarding him curiously. With her gone, it seemed somehow darker in the barn, and very empty.

"She's good," Giles said, standing by Simon's side with fists resting on his hips. "Wonder if she knows it."

Simon rounded on him. "You're not to put her onstage. 'Twas a foolish enough risk before. Do it now, and she'll be recognized."

"And lead the authorities to you, is that it?" Giles frowned at him. "I thought better of you," he said, and, turning, strode toward one of the small groups rehearsing. Simon started to call him back and then shook his head. Let Giles think it was his own neck he was concerned with. Let everyone think that. Better that than the truth be known.

Firming his lips, he bent to pick up the discarded swords. Swordplay, indeed. He wouldn't mind engaging in it with her again. Circumstances being what they were, that was the problem. He was not free to pursue her, or any other woman, not with the threat of hanging ever-present. Not when she thought he had committed the crime. Before he could move on with his life he would have to clear his name. The damnable thing was, he was beginning to doubt he ever would.

Mrs. Staples, the costume mistress, did indeed need Blythe's help. In most cases the actors wore contemporary dress onstage, and their clothing was their own. Still, someone had to see to it. Blythe's nose wrinkled as she took up a shirt that was not only thin at the elbows, but also stained with sweat. The conditions under which the troupe lived were primitive at best. She should wish to leave, to return to her own world. Odd, though, how that thought hurt.

She was sitting on a fallen beam against the wall of the barn, just about to take the first darning stitch in the elbow, when a shadow fell across the shirt, making her look up. Simon stood before her. "Should you be out?" she asked, before she could stop herself.

"Probably not." Simon sank cross-legged to the ground beside her. Behind her bulked the old barn, where now she wished she had stayed. Anything but to be so close to him.

"Well." She frowned over the shirt, concentrating on taking a precise stitch. "If you are not afraid of being caught, then why should I be?"

He cupped his chin in his hand. "If I am caught, you are, too," he pointed out.

"Oh? And do you really think they have any interest in me beyond you?"

"Yes. Like it or not, Blythe, you have broken the law—"

"And whose fault is that?"

"—and I suspect that our mysterious friend may be as interested in you as in me."

She frowned. "Why?"

"You've thwarted him."

"Is that how you would react in the same situation?" she asked, raising her head.

"No, though I don't like being bested."

"And bested you were." She grinned. "Admit it. You could not defeat me in our duel."

"Mayhap. But mayhap if we engaged in swordplay again, the outcome would be different."

She flushed. That insinuating tone was in his voice again, implying meanings she could only guess at, but that made her uncomfortable. And curious. And confused. "Mayhap. More likely not."

That made him laugh, a full-throated sound. She found herself staring at the strong column of his neck, lightly dusted with fine golden hair. The sun suddenly seemed very warm, her mouth very dry. "A worthy adversary, indeed," he said, his eyes brimming with amusement. "And here you hide as a plain companion."

She frowned as she took up the shirt again, unreasonably annoyed. He thought her plain? "Of necessity."

"You knew it, then?"

She looked up. "Knew what?"

"That you were playing a role?"

Then he didn't think her plain? Oh, what did it matter? "I know," she said, admitting it to him, and to herself, for the first time.

"I thought as much." He tilted his head to the side, studying her. "Who are you, Blythe Marden?"

"What do you mean?"

"You came with me."

"Not by choice, I might remind you."

"I'd let you go."

She paused, because that was an undeniable fact. He had let her go. When given the choice between staying with him in discomfort and fear or returning to her safe, suffocating, stultifying life, she had chosen to stay. Even now she wasn't sure why. "So you did," she said finally, her gaze on the shirt.

"And you haven't left yet."

"Because I am as much a fugitive as you are, in case you've forgotten."

"Don't fire up at me, princess," he said, and had the nerve to grin. "There's naught I can do about that."

She cast him a look from under her brows. "Naught," she muttered. "Hmph. And why are you staring at me so?"

"Your cap is askew."

"Oh, bother it," she said, and pulled off her mob-cap. Instantly her hair tumbled to her shoulders, thick and unruly. Why she had let him goad her into doing such a thing she did not know, except that suddenly the cap had felt as confining as her old life. "I do not know why you make me do such things. A lady should keep her head covered."

"I suppose you learned that at your mother's knee."

Blythe paused and then took up her stitching again. "Something like that, yes. Though it was my foster mother and her birch rod."

Simon straightened. "She beat you?"

"I sometimes needed it," Blythe said, keeping her gaze on her work.

"Where was your real mother?"

"Dead." She set the shirt down, looking at him at last. "My parents were young when they married, young and foolish, many said. Father had only a small plot of land, and Mama no portion at all. But they were happy." Her voice softened. " 'Twas why they called me Blythe."

"What happened?" he prompted, his voice almost gentle.

"A fever took them. There, that's done." She knotted the thread and bit the end off. "A neat piece of work, if I do say so myself, but then my mother—my foster mother—would have no less."

"How old were you?"

"Barely two. I've much mending to do, sir, so if you don't mind . . ."

"Not at all. I'll keep you company while you work."

She glared at him. "That was not what I meant."

"No offense taken. So you were orphaned young." Chin still resting on hand, he regarded her. "We've that in common, at least."

That made her look at him. "You, too?"

"Aye. Except that in my case, 'twas just my mother I lost." He looked away, his eyes curiously opaque. "No one knew who my father was."

Blythe's breath drew in sharply. "I am sorry."

" 'Tis long ago." He waved his hand in dismissal. "My Uncle Harry and Aunt Bess took me in, bless 'em, gave me as good a home as they could, and a family besides."

"I've always missed that."

"What?"

"Family."

"Yet you had foster parents."

She nodded, frowning down at the shirt. "The fever took many people, but I was the only one left without family. Parents, grandparents, all gone. I've relatives elsewhere, but they never came to claim me. So Dr. Temple took me in." She took a very careful, very precise stitch. "I'm sure he thought he was doing the right thing. And he was, of course. I needed a home."

"But?"

"But?" She shrugged. "His wife had other thoughts. They had a son, but they were older and could have no more children."

"Then I'd think she'd be happy with you."

"Mayhap if I'd been her idea of what a proper daughter should be, but I wasn't," she said flatly. "I couldn't seem to do anything right. I tried, but I kept getting into mischief. And when John—my brother—was tutored, so was I."

"Hence the fencing lessons."

"Yes, and Latin, and mathematics, and a great deal of other things that my mother thought a girl didn't need to know. And I think she resented me for that, as well."

"More than likely," Simon agreed. "Yet you changed."

"Well, I had to, didn't I?" Once again she knotted and bit off the thread, aware of Simon watching her with peculiar interest. "I had to try to be what she wanted. And I was."

"On the outside."

Blythe busied herself with folding the shirt. "Yes," she said finally, and jumped to her feet. "There! That's done. I believe I'll return this to Mrs. Staples and see what else she has for me."

Simon remained sitting. "Blythe."

She looked down, caught by his serious tone. "What?"

"If you could have one thing in the world, what would it be?"

"One thing? I don't—family," she blurted out. "A real family, of my own."

His eyes were opaque again. "Yes, I can see that."

"What of you?" she asked, caught by his gaze.

He shrugged and rose, untangling his long legs easily. "Freedom, I suppose. To clear my name."

He was standing very near, so that she had to crane her head to see his face. There were lines of strain about his eyes that were new, and a tightness to his mouth. "Do you think you can?"

"I need to try. Can I trust you?"

She didn't think twice. "You know you can."

"Aye." His gaze was so searching she wanted to look away, but she couldn't. "I do know that. I am going to leave the troupe," he said, turning and walking away.

"What?" She hurried to catch up with him. "You can't, 'tis too dangerous—"

"I have to clear my name," he repeated, stopping and turning to her. "I cannot do that here."

Blythe pursed her lips. "Where will you go?"

"Wherever I can find the answer." He looked down at her at last. "I have to do this, Blythe."

She bit her lip. She understood the pull of a long-held and cherished dream, and yet she feared for him. "Simon."

He turned to her. "What?"

"Did you—oh, it doesn't matter."

"What is it you want to know, princess?" His eyes had narrowed. "What you've asked me before?"

"No, 'tis none of my concern."

"But it is, princess, it is." He laughed, a bitter sound. "You want to know if I committed the crime I'm convicted of. How would you feel if I said I did?"

Chapter 13

Blythe's breath drew in sharply. "Surely you aren't."

He gazed down at her, keeping his face still. "What do you think?"

"I . . ." She held his gaze for a moment and then looked away, giving him his answer. It shouldn't have hurt as much as it did. "I don't know," she said. "We all play roles, Simon. You've taught me as much."

"Then tell me, Blythe. Am I playing the role of murderer or of an innocent man wrongly accused?"

"I don't know," she said again.

"Of course you don't." He turned away, thrusting his hand into his hair. "And that is why I have to leave. Because no one will ever know unless I prove it to them."

She didn't answer right away. "When will you go?"

"Soon. I'd rather not say exactly. Don't look so glum, princess." He forced himself to smile. "You'll be free of me at last."

"Yes, but too late to help me! The damage has been done."

"Go home, princess," he advised. "Go back to where you truly belong."

Her eyes were a stormy cobalt. "I don't know where I belong anymore. Another lesson learned from you."

"You'll figure it out. By the by." He glanced back at her. "Giles is thinking of giving you a part. If you're wise, you'll not accept it."

"That, sir, is my decision," she retorted, and walked away, costumes bundled into a ball at her hip and her head held high, as if she really were the princess he called her. In spite of himself he felt a stab of admiration for her courage. God, she was brave! He knew he'd hurt her by his apparent indifference, but what else could he do? He had already done enough to ruin her life. He would not add to his sins. He would, indeed, he vowed, watching as she disappeared into the barn, clear his name and thus prove himself to her. Then, and only then, would he come back to her. Only then would he have anything to offer her.

The barn was dark after the bright daylight outside. Blythe paused a moment in her headlong rush, letting her eyes adjust. Drat the man! What right had he to order her about, as if she were his property? She was no man's, no person's, for perhaps the first time in her life. She could make her own choices. Just now, though, she had no choice, because he was leaving her. Because he didn't want her.

"There you are," Giles's voice boomed out, and she stopped, watching him stride across the barn to her. "I've been looking for you."

"I was just outside, sir, and I do need to return these costumes to Mrs. Staples."

"A moment only." He took her elbow in the overly familiar manner that she had learned was simply his way, forcing her to walk with him. "I've a proposition for you."

She stopped. "Oh?"

"Yes." He glanced at her and chuckled. "Not like that, lass. Not with Phoebe to keep me happy."

"Oh," she said again, feeling herself color.

"No, 'tis something totally different. You've talent, lass. I wonder if you realize it."

"I don't know. It isn't something I've ever thought about."

"Think about it now, then, eh? I've a role in mind I'd like you to try."

Blythe bit her lip. Simon had forbidden her to take the role, though he had no right. He wouldn't even be here, anyway. "I'm not sure 'tis a good idea. I'm sure to be recognized."

"Not in proper costume. You're an unknown, lass,

and 'tis only your hair that gives you away." Giles stepped back, studying her with pursed lips. "That blond streak—'tis unusual. If that were covered, though, no one would remark you. You're much like Phoebe, you see," he went on, taking her elbow again and leading her deeper into the barn. "You do not draw attention to yourself unless you wish it."

That made her frown. "I'm not so sure of that, sir, and one thing I do know. I don't have Phoebe's talent."

"Likely not," he agreed. "Her talent is rare. But you've some, and presence, lass. Not everyone has that."

"I'm not sure what you mean."

"When you are on the stage, you command attention. You make people look at you."

Her frown deepened. "Are you sure? That doesn't sound like me at all."

"You become the part you act. I've watched you do it. And you draw people's eyes. Now, here." He stepped back, studying her. "You're pretty, lass, but not remarkable. Put you in costume, cover your hair, and give you a role, and no one will know you. Unless you wish it."

"I don't think that I can do it."

"You can," he answered her, putting his arm around her shoulders in a companionable way. "I wouldn't suggest it if I thought otherwise."

"I never thought of myself on the stage." It was oddly tempting, what he'd offered her. She'd enjoyed those moments when she'd helped Phoebe, or one of the other troupe members, rehearse; she'd wondered how it would feel to step out onstage and say lines herself. Frightening, yes, but it wouldn't be her, Blythe, up there. It would be her character. And how wondrous that would be, to bring to life someone who hadn't previously existed. To live someone else's life. "I'll do it," she said, before she could change her mind. "Yes. I'll do it."

"Good lass. I thought you might." He squeezed her shoulders and then released her. " 'Tis a small part, only seven lengths long, but important. You'll have no trouble learning it."

"Seven lengths." Blythe did some calculating. A length was the page upon which an actor's part was written, and it usually contained forty-two lines. Seven pages of forty-two lines each. "I don't know if I can!"

"Of course you can. It is a part Odette usually plays, but I want to try you in it."

"She'll be angry," Blythe said. If Odette had been incensed when Blythe had innocently sat in her chair, how would she react to this?

"No matter. You'll play a maid who spies upon her mistress."

"It's not a breeches part?" she asked in surprise.

"Nay, lass, and why should it be? Ah, because of the soldiers. No, you can do this. Besides"—his glance was shrewd—"play a breeches part and there's too good a chance you'll be recognized."

Blythe went still. For a moment she had forgotten. She was being hunted every bit as much as Simon was. If she was wise, she would refuse the part. Certainly acting would do her no good if she wished to clear her name and return to her real life. Or rather, what she had thought was her life. "I'll do it," she said again, in that moment defying everyone who had ever dismissed her as the orphan child of foster parents, or as a woman fit only to be an elderly lady's companion. Let them think as they would; let Simon think as he would. This was something she had to do.

Sir Hubert Winterborne had rarely felt such excitement in his life. As magistrate for the area, he dealt with matters that were boring and sometimes bewildering: the occasional theft of a horse or sheep or goat; complaints about this or that tradesman in Rochester, most of which Sir Hubert handled with great gusto; a dispute or two over property lines. Sir Hubert hadn't been trained in the law—he was a gentleman, not in trade!—but he knew his duty. He was the leading gentleman in the neighborhood. Justice was his to dispense as he saw fit.

And now this man, this fop, was standing there and telling him what to do! "You say we've a murderer in our midst," Sir Hubert rumbled, linking his hands upon his ample belly. "I've yet to see a sign of him."

"He has been in hiding," Quentin said, as calmly as possible. God save him from foolish men. Most men were stupid, easily manipulated, and thus good tools to Quentin's hand. Occasionally, however, the quality that made them valuable also turned them bullheaded. He was having the devil of a time convincing this fool that Simon Woodley was, indeed, in Rochester.

"With a bunch of actors?" Sir Hubert snorted. " 'Pon rep, the man is not stupid, is he? A theater is the first place anyone would think to look for him."

"I disagree." Quentin sat back. "It is the perfect place for him to hide, for that reason."

"Eh? I don't take your meaning, man."

"I know he is there," Quentin went on, forbearing to explain, yet again, his logic. "I have it on reliable information." From Odette, as it happened, who was furious that her part had been taken from her.

"Still seems havey-cavey to me. I can't call out the county on mere rumors, sirrah! If the man is there, bring me some proof."

"I have it on the word of one of the members of the troupe. She tells me—"

"An actress?" Sir Hubert perked up. "Damme, but I've heard of what actresses are like. Little more than strumpets, eh?"

"If you would like, I'll introduce you."

"I say!" Sir Hubert sat up straight. "That is decent of you, sirrah, dashed decent. But"—he sank back—"a man in my position can't be seen with someone like her."

"Of course not. No one need know, I assure you of that. The meeting will be . . . private."

"Private," Sir Hubert mused, lips pursed, and then nodded. "What is your plan again?"

Quentin kept his face straight. So. The fool was finally coming around. "Woodley has been in hiding, I don't know where," he explained again, sitting back with one elegantly hosed leg crossed over the other. "Not in the lodgings with Rowley and the others. He may be at Shepard's barn with the rest of the troupe, but he does not come to the theater. Miss Marden, however, does." And an intriguing opponent she was turning out to be, taking the stage as a soldier, of all things. As he remembered, her legs in breeches and silk stockings had been fine. But that was not his purpose, he reminded himself sternly. "I have kept watch this last sennight."

"Then we'll take her," Sir Hubert blustered.

"Oh? And give warning to Woodley what we are doing? I do not want the Marden woman." He recrossed his legs. "I believe if we capture her Woodley will escape. But I also believe that she may be used as a lure for Woodley. Like a fox to hounds."

"So we flush him from his cover—"

"And capture him." Quentin sat back. "Precisely."

"And the woman?"

"You may leave her to me." And she might prove to be tolerably entertaining. "Woodley is the prize, Sir Hubert."

"Indeed. Indeed." Sir Hubert pulled a crumpled handkerchief from his waistcoat pocket and blew his nose vigorously. "I like your idea," he said, stuffing the handkerchief away. "How do you plan to do it?"

"It's rather simple." Quentin leaned forward, keeping the elation from his face by force of long habit. It was a gamble, what he was doing, but then, much of his life had been. Much had depended on the turn of a card—whether he faced success or ruin. So it was now. "First you must gather your men together . . ."

"Better that time," Katherine said placidly. "Try it again, with more emotion."

"I don't have any emotion left in me." Blythe's voice was ragged, and her throat ached. So did her head, while her limbs were weak with exhaustion. Never had she realized that acting was such physically demanding work.

"*Tch*. Of course you do. Anger is emotion, is it not?

And you are close to anger. Use it." Katherine leaned forward, dark eyes intent. "Use the energy the anger gives you."

Blythe rubbed her throbbing temples. The play was a frivolous thing, a silly story of misunderstandings and mistakes, in which a gentleman, convinced his wife had taken a lover, set a maid to spy on her. But the faithful wife, noticing that her husband was abstracted and fearing that he had a mistress, convinced a footman to spy on him. When maid and footman met, there would be yet another dalliance. " 'I would that you would not dally with another.' "

"No, no." Katherine held up her hand. "That had all the feeling of a stone! You are supposed to be in love. Haven't you had a sweetheart?"

"No," Blythe replied firmly, though into her mind strode an image she'd as soon ignore. Simon.

"You lie, I think." Katherine's voice was prosaic. "But that is not my concern. Try again."

"I can't." Blythe dropped down upon a bale of hay in the barn, head in hands. "I'm just so tired."

"You go on tonight. You must be ready."

The panic that always accompanied that knowledge bubbled up within her again. "I know, but—"

"No buts! Try again, or do you think you have no talent?"

" 'I would that you would not dally with another!' " Blythe snapped, glaring at her.

"Brava!" Katherine applauded. "Very good. Now if you would compose your face, we shall be getting on. It's a thin line between anger and love, is it not?"

"I don't know," Blythe muttered, looking down at the length. True it was that anger had been behind her passionate outburst, and yet, while she was speaking, she had felt an undeniable jolt of emotion. For a moment she had actually become the lovelorn girl she portrayed. Amazing how that instant of feeling had changed things, made her speak her words differently, made her look at things differently. Like a woman in love.

"Good. Again, then?"

"Again," Blythe agreed, resigned, and recited the lines. If they didn't have the emotion of her previous attempt, if she didn't feel that current of energy again, still even she knew that she was doing a creditable job. Her voice had a ring of conviction that earlier it had lacked. Whether she could repeat the performance onstage was another matter. Why, oh, why had she agreed to do this?

"Katherine." Lester stood before them. "We were supposed to rehearse our scene this afternoon."

Katherine frowned. "I am busy here—but you are right. I'm sorry, Blythe. I must do this."

Blythe let her breath out. "I don't mind." She could rest at last. Heavens, but she was tired. "I'm glad for the rest."

"But you're not ready," Katherine fretted, her brow wrinkled. "If there is someone else—ah! Mr., er, Smith."

Simon, just coming down the ladder from the loft, continued on. "Mr. Smith," she called again, and this time he stopped. Smith. That was supposed to be his name, at least to this theater company. That they all knew who he was he didn't doubt, just as he knew they wouldn't betray him. "Yes, Katherine?" he asked, crossing to her. Beside her Blythe sat, head bent over a length, not looking at him.

"You're needed. Come." She pushed a sheaf of papers at him. "You are better to rehearse this scene than I am. Sit."

"Of course." He smiled at Katherine as she turned to leave, but the smile quickly faded as he scanned the lengths she handed him. So he was to rehearse a scene with Blythe, was he? No matter that he was opposed to her going onto the stage. No matter that this was a love scene. *Hell.* This was all he needed.

"You needn't rehearse with me if you'd rather not," Blythe said stiffly.

He looked up. They'd conversed little in the days since he'd made his decision to leave, and that was just as well. At least, he'd thought so. But, bloody hell, he'd missed her. He hadn't realized it until now.

He'd missed her quick smile, her willingness to help, her sometimes tart observations on life. He'd missed holding her hand, touching her hair. God help him, but he was in bad case. "Do you know your lines?" he forced himself to say, aware that the silence had dragged on for much too long and that she was staring at him.

"Well enough."

"A quick study, are you? Well, let us see," he said, and read out the first line of the scene. Blythe answered promptly, launching into her part with gusto and flair surprising in an amateur, and he was well and truly caught. For she was not the Blythe he'd come to know: the staid companion, the intrepid adventurer, the stubborn survivor. She was a different Blythe, her lips curved in a soft smile, her eyes alert and teasing and flirtatious beneath their lashes. She was a coquette, speaking the suggestive lines with an intoxicating mixture of innocence and beguiling sensuality. Who had taught her? he wondered. What man had put that smile on her face?

"Simon," she said, her voice impatient, and he realized at last that she was waiting for him. "Are you going to give me the cue or not?"

"What? Yes." He looked down at the paper, though he knew the part of the footman well. " 'My dear heart,' " he began, in a teasing, confidential tone, sidling a bit closer to her. " 'Do you not know there is no one for me but you? For I fear I love you.' " If she could go into character, then so could he. It was acting, nothing more.

" 'I would believe that if I could, sir. For I fear I love you, too,' " Blythe answered, laying her hand on his arm, lightly at first, and then with more assurance. The barn was warm. No wonder that her touch burned.

" 'Then let us not talk of parting.' " He turned, catching her hand in his and bringing it to his lips. Her breath caught, her eyes widened, and suddenly what had been only acting, only stagecraft, was more. It was real, her hand in his, the softness of her skin under his lips, the taste and smell and feel of her. It was real.

"Ah, my lady," he murmured, brushing his lips across her hand again. This time she tried to pull away, but he tightened his grip, keeping her captive. Soon he would go, and leaving her would be one of the hardest things he had ever done. But now . . . now she was near, and though it was sweet torture, he could not make himself move.

"Simon," she whispered.

His lips had moved to her knuckles now, touching and tasting each one individually. "Yes, princess?"

"This . . . isn't part of the scene."

He brought her fingertips to his parted lips and her hand jerked. "No?"

"No."

His grasp made her thumb move against his mouth, his teeth, his lips. "Shall I stop?"

"Y-yes."

He looked up, the tip of his tongue still grazing her skin. Her cheeks were flushed; her eyes were heavy and bright. "And if I don't?"

"I'll make a fuss."

"Will you?" His arm slid about her waist. He had to be closer, had to feel her near him. "Will you, indeed?"

Her mouth was close to his, so close that he felt her breath as she spoke, felt it as his own. "Yes."

"I don't believe you, princess." He lowered her hand, though he didn't release it, and was gratified to feel her fingers cling to his.

"Simon, this is acting."

"Not for me," he said, and lowered his head. Her lips were near, lush, sweet, his for the taking. His lips parted, his eyes closed—and someone nearby, much too close, began clapping.

"Brava. And bravo." Giles stood over them, genial, smiling. "Not the usual bit of business for that scene, but affecting, my boy. Think I'll instruct Thomas to do just that in the role."

"No." Simon straightened, face set, as Blythe slipped from his embrace.

"My company, my boy. I decide who plays what."

Simon rose, hands balled into fists at his side. No one was going to kiss his Blythe. No one. "No," he said again, punctuating the warning by stepping forward.

Giles peered thoughtfully up at him. "No? Eh, well, maybe not. Thomas wouldn't play it as well as you."

"Simon," Blythe said from behind him, and he turned to see her still sitting on the bench, hands folded in her lap, looking remarkably composed. " 'Tis only acting."

His eyes narrowed. "Is it?"

Her gaze didn't waver. "Yes."

"Like hell," he snorted, and swung away. "Find someone else to rehearse with you, princess. I am leaving."

"Simon!" Blythe started up. "Don't—"

"Leave the boy go." Giles caught her arm. "He needs to cool off."

"You don't understand." She stared past Giles to Simon stalking out of the barn. "He's leaving."

"Aye, lass." Giles's voice was unexpectedly kind. "I know."

That made her look at him. "You do?"

"Aye. He can't stay, lass. I've known that for a time."

"But . . ." She swallowed, hard. "I don't belong here."

"More than you think, lass. Come." He slung an arm about her shoulder, turning her away from the door. "Thomas will rehearse with you."

Blythe planted her feet firmly on the floor. "I'm not going on tonight," she announced. Not if Simon was leaving. She could not go onstage and act a role, act as if nothing were amiss, when Simon was leaving.

"But you are, miss." Giles's voice was firm. "Aye, and we'll get you to your family, too. He made me promise that much."

She looked up, some of her resolve fading. "He did?"

"Yes." His face softened. "He's a strolling player, lass. Leaving is what he does best."

Blythe stared at the opening to the barn, which was empty, bright. "Yes," she said, finally admitting what she had always known. Simon was not for her. And why she should care, with all he'd done, was beyond her.

"It's better this way, lass."

"Yes," she said again, and this time allowed herself to be turned away, to the safety of the barn and the theater company. Easier, yes, but better? No. Not with Simon gone. She didn't imagine that life would ever be better again.

The barn was empty. In the loft Simon finished rolling his few possessions together and looked about him, though he knew he'd left nothing behind. That was the way his life had always been. He moved on to the next play, the next theater. The other actors were his family, and so he didn't mind not having a stable home. This time was different, though. This time he was leaving behind the hangman's noose. And this time, he was leaving Blythe.

Lips set grimly, he hefted the roll onto his shoulder. There was no real need for him to go, at least not for his own safety. It had been over a week since anyone had seen the mysterious man who pursued him; nor had any officials harassed the troupe about him. He was safe enough. He might have stayed, were it not for Blythe. Sweet Jesus, what had passed between them this afternoon had held as much sweetness, and as much danger, as anything in his life. And not just to him. He would do Blythe no good if he stayed.

For just a moment he let his thoughts stray to the theater, where Blythe would soon be making her debut. Likely she was nervous. Her first appearance, and she had a leading role. That wasn't unusual; in such a way managers and actors alike quickly learned who could handle themselves and who couldn't. He suspected that Blythe would do well. His only regret was that he wouldn't be there to see her.

A sunbeam streamed through a chink in the wall, mellow, golden. It was getting late. If he was to be going, he would need to leave soon. Squaring his shoulders, he stalked across the loft. He was halfway down the ladder when the barn door below creaked open.

Simon froze. No one but he was in the barn; the entire troupe was supposed to be at the theater. Hell, if someone had gotten curious and decided to investigate . . .

"Woodley!" a voice hissed, and in spite of himself, Simon looked down.

"McNally." Relieved, annoyed, he scrambled down the ladder. "What the hell—"

"No time, lad." McNally grabbed his arm, dragging him out of the barn. "You've got to leave."

"Hell, I am, but why such a hurry—"

"They've found you," McNally blurted. "At least, they think they have."

Simon went very still, eyes alert, nostrils flared. "How do you know?"

"Heard someone near the theater, some local person. They know you're around."

"Bloody hell. Do they know about the barn?"

"It's not the barn they're interested in just now. It's not even you. Yet."

Simon, halfway out the door, turned. "You'd best explain that."

"They know you're here, but not where. We hid you well. But they think they know who will lead them to you."

Simon's bundle dropped to the ground with a thud. "Blythe."

"Aye." McNally's face was grim. "They plan to arrest Miss Blythe."

Chapter 14

Blythe stood in the wings, her hair powdered, her bodice tighter laced than usual, awaiting her cue. Odd, she'd thought she'd be scared. Nervous, at least, as she had been when she'd gone on as a soldier. She wasn't, though. She knew her lines, knew even what gestures she might use. What she chiefly felt was impatience to get it all over with. It was all playacting. Her life with Simon was, however, all too real.

"Lass." Giles grabbed her arm, pulling her back farther into the wings. "You can't go on."

"What?" She glanced out at the stage, lowering her voice in deference to the action, though how anyone could hear the play over the constant applause and conversation in the audience was beyond her. "But my cue is in just a few lines—"

"Odette is preparing now. If we have to, we'll ring down the curtain until she's ready."

"But I don't understand. I'm prepared—"

"We've word of a plot." Giles's voice was low, terse. "The local magistrate plans to arrest you."

Blythe drew in her breath sharply. Oh, dear heaven, then she'd been discovered. She knew all too well what that meant. Disgrace, certainly, and possible—no, she would not think about the ultimate punishment. But why would they pursue her when it was Simon they wanted?

"Bloody hell," she swore, hardly aware she did so. It was clear to her now. "They don't want me. They want Simon."

"Aye, lass." Giles shook his head. "I fear they're here for you. We'll get you out."

"Did you send someone to warn Simon?"

"Aye, McNally went."

"Then what do you think he'll do?" she demanded, hands on hips. "I don't care what anyone says about him or about actors. He's no coward. He won't run."

Giles's breath hissed out. "You think he'll come here?"

"Yes." Blythe set her lips in a thin line. "They'll use me to catch him."

"I'll set someone to warn him off. But you," he said, as Blythe glanced back toward the stage, "we'll have to figure out what to do with you."

"I'm going on, of course."

"Don't be foolish, lass! Do you want to be caught?"

"Of course not." The thought of prison, of what might ultimately happen to her, turned her knees weak with terror. "They won't arrest me while I'm onstage."

"That won't stop them." Giles sounded thoroughly exasperated. "They'll care not for stopping the show."

"Then you must keep them back. And you must get Simon away from here. There is my cue," she said coolly, and slipped away onto the stage.

There was no burst of applause when she entered, which was just as well and which she hadn't expected; she was new on the stage and the audience wouldn't know her. On another night, that might have meant something to her. On another night, as when she had played the role of soldier, she would probably have been very aware of herself, of her actions and her lines; aware of the audience, as well. Tonight, though, the mass of people in the auditorium barely registered. Oh, she knew the pit was crowded, that finely dressed people sat in the boxes to either side and above, but no one stood out, no one mattered. Nor did she, not just now. She was a lure to the hunter, no more, and as such she would have to be very, very careful.

Later her memory of that night, her debut onstage, would be hazy at best. She would not remember how she spoke her lines or how she moved. She would remember that occasionally the audience laughed or applauded, startling her out of her trance, but for the most part she remained concentrated upon one thing. While she was onstage, while the hunter knew where she was, he would not be on the watch for Simon.

It was during the second act that activity in the theater began to penetrate even Blythe's concentration. The crowd, up until then appreciative, began hissing and booing. Faltering just a bit on her lines, she glanced out at the audience and froze. Soldiers, too many of them, making their way toward the stage, from the back, from the sides. More chilling still was the sight of a man half in the shadows and yet recognizable: the man from Lambeth Bridge, from the Tabard Inn, from the audience last week. The man who, for reasons unknown, was unflagging in his pursuit of Blythe and Simon.

"Pay heed, princess!" a voice hissed beside her on the stage, and she whipped her head around. As she'd expected, she saw the character of the footman, her lover in the play, attired in rich brocade and powdered wig. It was not Thomas in the role, though. It was Simon.

"Oh, my God," she said, before she could stop herself. Oddly enough, that provoked the audience to laughter. "What are you doing?"

"'Such coils as you are in will only lead you to more trouble,'" Simon said, the next line of the play. "Go along with me!" he added in a fierce whisper.

"'I care not for what you think.' But you'll be caught."

"'You care more than you care to admit.' There's a plan. Pay heed."

Mechanically Blythe spoke her next line, and in the audience someone booed. A day ago, this morning, such a reception would have devastated her. Now it seemed beneath her notice. They were trapped, she and Simon, here on this stage. If there were soldiers out front, then surely they were in the back of the theater as well. "Oh, Simon—"

Something plopped onto the stage at her feet, spattering her with moisture. It took her a moment to realize that it was an overripe tomato. "We want Odette!" someone yelled in the audience, and others took up the call. From all corners of the auditorium shouting went up, some siding with the call for Odette, but many yelling for the play to proceed. Two men in the pit, apparently not content with verbal abuse, suddenly started swinging at each other, their arms flailing and pumping. "What do we do?" Blythe said, no longer trying to stay in character.

"Wait." Simon's eyes were sharp as he gazed into the auditorium. Chaos had spread across the pit; now a good many of the audience were fighting, spilling into the aisles at either side and halting the progress of the soldiers. "We'll have a chance."

"Redcoats, by God!" someone shouted, a familiar voice, though Blythe couldn't place it. In that instant the audience's aggression switched from each other to the soldiers. Within moments the entire theater seemed to rise up as one, screaming, shouting, scrambling across the benches, scuttling into the aisles, a teeming, riotous mass of humanity. All but forgotten were the actors onstage.

"This way!" a voice barked at Blythe's side. She turned just as McNally grabbed her arm, dragging her from the stage. Now she knew who had incited the crowd to riot; it had been his voice she'd heard. "The soldiers have enough to do putting down the riot."

"In back?" Blythe gasped, letting Simon grasp her other hand, trusting McNally, trusting him.

"Taken care of for now. The soldiers are busy out front."

"You're a devious soul, McNally," Simon said, pulling off his wig and tossing it aside as they pounded through the wings and into the corridor.

"Aye, so I am. We've not much time. Put this on," he added, thrusting a huge black bonnet at Blythe.

Through the corridor, past milling people trying to find out what was causing such a commotion. "He's out there," Blythe gasped, less concerned about the soldiers than about the man who pursued them. "The man I saw before—"

"His name's Heywood." McNally stopped abruptly at the stage door. "Wait here and let me check outside. Ah, good, the soldiers are busy here, too."

"Who?" Simon said, as McNally hustled them out into darkness and the sound of uproar in the distance.

"Quentin Heywood. Know that much about the man, but little else. Mind your step, now, 'tis dark on these stairs. There." Down the stairs, out into the alley that ran alongside the theater. From the end of the alley at the front of the theater came ringing, discordant sounds, voices raised in anger, fists meeting flesh, booted feet running hard. "This way." McNally caught Blythe's arm again, pulling her toward the darkness in back of the theater. "There's a lane here. Follow it and you'll come to a—"

"There they are!" A shout from the other end of the alley, suddenly illumined by torches. Blythe had time for only a quick look before Simon grabbed her other arm and began running. In that look she'd seen not only soldiers with muskets at the ready, but the mysterious, menacing man McNally had just identified as Quentin Heywood. Why was he after them?

"Go!" McNally gave her a push. "I'll hold them off."

"I'll repay you for this someday," Simon said, and took to his heels, Blythe's hand firmly clasped in his.

"Will he be all right?" Blythe gasped, pounding along beside him. She was a fugitive again, running from a world that had begun to feel familiar, safe. Yet somehow it didn't bother her. Somehow she felt almost happy.

"Save your breath," Simon said, as she was contemplating her odd reaction. "But, yes, he can take care of himself."

"Do you know where we're going?"

"Not really. McNally told me roughly where to go on the way to the theater, but that's all." The lane ran between neat rows of cottages edged by hedges and the backs of shops, all in darkness. "We need to find a place to hide. Bloody hell."

"What?" Blythe asked as Simon slammed them

both back against an ivy-covered wall. But then she saw them, too. Torches, at the other end of the lane. "Oh, no."

"We can't go back." From the direction of the theater came shouts. "If we hide—'tis too dark for them to see us yet—"

"But they'll know we're trapped here, and they'll find us."

"This way," he said, and to her immense astonishment put his hands to her backside, boosting her up. "Over the wall."

"Simon—"

" 'Tis our only choice. Go!"

" 'Tis a good thing I grew up with a brother," Blythe grumbled, using the ivy that covered the wall to hold to, until she reached the top. Good heavens, it was at least a ten-foot drop to the ground, and no ivy here to provide a grip. Nothing for it, then, but to jump. She took a deep breath, preparing herself, when Simon scrambled up beside her. With only a quick glance he jumped, landing lightly on the ground, and held his arms up to her. She didn't wait; she only trusted. She jumped, and his arms, strong, hard, caught her.

"This way." He pulled her across someone's neatly tended garden toward a hedge. A dog barked, too close for comfort, and in a window light suddenly bloomed. "Let's not make it easy for them."

"Someone will hear us."

"Probably." He stopped just past the cottage, peering into the darkness, and then pulled her forward again, past a trim hedgerow, through a lane and into yet another garden. "I think I know where we are."

"Are we hiding here?" she gasped.

"No, too open. But I've an idea."

"Why don't I trust you when you say that?"

"I don't know, princess. Have I never led you wrong before?"

"Ha. What about—"

"Save your breath for running," he said, and tugged on her hand. Reluctant to leave the shadowed quiet of the garden, and yet anxious to escape, she followed, pausing only a moment when they came to the banks of a stream. "It's not deep."

"I always seem to get my feet wet when I'm with you," she complained, splashing beside him, and behind them dogs barked again.

"Hush. You'll dry."

They were across at last, scrambling onto solid ground. "If I catch my death, it'll be on your head."

"Sweeting, that's precisely what I'm trying to avoid. Careful, there's a hill here, it's steep."

Blythe's breath was coming quick and hard by the time they reached the top of the small rise. She had the sense of land spreading out before her, with the bulk of a building rising to her left, blocking out the stars. "Where are we?"

"Churchyard." He spoke absently, leaning down to unlatch the gate, leading her inside. "If I remember aright, McNally found us a place to hide."

"Simon, not in a graveyard!"

"There's no place else."

"Could we not go into the church—"

"They'd find us there too easily." He glanced behind them. "We're leaving a trail."

"You would have it that we go through water," she said, following him as he threaded his way through the gravestones, faintly visible in the dim light.

"We couldn't very well use the bridge. Yes." He stopped so suddenly that she collided with his back, knocking him briefly off balance. "Careful, there."

"Ouch." Blythe rubbed her nose. "Simon, what are we doing here?"

"Hiding. There's a crypt—bloody hell." Far off behind them came the sudden gleam of light and the low murmur of voices. "They're nearly upon us."

"A crypt." Blythe set her heels as he grabbed her hand again. "You can't mean—"

"Oh, yes, I can. This one, here."

"Oh, no." This was the end of enough. They were stopped before a small, yet solid building of white marble in a gothic design. Blythe shuddered. "There's a lock."

"Which is broken." Simon pulled the door handle. "In with you."

"No." Blythe grasped the top of the railing that enclosed the crypt. In the past weeks she had been taken captive, had gone upon the stage, and had been chased more times than she cared to count. She had seen her reputation fall into shreds, and she had faced the reality of a bleak future. If she didn't escape she could end up in prison, or worse. Somehow, though, that was preferable to what was ahead now. "I'm not going in there."

"You have no choice," Simon said, and caught her about the waist. She tightened her grip on the railing, but he was stronger. Her fingers slipped, and before Blythe quite knew what was happening, she was being swung off her feet. Struggling, kicking, she was nonetheless borne into darkness and set down with an unceremonious thud. She had just a chance to see a tiny room, its floor littered with last year's leaves, before the door boomed shut.

Darkness, dank and complete. Disoriented, unnerved, Blythe stumbled backward, coming up hard against a ledge of some kind at waist level. Scrabbling for support, she grasped the ledge, finding it solid and substantial, something she could lean against. Something not flat, but oddly sculpted. Her hands moved over the surface, the shape of what she was feeling not quite making sense. Fingers? Oh, mercy! Fingers!

She shrieked and stumbled forward, only to encounter something else strong and hard. This time the obstacle was warm and just a bit yielding. "Hush, princess," Simon whispered into her hair. "Hush, now."

"Fingers," she babbled. "Someone's back there, Simon, someone dead and laid out—"

"An effigy, princess."

"What?"

"An effigy. A carving. No bodies, princess. I promise."

Her hands clung to his shirt. "I don't like it here."

"I know. I know." His arms were about her, strong, hard, protective, his chest a bulwark against the terrors that beset her. "It won't be for long."

She could hear his heartbeat, strong, a trifle fast, a trifle erratic, under her ear. "Do you promise?"

"I promise. Only until 'tis safe for us to leave."

"When will that be?"

"Soon." In the darkness she felt his head rise. "Someone's coming."

"How can you tell?" she asked, and at the same time heard sounds, distant voices and tramping feet. Suddenly the imagined terrors of the crypt gave way to the very real threat outside. "They've found us."

"Not yet. Hush, now, princess." He cupped her head with his hand, holding her close against him. "We must be quiet."

Blythe bit her lips, burrowing her head against his solid warmth. Dear heavens, how would she survive this night if not for him? Never mind that she was here because of him, that it was his fault that her safe, comfortable world was gone. Safe, comfortable, and boring, she confessed to herself, while outside, the voices came closer. Stifling, smothering life. She'd felt more alive in the past weeks than ever she had. And what she was feeling now. She raised her head, though she couldn't see Simon's face. What she felt for this man came perilously close to love.

"No one here, Sergeant," a voice said, much too close.

"Look in the tomb," another, more distant voice ordered.

Blythe stiffened; Simon's hold on her tightened. "The tomb? But Sergeant—"

"The tomb, soldier. Now."

"Sir Hubert'll have my head, me disturbing the family tomb," the soldier muttered. His bootheels sounded hollow on the stone doorstep. "Not to mention the dead." The handle to the tomb rattled. "Lord Jesus, protect me. God, protect me. Mother Mary and all the saints . . ."

"Give me your handkerchief," Simon hissed in Blythe's ear, as the soldier continued with his litany.

"What?" she whispered, her voice lost in the scraping noise of the crypt door opening, but already she was obeying, pulling her kerchief from her pocket. She felt oddly bereft and abandoned as Simon's arms dropped from around her, and frightened. They were about to be discovered, and he was concerned with her handkerchief.

The bottom of the door rasped as it opened, bronze against granite. Against the pale rectangle of the night sky, the soldier stood silhouetted, hesitating. "Oh, sweet Jesus," he muttered, and Blythe shrank back. It was only a matter of moments before they were discovered.

From her side came a strange sound, a low groan that rose and lengthened into a moan. Her arms prickled, even as she recognized the voice. Simon. But what in the world was he doing?

Simon moaned again, longer, louder, and the soldier stumbled back. "Who is that?" Simon demanded in a harsh, rusty whisper.

"I—I—oh, sweet Jesus!" The soldier fell back again. "Don't hurt me, I swear I mean no harm—"

Simon came forward, his head covered by Blythe's kerchief. The effect was remarkable: his clothing blended into the darkness, while the white cloth appeared as a floating, disembodied head. "Who dares disturb my rest?" Simon growled.

"Unhh," the soldier grunted, and with a clatter of sword and musket fell to the ground.

Simon pulled off the kerchief. "He's fainted. Come on."

"There are others," she protested, though she didn't resist the pull of his hand on her arm.

"Blythe, will you for once in your life do as I say without putting up a quarrel?"

"But—"

"We'll not have a better chance. Come."

This time she allowed him to pull her forward, past the still form of the soldier, onto the doorstep. The crypt had held only terror just a moment ago; it now appeared a sanctuary. Yet she knew he was right. They had to escape, now.

"This way." Simon tugged on her hand and dropped into a crouch. She followed, dodging behind tombstones and trees. At the other side of the graveyard torches flickered, the searchers apparently not having realized yet that one of their number was missing.

Simon stumbled to a halt behind a table grave, pulling her down to the ground with him. "We'll hide here," he muttered in her ear.

"They'll find us," Blythe whispered, her head close to his. It was oddly intimate talking this way, so close that their very breaths mingled.

Simon's lips grazed her cheek, and she jerked back. "They've looked here already."

"Oh." He hadn't kissed her, she told herself. He hadn't, and the pounding of her heart was from fear, not excitement. And she did not—did not!—wish that he would move his head again, just so, just there. She was frightened; he was familiar. That was all.

"Shea?" The sergeant's voice suddenly rang out. "Damn it all, where are you? Jackson. You and Martin there, go see what's become of Shea."

Simon gripped her shoulders. This was the moment. When the soldiers discovered Shea lying in the doorway of the crypt, they would know what he had found. They would know that the objects of their search were very close.

"Sergeant!" one of the men called, voice high and sharp. "You'd better come here, sir."

"What is it, Jackson?" the sergeant said, sounding almost bored.

"Shea, sir, here in this crypt. He won't wake up, sir."

"Won't he, now. Shea, lad!" There was the sound of a hand slapping flesh, followed by a groan. "Up with you."

"Sweet Jesus!" Shea yelled, so suddenly that Simon and Blythe, though some distance away, jumped. "Did you see him?"

"See who, lad? The criminal?"

"No, the ghost. He was there," Shea babbled. "Right there, protecting the tomb. All he had was a head, no body, no hands—"

"Rubbish. On your feet, soldier." There was the sound of scuffling, Shea apparently being pulled upright. "Are you saying you didn't see the criminal?"

"No, sir, a ghost as I live and breathe, sir. I swear, sir—"

"Rubbish," the sergeant said again. "They're not in the tomb, at any rate. Move out!" This, as he moved away from the crypt. "We've searched here, lads. Time to look elsewhere."

"But I swear there was a ghost," Shea was still saying, his voice fading as he moved away. His comrades answered, their voices lost to distance. From their hiding place, Blythe could see the small troop forming up at the churchyard gate. The torches wavered, then straightened, and the soldiers at last moved off. Within a moment only the echo of their footsteps remained.

Blythe sagged, her head resting against the cool stone of the tomb, her muscles atremble. "Dear heavens."

"Hush." Simon's hand on her shoulder was gentle. "We'll wait a few minutes."

She looked up at him, and though she was accustomed to the darkness, she could see little beyond his shape. "For what?"

"For them to be well away." He shifted, settling with his back against the stone and his legs outstretched. "Come here, princess." He drew Blythe against his side. "We're safe, for now. You're quite remarkable, you know," he went on in that same easy tone.

"No, I'm not, really."

"But you are." His thumb rubbed across the ridge of her shoulder, again and again. "I don't know another woman who wouldn't be in hysterics by now. Running from soldiers, hiding in a crypt—"

"Oh, yes, quite unladylike of me," she said tartly, pulling away. "You needn't remind me of that."

"Blythe." His breath touched her face in a gust of amusement. "I never said such a thing."

"And all because of you," she went on as if he hadn't spoken. Because of him she had left her life behind; because of him, she stayed. "I wouldn't be here except for you."

"No." He glanced away and then rose. "Come. They're gone. 'Tis time we left."

Blythe swayed with tiredness as she got to her feet. "Now where are we going? To another crypt? Or will I have to make do with a ditch?"

"Neither. Come, there's a barn nearby where we can stay. It's not far."

"How do you know about such places?" she complained. "First the crypt, now the barn—"

"McNally. He's been a great help. Come, princess." He tucked his arm about her waist. "You'll feel better after a good night's sleep."

"That I sincerely doubt," she muttered, but she let him lead her out of the churchyard, following him blindly, as she had from the beginning. As she would continue doing, as she was helpless to stop doing. He was a convicted murderer, an escaped criminal, and it didn't seem to matter. She'd realized that while he'd held her in the crypt, realized that she'd done something very foolish. She did not at the moment particularly like or trust Simon, but that was beside the point. Somehow, at some time during their adventure, she had fallen in love with him.

Chapter 15

Dawn was tinting the sky by the time Simon and Blythe reached their destination. The barn was old and ramshackle, with boards missing here and there, the aroma of long-gone animals still lingering. Nearby were the charred remains of a farmhouse, and fields long gone fallow. "What a shame no one uses this land," Blythe said.

"Fortunate for us." Simon pried open one creaking side of the barn door, peering around inside. "McNally found it on one of his rambles, thought it would come in handy. He said last night he'd try to get some supplies out here—oh, good man!" He grinned at her, looking tired but otherwise no worse for wear. She forced an exhausted smile. Why didn't he at least have the decency to show the effects of the night's ordeal, as she was certain she must? "I see blankets and a basket. Food, milady."

"At the moment, all I'd like to do is sleep." She wandered into the barn, vaguely surprised at how normal everything seemed. Just a few weeks ago, she would not have been able to imagine such an experience, let alone live it. And yet here she was, taking it for granted that she would be passing the rest of the day in a barn, in the company of a convict. "Life is strange."

Simon, engaged in shaking out one of the blankets, turned to her. "Why?"

"Why? Because." She gestured helplessly. "All this."

"It's an adventure, princess. Come, I see McNally's left bread and cheese for us, and water."

"I would kill for a cup of tea," she murmured, dropping to her knees on the blanket beside him.

"Aye, men have been killed for less," he said after a moment.

"I didn't mean—"

"I know what you meant, princess."

"It was just a saying," she said, lamely.

"You surprise me, princess." He broke off a hunk of bread and handed the loaf to her. "You face soldiers without turning a hair and get up onstage in front of hundreds of people, and yet you're concerned about my feelings."

The bread, though dry, was manna. "I'm afraid you'll hurt me."

"Blythe." He set down his food, and she could see that this time she'd truly shaken him. "You don't really believe that, do you?"

"No," she said. *Because you came back for me last night.* "Simon, why did you—oh!"

A sudden rustling, a stirring of air, was all the warning they had. A great dark shape hurtled past them, narrowly missing Blythe's head, and then was gone. It was too much. With a shriek, she threw herself into Simon's arms. "Wh—what is it?" she gasped, clinging to him. "Not a ghost, not—"

"A barn owl, sweeting." He sounded as shaken as she. "That is all. We must have disturbed him when we came in."

"A barn owl." She pulled back, managing a shaky laugh. "How silly. Everything that's happened, and I'm afraid of a barn owl."

"I think you've the right, princess." His gaze on her was peculiarly intent; his grip on her arms, though loose, was somehow possessive. She felt her muscles going slack, her mouth going dry, as she looked back at him, helplessly caught. He was so close, so warm, so solid. Dear Lord help her, but she kept remembering how his lips had felt on hers that night at the Tabard Inn, and his hand on her breast. And she loved him. That one little fact made her helpless. She did not protest, then, when his mouth came down on hers.

*   *   *

"They were here." Quentin stood at the gate to the churchyard. The pale light of morning illumined wildflowers growing in profusion along the stone wall, lilies and lavender, and the grass was an incomparable emerald. Quentin, however, was frowning down at the tracks that could be seen faintly in the dust near the gate, though they had nearly been obliterated by the passing of soldiers last night. "We traced them to the stream. It looks like they went across and then up the bank, and then?" He looked up at the sergeant. "Where did they go?"

"We searched here," Sergeant Thompson said stiffly. Why he must answer to this man, he did not know. "We looked into the church and behind every stone, and not a sign of them did we see."

"Except for Shea's ghost, Sergeant," someone said.

Quentin looked up. "Shea's ghost?"

Thompson shook his head. "One of my men's superstitious. Irish, you know, thought he saw something—"

"But I did," Shea protested. "Sir," he added belatedly, as Thompson glared at him.

"Back in line, soldier." Thompson's face was red as he turned away. Who Quentin was, he neither knew nor cared, except that he was quality of some kind. Sir Hubert, now, yawning and scratching behind Quentin, was another story. He was local, and a magistrate to boot. While Thompson didn't answer to him directly, being billeted in Rochester meant that he came under the squire's authority. And though he had heard of the escaped killer, everything had been quiet in the area until the arrival of the man with Sir Hubert. "We found nothing, sir," he said, addressing himself to Sir Hubert.

Sir Hubert yawned again. "Doubtless. You promised me the criminal, Heywood," he grumbled. "Where is he?"

"Sir." Shea stepped forward again, stiff, poker-faced. "I did see something, sir. In that crypt over there."

Sir Hubert peered through the morning mist. "Upon my soul! That is the family tomb!"

"What did you see, soldier?" Quentin's tone was silky, his face still; he was dressed as a gentleman, and yet Sergeant Thompson, watching helpless as events were taken out of his hands, had the impression of a taut, hungry animal, coiled to spring.

"Sir." Shea glanced toward the sergeant, who nodded resignedly. "A head, sir. Just floating-like. It had to be a ghost."

"In my tomb?" Sir Hubert stomped past him into the churchyard, trampling the grass still further. "We've had no dealings with ghosts in my family."

Quentin pursed his lips. "Perhaps it wasn't a ghost. Sir Hubert! Hold, there," he called. "Soldier, come with me to the crypt."

Shea swallowed, and Thompson grimaced in sympathy. He didn't know what was more threatening: the supposed ghost or Heywood, with his cool smile and hard eyes. "Yes, sir," Shea said woodenly. "This way, sir."

"Now, where," Quentin said conversationally, "did you see this—apparition—soldier?"

"Inside the crypt, sir." Shea's face was stolid as he pointed out the mausoleum where Sir Hubert awaited them, shifting from foot to foot. "The sergeant ordered me to check it."

"Was the door locked?"

"No, sir."

"It had to be," Sir Hubert blustered as they reached him. "Only time we open the place is for funerals."

"The door was open, sir," the sergeant put in.

"Well, I don't like it," Sir Hubert fumed. "Not one bit."

"Hold, there, sir." Quentin laid his hand on Sir Hubert's arm, preventing him from stepping into the enclosure around the crypt. "I see footprints."

"Of course there are footprints, man. These men defiled my family's resting place!" Sir Hubert spun around to the sergeant. "You'll answer for that."

"We were doing as we were bid, sir," the sergeant said stiffly. "By you."

"Someone was here." Quentin rose from his squatting position, a long green frond in his hand. "This looks distinctly like the grass from along the stream, and there is mud on the doorstep."

"A ghost wouldn't drag in mud or plants, sir," the sergeant said.

"No." Quentin studied the crypt. In the brightening sun it looked normal, quiet, almost serene. And to open the door would be bad luck, Thompson thought, dread shivering along his spine. "I do not fear ghosts," he said, and wrenched the door open.

"Upon my soul!" Sir Hubert protested. "You go too far, sir!"

"The crypt was unlocked." Quentin's voice was almost gentle, but Thompson wasn't fooled. His anger showed in the set of his shoulders, in the glitter of his eyes. "And this"—he stepped inside and bent down—"never came from any ghost."

"A handkerchief," Sir Hubert said dumbly, staring at the square of cloth. "Upon my soul, sir, but I don't understand."

"Do you not? It was no ghost the soldier saw. No ghost that started the riot last night." He frowned. "I lost an expensive wig in the riot, but . . . no matter. Woodley was here." Quentin's eyes glowed with dark light as he swung about, facing them all: Sir Hubert, the sergeant, the soldiers. "And we are going to find him."

Blythe had one clear moment of sanity, and then Simon's lips were on hers, blotting out all else. Emotions rioted through her in a chaos of sensations: the white heat of need; the dark rasp of his stubbled face against hers; the bright glory of her body coming alive, all at once. She was aware of his hand holding her head firmly against his, of his tongue ravishing her mouth; aware as well that the little sounds and whimpers she heard were coming from her, not him.

"Simon," she gasped when at last he released her mouth to brand her throat with his lips. "Simon."

He didn't answer, only slammed his mouth onto hers again, tongues meeting and clashing in an almost violent mating that made her blood sing. This wasn't like her, this passion, this need. She was quiet and prim and proper, not an actress, and certainly not a wanton. Oh, but she wanted this, wanted to sear his skin with her fingertips, wanted to burn with his touch, to glory in the fire of his loving. All her life had led to this moment, all the loneliness, all her vaunted independence. There was a woman inside her she'd never known, a woman with fierce desires and needs, and he was her other half. Rogue, actor, criminal— God help her, but he made her whole.

"Blythe." Simon wrenched his mouth away. "Hell, We can't."

She clung to him, pressing kisses on his neck. "Why not?"

"Why not?" He put her away from him, staring at her with his hair on end and his mouth slack, and a place on his neck just beginning to turn red. She'd done that, she realized with a mixture of astonishment and delight. "Because we can't."

She put her finger to the red mark on his neck; he flinched, and she let her touch trail lower, along his collarbone, down the open neck of his shirt. "Why not?" she repeated.

"Hell. I'm a convict, Blythe. You're a lady—"

"Oh, no, I'm not," she said, and looped her arm around his neck, bringing his face to hers. This was right. Maybe tomorrow she'd think differently, but she'd deal with that when it happened. "Simon, you have dragged me halfway across the country, through rivers and across fields and into theaters, for heaven's sake! Are you going to stop debauching me now?"

"Debauch . . ." He gaped down at her, and then threw his head back, laughing, making his throat muscles stand out like columns. "Only you would use that word." His eyes were brimming with amusement, and something more, something darker, hotter. "Debauch."

"You once asked me why I was named Blythe." She let her hand wander across his chest and felt his indrawn breath as her own. "I think I am better named than I know."

Simon caught her hand and brought it to his mouth. "I won't be able to stop."

"I'm not asking you to." Let tomorrow take care of itself. She was tired of being prudent, tired of being sensible and proper. Never before had she allowed herself to be swept away by feelings; never before had she had feelings like this.

Simon ran a hand through his hair. "I can't promise you anything."

"I don't expect you to."

"Bloody hell," he said, and sat up, turning away.

Well. And what was this about? She reached out to touch him. "Simon—"

"Don't." He shrugged off her hand. "Or I won't answer for the consequences."

"I'm not asking you to."

"And why not?" He rounded on her. "Do you know what you're asking? Do you?"

"Simon, I'm not stupid and I'm not naive—"

"You're as naive as a newborn babe! God." He pounded the wooden floor with his fist. "What kind of woman are you? I took you for a good woman, not a . . ."

"What?" she prompted when he didn't go on. "What am I?"

"Nothing," he muttered.

"I think I can guess." She sat up beside him, wrapping her arms about her knees, more puzzled than annoyed; chilled, without the heat of him surrounding her. If he so much as touched her now, she thought she might hit him. "All my life . . ." She picked at some straw, cleared her throat, and then went on. "All my life I've been what people expected me to be. I don't remember my mother, you know. But one of the worst things my foster mother could say to me was that I was just like my mother. But do you know something?" She looked up at him. "I was proud when she said that. I had to hide it, but I kept it inside me always, that I was like my real mother. She grabbed happiness when she found it. 'Twas why she named me Blythe." Idly she drew designs in the dust beside her. "But I learned to be what everyone else wanted me to be, and when the time came that I had to make my own way, there I was again, doing what someone else wanted. And then you came along."

Simon had turned to study her as she talked. "I disrupted your life."

"And expected me to be what you needed." She frowned. "Except that I like being this new person, Simon. I don't know who I am anymore, but I like it." And she loved him.

He hunched forward, arms on his knees. "I can't give you anything except disgrace. And maybe a child," he muttered.

Something leaped within her. "I've not asked for anything, Simon." Only his love.

"Lord, Blythe, don't you see that only makes it worse? I have no future. Even if I did . . ." He turned to her. "It wouldn't be with you, Blythe."

It hurt. It was no surprise and so should not have caused her pain, but it did. "Oh."

"I'm sorry." Quickly he stroked his fingers down her cheek. "I do want you."

She gazed back at him, intent now only on hiding what earlier she had so wanted to share with him. He didn't love her. Thank heavens he didn't know how she felt. "Do you?"

"More than you know. But not like this." He got to his feet, pacing restlessly away. "Not with my life in jeopardy and a cloud over my name." He straightened, mouth set. "And that is why I cannot run away."

She looked up from gathering the food that they had scattered across the blanket during their wild embrace. "Isn't that what you are doing?"

"No. Do you not realize where we are?"

"I've barely traveled away from my village before."

"Which is?"

"Hartley, in Kent."

He nodded. "Somewhat west of here."

"Where are we, then?"

"On the road to Canterbury."

She frowned. "Are you going on a pilgrimage?"

"Canterbury, Blythe," he repeated. "Where Miller was murdered."

Blythe looked up, mouth open in astonishment. "You aren't serious!"

He nodded. "Indeed I am."

"But if you're known anywhere, surely 'twill be there."

"I've plans," he said vaguely. "How else can I clear my name?"

"Clear your . . ." She clamped her mouth shut. "You are saying you are innocent."

"Yes. At least, not guilty."

"I don't understand."

"I've thought a great deal about this." He laughed, mirthlessly. "For a long time I had nothing to do but think. And I reached the same conclusions every time." He pounded a fist on his knee and rose. "But why? That is what bothers me. Why would someone want him dead? And why"—his voice was baffled—"does someone want me to pay for his death?"

Blythe sat straighter, cautious. They had never before discussed his crime. "Who was he? Miller?"

Simon's face tightened. "A rather unpleasant man."

Her heart sank. She had hoped to hear that the murdered man was a stranger to him. "So you did know him."

"Oh, yes. Better than I would have liked."

"Oh." She looked down. "I'd heard—I understood it was his wife you knew."

"Bloody hell, then you've heard that story?"

"Is it true?"

"No." He shifted his shoulders in apparent irritation. "I don't know how that tale started."

"I can't imagine," she said icily.

He slanted her a look. "Don't sound so disapproving, princess. I never claimed to be a monk."

Only with me, she thought, wrapping her arms

around her bent knees. "Didn't he have some reason to be angry with you?"

"What? No. The rumor I'd seduced his wife didn't begin until after I was arrested. No, he had no quarrel with me." He stood for a moment, his back to her, hands jammed into his pockets. "He had every reason to want me alive and well, being a moneylender."

Blythe's head jerked up. "I'd not heard that!"

"No? But 'tis true."

"I thought he was a merchant."

"That, too. He traded with foreign countries. The Orient, in particular. But his main trade was lending money."

"There was a money bag found near him," she said, pursing her lips as she tried to recall the details.

"Aye. Filled with gold sovereigns."

She looked up. "Were you holding it?"

"No. 'Twas the knife I was caught with. The money was in my room."

She drew in a breath. "Then you admit it?"

He gazed at her for a moment, so steadily that she had to look away. "I admit to being foolish enough to pick up the knife, nothing more." He dropped to his knees beside her. "Blythe, he was dead when I found him."

Blythe looked down at her hands, wanting, needing to believe him. "Then who killed him?"

"I don't know." He rose again, pacing the earthen floor. "I'd think someone was trying to rob him, except the gold was still there. Blythe." He turned to her. "This may sound mad, but I think whoever did it wanted to make sure I was blamed."

She frowned. This was beyond protesting his innocence. This was fantasy. "Whatever for?"

"I don't know." He sat next to her, one knee cocked, the other straight. "I've asked myself that many a time."

"There's a problem," she pointed out. "How could this person have known you would be there at the proper time?"

"I'd an appointment with him," he said after a moment.

She stared at him. "Why?"

"He'd lent me money. No, never mind why. He was charging such high interest, I'd never be able to pay it back, and I wanted him to lower the rate."

Blythe looked down at her hands. "You had reason to want him dead," she said softly.

"Aye," he said, to her surprise. "So I did. But I didn't kill him. I swear that to you, Blythe." He looked at her. "Do you believe I'm innocent?"

Blythe opened her mouth, closed it again, and looked away. "I'd like to."

"But you don't," he said flatly.

"I don't know what to believe!" She spread her hands in exasperation. "You were found standing over a dead body with a knife in your hands."

"Someone else's knife."

"I know you were convicted. I know you abducted me."

"Which you will never let me forget."

"It isn't an easy thing to let go." She paused. "But you came back for me."

"When?"

"Last night, at the theater. You didn't have to."

"Yes, I did."

She nodded. In some way that she didn't quite understand, she had known he would come for her. "I want to believe in your innocence."

"But you don't."

"No. Simon, I'm sorry—"

He shied away from her touch. "Don't."

"I wish there was something I could say."

"There's nothing," he said, and rose. " 'Tis early yet. We should sleep before we head out again."

Blythe stayed sitting. "I'm not sure I'm going with you, Simon."

He rounded on her. "So what will you do? Stay here and let them take you?"

She pushed her hair away from her face. "Maybe." Just now that seemed preferable to the pain of being with him. She loved him, loved him, but he didn't feel the same. She couldn't bear it.

"Don't be stupid." He bit off the words. "Do you think I'll let you stay to tell them where I've gone?"

She lifted her chin. "Would you force me to go with you?"

"Why not? I've done so before. As you've pointed out."

"So you have." She sighed. She had little choice: facing arrest, with its notoriety and disgrace, or being with him. Both hurt. Only one drew her, a moth to the flame. "Very well. But if I have a chance to go home, then I will."

Simon nodded. "Best we get some sleep," he said, and rolled himself into a blanket, facing away from her.

Well. One would think that he was the injured party rather than she, Blythe thought, looking at his stiff, unresponsive back. Her life had been permanently altered because of him, and her future was clouded. None of that would matter very much, though, if only he loved her. If he loved her, she felt she could face anything. Or could have, were he an innocent man. And that she still very much doubted, no matter how much she might wish to believe otherwise.

Heaving a rather theatrical sigh, she took up the other blanket, spread it a distance away from Simon, and wrapped herself up in it. She was growing used to living under strange conditions, but she doubted she'd sleep.

Some time later, a sound startled her into awareness, making her sit bolt upright. Heavens, she'd slept after all. A quick glance showed her that Simon was still asleep. Either he hadn't heard the sound or her adventures had caught up with her, making her fear pursuit even in her dreams. Clearly all was well, and they were safe—

The sound came again, and this time she recognized it: a horse whickering outside, followed by footsteps. Blythe stumbled to her knees. Dear heavens. They'd been found.

The blanket hampered her as she tried to crawl across the floor to warn Simon. She was just about to shake his shoulder when the barn door creaked open, letting in a shaft of sunlight. Simon shot to his feet, fists bunched. "Simon," she gasped, rising at last.

He grabbed her arm, dragging her behind him as the door opened more fully. From her hiding place behind his shoulder, she watched as the broad figure of a man, silhouetted in light, stepped inside. "Well," a voice said. "It appears I've found the fugitive."

Chapter 16

"Oh, no," Blythe moaned, digging her fingers into Simon's shoulders. All they'd gone through, and it wasn't enough. They were caught. Did it matter now whether or not she believed Simon to be innocent? She was going to prison, while he . . . She swallowed against a lump in her throat. He would be hanged.

"Have you nothing to say for yourself?" the voice said.

"Yes," Simon said, and Blythe felt him inexplicably relaxing. "What took you so long?"

"We had the devil of a time getting out of Rochester." The figure in the doorway stepped forward, tugging absently at one ear. "Seems there's a dangerous killer escaped."

"Simon," Blythe whispered.

Without turning, he reached behind him, and his hand settled on her breast. Startled, Blythe jumped back, and this time he did look at her. Odd, but she could swear that there was embarrassment in his eyes. "Blythe." His hand slipped down, settled on her arm. She could breathe again, yet the heat and power of that one touch seemed to seep into her very being. "He is a friend."

"We'd heard you'd picked up a traveling companion," the man said, and let out a low whistle as Blythe stepped out at last from behind Simon. "And a fair sight she is. May I introduce myself, madam?" He swept into a deep bow. "I am Ian Montaigne, and may I tell you, you have been keeping low company."

"Indeed?" Blythe stayed still as the man straightened. He was young, she could see now, and attractive in a smooth, civilized way, with his unpowdered hair carefully clubbed back, and his features regular. She much preferred Simon's more rugged good looks. "And who are you, sir?"

"A member of the Woodley troupe, Blythe," Simon said, stepping forward to clap Ian on the shoulder. You're a sight to gladden my heart. What happened to Rochester?"

Ian grimaced. "Trouble. The local magistrate—rather a foolish fellow, do you know him? No? He was roaring that he would not be so insulted, upon his soul, and demanding that every man-jack of us be put into gaol until we told him where you were."

The impersonation of an angry, bullheaded country gentleman was so apt that Blythe found herself smiling. "Was that Quentin Heywood?"

"No. Sir Hubert somebody-or-other, though Heywood was there. He was the one who said we should be let go." His face was grim. "You know of him?"

"He has been dogging our footsteps," Simon said grimly. "He is determined to catch us."

"You're lucky he let you go," Blythe put in.

"Unless he expected you to lead him to us."

"Damnation! I'd not thought of that." Ian snapped his fingers. "I'll be off, then. You know where we're to meet?"

"Yes."

"Good. I'd see you there, but in light of what you just said, mayhap I should lay a false trail." He stepped forward, embraced Simon quickly, and turned. "Good luck, my friend."

"And to you, too. We have to get out of here," Simon said. From outside they could hear Ian talking to his horse and then riding away. "And quickly."

"Oh, why not?" Blythe stooped, gathering up the blanket. "We may need this," she said at his inquiring look.

"Nay. Leave it and come." He caught her hand and led her to the door. There they paused, peering cautiously out, and seeing nothing more alarming than leafy trees swaying in the breeze. "I think we might be all right yet. Soldiers usually make enough noise for us to hear. The worst will be getting across to the trees."

"I'll go," she said, suddenly terrified, but not for herself.

"Don't be silly." He dropped a quick, hard kiss onto her forehead and then broke out into the open, running across what had once been a busy barnyard in a zigzag pattern. No one appeared in either the trees or the lane; no strange noises rose to disturb the peaceful morning. Simon signaled to her from the trees. She would have to trust him that it was safe.

A moment later she was across the clearing and dropping to the ground beneath the trees where Simon waited. He nodded at her and turned, starting off through the woods on a track roughly parallel to the road. "Wait," Blythe gasped, trying to catch up. Fear and her dash to safety had made her breathless. "Are you going to tell me what's about?"

"There's no time, princess." He didn't look back at her, but merely continued on his way, stopping occasionally to hold back branches that otherwise would have caught her in the face. "If we're to meet the others and be on our way, we must hurry."

Blythe barely avoided tripping over a root in the ground. Since it was spring, there was little undergrowth, but the footing was treacherous. "What others? And when did you plan this?"

"McNally planned it," he said over his shoulder, and then stopped, appearing at last to take pity on her. His face a mask of patience, he waited for her to catch up. "I need—we need—a place to hide. McNally took care of everything."

"And that man back in the barn?"

Simon stopped again, so abruptly that she walked into him, banging her nose on his shoulder. "My apologies, princess." He smiled faintly. "I keep forgetting that you're in this as much as I am."

Blythe rubbed her nose. "Oh, by all means. Since I've done nothing wrong."

"Of course not." His voice was cool again, making

her feel as if she were indeed the one in the wrong. He had been convicted, she told herself. Surely that meant he was guilty. "My apologies, again. Ian is a member of the Woodley troupe of strolling players, my uncle's troupe. We're to meet with them upon the road."

"But surely that's dangerous! Won't people suspect where you're hiding?"

"'Tis a risk, that's true. However, you should know that my uncle publicly disowned me when I was convicted. An act, princess," he said, his tone softening at the dismay she knew must show on her face. "'Twas all an act."

"I don't understand—oh. So no one would think he'd have anything to do with you."

"Precisely." He turned and began walking again, still briskly, but somehow less remote. "I'm not sure what the plans are, but I know that there are plans."

"They won't expect me."

"They will now, with Ian going back to tell them. Don't worry, princess. They'll find a way to hide you." He stopped abruptly. Past his shoulder, Blythe could see that they'd reached the road. "Looks like we'll have to wait a bit."

Blythe sank gratefully upon a fallen log. "So they'll shelter you until you have a chance to leave the country."

He shot her a look. "Is that what you think I plan?"

"It seems the wisest course."

"Mayhap, but it's not mine. I told you at the barn, princess. I intend to clear my name." He crouched before her, hand held out. "Will you help me?"

"How can I?" she protested. "When I'm not even sure if . . ."

"If I'm innocent." He got to his feet, his mouth a grim slash. "So be it."

"Simon, I'm sorry." She followed him, placing a hand on his sleeve; he shrugged it off. "But I'd be of no help to you. I wouldn't know how to begin, and if people realize who I am, I'll likely be arrested—"

"So be it," he said again, and held up his hand.

"Ah. I hear horses—ah, yes." His face lightened just a bit as a ramshackle cart driven by an old man rounded a bend in the road. "There's Old Gaffer. We've someplace to stay, for now."

"Simon," she said urgently. "I want to believe you. I do. 'Tis just—I can't."

He nodded. "You needn't explain, princess. I understand well enough." And with that he stepped out of the trees and hailed the cart. Blythe followed more cautiously. She did want to believe him. Everything would be so much easier if she did. Why, she wondered, at last approaching the cart, had no one ever told her that love could feel so perfectly wretched?

" 'Tis good to have you back," Harry said yet again, raising his glass of port in a toast.

Simon, seated across the table from him, raised his glass as well. For once the Woodley troupe appeared to be doing well. Here in Maidstone, where they would play for a week, the manager and principal players had taken lodgings over a bakeshop. It was in the room shared by Harry Woodley, his wife Bess, and their daughter Henrietta, that Simon sat now, as much at ease as he had been since finding Miller's body. For the time being, he was safe. " 'Tis good to be here," he admitted. "For however long it lasts."

Bess refilled his glass. "Oh, tush, we won't think about that now."

"But we have to." Henrietta, commonly known as Young Harry, sat cross-legged on the bed. At first glance a stranger could be forgiven for taking her for a lad. Tall as she was, and thin, she was well suited to the breeches parts she played so well. Even her hair, close-cropped curls, added to the effect. "I believe our disguises will deflect suspicion for a time, but as we are near Canterbury, we will be watched more closely."

Simon grinned at her, this cousin he'd always looked on as a younger sister. "Still a bookworm, brat? You sound like a schoolmaster, the way you speak."

"I intend to improve myself. Something you wouldn't understand."

"I'm not in any need of improvement. Though now that you mention it"—he cast his gaze over her—"I can see that you are."

Henrietta leaned forward. "I'd forgotten how perfectly despicable you are."

"Don't worry. Blythe reminds me of that whenever she can."

"Miss Marden? I'm not surprised." Henrietta settled back onto the bed, her brief spate of temper fading. "How lucky for you to meet her."

"More than you know."

"But what are you going to do about her, Simon?" Bess looked up from the sock she was knitting. "She is as much looked-for as you."

"I know."

"She can't go back to London," Bess went on, the needles clacking together. "And gracious, life in the theater isn't for her."

"You'd be surprised." He turned to Henrietta, serious now. "You're sure she is safe?"

"No one will suspect her, Simon," Henrietta said serenely. "She's safe enough."

"Our Young Harry's worked out a good plan," Harry put in, setting down his glass. "Smart thinking, to get Old Gaffer and Dolly to leave for a time. Anyone watching us will see we still have the same number of people." Harry grimaced. "Had to promise Dolly a benefit, but I don't know what else we could do. We owe Miss Marden a powerful amount."

Simon took a long swallow of wine. "I'm well aware of that," he said grimly. "So, Young Harry, what is your plan exactly?"

Henrietta looked up. "To keep you both in disguise until you may cross the Channel to the continent."

Simon frowned. "That is it?"

"What else would you have us do? You've made yourself notorious, Simon, especially in this area."

"And if I don't want to leave England?"

Three faces turned to him in dismay and shock.

"But what else can you do?" Harry asked. "If you stay here they'll be sure to catch you. And us, too," he added gloomily.

"Unless I clear my name," Simon said, and was met by silence. Setting the glass down, he scanned the faces that now were downcast or turned away from him. They were the dearest people in the world to him, the only family he had ever known, and yet even they did not fully believe in his innocence. "I didn't do it," he said flatly, and rose.

"Oh, Simon, no one says you did," Bess protested.

"No?"

"No." Harry had risen, too, a stocky, burly figure, and placed his hand on Simon's shoulder. "But it'll be hard to disprove."

"Even I can't think how, Simon," Henrietta chimed in. "And I have tried."

Simon sat down again. "There's a way."

"If so, I can't see it."

"It's right before your nose, brat," he said, reaching out to tweak that appendage. She pulled back, scowling. "We find out who did kill Miller."

His relatives exchanged looks. " 'Twill be dangerous," Harry said finally. "If you're recognized—"

"I'll trust Young Harry not to let that happen."

Henrietta frowned. "You aren't so easy to disguise, Simon, but I'll do what I can." She leaned forward. "How can we help?"

Simon sat back, light-headed with relief. No doubts about his innocence here; only a profound distrust of England's justice system. Why couldn't more people trust him so? Why couldn't Blythe? "We'll need to learn if he had any enemies," he began, when there was a sudden pounding at the door.

The occupants of the room froze. Bloody hell, Simon thought. Had he been discovered already? Gesturing wildly to the others to keep still, he dashed across to the small casement window and looked out with dismay. Thirty feet to the ground, and no way to climb down. *Hell.*

Henrietta was holding up the bed skirts and pointing beneath the bed when the pounding came again. "Harry? Bess? Are you there?"

" 'Tis Tom," Harry said, crossing to the door, and Simon sagged in relief. Not capture, then, but another member of the troupe. Not yet. "Yes, Tom, what is it?"

"Something's happened." Tom tumbled into the room as Harry opened the door. "I'm sorry to disturb you so late, but I thought you should know."

"Soldiers?" Simon said, tensing.

"No, not that I've seen. It's that Marden woman."

Simon had relaxed, but now he stiffened again. "What about her?"

"She is sharing a room with Susan. But Susan went to bed a little while ago, and that's when we realized."

Simon sprang forward. "Is she hurt?"

"That's just it. We don't know." Tom spread his hands, turning to Harry. "We looked everywhere, but we just can't find her. It looks like she's gone."

"The morning post, my lady." The footman bowed as he presented the silver salver to Honoria. Without sparing him a glance she reached for the missives and carelessly tossed them onto the polished mahogany surface of the breakfast room table. That quick glance had been enough to show her that one of the letters was from Quentin, an ominous sign indeed. Had he good news for her he would most certainly be here to share it. Instead, his absence made her suspicious.

Thoughtfully, Honoria took a sip of tea. She liked this time of morning, free of visitors and other interruptions, when she could plan and plot and scheme as to how to spend her day. She liked having Stanton House to herself, though it wouldn't be for long. Soon she was to return to Moulton Hall, her husband's country estate, by his order. And he was staying behind all because of his silly preoccupation with politics and Parliament. If she had run up some gambling debts, what was that to a man as rich as Stanton? Debts of honor must be paid, surely even he knew that. And it wasn't even as if she had been playing very deep. She'd lost only a trifle, several hundred pounds here, perhaps a thousand there. Not enough for her to be banished from London. Unless Quentin's letter held better news than she expected, however, she might very well have to return there, no matter what Stanton would think.

Tossing her napkin onto the table, she rose, snatching up the letters with apparent disregard. Behind her and before her footmen bowed; she swept past them in her open gown of lavender silk, the scent of lilacs hanging heavy about her. They bowed again as she chose a chair at random in the drawing room, and then they closed the door, leaving her alone at last.

Only then did Honoria pick up Quentin's letter, and then only after casting a quick glance about the room, to be certain she was completely unobserved. Her hands were steady as she broke the seal and unfolded the letter, her face inscrutable as she read it. Only when she set it back down did a little crease appear between her brows. Had anybody been in the room, the signs would have been clear. The viscountess was angry.

This was what happened when one trusted someone else to deal with one's problems. This came from dealing with inferior tools. The pity was, Quentin had seemed acceptable, until recently. He was adequate in bed, quite good at looking out for himself, and almost as devious-minded as she herself was. That was the pleasure of it, of course, the satisfaction of devising ways around other peoples' humdrum lives, to accomplish whatever one desired. Look how masterfully Quentin had arranged for the actor to be charged with murder. When it came to more direct action, however, as was called for now, Quentin was lamentably laggard.

The actor had yet to be caught. Honoria frowned, and then relaxed her face, carefully smoothing her forehead with her fingertips. Few wrinkles dared mar her complexion, and those that did she could disguise with a coating of powder and an application of rouge.

It was vital that she remain looking young, attractive. Men were allowed to age gracefully, to grow bald and fat. A woman, however, lost her power when she lost her looks. It was not going to happen to her. There wouldn't be even the threat of it just now were it not for the actor.

Another frown, quickly eased. Galling as it was that he still ran free, what made matters worse was Quentin's inability to catch him. With each day the actor remained loose, the danger to Honoria increased. Oh, Quentin's danger was the greater, no question about that; but if he were found out he would implicate her. There was no question about that, either. And though she knew that Quentin was doing what he could, it wasn't enough. More action was needed.

Crossing the room, she stood before the huge pier glass, studying her reflection, assessing the flesh beneath her jawline. Was there just the hint of softening there? No, it was just a trick of the light. She was still, by any measure, a beautiful woman. Perhaps it was time for her to use that beauty. Past time.

Nodding decisively, she swept from the room, again ignoring the footmen. In her chamber she snapped her fingers at Clothilde, her maid, who came forward with the lavender satin overskirt that would go so well with the pale lilac petticoat she'd chosen for today. She watched her reflection in the mirror dispassionately as Clothilde clothed her. There was more than one way to catch a thief, or a killer. She would find that way. Soon, before the accursed Simon Woodley could do any further damage. She would do anything she had to, to protect the life she'd fought so hard for. Anything.

Blythe slipped from tree to tree along the side of the road, the lessons of travel learned in the past weeks coming in handy. It was dark, but a crescent moon gave fitful life to the trees that surrounded her, shadow and shade and the occasional shine of light on silvery bark. There was danger in the night, and yet she felt far safer here than she ever had in London, among the trees and plants that had formed part of her childhood. Hartley, her village, was not so far distant, she'd realized when the Woodley troupe had reached Maidstone, the journey perhaps of a day. No matter what awaited her there, it would surely be better than life with a troupe of strolling players, or with a man who could offer her no future. Wouldn't it?

Blythe looked back, but the road was an empty ribbon stretching away into darkness. He wouldn't come after her. She didn't know why she thought he would. Since they'd met she'd been a necessary encumbrance to him, to be discarded when she was no longer convenient. Not that he'd said so, though he'd made it clear to her that morning in the barn. She would have given herself to him, and he would have none of her.

Blythe's cheeks burned. Bad enough that she'd been so wanton, so lacking in proper behavior; worse that he hadn't been. It was her own fault, of course, for being so impulsive, a trait her foster mother had warned against time and again. Her fault, for forgetting that he was an actor, able to simulate emotions when it suited him. Reality was not in his smiling face, nor in his passionate kisses. Reality was that he was a cool, desperate criminal on the run from the authorities, and she had been useful to him. For a time.

And so she had decided to go home, no matter what awaited her there. There was no place for her in Simon's life. Sooner or later he would either be retaken by the authorities or would flee the country. The thought of never seeing him again hurt. She loved Simon, fool that she was. She'd liked his family, what little she'd seen of them, and she had even enjoyed her time in the theater. It wasn't real, though, any of it. Blythe knew about pain. She knew from helping her father doctor people that a clean break, though painful, healed quickly. One day Simon would no longer be in her life. It was far better that she make the break now. But oh, if that was so, why did it hurt so badly?

Not so far behind her she heard hoofbeats, forcing her deeper into the woods. Since Simon no longer traveled by her side she was probably safe from arrest, but who knew what other dangers were abroad? A woman alone had always to be careful. That was a lesson she'd learned all too well.

The rider came closer. Blythe's heartbeat speeded up in time with the hoofbeats, faster and faster, louder and louder. Rationally she knew that, standing in shadow as she was, she wasn't likely to be discovered. Still, she pressed herself against a tree trunk, her breath coming in quick, shallow gasps, her fingers clutching the rough bark. She was alone. Should she be seen, and should that person have evil intentions, she would have no one to help her. Alone, as she had been all her life. And now, when it was too late, she wished she had never left the security, dubious though it was, of the Woodley troupe. She wished she'd never left Simon.

The horse was very near now. Blythe bit her lips, barely breathing; the rider seemed to have slowed, or was that her imagination? But no, the horse was at a walk, coming nearer, nearer. She hugged the tree, praying that she wouldn't be detected, and in that instant the rider stepped into a patch of moonlight that illuminated the road. It was Simon.

She gasped, startled, dismayed, overjoyed. The horse gave a quick nicker, tossing its head, and Simon pulled on the reins. "What is it, boy, eh?" he said softly, looking into the trees. Looking right at her. "What do you hear?"

"Me," Blythe said, stepping away from the tree, and the horse nickered again. "How did you know I was here?"

"What the devil? Blythe?" Simon tossed the reins over the horse's head and jumped down to the ground. "What are you doing hiding in the trees?"

"I didn't know who was on the road." She stepped out at last from the trees' shadow, leaving their protection behind and not regretting it. "Though I'm not sure I'm any safer with you."

He was shaking his head. "If you'd not spoken, I wouldn't have seen you."

"Oh." She looked away. She could have avoided this meeting had she only stayed still. She should be annoyed with herself. Instead, her heart felt lighter than it had for hours. "Where do you go?"

He took her hand. "I was looking for you, princess. Come, I'm as leery of discovery as you—"

"Looking for me?" Blythe stopped. "Why?"

He shook his head. "Not here," he said, and pulled her back under the trees, leading the horse behind him. "We need a place to talk in private."

"Simon, I'll not tell anyone about you."

"I know that. Here. Sit down." His hand, now on her shoulder, pushed her down onto a fallen log she hadn't noticed before. "Let me just tie up old Hazel here."

"I didn't even know you could ride," she said blankly.

"There's much you don't know about me, princess." He settled beside her, and she shifted away. They were alone. He could do what he would with her, and no one would know. Odd that she wasn't scared. "Why did you go?"

"Why do you think?" She turned toward him. "What life would I have, Simon, constantly running? I'm tired of it. I want a home, my own home. Surely you can understand that."

He shrugged. "I suppose, though 'tis not something I've ever missed. Home has always been with my family." For a moment he stared ahead, brow creased in a frown. "Why didn't you tell me you wished to go?"

"You would have stopped me."

"No, princess. I wouldn't have."

Blythe's breath caught. Foolish of her to feel hurt at his words, when she'd known all along that someday he would let her go. Wasn't that why she had left? "Oh."

"Though I'd have made sure you weren't alone. Hell, Blythe, 'tis not safe for you to travel like this. Who knows who you might meet?"

"Such as escaped murderers?"

"Yes." His tone was grim. "Trust me, princess,

there are many more desperate characters in the world than I.''

"Really."

"Have I hurt you at all?"

"For heaven's sake, Simon, you abducted me—"

"But have I hurt you?"

She bit her lip. Oh, yes, he'd hurt her, if not in the way he meant. "No."

"You didn't even say good-bye."

"I didn't think you'd notice I was gone."

"Not notice! Bloody hell. I owe you my life."

"And I shall keep my word."

"That's not what I'm concerned about." He grasped her shoulders. "Where are you going? Have you any idea?"

"I told you, Simon." His grip was hard, punishing, and yet in a way she welcomed it. Before this moment she'd thought he'd never touch her again. "I'm going home."

"Home?"

"Yes. My village is not above a day from here."

Slowly his fingers relaxed, though he didn't pull away. "I didn't realize that."

"I have to go somewhere," she went on, explaining as much to herself as to him. "Mrs. Wicket won't have me back, that much is certain, nor will she give me a reference. I won't be able to find another position in London."

"My family would have taken you in."

"No." She shook her head. "I don't belong there, either. I wasn't trained to be an actress. Surely you realize that. 'Tis not the life I was raised for."

His hands at last dropped away. "What do you want in life, Blythe?"

"What I want and what I'm likely to get are two very different things," she said lightly. "In London at least I was earning my way. Now I'll need to go back with my family, for a time, at least. I'm quite on the shelf, you know. It's not likely I'll marry."

"Then the men in your village are fools."

" 'Tis sweet of you to say so."

"I'm not sweet," he growled.

"I will be the village spinster, I imagine. A maiden aunt to my nieces and nephews. I shall perform good works and arrange flowers upon the church altar. I may even assist my father in his surgery." She shifted on the log, hugging herself. "And people will wonder all my life just what happened when I met up with an escaped criminal."

Simon's lips pursed. "It sounds deadly dull, Blythe."

" 'Tis what I've expected."

"That may be, but things can change." He turned to her again. "You've changed, Blythe. Don't you realize that?"

"Oh, yes," she murmured. "But with circumstances as they are, I really have little choice."

"Hell." Simon slung his arm about her shoulder. "I'm sorry, Blythe. If I hadn't grabbed you on the street—"

" 'Tis past. And to be honest with you, I'm not sorry to leave London behind."

"But, hell, Blythe, for you to wither away a spinster . . ."

"With a reputation."

"Hang your reputation. It sounds damned lonely."

She nodded. Of course it would be lonely. Any life without him would be. "I shall just have to manage."

"I cannot change your mind?"

Only if he said he loved her. "No."

"Hell," he said again, resting his forehead against hers. "I'm going to miss you, Blythe."

"You'll forget me soon enough," she said lightly. "When you meet a pretty woman."

"No." He pulled back, and in the dim light his eyes were dark, liquid. "I don't think I'll ever forget you, Blythe."

Her gaze locked with his. For the life of her, she could not look away. "Nor I, you." She traced his lips with her fingertip. "Shall we kiss good-bye and part as friends?"

He regarded her for a moment. "A kiss is a fine idea."

Merciful heavens, did that mean he was going to do it? She stiffened, but then his arms urged her closer, his mouth lowered just a fraction. Just enough for her to realize how much she wanted him to kiss her. Oh, she wanted it. Never in her life would she feel this way again. Why not, just this once, take what life offered her? "A wonderful idea," she said, and, surging up against him, placed her mouth full on his.

Chapter 17

Simon's arms tightened in reflex as Blythe's body came up full against his. Sweet Jesus, but he'd not dreamed this would happen when he'd set out to find her. Truly, his intent had been to ensure her safety, and yet, now that she was here, he wanted never to let her go. She was soft and warm in his arms, her curves lush and familiar to his hands. How many nights had he thought of this? How many nights had he ached for her, longed for her? Though he'd known her but a few short weeks, it felt as if the yearning had been inside him forever. She felt so real, so right, a part of himself he'd not known was missing. How he would live without her, he did not know.

Her clever lips were at his, warm, wet, suckling, kissing him as he'd taught her to do. It was heaven, it was hell. With almost any other woman he'd enjoy the heaven, and damn the consequences. Blythe, however, was indisputably and completely herself, and that made him pull back, difficult though it was. "Princess," he rasped, his forehead resting against hers. He felt he'd run a race to her, so breathless was he. "Will you come back with me?"

She started against him. In the moonlight all he could see of her eyes were that they were dark and huge. "Why?"

He couldn't help it; he chuckled. Trust his Blythe to ask such a question. He moved his hips against her, felt her jerk back again, gasping. "Sweeting, do you really need to ask?"

"Actually"—her voice was as rough as his—"yes."

"I want you with me. I know 'tis not much," he

rushed on, before she could answer. "I cannot offer you a life. Even if my name was cleared I'd still be a strolling player, and I know that's not what you want. But Blythe"—he stared at her intently—"I want you."

Unexpectedly, she buried her head against his shoulder. "Oh, it's so hard," she murmured.

Oh, yes, and it was all for her, because of her. "I aim to oblige, sweeting."

"What?" She looked up at him blankly. "You enjoy making my life hard?"

"Your life—oh." Simon didn't think he'd blushed in his life, but he could feel hot color flooding his face right now. "No, of course not. Why is it hard?"

She shook her head, easing away from him to sit by his side. He would not let her go, however, keeping his arm about her shoulder. "Everything was simple. I knew who I was, where I belonged, what my life was to be. And then—"

"I came along."

"No. I went to London."

He frowned down at her. "I thought 'twas what you wanted."

"So did I." She worried her lips with her top teeth, and the urge to kiss her again slashed through him. "But now . . . Simon, these last weeks, they've been terrible, and yet in some ways I've never felt more alive." She shook her head. "It makes no sense."

"Why not?"

"Because I'm not like that. I'm not an actress, or someone who goes off on adventures, or—"

"But you are, sweeting," he said gently. "You are, and have been. Mayhap you never really were meant to be a doctor's daughter or some old woman's paid companion."

Her mouth opened and then closed again. "But that is what I was. Am."

"No." His finger trailed along her cheek. "You are so much more. Will you come back with me, sweeting?"

"I do believe this is the first time you've ever actually asked me."

"Then I've been a fool," he said, and took her

mouth again. She stiffened briefly, and then she was yielding, clinging. Dear lord, he shouldn't do this, not when the results could be so serious. She was not a woman of easy virtue, accustomed to casual encounters, but a lady, in spite of his earlier teasing. His lady, and that made all the difference. His, and if he made her his in every way possible, she wouldn't leave him. She couldn't. It made the risk almost worthwhile. "Come with me," he muttered against her throat.

Her head arched back. "I shouldn't—"

"Come with me, Blythe. Of your own choice this time."

Of her own choice? When he was holding her and kissing her so that she could hardly think? All Blythe knew was his embrace; all she wanted was for it to go on forever. It couldn't, of course, and yet somehow that didn't seem to matter the way it had earlier. What was important was now. "Yes," she said, and gave herself up to the moment.

He made a sound deep in her throat, an inarticulate noise, and suddenly he was kissing her in a way she'd never experienced before, fiercely, passionately, with a possessiveness that took her breath away. *His.* She let him bear her back, threading her fingers into his hair, meeting the thrust of his tongue with her own. *His.* His hand at her bodice, struggling with the laces; her own fingers, fumbling to help him. *His.* Cool air on her flesh, and then something warm, moist, his tongue against her breast, his lips at her nipple, hardening from the caress, making her whimper. His, only his.

Simon made that inarticulate noise again and sat up, leaving her bereft, forlorn. But it was only for a moment, only so that he could sweep off his cloak and lay it down, lay her down upon it. He settled atop her, one knee between her thighs, his arms bracketing her face, his mouth devouring, demanding. He was warm, so warm, and hard; her hands swept over his back, urgent, delighted. *Hers.* The hard sinews and muscles of his back, bunched now with strain. *Hers.* Impatiently pulling at the laces of his shirt, and helping him pull it up over his head. *Hers.* The soft, golden hair curling on his chest; his brown nipples, exciting and enticing to her hands, her lips. Hers, hers, hers. Mercy, she'd never imagined such feelings existed, never known that she was capable of such freedom, such need. She was changed, not the dutiful daughter she had tried so hard to be, not the lady, not the companion. Neither was she the woman Simon thought, but someone else, someone more. Someone she didn't know, but whose very existence tantalized her. She was herself, elemental and real and his, every bit as much as he was hers.

Simon abruptly reared up on his hands. In the dim light he looked like a bronzed statue, a pagan god come to life. And oh, she worshiped him, her hands moving over his chest and stomach, making his breath draw in sharply. "Blythe . . ."

"Come to me," she whispered, and twined her arms around his neck, bringing him back down to her. What was it she'd seen in his face? A fleeting emotion, somehow out of tune with the moment. Whatever it had been, it was gone now. He leaned on his elbow over her, smoothing back her hair with a hand that, oddly enough, trembled. "Blythe," he said again, quietly determined, and his lips met hers again. Sweet, so sweet, moist and soft and yet possessive; his hands on her, firm, tender, the earlier frenzy replaced by sure confidence. She rose up to meet him, pulling at his shoulders, his back, his hips, and he came down to her, his knee riding higher. She gasped, flooded with warmth low in her belly, helplessly arching against his hard thigh. And just when she thought she couldn't bear it anymore, that she would die if he didn't touch her, his fingers moved against her thigh in exploration, in possession. She tensed against the sensation of his touch, feather-light, on her skin, stroking surely upwards, readied herself, but she still wasn't prepared for the jolt of pure pleasure that streaked through her. She cried out, jerking against his chest, and his fingers moved again, firmly, rhythmically. She moved with them, helpless to stop, whimpering, needing, wanting. His. Her hands moved frantically on his hips, his buttocks. "Simon—"

He groaned, low, guttural, and caught her hand in a tight grasp, bringing it around to the front of his breeches. Oh, Lord, he was hard and huge, and she couldn't stop her fingers from exploring his contours. He made that strange sound again, and fumbled against her hand, and suddenly he was in her grasp, the entire hot, hard length of him. From instinct came the knowledge of what to do, of how to surround him with fingers and palm and caress him with the same rhythm as his fingers against her. The same rhythm that pulsed inside her, urging her to him, making her clutch at his shoulders with her other hand. Inside her, she wanted him inside her, completely and totally hers, but he was stronger, immovable, relentless. They moved in unison now, her hand, his fingers, quicker, harder, separate yet together, and when at last the pleasure crested inside her in a great cataclysm that threatened to tear her apart, she felt his seed, warm against her hand, and knew, in her pleasure, desolating emptiness. She was his, oh, yes, there could be no question. But he was not hers.

There was quiet under the trees, save for the horse's occasional nicker or stamp, and their own breathing, growing slower, more regular. Simon was beside her, and yet not with her, on his back with his arm flung up over his forehead. She sat up, tugging up her chemise, lacing her bodice, smoothing her disordered skirts. And when she could bear the silence no longer, she turned to him. "Why?"

He lowered his arm, eyes grave. "Because you could get pregnant."

"Oh." Strange, but that hadn't even occurred to her, and yet it would be a calamity for her to have a child, with no husband. Wouldn't it? Simon's child, with his father's dark, penetrating eyes and hair several shades lighter, like cornsilk. A great yearning filled her, and she rolled toward him. "But I'd like—"

"To bear a bastard? I think not."

She flinched. "How could you label your own child so?"

"As I was labeled? No, I'd never call him so. But others would." Not looking at her, he rose, casually straightening his own clothes. "I can't offer you marriage, Blythe."

"I'm not asking it of you, Simon."

"You will." He looked at her then. "It's what you're made for, princess. You were meant to be somebody's wife, someone's mother. Not the doxy of an escaped criminal."

She flinched again. "You're hard on yourself, Simon," she said, ignoring the times she had reminded him of his status. "And on me. But you don't know me." She raised her chin, glaring at him. "I begin to think I don't know myself."

He returned her gaze, solemn, enigmatic. "This changes nothing. Come." He held out his hand. "We need to go if we wish to reach Maidstone before dawn."

Blythe ignored his hand. Could he really dismiss all that had happened between them so easily? "If you feel this way, why do you want me to come back?"

"I need help to clear my name."

"Why should I help you, after all you've done?"

"Because"—he went down on one knee before her—"you will wonder for the rest of your life if I'm guilty, or innocent."

She searched his face. "What I think shouldn't matter to you, Simon."

"No, it shouldn't, should it." He got abruptly to his feet. "Come or stay, then, it makes little difference to me."

That had the effect of making her stand, though she was stiff after their interlude among the trees, and little tremors still ran through her body. His back was turned as he freed the horse's reins, and she could see that his shoulders were bunched tight. "Then I'll come."

"Good." With one fluid movement he mounted the horse; a moment later, he reached down and pulled her up before him. "At least this time you won't have to walk."

"Small consolation," she retorted. She had no desire at the moment to be close to him, and so she tried to hold herself stiff, away from him, as they rode out onto the road. The lack of space and the horse's swaying movement defeated her, though, and after a moment she leaned back against Simon. It was going to be a miserable ride. She doubted she had ever felt so confused, unhappy, or lonely in her life.

Dawn was breaking as Simon trudged wearily up the stairs to the rooms above the bakeshop in Maidstone. Blythe was elsewhere, in rooms occupied by other members of the troupe. He wasn't sure how he felt about that. What had happened between them in the woods—sweet Jesus, it had been heaven and hell all in one. He'd come close to consummating the act, so close, and he knew that it confused her that he hadn't. She had been very quiet during the ride back, and though he had been acutely aware of her, her breasts just under his arms, her bottom nestled intimately against him, still he had remained quiet, too. There were no words to explain what had happened between them, no words to describe his feelings.

Harry met him at the top of the stairs, a finger to his lips. "Did you find her?" he whispered.

Simon nodded tiredly. "Aye, and brought her back, though mayhap it would have been better had I let her go."

Harry frowned, glanced into the darkened room behind him, and then closed the door. "There's much you haven't said about her, lad," he said, settling on the top stair.

"I know." Simon sat several stairs below him, leaning his head against the wall. "Upon my honor, I never meant to involve her as I have, but at the time I needed help getting out of London. She happened to be nearby."

"You could have let her go once you were out of the city."

"Circumstances," Simon said, and related briefly all that had happened since he'd first seen Blythe on a quiet London street. Almost all. The night's events were no one's business but his. "She was going home," he concluded. "I probably should have let her go."

"Mayhap. Mayhap not." Harry hunched, with his hands loosely clasped between his parted knees. "There's no way of knowing how she'll be received. 'Tis a long time she's been with you."

"Aye, I know, and her reputation's ruined. I know." He rubbed his eyes. "What I don't know is what to do about it."

"There's an obvious answer."

Simon looked up sharply. "You're not suggesting marriage, Uncle."

"There are worse fates, lad."

"Not for her, there aren't." Simon straightened, face grim. "What kind of life would that be for her, Uncle, the wife of a condemned man? Even if by some miracle I clear my name, I'm still naught but a strolling player. And a bastard," he added bitterly.

Harry rested his hand on Simon's shoulder. "You know that's never mattered to us, lad."

"It matters to everyone else."

"Not to anyone who cares about you."

"Huh. 'Tis a word that's been used against me many a time, Uncle. And a word no child of mine will ever hear."

Silence fell between them. "I believe I've done you a disservice, lad, and I never meant to," Harry said finally.

"What?"

"Your parents met in Dover. Did I ever tell you that?"

Simon straightened. "No. You know damn well you didn't."

" 'Tis not something I've ever cared to discuss. As far as Bess and I are concerned, you're our son." He let out his breath. "And I had no liking for your father."

"You knew him. You knew him? Did you? When all these years you've told me—"

"Hush, lad." Harry's hand was heavy on Simon's shoulder. "No, I've not lied to you. I never met the man, nor did I ever know who he was."

Simon sat forward, intent. In all his life Harry had rarely talked about Simon's parentage. Simon had long ago learned to stop asking. "Didn't my mother say?"

Harry shifted on the stair. "Of course she said, lad, but I didn't want to listen to her, I was that angry." He shook his head. "She had talent, did your mother. Most talented actress I've ever seen, except maybe Henrietta." He nodded. "Aye, we'll see about Young Harry. She has time yet. But Maggie . . ." His eyes went distant. "She could read a part once, know it immediately, and become that character. I've never seen the like. And she didn't care."

"I thought she liked being onstage."

"Not really, no. It was a way for her to live." Harry passed a hand over his hair, sighing. "You know that our parents died young. You know that we became strolling players because our aunt was one, much as what's happened to you. But what you don't know is that your mother hated it." His voice was quiet, emphatic. "She hated everything about the life, the traveling, the constant work, but I think what she missed most of all was not having a steady home. A family. Me, I thought 'twas a great adventure."

"And yet, she did well," Simon said, loath to interrupt this flood of reminiscence.

"Aye, that she did. I told you she was talented. It just didn't mean much to her. Not the way it did to me." His hands fisted on his knees. "I'd've given my eyeteeth to have half her talent, and she'd've been glad to give it all away. We never did understand each other, and when we were older it caused trouble between us."

"So she met my father."

"Aye." Harry's voice was heavy. "Men had paid court to her before, but she'd never paid much heed.

But this one—I don't know what it was he had, but
Maggie was besotted with him."

"Was he really gentry?" Simon asked, remembering
one of the few tales he'd been told of his birth.

"I don't know, lad. She said he was. Said he wanted
to marry her. And I'd have none of it. None of it. She
was a success on the stage, was destined for great
things, London—even—and I wasn't going to let her
give it up. Not for some man who'd likely seduce her
and leave her with child."

Simon grimaced. "Which he did."

Harry didn't answer right away. "Mayhap."

"What do you mean?"

Harry rested his arms on his knees. "There's something you've never been told, lad, something you
should have known long ago."

Simon leaned forward, trying in vain to catch Harry's eye. "What?"

"Your mother . . ." He took a deep breath. "Maggie
always said your father had married her."

Chapter 18

It slammed into Simon's stomach like a blow. "That can't be."

"Oh, aye, so I said, since she didn't have the marriage lines. But married good and proper, she said she was."

"Who?" Simon's hand gripped Harry's. "Who is my father?"

"I don't know, lad." Regret was heavy on Harry's face. "I've a temper, you know that. When she met this man—"

"How?"

"He was in the audience one evening."

"Then you saw him?"

"Aye." Harry leaned back, studying Simon. "You favor him."

"God."

"When she met him I was angry. I told her I was responsible for her, that she'd not be taking up with some strange man who'd seduce her and leave her behind. But she was stubborn, our Maggie." He looked away. "When she wanted something, she went after it."

"She went with him anyway."

"More than that. She ran away." He looked at Simon. "With him. I didn't know where, what had happened to her, if I'd ever see her again. And I searched. By God, I searched, but I couldn't find her."

"God," Simon said again. His memories of his mother were dim, he'd been so young when she died. In his mind he saw her always as sad, her smile always distant and distracted, her voice lifeless. It had been

Aunt Bess he'd turned to for mothering, Bess who'd patched up his little-boy scrapes and given him a kiss to make them better, and when his mother died, he'd hardly noticed her absence. The only legacy she'd left him was the knowledge of his bastardy. Now he'd lost even that. "How did you find her?"

"I didn't. She came back."

"Alone?"

"Aye. Alone, and several months gone with child."

"Did she say—"

"She never would, lad, never. I yelled at her, raged at her—God help me, I even struck her—but she would never say. She told me she was married and I wouldn't believe her. And after that, she'd not tell me a thing." He took a deep breath. "But after you were born, lad, she left again, carrying you, and when she came back she was different. All the anger was gone, all the spirit. All she would tell me was that she was a widow, and so who your father had been didn't matter."

"It matters." Simon's voice quivered with the force of restrained anger. "If I had a legitimate father, if I've family somewhere—"

"We're family, lad."

"My father's family." It exploded out of him. "God, all these years I thought I was a bastard, I was told it enough, and now I find . . ." He stood abruptly. "I have to get out of here."

Harry was behind him on the stairs. "Where are you going?"

"Out." Simon turned in the doorway, fingers shoved into his hair. "Just . . . out. I have to. I have to think. Damn it!" He took a step outside and then whirled to face Harry. "Why didn't she ever tell me?"

Harry lifted his hands helplessly. "I don't know, lad. But I think it was to spare you pain."

"Pain. My God."

Harry held his hand out. "Simon—"

"I have to go," Simon said, and, turning on his heel, stalked out into the gathering day.

He was legitimate. All those years he'd believed

otherwise. All those years . . . Anger sliced through him, making him pound his fist against his palm. Bloody hell, why hadn't his mother told him? Why hadn't Harry told him? All these years, with their shame, their pain, and now to find out he'd endured them for naught. His father, the man he'd always refused to think about, had married his mother. Or so she claimed.

The thought made him slow his pace; made him glance about, as well, as caution returned to him. It didn't matter how earth-shattering the revelation he'd just received was. It had nothing to do with his present situation. He was legitimate, aye, but he was also still an escaped convict, with a cloud over his name. If he had family he'd never known about, what good did that do him? They'd not be eager to claim him now.

Heart heavy, arms and legs heavy, he turned and trudged back to the bakeshop. The past was past. No good in mourning something that never was. Besides, hadn't he had a fine life with Harry and Bess? Hadn't they been about the best parents a boy could have, and hadn't they helped him find his talent? Aye, and yet they'd never told him the truth. Never, until now, and he wondered why Harry had chosen today, of all days, to do so. Today when he had to decide once and for all whether to make the possibly fruitless, and definitely dangerous, effort to clear his name or to flee.

But that decision had already been made, he reminded himself, when he'd suddenly been given a second chance at life. Too many people had risked too much for him to waste this opportunity. He wanted his old life back, and that meant finding out what had really happened in Canterbury. If he failed—and that was possible—at least he'd know he'd tried.

Determined, and at the same time lighthearted, he walked into the garden of the bakeshop, checking to make sure that no one noticed him. He had a purpose now, a goal. He would not let anything distract him from it. Not even Blythe, sitting now on the stone doorstep, chin propped in hand. Especially not Blythe.

"Good morrow, princess." He dropped down beside her, stretching out his legs and propping his elbows on the threshold behind him. "I thought you'd be asleep."

Blythe shook her head. "I've been thinking."

"Dangerous thing to do."

"Mayhap. But I couldn't sleep." Not with the memories of their time together in the woods running through her mind over and over. Not when she had tossed and turned and yearned so much that the actress who shared the bed with her had given her an uncompromising thump on the back. "What of you?"

He shook his head, his brow furrowed. "Too much has happened."

"I know." She leaned forward, elbows on knees. "You do realize that the only way to clear your name is to find out what really happened."

Simon straightened so fast that his back slammed against the edge of the threshold. "What did you say?"

"Someone killed that man, Simon. Maybe it was you, but maybe it wasn't. And if it wasn't, we have to find out who did."

"My God." He stared at her. "Did Henrietta talk to you?"

"No. Why?"

"She's thinking of a plan."

"I'm not sure 'tis a good idea to involve your family in this."

"I need help, princess."

"Of course you do. I'm offering it to you."

"My God," he said again. "Why?"

She shrugged. "What else is there for me to do?"

"Oh."

That had made his frown return, Blythe noted. Good. Let Simon feel as off balance as she did with him. In the last weeks she had let too many other people tell her where to go, what to do. If she had complied, it was partly because she had always done so, always seeking acceptance and approval. And where had it got her? Into some very strange circumstances. She could not chance the past. She could, however, control her future. She was not going to run away. "If you didn't commit the murder, someone else did."

"So you've pointed out," he said dryly.

"And to find out who that is"—her brow wrinkled—"we need to find out why. Why would someone have wanted the man—what was his name again?"

"Miller."

"A true Miller's Canterbury tale, then."

"Ha."

That, too, had made him frown. Very good. Let him know how it felt to have someone making sport of his life, as he had with her. Petty of her, but satisfying. "Why would someone want to kill Miller?"

Simon looked at her a moment longer. "Mayhap I had reason."

"Don't dismiss me so lightly," she scolded. "I'm trying to help you."

"You're trying to condemn me."

"Is that what finding the truth will do?"

"No." He looked at her, his eyes puzzled. "Why are you doing this?"

Because I love you, you idiot. "Because I've no chance of getting my life back while you remain a fugitive, of course. What was your reason? You might as well tell me," she went on, when his mouth set in a tight, thin line. "You never have told me your side of the story."

"You wouldn't listen."

"I'm listening now, Simon."

He looked away, and for the first time she realized how tired he appeared. It must hang heavily on him, she thought, all that he'd gone through, guilty or not. What she had experienced these past weeks was as nothing compared to that. "I owed him money."

"And?"

"And I've already told you I could never have paid it back." He looked over at her. "Some people would consider that a reason."

"Mmm. How did you meet him?"

"Through the stage, of course. He fancied himself an actor. Sometimes a troupe will let an actor take the stage if he pays enough."

"Was he any good?"

"No. Terrible. But he was a good sort, willing to take any part, which many an amateur won't. Everyone liked him."

"Except you."

"No, no, I liked him, too. But you've seen for yourself, Blythe, we players don't mingle with ordinary people."

"Civilians."

He grinned. "Precisely. Because sometimes being in the theater is like being in a war. I made a mistake in judgment. In any event, I needed money." He straightened, shoulders stiff. "Miller learned of it and offered to lend it to me. All very friendly."

"Was it?"

"Aye. Until he charged that high interest rate. The total I owed grew faster than I could pay it. Amazing how serious he got after that."

"But didn't you know that when you took the money?"

He shifted on the stair. "I'm an actor, Blythe, not a scholar. When he told me the rate, it seemed paltry. 'Twas only later that I'd learned how bad a bargain I'd made."

"So you went to see him."

He shook his head. "No, Uncle Harry tried to help at first. He tried to get the rate lowered. It didn't work."

Blythe pursed her lips. "How many people knew about this?"

"Everyone in the troupe, of course. Hard to keep that kind of thing a secret, with the life we live. Why?"

She shook her head. "I don't know yet. What happened next?"

"Next was that Harry would have repaid the debt, though it would have bankrupted him. I didn't let him, of course. But I had to solve the problem myself, or I would have gone to debtor's prison."

"So?"

"So I decided that I would go to see Miller myself."
He took a deep breath. "It was—"

"Who knew of that?"

He frowned. "I don't know. Why?"

She shook her head again. "Go on."

Simon's gaze was hard. She made herself meet it
without flinching. For the life of her she didn't know
if he was innocent or not, but she wanted him to be.
Oh, how she wanted it. And that meant she'd set herself a difficult task.

"I wish I knew what you were thinking," he said.

"You will. Go on."

"All right." He shrugged. "Miller wouldn't see me
right away, told me to come back that evening. I had
no part in the play we were doing, so I was free."

"And?"

"He was dead when I got there, Blythe. I swear it."

"Tell me from the beginning," she said gently, aching to place a comforting hand on his shoulder. Guilty
or no, he was suffering.

"Not much to tell. He'd told me to come to his
home above the shop. No one answered when I
knocked, but the door was ajar, and so I went in. It
was dark. Sun had set, and there was only one candle,
burning low. But it was enough." He swallowed, hard.
"It was quiet. That's what I remember most, how
quiet it was. Like a tomb."

"Simon—"

He shook off the hand that she did, at last, place
on his shoulder. "And there was a smell; I thought
maybe the room was filled with metal. I called, and
there was no answer. I decided not to wait, but when
I turned I saw . . . something. There was a cabinet in
the corner, a large thing . . . black with Chinese
design?"

She nodded, to show she knew what he was talking
about. "What did you see?"

"A foot. Just a man's foot, sticking out from the
side of the cabinet. I said something, I think, asked if
it was Miller and if he was hurt. And then I saw him."

He rose, took a few paces about the garden, and turned back. "I didn't know what I was seeing at first. I was in shock, I imagine. But then I realized. He was lying on his back, and he was dead."

"How could you tell?"

"His throat had been cut, Blythe," he said bluntly.

Blythe's hand flew protectively to her own throat. She had invited this, she thought. "Oh."

"And his eyes were open. There was blood—but never mind that," he said hastily, looking at her at last. "There was a knife on the floor. I picked it up—I don't know why—and that was when the door opened."

"Dear heavens."

"It was Miller's wife. She screamed. I tried to explain, but she kept screaming. And then the night watchman was there, and the neighbors, and the next thing I knew I was being taken off to gaol." He dropped down onto the stair again. "And that is my Canterbury tale."

She didn't smile. "It looks very bad, Simon."

He nodded. "Aye, that it does. I had quarreled with him and I owed him money I could never repay. Being found as I was was just the capper."

"Mmm." Blythe's brow was wrinkled. It was no wonder he'd been convicted, so strong had been the evidence against him. And yet, he was no killer. At least, she didn't think so. "I'm tired," she said, surprising herself by yawning.

"I'm not surprised." He glanced at her. "What think you of my tale?"

She shook her head. "Right now I frankly don't know what to think. It doesn't look good, Simon."

"I'm aware of that."

"But if Mr. Miller made an enemy of you, mayhap he had others."

" 'Tis possible."

"Aye. And 'tis what we'll have to look for. Have you any plans?"

"Yes." He grinned, the derisive, mocking grin that she'd learned was aimed as much at himself as at anyone else. "I was thinking of bed."

"Oh, you're always promising me that," she said lightly, and rose, aware that he was gaping at her. Good. "We'll make our plans later."

He stood up, stretching his arms in a prodigious yawn that emphasized his chest, making her look hastily away, cheeks warm. "Aye. We'll have to go to Canterbury sometime. Blythe." His hand reached out, cupped her shoulder. " 'Twill be dangerous."

Deliberately she twitched her skirts. "And what is that to me?"

He gave her a little shake. "I'm serious, Blythe. I may be recognized, and if we're caught—"

"There's danger now, Simon. Do you wish to wait for it to come to you?"

"No," he said slowly. "No. Very well. We'll do it."

"Of course we will," she said, and turned away. If he touched her once more she would melt into a puddle at his feet. "I need to sleep."

"Yes. Blythe?"

She turned in the doorway. "What?"

He frowned, tightened his lips, and then let his breath out in a gush. "Thank you."

"Fair payment for all you've done for me, sir," she said sweetly, and turned away, twitching her skirts again. She'd won that encounter, a rarity in her acquaintance with him, and it was rather pleasant. It wouldn't last, of course. Her smile faded as she started up the stairs, the full weight of her exhaustion settling upon her shoulders. Soon they would be on the road again, and who knew what the future would hold?

It was market day in Maidstone, and fine weather for it, too. Farmers from all over the area converged on the town to sell their wares and to purchase others. They would stop in at alehouses and inns, at the shops, at the other market stalls. Some might even decide to watch the play that was being given that very afternoon by the Woodley strolling players. It was noisy, crowded, warm, and confusing. Among all the farm carts and barrows, no one would notice one more leaving the town, or the people it held.

Blythe gazed up at the bed of the rickety old cart, fists on hips, mouth set in a thoughtful line. Yesterday and the day before she and Simon had worked out the plan, with the help of Henrietta. Disguised as a farmer and his wife, they would travel the back roads to Canterbury. Were they stopped, the hay-strewn cart, littered with old onion skins and fragrant with the earthy smell of potatoes, would make them appear more credible. Both would be disguised: Simon with a false beard, Blythe with brown powder dulling her hair to a uniform shade, and padding inside her clothing to make her appear heavy. A few streaks of rouge on her face, and she'd been transformed. Staring at herself in the mirror, she was startled at how little it took to change her appearance. It was almost like being another person, and that was almost fun.

A footfall beside her made her look up to see Harry studying the cart with the same concentration. "You've everything you need?" he asked abruptly.

"Yes, I believe so. Food enough for several days, blankets, a change of clothes"—she counted off the items on her fingers—"and money." She smiled at him. "We've had to make do with far less. I do thank you, sir, for your generosity."

Harry leaned his hand against the cart, his frown massive. " 'Tis us should be thanking you, lass. Simon's got himself into a right proper mess, and none of us can help him."

"Ah, well, by helping him, I help myself," she said breezily, stepping away from the cart. "I believe we're ready."

"If your plan does work, what will you do?"

Blythe sighed. "I don't really know, Mr. Woodley. I suppose I could go home, but . . ."

"You don't really want to, do you, lass?" Harry said, when she didn't go on. His eyes beneath his shaggy brows were keen and kind.

"Not particularly, no. And I don't know why," she went on. "I've family there, and they'll take me in." But not family like Simon's, she thought, a lump rising unwanted in her throat. Not family that took you in and helped you, no matter what you'd done, no matter the cost to them, and with never a word of complaint. Not family that laughed and scolded and hugged, or looked at you with troubled, loving eyes. Blythe wondered if Simon had any idea of just how lucky he was.

"You've changed, most likely." Harry fell into step beside her as they turned from the lane into the yard of the bakeshop. "Bound to happen."

"I don't know." She frowned. "I've changed, yes, but I think what I've become is what I always was."

He shot her a quick look. "I don't follow you, lass."

She smiled. "Actors aren't the only people who play roles, Mr. Woodley. I'm not sorry this happened," she said, and, as she did so, realized it was true. "I should be, but I'm not."

Harry studied her. " 'Tis a pity Simon didn't meet you sooner, lass, else he might not be in this coil at all."

"But I might be." She flounced away, unreasonably annoyed. She knew quite well that Simon would never have taken a second glance at her had he not needed her help.

"There's naught wrong with the boy," Harry rumbled on, falling into step beside her, as if she hadn't reacted in any way. "He's a good lad. A trifle wild, mayhap, but that's to be expected. Aye, and he's outgrowing that, too."

"And he takes nothing seriously," she burst out, stopping dead.

"Does he not, lass?" Harry's fingers cupped her chin, forcing her to face him. "Do you really know him so little, then?"

"No." She twisted her face away. "I understand why he acts as he does. 'Tis a good defense. But it can be rather wearing on other people."

"So it can. Though mayhap you've noticed that he's not like that with his family."

"Yes."

"Or with you."

Her head came up sharply. "He is at his absolute worst with me! I—"

He smiled. "Aye, lass, and shouldn't that tell you something? I've worried about the lad," he went on before she could speak, resting a heavy hand on her shoulder. "Even before all this happened, I worried. There's been a restlessness to him, like he needs more."

"More of what?"

"I don't know, lass, or I'd give it him. But I've noticed something about him the past few days."

"What is that?"

"That the restlessness is gone."

She frowned. "Yet he has always been heading to Canterbury."

"Aye. To a goal, not away from something. You mentioned playing roles, lass. 'Tis a handy way to escape."

"From what?"

"From reality. From your life. Take on someone else's problems and you can forget, for a time, that your own exist."

Blythe bit her lip. Hadn't she felt something of the sort when she'd taken the stage in Rochester? Hadn't she almost believed she was someone else, and felt a peculiar freedom in doing so? "But I think he's facing his problems now."

"Aye, lass, that he is, and I think you're in large measure the reason."

"Me!"

"Aye."

"Well, I'm sure I don't know why." She turned again, heading for the garden gate. What Harry was saying wasn't true, couldn't be true. Simon saw her as a traveling companion, and no more. "Tell Simon I'll return shortly."

"Where you are going, lass?" Harry called.

"Just for a walk." She waved at him and walked quickly away, leaving Harry to stare after her, frowning. Made a mull of that, he had.

"And what was that all about?" Bess asked at his side.

"I spoke out of turn." Harry's voice was rueful as

he slipped his arm about her ample waist. "Mayhap said some things I shouldn't."

"Oh?"

"Yes. I think our Simon fancies her."

"Of course he does." Bess nestled a bit closer. "She's a brave girl. He could do worse."

"Aye, and so could she. But does she see that, Bess?" He turned troubled eyes on her. "All she knows of Simon is that he's a criminal."

"I think she sees more than that, Harry. 'Tis a pity they didn't meet before."

"Aye, though likely it would have changed nothing." He rested his head briefly against hers. "What makes it worse is that we cannot help."

"We're doing what he can." Bess sounded resolute, but her fingers clutched him just a bit hard. And so they stood together, taking comfort from each other, and wondering what was going to become of their boy.

Caution took over Blythe's steps before she had gone far from the bakeshop, caution born of her upbringing and of the recent events in her life. The square was thronged with people of all kinds, farmers in smocks, a soldier or two, and even a juggler, whose antics held several children fascinated. Against the buildings of dull Kentish ragstone, the effect was colorful and vivid. Under such circumstances it was unlikely she'd be noticed, and so she was fairly safe. Still, away from her lodgings, away from Simon, she felt nervous, exposed, as if someone were watching and would pounce at any minute. Best she return, then.

Her back crawling with the sensation of being watched, she turned and began fighting her way back through the crowds of jostling, preoccupied people. She shouldn't have run as she had, even if she'd needed to escape from Harry and the pain of what he had said to her. He meant well, of that Blythe was certain. He worried about Simon and wished to see him settled. What he did not know, what he could not know, was how his concern stung. She loved Simon and would make him a good wife, if that was what he wanted. Unfortunately, it wasn't, and never would be.

The crowd lessened as she reached the edge of the square, and she stopped, catching her breath and looking again at the colorful stalls and the people who went about their business, unaware that a desperate fugitive was nearby. It was all so very normal that it made her heart ache. Her life would never be so simple again.

She was turning away, ready to return to the bakeshop, when of a sudden a hand clamped onto her arm. "Hey. Blythe Marden? It *is* you," a male voice said, amazed and pleased at once. "And I've got you now."

Chapter 19

Blythe froze, as always she reacted to danger, though her mind was calm and clear and registering events, seemingly independent of herself. Foolish of her to come to the market and to think that her disguise would fool anyone. Now she was caught, and she and Simon both would pay the consequences.

The pressure on her arm increased, forcing her to turn and face her assailant. Against the morning light all she could see at first was that he was a man, taller than she, and broad-shouldered. "Please," her voice quavered, while her mind mocked her weakness. "I've done no wrong."

"I wouldn't say that. You always were one for landing in a fix."

Blythe tugged away, to no avail, but the movement brought the man more into shadow. It took her a moment to realize that he was neither a soldier nor a watchman, nor Quentin Heywood, her inexplicable enemy. "John!" she gasped, and threw herself into his arms.

"Hey." John held her a bit awkwardly, his arms stiff. "What is this?"

"Oh, 'tis just that I'm so glad to see you!" She pulled back, patting his face. "When I came to the market I'd not expected to see my brother."

"Nor I, you." John pulled back, frowning. "Have you gone to fat?"

Blythe let her breath out in an explosive laugh. "Trust a brother to be so tactless! No, I'm not exactly as I appear." Glancing first over her shoulder to see if they were being watched, she slipped her arm through his and began to stroll, away from the bustle of the market. "Is Mother here? And Father?"

"Yes, and Polly, too." His frown deepened. "What the devil's happened with you, Blythe? We've heard all sorts of rumors."

"I've had quite an adventure," she said, and gave him a brief recitation of recent events, omitting the fact that she had actually gone on the stage. Even so, John was frowning when she finished.

"It sounds deuced bad, Blythe." They were sitting on a bench before the Star Inn, and his face was somber. "Your reputation is entirely in shreds."

That hurt. "What of my well-being, John? Shouldn't that be a greater concern?"

"Yes, yes, of course, but you know our mother."

Blythe nodded. Oh, yes, she did indeed know what her foster mother was like. "I almost came home, you know, when I realized how close I was."

"Why didn't you? We'd've welcomed you, Blythe, you know that."

"Would you?" She gave him a long look, her lips tightening when he wouldn't meet her gaze. "I'm a wanted woman, John."

"That doesn't matter to me, Blythe, you should know that! Or to Father. It's just that—"

"It matters to Mother," Blythe said flatly.

"And Polly. She is with child."

Blythe's eyes lit up. "But that is wonderful news, John! I'm to be an aunt at last."

"Yes. The trouble is, her health is not good."

"Oh, dear."

"We've been very careful not to upset her."

"Oh." Blythe gazed ahead. Were she to go home, the situation would be worse than she had realized. Neither her mother nor her sister-in-law would want to take her in, though for family's sake they probably would. They would also talk about her, and shun her, and she would have no life. A high price to pay for safety. "Then I'd best not come home."

"But we're your family," John protested. "Of course you'll come home."

"No." Gently Blythe freed her hands and rose. Her life as she had known it was over. What would happen next she couldn't even guess. Strange that she felt so light. "I'll not put anyone in danger. No," she went on, as John drew breath to protest, "I've quite made up my mind about this. 'Tis best if I stay away."

"I won't have it." John's mouth was set in the stubborn line she remembered from childhood. "I am your older brother, and you should do what I say."

Blythe couldn't help it; she smiled. "Oh, John, I do love you," she said, leaning forward to plant an impulsive kiss on his cheek, and then spinning away, before he could see the tears welling in her eyes. The last bridge was burned behind her. She had cast her destiny with Simon, no matter where it might lead her.

Behind her Blythe heard John call her. She stepped up her pace, pushing through the market-day crowds and stumbling upon the cobblestones until she reached the relative safety of a shopfront. A quick glance back showed her that she had lost John. Relieved, sorry, she turned to be on her way and was blocked by a man stepping in front of her.

A small scream escaped her, even as she recognized him. "Be quiet," Simon hissed, his hand clamping on her upper arm as he dragged her into the lane next to the shop. "You've attracted enough attention today."

Blythe pried at his fingers. "Pray unhand me, sir. What I do with my time is no concern of yours."

"It is when you might bring disaster upon us. 'Tis a good thing I thought to look for you."

"I caused no trouble."

"No?" He stepped before her again, brows lowered in a tremendous frown. "Who was that man I saw you with?"

"No one you need fear, I assure you—"

"Who was he?" Simon's hand shot out and caught her arm again. "You had best tell me, madam, or—"

"You're hurting me," she said, her voice very small.

Instantly he released her, his glower softening. "I am sorry, Blythe, but when I found you'd left the bakeshop I grew concerned."

Blythe sighed, suddenly tired. Why did men feel they needed to be so overbearing? "There was no danger, Simon. Not to you."

"And what of you? Bloody hell, Blythe! You could have been caught and hurt."

"Were you worried about me?"

Simon looked away. "No."

Her spirits, a moment before so low, suddenly rose. "You were, weren't you?"

"It matters not." He pulled at his ear and then, gently this time, reached for her arm. " 'Tis not wise for us to be seen, Blythe. I shouldn't have to explain that to you."

"You don't, and you're right. I was taking a chance. But it felt—"

"As if you hadn't taken a free breath in years."

"Yes, that's exactly it! I'm sorry, Simon." She glanced up at him through her lashes. "I'll be more careful in future."

"Good." They walked on. "Who was he?"

Blythe bit her lip. Simon's family cared about him, had come to his aid in time of trouble, even if his innocence was in doubt. "My brother," she said, her throat tight. "My foster brother."

"Your brother! Good God, if anyone else knows—"

"John wouldn't give me away," she protested. "He wants me to be safe."

"Ah, but did he ask you to come home?"

"Of course he did."

"Then why didn't you?" He went on as she hesitated in answering, "Because he really didn't want you to, did he?"

"No! He said . . . well." She looked away. "He wants me to. 'Tis the rest of my family that is the problem."

Simon slung his arm about her shoulders. She had to force herself not to nestle against his sheltering, enticing warmth. "It appears I've made you an outcast. I'm sorry, Blythe. 'Twas never my intention."

"I'm not," Blythe said, startling them both. "No, truly, I'm not. And I'm just now realizing it."

He frowned. "Why not?"

"It matters not." For the first time since leaving John, she felt like smiling. That part of her life was over, and she was glad. Until she'd had the chance to return to it, though, she hadn't realized it. "Come, we should return. We don't want to take the chance of your being seen."

Simon was still frowning. "Sometimes I don't understand you," he complained.

"Good," she said, and slipping her arm through his, walked on, to seek whatever the road ahead brought her.

John Temple stopped at the entrance to the lane, squinting into the shadows. That was a dammed large man who had accosted Blythe just now, though she didn't seem alarmed. They walked together ahead of John, so intent on their discussion that they appeared unaware of him. Deuce take it, but could that be the actor whose accomplice Blythe had become? If so, he, John, should do something about it. He was her brother, and concerned for her safety. He was also, he thought, something of a coward. Morosely he regarded his hands, callused but pale. Surgeon's hands. It had always been assumed that he'd follow his father into practice, and so he had, though he sometimes found it difficult. He'd always been careful of his hands. Not even for Blythe did he wish to get into a brawl and risk damaging them.

And what his wife would say to that he could well imagine. She considered life with a country doctor difficult enough and nagged him continually to go to London, where his talents would be appreciated. It did no good telling her that the country was where he was needed, and that it was where he wished to be. She resented his seeming lack of ambition and his closeness to his family. If he returned home with Blythe in tow, there would be deuce to pay.

He shuddered, glad enough to have forestalled that fate for now. Not that he should leave Blythe to her own devices. He frowned as the man with her put his arm about her shoulders. Blythe was his sister in name only, and yet from the time she'd arrived in his home, a tiny, bewildered orphan, he'd been enchanted with her. Together they had shared his lessons and assisted his father, with Blythe often more intrepid than he. Yet he was the trained surgeon. That was as it should be, of course—women weren't meant to be doctors— and yet sometimes John wondered why one person had such a talent and not another. He wondered what was in Blythe that had made her take up with a con- victed felon.

Blythe and her companion had disappeared around a corner. John hesitated and then stepped forward. His wife and mother would be at the market awaiting him, and both would scold him if they knew what he was doing. Blythe had made her bed, his mother had said; let her lie in it, as undoubtedly she was doing. But he couldn't let it go. Blythe was his sister. Should anything befall her, he would never forgive himself. For once in his life he had to forget others' opinions and his own doubts and take action.

The least he could do was discover where Blythe was staying. Squaring his shoulders, he stepped from the shadows and moved at a quick pace to follow the couple.

The farm cart rumbled along the lane, turned, and was out of sight. Harry lowered his hand, raised in farewell, and gazed at the dust that was the only sign of the recent departure. Simon was gone again, facing who knew what danger now. As a man, Harry could understand Simon's need to clear his name. As a fa- ther, though, or as good as, the idea terrified him. It had taken all his strength not to try to convince the boy to make for the coast instead, and safety. For the boy was not a boy any longer, but a man grown, and with an apparently intrepid companion. Of all the things that had happened to Simon in the past weeks, meeting Miss Marden had likely been the luckiest.

Beside him, Bess sighed. He laid a solid, reassuring hand on her shoulder. "Time we got to the theater," he said briskly. Talking about Simon would do no one any good. The lad was gone, that was that. "Come, woman, we've work to do."

"I suppose we do," Bess said, not the teasing rejoinder he had expected, but delivered with a hint of the smile that had first drawn him to her. "I'd best be seeing to your costume—gracious, who is that?"

Harry was already turning at the sound of feet tramping along the lane, accompanied by hoofbeats. Soldiers! A battalion of them, it looked like to Harry's untrained eyes, led by an officer on a brown horse and followed by another man, this one apparently a citizen, clad in sky blue. Harry's heart pounded, with the little catch that reminded him all too often that he was growing old. Simon. Dear God, they had discovered Simon had been here.

Bess shrank toward him. "Harry—"

"Let me do the talking," he said, voice low, and stepped forward. "Soldiers." Hands on his hips, he surveyed them, frowning. "I assume you've come about my scapegrace nephew."

The officer in charge of the group looked briefly startled; the other man merely sat back in his saddle, eyes narrowed thoughtfully. "Are you Henry Woodley?" the officer barked.

"Yes, sir, that I am." Harry slumped his shoulders just a bit and lowered his chin; had he been wearing a cap, he would have twisted it between his hands, the very picture of submission. "Who do I have the honor of addressing, sir?"

"I shall ask the questions! I have here"—from a pouch at his belt he produced a folded sheet of foolscap—"a warrant for the arrest of one Simon Woodley."

"May I see that?" Harry said, still meek.

"The likes of you wouldn't understand it. Be assured it has been properly executed by a magistrate, and that I have the authority to enforce it."

"Oh, I don't doubt that." Harry scratched his chin. "Not that it'll do you any good, mind. Simon's not here."

"We have information that he is."

"Nay. I was hoping you could tell me aught of him, sir? A fine old time of it we've had, going about our business," he whined. "We've been bedeviled by soldiers—"

"And the local watchmen," Bess put in.

"—in every village in England. I swear, sir, if I knew where Simon was, I'd hand him over, so we could be about our business. 'Tis no way to run a theater company."

"That is no concern of mine." The officer swung off his horse, its reins being held by a soldier. "I intend to find this man, with or without your help."

Harry gestured toward the bakeshop. "Oh, search all you want."

"Harry," Bess hissed.

"Be quiet, woman. This is man's work." And he'd hear about that later, he thought briefly, even though he was acting a role as never he had before. "We've nothing to hide."

"Henrietta."

"What?" He frowned, not having to feign looking puzzled. "What of her?"

"She is still abed."

"That lazy jade," he roared, picking up his cue with relish. "When she knows what's to be done today? I'll—"

"Mr. Woodley. Mr. Woodley!" The officer was standing before him, mouth twisted. "I haven't all day to stand here listening to you. Step aside, sir, or I shall have to use force."

"But I told you. Simon's not here."

"Indeed?" The officer's frown deepened, but there was a flicker of uncertainty in his eyes. "Where, pray tell, is he?"

"Do not bother with this one." It was the other man on horseback, the one all in sky-blue satin and white lace. Harmless, Harry would have thought, except for the jut of his chin and his strange, pale eyes. "Remember that they are actors and are used to lying."

"I say!" Harry blustered.

"And my information is good," the man went on. "From Miss Marden's brother."

The officer stepped forward; Harry blocked his way, though a moment before he had been quite willing to allow the soldiers access. He didn't like the man in sky blue, the man with the soulless eyes. "And who are you, and what do you want with Simon?" he demanded.

The man smiled, a mere grimace with his lips. "Who I am is of no moment. But as it is better to be civilized, you may call me Mr. Heywood."

Mr. Heywood, indeed! So this was the villain Simon had spoken of. What his part was in Simon's troubles, Harry couldn't fathom. All he knew was he had to keep Heywood away. Far away. "Yes, sir, Mr. Heywood." He reached up his hand as if to tug at a forelock, hesitated as if just realizing that the hair was no longer there, and ran a hand over his balding head instead. "Go in if you must, and if my daughter is still abed, tell her to get her lazy—to rise. After you've left, of course," he went on quickly, seeing one or two of the soldiers grin.

"Thank you for your permission," the officer said with sardonic, perfect politeness, and stepped past him. Harry moved back, slipping a protective arm about his wife's waist. Where was Young Harry, anyway? She'd been down earlier, to see Simon off.

Heywood's horse now stood beside the fence; the man stared at the bakeshop as the soldiers went in and the baker's wife began to protest their intrusion. "He's not here, is he," he said, and it wasn't a question.

Harry lowered his eyes. "I told you, sir. We've not seen hide nor hair of him."

"Hmm. Well. Whether you tell the truth or lie, it matters not. He's not here." Heywood pursed his lips. "I hardly expected him to be. But you." He fixed his gaze on Harry like a spear. "You know where he is."

"I, sir?" Harry's tremor wasn't completely feigned. "How would I know that?"

"Because he was here." Heywood crossed his arms

on the pommel, gazing meditatively down at Harry. "And because you are going to tell us where he is or suffer the consequences."

"He's not here, sir!" a soldier called from the door before Harry could answer. Heywood nodded, seeming unsurprised. The man's calmness was eerie. Did he know more than he was letting on?

A scream from behind him made Harry swing around, startled, to see his daughter struggling with one of the soldiers, who was dragging her outside. Harry took a quick step forward, to be stopped by another soldier blocking the way. "Your daughter is spirited," Heywood said dryly.

Yes, that she was, but she usually didn't become hysterical—ah. It was an act. Harry relaxed slightly. Henrietta's eyes were rolling; her screeches were almost mechanical. An appalling bit of overacting. He'd speak to her about it later. But what was she up to now?

"Papa!" Henrietta cast herself onto his chest, draping limply against him. "Please make these horrible men go away!"

"There, daughter, you're safe. What have you done to her?" he demanded, now very much the outraged parent.

"Your daughter is unharmed, sir," the officer drawled. "Which is more than I can say for the soldier she assaulted."

Harry noticed for the first time that one of the soldiers bore long scratches along his cheek, and bent his head to hide a smile. "Oh."

"We merely asked her a question."

"Papa, I don't know anything!" Henrietta clutched at his arms and rocked back, eyes wild. "Please tell them that."

"Sir," the officer said before Harry could answer. "Be advised that we will find your nephew. It will go better for you if you tell us his whereabouts."

"But we don't know!" Henrietta cried, turning to him. "Oh, please, can't you see we don't know anything?"

"You're lying," Heywood said pleasantly, and, just like that, Henrietta subsided. "Ah. Didn't think I'd catch on, did you? You protest too much, I think."

"I don't know anything," she repeated, but her voice quivered.

"Don't you? I think you do. You had best tell us." His voice hardened; his face sharpened, like a hawk after prey. "Or it will go very ill with you and your parents."

"I don't know—"

"You will end up in gaol, Miss Woodley. Not a pleasant place. Shall I tell you what happens to young ladies in gaol?"

"For God's sake, man," Harry protested.

"All right!" Henrietta cried at the same time, and suddenly drooped, head down shoulders slumped. "All right."

"For the love of God, Henrietta—"

"Very wise of you," Heywood broke in. "So you do know where Woodley is."

"Of course I know." Her voice was flat, and all the more convincing for it. "We all do."

Harry stepped forward. "Henrietta, don't—"

"It's no good, Father." She looked up at him, eyes blank. "For your sake, I have to tell him where Simon is."

Chapter 20

"Oh, stop!" Blythe cried suddenly.

Simon pulled on the reins of the farm cart, so that it slewed across the road. "What is it?" he asked, alarmed. They were two hours out of Maidstone, with signs neither of pursuit nor danger. Though they had passed other travelers, none had paid them much heed, which was a relief. Traveling like this, even in disguise, made Simon feel exposed. Yet it seemed that this last leg of their journey, the most perilous, might also be the dullest.

"There's feverfew." Blythe jumped nimbly down from the cart, belying the bulk of an advanced pregnancy, simulated by pillows. "Just let me collect some."

"Why?"

"I need some in case either of us falls ill," she said, breaking off the plant and stowing it carefully in the bag tied about her nonexistent waist.

"You have enough herbs there to heal all of Canterbury," Simon grumbled.

"Not quite." Clinging to the side of the cart, she climbed back in. "There. Now we can go."

"This is not meant to be a pleasure jaunt."

"I'm well aware of that." She slanted him a look. "Why are you so downcast this morn?"

"Why are you in such high spirits?"

"Blithe spirits, you mean."

"Oh, Lord."

"I don't know." She arched her head back, gripping the side of the cart bench to keep her balance. Her neck was soft, white, tempting, an emblem of all he couldn't have. " 'Tis such a fine day, and I just feel that all will be well."

"Ha."

"Well, I do." She shifted to face him. "What are your plans, once we reach Canterbury?"

"We need first a place to stay."

"Do you mean instead of a barn or a hedge?"

He deigned not to dignify that with a reply. "I know people there. Harry has passed the word along that we're coming. So long as we're not recognized, we should be all right."

"Imagine. Adventure without sleeping rough or eating cold food."

"This is still the most dangerous part," he said quietly.

"I realize that." Blythe's voice was as quiet as his. He chanced a look at her, and saw understanding and compassion in her eyes, and something else. Whatever it was, that warm gaze, it made him turn quickly away. "Believe me, Simon, I don't take this lightly."

"If we run into trouble, I want you to leave."

"What?"

"Make for Rye or Dover and leave the country. 'Tis the best thing."

"And leave you?"

"Aye. You'll be arrested, else."

"And what makes you think I won't be, anyway?"

"I don't know. But 'tis me they're after, not you." He held out his hand, gripping hers. "Promise me, Blythe."

"I can't."

"Promise me, or I'll turn this cart around and leave you with my family."

"Simon—"

"I want to know you'll be safe."

"Of course I'll be safe." Her hand turned, clasped his. "But if it will ease your mind, of course I promise."

"Good." His tight shoulders relaxed, but he didn't pull his hand away. Nor did she move hers. Her gaze met his and held, and this time he didn't turn away from what he saw there, though it frightened him as much as anything in his life ever had. There was a future for him. For the first time, he could see beyond the trials ahead, the fight to clear his name; the possibility of flight. He could have a future.

"Simon." Blythe tugged at his hand, making him tighten his grip. He didn't want to let her go, not now, not ever. "Simon! There's someone coming."

"What?" he said, but then he heard it, hoofbeats coming from behind them. He released her hand slowly, reluctantly. She pulled hers back with startling haste, facing forward and quickly assuming the expression of a placid, content farm wife. She was a mass of contradictions, his Blythe, as adept at hiding as he was, and that only fascinated him more. She was also, regrettably, correct. Because this road was not heavily traveled, anyone using it would be remembered. It was best to look as unremarkable as possible.

The noise behind them increased, the sound of a sizable caravan. Simon glanced back to see several outriders coming toward them, followed by a large traveling coach pulled by four horses. He had barely time to pull his own slow-moving cart to the side before the outriders were upon them. The carriage followed, an elegant coach with a crest on the side. Then there was only dust, making them cover their faces and cough.

They were alone again. Simon did not, however, reach for Blythe. Instead, not looking at her, he picked up the reins and set their horses to a slow, jouncing walk. Canterbury lay ahead, with all its perils and promise, the very thought of it making him tense. He had lost the elusive sense of a bright future, brought back to reality and to his fears. He could not let Blythe become important to him, not when so much was uncertain. For he did not yet know whether he would live or hang.

"Henrietta!" Harry stared at his daughter in blank horror. "Be quiet, girl."

"Let her speak." Quentin's horse daintily picked its

way forward, stopping at the low stone wall edging the bakeshop's garden. From the other side the girl, tall, disheveled, defiant, glared at him, though she was held back by soldiers. A game one, even in defeat, he thought with some admiration. Terrible clothes, of course, and the coiffure was beyond repair, but there was something there. He wasn't surprised that she, the weak link, had broken. "Where is he, then?"

"Gone," she said, and sagged so that the soldiers had to grab at her to keep her from falling.

"So he was here, then." And Quentin had missed him yet again. No matter. He would catch Woodley sooner or later. In the meantime, he had the bait for a trap. "Where is he?"

"Oh, please don't arrest us, sir!" The girl fell to her knees, her parents watching in slack-jawed shock, confirming her words. "We didn't ask him to come, and we didn't let him stay. 'Twas just for a while."

"When?" Quentin said again.

"Yesterday, sir." The girl dropped her head. "He was here and then gone."

Quentin dropped the reins over his horse's head and dismounted leisurely. "Which does not help me now, does it?" He lifted the girl's chin with his fingers and saw something flash briefly in her eyes. So she had some spirit left. That would not last. "Where is he? I am growing impatient," he went on, as she pulled back from him. "Tell me what I wish to know, or it will go ill with you."

"Oh, please, sir—"

"Tell me."

"The coast!" she burst out, and behind her her mother gave a cry of dismay. "He's making for the coast."

"Is he, then. Where? Rye? Dover?"

"Neither." It was a whisper. "Margate."

"Margate." He stepped back, waited until he saw her shoulders loosen, and then pushed her face up again. Her eyes flared wide. "I don't believe you."

" 'Tis the truth." Her face was flat, her eyes dull and yet defiant. "I am not going to risk my neck for him."

"Oh, Henrietta," Mrs. Woodley moaned.

"We can't, Mama." Henrietta tried to twist around to face her parents, though the soldiers still held her. "You and Papa both told him to leave, him and that woman."

"She is still with him?"

Henrietta blinked. "She went with him, sir."

"Ah. Go on. Why did your parents tell him to go?"

"Because of the danger." She sighed, her eyes closing briefly. "He thought we'd take him in. 'Tis why he came so far out of his way."

"And chose to go north, rather than south, to throw us off the scent," Quentin ruminated, and pulled back, releasing the girl's chin. Sullen rebellion mingled with defeat in her posture, while her parents looked dazed, bewildered. "Did you hear that, Lieutenant?"

"Yes, sir." The officer nodded. "The garrison there must be alerted."

"Indeed. You have done well, Miss Woodley. Such forthrightness deserves a reward."

She looked up at him at that. His gaze rested on hers, swept over to her parents, and then returned. "Indeed, it does. Arrest them," he barked to the lieutenant, and swung up onto his horse, ignoring the cries and protests behind him. His work here was done. He was needed now in Margate. And if Woodley refused to give up . . . Quentin grinned. If that happened, Quentin had a tool he would use well. Hostages. Woodley would pay at last.

Midmorning, and the city of Canterbury was bustling. Blythe stood just outside the door of the old timber-framed house, taking in the view of small houses clustered together, along with the remarkable sight of a large, ancient building straddling the River Stour. So much of Canterbury was medieval that she almost felt as if she belonged in one of the tales. The Actor's Tale, she thought, and smiled. Last evening she and Simon had entered the city through the Westgate—which he hadn't told her until afterward served as the city gaol—and had immediately gone to the home of a friend, a former actor. He had put them up with few questions asked. The long pilgrimage from London was nearly over.

A man stepped out beside Blythe, an older man, his hair graying at the temples, his figure ample without being stout. His coat was of good, if not excellent, cloth and cut. So obviously was he a prosperous tradesman that it took Blythe a second to recognize him. "The sun shows up the powder in your hair," she commented. "Maybe you'd better keep your hat on."

Simon grimaced. " 'Tis too hot to be dressed with all this padding. And I can't wear a hat inside, not for politeness. I'll be glad when this escapade is done."

Something shot through Blythe, something akin to pain. She decided not to think about it. "We may find what we need today. Come." She slipped her arm through his, leading him out onto the lane. She still wore padding, though not so much as earlier, and she kept her pace measured, serene, as befitted the wife of a prosperous merchant. "Lay on, MacDuff."

Simon scowled. "I think I'll regret ever introducing you to the theater," he said, but continued walking, all too aware of her light touch on his arm. He would need help to clear his name. That was indisputable. That he'd rather the help come from anyone but her was also fact. Lord help him, what if he didn't succeed? For himself he didn't care so much as he had; he knew who he was and what he was capable of. Blythe, however, did not. Without incontrovertible proof that he had not killed Miller, she would never believe him innocent. It was a depressing thought.

From the High Street they turned onto a narrow lane he'd once known all too well, its high, timbered houses overhanging the street. In spite of himself, his muscles stiffened, his steps slowed. Here was where everything had come apart, in that house just along there. There was where he had found Miller's body.

"Simon?" Blythe's voice was soft. "If we stand here like this we'll be noticed."

"I know."

She squeezed his arm. "You don't have to go through with this if you don't want to."

"Yes, I do," he said grimly, and surged forward. "If 'twere done, 'twere best done quickly."

"Another quote from the Scottish play? Surely an evil omen."

"There's more to fear in this world than superstition," he said, and pushed at the door handle of the shop next to what had once been Miller's home.

Bells jingled on the door overhead as it opened. A pewtersmith's shop, Simon realized, seeing all about him on display shiny tankards and various dishes, and some cutlery. "Good morrow," a cheery voice came through a back room, and in bustled a man, short, tubby, his red face surmounted by an absurd fringe of white hair. "And what might I do for you?"

"You are Mr. West?"

"Aye, as it says on the sign. And you, sir?"

"Benjamin Bowles." Simon bowed briefly, hoping he gave the impression of a busy, businesslike man. "And a right pleasure it is to make your acquaintance."

"And yours, sir." West frowned. "Have we met?"

"I do not believe so, no."

"I did not think so. May I assist you in your purchase?"

Simon relaxed. One hurdle passed; West didn't recognize him, though he had been at Simon's trial. "Mayhap you could."

"Some tableware, perhaps? Those forks are particularly fine," West went on, and Simon realized that Blythe was fingering some of the merchandise. "Three tines, very handy, yes."

Blythe turned huge eyes up at him. "Oh, may we buy some, please, Mr. Bowles?" she breathed, very much the character they had decided upon for her. No one, they agreed, would pay much heed to a seemingly silly younger wife, which meant that Blythe could probably ask what she wished, without anyone wondering why. Her speech was careful, precise, with only the slightest hint of Yorkshire, in contrast to his own broad accent. She was really quite good at this. "Please?"

"We are here on business, wife." Patting her hand, he turned back to West. "Has summat happened to Mr. Miller? His shop's locked right and tight."

"Upon my soul. Haven't you heard?" West stared at him. "Miller is dead."

Simon stepped back a pace. "Dead? Well, I'm flummoxed! When?"

"This six months and more. And a terrible deed it was, him stabbed through the throat in his own house. I beg your pardon, ma'am." This as Blythe sagged against Simon, who put his arm around her.

"I heard nowt of it. He and I were in the way of doing business."

"Oh, a terrible scandal it was," West said with relish. "You're better off without him, too, though I don't like to speak ill of the dead. Not an honest man."

"I'd no trouble with him. I've t'shop in Leeds."

"Then likely you paid too much. No, we all knew to steer clear of Master Miller. Where did you say you met him?"

Simon shook his head. "My wife needs a place to sit, she's that pale. T'news has upset her."

"Of course, of course. Come through here." West led them through a doorway, into what was obviously a kitchen. Pewter plates, not so well burnished as those in the shop, were arranged on a rail, while the fire in the wide stone hearth made the room very warm. "Martha? Where are you, woman?"

"Cease your racket, sir," a woman scolded, stepping into the room from the outside, her arms filled with vegetables. "Can a body not step out to the garden for a moment?"

"We've guests. Here." West pulled a chair forward. "Sit you down, Mrs. Bowles."

"Thank you," Blythe said, sinking into the chair as if she were, indeed, feeling faint. They had planned this, of course, to give them each a chance to talk with both people. It was her idea, and she was rather proud of it. "I'm that sorry to discombobble—that is, to inconvenience you, ma'am."

"My wife is breeding," Simon said bluntly.

"Mr. Bowles!" Blythe exclaimed.

"And the tale of what happened to Miller upset her," West put in.

"It would. Sit you, then." Martha nodded at Blythe and dumped the greens onto a table already laden with a slab of beef and a huge turnip. "And if you plan to speak more of it, do so in the shop."

"Yes, dear," West said, surprisingly meekly, and turned to lead Simon back into the shop. Blythe, momentarily distracted, watched him go, until a loud *thwack* from behind her made her turn, startled.

"So you're breeding," Mrs. West said, bringing the cleaver down again, cutting chunks of beef.

"Yes." It wasn't hard to sound breathless. If she hadn't been ill before, she certainly was queasy now. The bloody beef, along with the way Mrs. West wielded the cleaver, was cause enough. "But such a tragedy as you have suffered."

"A tragedy? Him?" She jerked her head in the general direction of Miller's shop and brought the cleaver down again. "No loss there. Seems I'm not the only one who thinks so, neither."

Blythe perked up. Despite the sour appearance, Mrs. West apparently enjoyed a gossip as much as anyone. "No?"

"No. Didn't take his widow long to find herself another man. Not that I thought it would." She shoved the cubed beef aside with a careless push and went to work on the turnip. "Miller should have known what she was doing, that, he should have."

"I don't follow you."

"Don't you?" Mrs. West fixed her with small, shrewd eyes. "I thought you knew him."

Blythe shook her head. "No, I never had t'pleasure."

"Pleasure. Ha. Well, let me tell you, no man deserves to die as he did, not even him. And she didn't even have the courtesy to wait till his body was cold, either."

Blythe leaned forward, intrigued. "My husband said Mrs. Miller is a beautiful woman."

The cleaver came down again. "Mrs. Selley, she is now, and aye, she's well enough. If you like the type. Miller was a fool to marry her."

"Oh, but surely ye're too hard on 'er."

"Am I?" Mrs. West stared at her. "Would you like it, then, if she came in here and flirted with your husband?"

Blythe didn't have to feign indignation. "I should say not!"

"Didn't think so." She nodded. "Well, she did, and with anything else in pants. Many's the fight they had over it, too."

"Did she kill 'im?"

"Her? No. Wouldn't get her hands dirty, No, 'twas some actor fellow."

"An actor! Was he her lover, too?"

"Are you well?"

Blythe coughed. That had been a difficult question to ask. "Yes, nowt wrong, just went down the wrong pipe. Was the actor her lover, too, then?"

"Him? No. Least I never saw him around here. No, he had some kind of business with Miller. Borrowed money, I heard, and couldn't pay it back. And he was found with the knife in his hand."

"Oh." Blythe sat back. What Simon had told her was true, then, as far as it went. "It must have been a shock."

"That it was, and a scandal. Never seen St. Martin's Church so filled as it was for his funeral. Even Viscountess Stanton showed up, aye, as well she should, all the business she did with him, and some heathen-looking foreigners. If they hadn't caught the actor, I'd say they did the deed, that I would. Nasty-looking fellows."

"Oh?" Blythe said. Now, who could this be? Someone else Miller had dealt with? "I wonder if—"

"Are ye better, wife?" Simon's voice boomed from the doorway. "We'd best be off. Seems we came this way for nowt."

"Oh." Blythe let her hand drop from her heart; he had startled her. "Yes, I am well, Mr. Bowles."

"Good. Good. Come along, then. We've trespassed enough upon these good people."

"Mind you take care of her," Mrs. West scolded. "Breeding is a difficult time for a woman. And if you take ill again, just you come to me." She patted Blythe's hand. "I've some herbs will set you up, right as rain."

"Thank you," Blythe stammered. "I'll do that."

"Come, wife," Simon said, and led her out of the shop.

In the lane, Blythe scrambled to keep up with Simon's long strides. His shoulders were squared and his expression was, for the first time since she'd met him, hopeful. He'd learned something, and though she wondered what, she also wished he would acknowledge her own efforts. Just a little. "Do you intend to drag me all over Canterbury?" she demanded, digging in her heels. "If so, I may just as well stay at home."

Simon turned, frowning. "There's no time! I have to find someone West told me about."

"And that is why you wouldn't let me stay? Simon, I was just about to find out about some people Miller traded with. Someone from a foreign country."

"Dark, heathenish men?"

"Yes." She gripped his hand. "West told you. Are they here?"

"Aye, at the King's Head Inn, but not for much longer. They return to Persia tomorrow."

"Persia."

"Aye. Miller dealt with Oriental goods."

"Simon." She ran a few steps, catching up with him again. "Do you really think they're involved?"

"I don't know. All West could tell me was that the day before Miller died he and these men had a quarrel. A regular row, so I understand. And you heard West say that Miller was a hard man in business."

"With a young wife."

"Yes, so?"

"Who liked to flirt with other men, and who remarried in haste."

That made him stop at last. "And it was his wife's knife—that's bloody marvelous!" Swinging about, he caught her around the waist, lifted her into the air, and planted a sound kiss on her mouth. "Marvelous." He dropped her to her feet and started off, apparently as oblivious to her bemusement as he was to the amusement or shock of people passing by. Blythe, whose lips still tingled, was not so lucky. She stood on the cobblestoned lane, hand to her lips, realizing for the first time the enormity of what she had taken on. She loved him. Oh, she loved him, but his affection came in careless kisses and caresses. If she stayed with him things would never change. They had been together now for weeks, and even during their most intimate moments he'd held himself aloof from her. He didn't need her, not the way she needed him, and that hurt. Oh, it hurt, and yet how could she leave?

Simon had finally stopped, a few paces ahead, and was looking back at her. "Are you coming?" he called impatiently.

"Yes," she said, and moved at last. Of course she would stay. She had no choice, not with her whole being urging her to go to him, and if she stayed, she would do her all to prove his innocence. The alternative was unthinkable.

Honoria stood at the wide leaded window, gazing out at a dreary day. Though it was summer, all was gray, with fog that had rolled in from the coast last evening and had yet to burn off. The sounds of waves, from the Straits of Dover, hidden by the fog, were faint, distant, ominous. Honoria's hands clenched, her nails digging into her palms. Home again, she thought ironically. Home to Moulton Hall.

Turning from the window, she gazed for a moment at the portrait of her husband's grandfather, the third viscount, and then drifted to a chair. She hated Moulton, though it was her husband's principal country estate and was considered quite fine. She hated the dampness, the ever-present fog, the old-fashioned brick house. She hated the reminders of previous occupants that, unlike Stanton House in London, remained by express order of the viscount. She hated being away from town, away from the games of chance she loved so well, though even she knew it was for the best. Not only had the tradesmen become importunate of late with their bills—as if she cared!—but she needed to be here for the endeavor in which she was engaged. It was crucial that she behave as she always had, so that no blame, not the merest breath of suspicion would attach to her. Not that it would. Matters, however, had not gone as planned recently. It was best to be prepared.

There was a knock on the drawing room door, and Goodfellow, their butler, entered, holding a silver tray. "Your pardon, my lady. This just arrived for you."

She nodded, taking the letter from the tray and recognized at once the black, slanting handwriting. Quentin. Her lips tightened. In the past he had come to her with news. Now he sent letters, which could so easily fall into the wrong hands. And since he hadn't the courage to face her, she suspected she would not like the letter's contents.

She didn't. After letting out a tiny breath of relief that apparently no one had tampered with the wax seal, she unfolded the letter and scanned it quickly. Quentin was writing, in haste, from Maidstone. He had good information that their merchandise had been shipped to Margate and might be exported. He would endeavor to learn the details. He remained, obediently hers, her servant, & C., Quentin Heywood.

In spite of her annoyance, Honoria smiled. A nice touch, calling the actor merchandise, and thus transforming potentially dangerous news into something innocuous. Still, it would not do to leave this letter lying about for anyone to see.

Honoria dropped the paper into the fireplace, alight on this cold, damp day. The flames flared briefly and then lowered again, the letter transformed into ash. One less danger. The real danger remained, however.

If the actor left the country, that would be just as well. Not so final, perhaps, but he would be unlikely ever to return. If he did not leave, if Quentin at last managed to catch him, then he would be arrested and would meet his fate, perhaps there in Margate. She frowned. An odd place for him to go from Maidstone, through which she had passed on her recent journey from London. The Channel ports were closer. In fact . . . She frowned. Quentin had been wrong in the past. He might be wrong again.

Whirling about, she strode across the room and tugged on the bellpull. Quentin had outlived his usefulness and was fast becoming a nuisance. Nor was he her only tool. Though this was her husband's estate, there were those on the staff who were loyal to her.

The door opened behind her. "Goodfellow, have Crenshaw sent to me," she ordered crisply.

"Crenshaw?" a bemused voice said, and she turned to see a man of middling height, with middling brown hair thinning on top and bits of hay clinging to his undeniably rustic coat. Edward Vernon, the Viscount Stanton—her husband, God help her. He looked like a farmer, which was, she thought dispassionately, exactly what he was. She wished she'd known that when she married him. "What do you want with Crenshaw?"

"I've an errand for him in Canterbury," she lied smoothly, as she had so many times before.

"Extraordinary. Why not send one of the footmen, rather than outdoor staff? I'll tell you, Honey, I can't spare a man from the fields this time of year."

She smiled brightly, hating the silly little nickname her husband persisted on using. "Perhaps I'll do so. I didn't expect you."

" 'Tis time for nuncheon." He held out his arm. "Are you ready?"

Honoria let her gaze go blank as she quickly reviewed her plans. If all went well, the actor would not set foot in Margate, the continent, or anyplace else ever again. "Yes, I am ready," she said, and allowed him to lead her to the dining room.

Chapter 21

"I still don't understand why I can't go," Blythe said, watching as Simon bundled his clothing together.

"I told you, princess." He frowned as he placed the clothes in a battered leather bag. " 'Tis likely to be dangerous."

As if she hadn't already encountered danger. "Two foreign tradesmen? What danger could they be?"

"Two heathen foreign tradesmen, who might have borne some ill will against their friend Miller." He straightened. "Remember, the knife used on Miller was imported."

"Yes, and it belonged to his wife. Simon, I really think you should look at her."

"She's likely to recognize me, princess." He closed the bag. "If these tradesmen had still been at the King's Head Inn I'd agree with you, but it sounds as if they're making for London. I'd like to speak with them while I've the chance."

"Bad luck that they left this morning."

"Yes, but at least they didn't head for the continent." He glanced up and smiled. "Don't worry, Blythe. Nothing will happen to me."

Blythe, sitting on the one chair in the cramped bedroom, propped her chin on her hand as she watched him finish his preparations. Most probably he would come out of this particular adventure unscathed. He had, after all, managed quite well before abducting her. Yet since then they'd rarely been apart, and then she had been the one to leave. Waiting for his return would be difficult. "You will come back, won't you?"

Simon straightened. "Of course I will. Why shouldn't I?"

"If you find these men and they did have something to do with Miller's death, you'll be free."

He frowned. "Not quite. There's the small matter of proving they were involved."

"Yes. But after that, you'll be free to do what you want."

He gazed at her a moment and then swiftly crossed the room to her, going down on one knee. "I'll come back for you," he said, hauling her into his arms. "I promise you that."

"Just you make sure you do." Her fingers dug into his shoulders. "I've been through quite enough with you, Mr. Woodley."

"So you have." He pulled back, studying her face. "Of course I wouldn't leave you alone, Blythe. I'll make sure your name is cleared, too."

"Oh."

"Is that all you have to say? 'Oh?'"

She focused on his cravat in an effort to hold back the tears. "Yes." Because she should know better by now, she really should. Her usefulness to Simon would end once he resolved his problems. She was a chance-met companion on his road, nothing more.

"For the Lord's sake, Blythe, isn't that what you want?"

"Yes," she said again, still not looking at him.

"The hell it is," he growled, and brought his mouth down on hers. She jerked back, made a startled little noise, but quickly cooperated, opening her mouth to his ravaging tongue, clinging to his neck. And then, as quickly as he'd started it, Simon ended the kiss, breaking away and yet still holding her. "Ah, Blythe, if I could give you what you want . . ."

"I know," she gasped, and clutched at his shoulders, her whole being on fire from that kiss. *Stay with me. Love me.*

"I can't, Blythe. I don't know what the future holds."

Her fingers touched his cheek as he pulled back again. "But you'll come back?"

"I promise. I must go." He bent his head, and this time the kiss was quick and hard, leaving her shaken and exasperated. Oh, no, not this time. She grasped at his neck, holding him to her, and this time she was the one in control, she was the one whose lips moved and suckled and coaxed. With a growl Simon hauled her into his arms, and they toppled together to the floor, his hands roving over her body, her fingers grasping, greedy. She shifted so that he lay atop her, his desire for her pulsing against her stomach, and let herself melt. This was right. This was good.

"Sweet Jesus." Simon reared up, hair on end, breath coming in gasps. "We can't do this, Blythe."

"Why not?"

"On the floor? When I must leave? No." He rose on shaky legs. She watched him for a moment, lips tight, and then sat up, smoothing her skirts. He was right, curse him. "But when I come back . . ."

"I'll be here," she whispered, and watched as he grabbed his valise and stalked from the room.

Blythe closed her eyes, put her fingers to her lips, swollen and hot to the touch. His. With that kiss, he had made her his, and there was nothing she could do to change it. For the rest of her life she would belong to a laughing-eyed rogue. It was not what she had expected.

Frowning, she let her hand drop. No, it wasn't what she'd planned, but it was what she had. Simon seemed to be a decent man, except for his conviction for murder. Rather a large exception, she thought, but that was of no importance, either. Whether or not he had committed the crime for which he nearly had hanged, she loved him. She always would. Perhaps she always had.

That bit of self-knowledge made her squirm. She liked to think of herself as virtuous, and certainly no good woman would love a convict. But there it was. She was his, heart, soul, and body, if only he would claim her. If only he loved her. And because she did love him, she could not sit idly by while he took the risks in this venture. Her future was at stake.

Sometime later Blythe stood across from a rambling old house, its windows and walls covered by rose vines, on St. Peter's Street, the main road into the city. It was where Miller's widow, now Mrs. Selley, lived, and it was a distance, in more ways than one, from the narrow lane where Miller had once had his shop. Blythe was again subtly disguised, her hair neatly covered by a lace-trimmed cap under a huge bonnet. Beneath the padding at waist and arms that made her appear stout she was sweating, for it was a warm day. She also had no idea what she would do next. The purpose that had driven her here was gone, leaving in its place uncertainty. It was all very well for her to decide to investigate Mrs. Selley, but just how was she going to do so? She could hardly knock on the door and proclaim her purpose. Nor did a suitable identity come to mind. Simon could present himself as a tradesman, but who would believe a woman in the role? And she could hardly claim to be an old neighbor or acquaintance.

She was still dithering when the door to the townhouse opened and two women stepped out. Mrs. Selley, by her dress, Blythe thought, stepping back, and her maid. The former widow wore a richly embroidered shawl tossed over her gown of fine-looking green broadcloth, and blond curls peeked out from under the brim of her peacock-blue bonnet. No mourning for her first husband, apparently. Glancing along the street to make sure she wasn't noticed, Blythe fell into step behind the two women.

They set a quick pace, never looking back, so that Blythe found it relatively easy to follow them. Since Mrs. Selley had her maid with her, Blythe doubted she was involved in anything clandestine, but anything she could learn would help. Traffic increased as the three of them, Blythe trailing, crossed the King's Bridge over the Stour and entered the High Street. There were more vehicles in the road, more people along the walkway. Blythe dodged carts and people alike, glad of the camouflage they provided, glad as well that Mrs. Selley wore such a distinctive bonnet. Here the tall medieval buildings pressed even closer together, many housing a variety of shops. Mrs. Selley passed them all with no signs of shopping. Where on earth were they going?

Onto Guildhall Street now; to the right and ahead, the mismatched towers of the cathedral loomed ever larger against the pewter-dull sky. The flow of people was much greater here, and Blythe was hard-pressed to keep her quarry in sight. She would like to see the cathedral someday, she thought wistfully. It would make her pilgrimage complete.

A man unexpectedly bobbed up before her. Startled, she sidestepped, and he did, too. "Oh!" she exclaimed, stepping the other way, but the man had the same impulse, blocking her way yet again. "For mercy's sake—"

"Stay still, little lady." His voice boomed out, genial and amused. "If one of us would just be still we can both make progress."

Blythe stood on tiptoe, trying in vain to see past the bulk of his shoulder. "If you would just please move . . ."

The man swept her a low bow, still grinning. "My apologies," he said, and stepped aside, just as Blythe decided to get past him yet again. "Now we can both be on our way."

She nodded, too concerned about her task to pay him much heed. The way ahead was clear. She could continue, except for one problem. The peacock-blue bonnet was no longer in sight.

Frantic, Blythe ran forward, searching, searching. A horn blared to her right; she jumped back just as a coach rattled by, the driver vigorously blowing the long tin horn and the people riding atop glancing down at her curiously. She'd lost her quarry. Mrs. Selley was gone—no, wait! Wasn't that her bonnet? Blythe glanced in both directions and then dashed across the road into a narrow street. Yes! There under that gateway, hemmed in by a crowd of people, bobbed a bonnet exactly like the one she had been following.

Blythe went through the gate into the cathedral yard at a less than worshipful pace, afraid of losing her quarry. Reaching the west entrance, she took a deep breath and plunged into the cathedral, a pilgrim on a quest for she knew not what.

Quentin glanced out the narrow barred window, seeing only a paved courtyard and the feet of passersby. Not a pleasant view, but then, Maidstone's gaol was not a pleasant place, he reflected, turning and facing the room's other occupant. The room was dark and drab and bare, save for a stool and one straight chair. The cells must be truly uncomfortable, if this visitor's room was any indication.

Henrietta Woodley stood in the middle of the room, head down, fingers knotting together. A most resourceful girl. Quentin had believed her when she said that her cousin had gone to Margate. More fool, he. What he had allowed himself to forget was that he was dealing with actors—low, cunning people who thought little of telling lies. He would not make that mistake again.

"You are quite good at your trade," he began, pleasantly enough. Her head twitched, but otherwise she showed no response. "I believed you, you know. Come, no need to stand there like that. Sit down." He took the chair, frowning a little when she continued to stand, very still, very quiet. The chair was old, unsteady, feeling as if it might give way under him at any moment, but still Quentin sat, one leg crossed comfortably over the other. Let her stand, then, like an abject penitent. It gave him a measure of power.

"You're quite clever," he went on, "telling me something I knew would be a lie, so I would think I'd forced the truth from you. I would have believed you, too, if"—he held up a finger—"there was the slightest sign of your cousin in Margate. But there wasn't." He let a moment pass in silence. "He was never there, was he?"

Henrietta raised her head at last, weary lines that were not an actor's illusion underscoring her eyes. "No," she admitted, pushing back her heavy hair. Not very remarkable hair, really, rather a pale brown and straight, and yet even in this dank gaol it shone. She wasn't pretty; she was too tall, too sturdy, for that, but she was striking. Under other circumstances Quentin might have found her admirable.

"I thought not. Where is he?"

She pushed her hair back again. "I really don't know," she said tiredly. "No, really, I don't. I know where he said he was heading, but that was days ago."

"And that was? Come, you'd best tell me," he went on, as she hesitated. "I can make life quite uncomfortable for you. And your parents."

Something sparked in her eyes and then was gone. "He mentioned the Channel ports." Her voice was low, defeated. "Dover, of course, but he thought he might go to Rye, or Deal, if he had to."

"Ah." Quentin sat back, arms crossed, regarding her with narrowed eyes. Her answer had the ring of truth, but he would not be so easily gulled this time. "Am I to believe you, just like that?"

She sighed. "I've no proof, of course, nothing written. Only my word." Her mouth quirked. "And I know what you think of that."

In spite of himself, Quentin bit back a smile. She was brave, he'd say that for her. "Not very highly, I will admit. Tell me. If I question your parents, will they say the same?"

"I doubt it."

"Really." He steepled his fingers. "Would that be because you're all lying?"

Her eyes flashed. "They will lie to you, yes. They'll do anything they can to protect him. Anything." Her voice was bitter. "He's the son they never had."

Quentin's interest rose, though he was careful to keep his face expressionless. "They'll protect him, you mean."

"Yes. No matter what it means to me." All at once

she sank onto the stool, shoulders slumped, lips set. "I'm not a boy, you see."

"Ah." And he was beginning to see. The united front the Woodleys presented had cracks in it, after all. "So you were named after your father," he mused, "yet you're not a son."

"No. Not a son to carry on the grand Woodley theatrical tradition. Women might go on the stage, but heaven forfend they become managers."

"I see." He pursed his lips. "So 'tis safe to say you dislike your cousin."

"Oh, no." She raised her head. "I like him well enough. I just wish . . ."

"What?" he prompted.

Her head was lowered. "It matters not."

"But it does. Come, tell me."

"Why?" She stared directly at him. "What can our family concerns have to do with you?"

"More than you might think." For if he could widen the crack between her and her parents, he would have an advantage over them. "What is it you wish? That he be captured? That he be hanged, and—"

"No!" she burst out. "Not that. I just wish he'd go away and leave my parents to me!" Her hand flew to her mouth and she stared at him, eyes stark. "Oh, no."

"I see," he said again, and leaned back, vastly satisfied. "So you will tell me, then, where your cousin is."

She stared at him a moment longer and then looked away. "Will you let my parents go?"

"Mayhap. Where is he?"

She sighed. "I told you. He made for Dover." She pushed her hair back again. "There's an inn where we've stayed, the George. I doubt he'd go there, yet he might."

"Ah." The truth, at last. "And the woman?"

"Miss Marden? She went with him, poor thing."

He paused in the act of rising. "Why do you say that?"

"She's quite besotted with my cousin, 'tis plain to see. And 'tis just as plain that he's using her." Her mouth twisted. "Do you know that he abducted her off a London street? That is what he is like. He will use anyone to his own ends."

"Interesting. Of course, she didn't have to stay with him."

"She had no choice. He couldn't let her go. Please, I've told you what I can. Please set my parents free."

"How would he keep her with him?" he asked, ignoring her plea. "By force?"

"I—" She stopped, eyes closed. "Maybe. Did he . . ."

"Did he what?" he asked, when she stopped.

"Did he kill that man?" she whispered.

"Miller?" In spite of himself, surprise crept into his voice. "Don't you know?"

"Lord, help me." She bit her lip. "No."

"Ah." Interesting, that, that Woodley's own family apparently thought it was possible he was guilty. It would make his eventual capture that much more plausible.

Quentin turned and strode toward the door. "Guard!" he called through the barred opening. "I wish to go now."

"Am I free?" Henrietta asked behind him.

"Free?" He turned, lips twisted. "Of course not. Until I find Woodley, you're too valuable to let go."

"But I told you what you wanted to know!"

"If it proves to be true, perhaps you won't be prosecuted for aiding a criminal."

"But my parents—you said you'd let them go."

Keys jingled in the door, which then swung open. "I've changed my mind. Adieu, Miss Woodley," he said, and swept through the door.

And, left alone in the dark, drab room, Henrietta at last allowed herself to smile.

Blythe plunged through the doors into the great Cathedral of Christ and found herself in the nave. It was swarming with people, most grouped across the nave near the stairs, and it was hard to see any one person. But there was that peacock-blue bonnet, its feather plume a jaunty signpost that was somehow more conspicuous than it had been in the street. Setting her lips, Blythe followed. She would find out what the widow Miller, now Mrs. Selley, was about, no matter what it took.

Past the screen, and into the choir. There were more people here, but the space was so huge the crowding was lessened. Blythe hastily stopped to admire a stained-glass window as the woman in the blue bonnet paused to speak to a man. It was a strange and yet elegant place for a meeting. An assignation in a cathedral seemed blasphemous, and yet who in this crowd would note two people meeting as if by chance? And who would notice if Blythe moved close enough to overhear their conversation?

She had just taken a step forward when Mrs. Selley nodded at the man and then continued on her way. Blythe frowned; where was Mrs. Selley's maid? And when had she misplaced her shawl? She had to step aside as the man walked toward the exit and past her. Not an assignation, then; it was too brief, and Mrs. Selley was continuing on deeper into the cathedral. What could she be doing?

Abruptly Mrs. Selley stepped into a pew from the aisle, sat for a moment, and then knelt forward, hands clasped, head lowered. Blythe gazed at her in blank astonishment. The woman was praying. Not so very remarkable, considering that worshipers filled other pews, but of all possibilities Blythe hadn't expected this. Baffled, she slipped into a seat a few rows back and prepared herself to wait.

And wait, and wait. Whatever cause Mrs. Selley prayed for was evidently important. It was a good quarter hour before she rose. Blythe, her own knees cramped, stayed where she was; she would continue her pursuit once Mrs. Selley passed her. She was startled, then, when after hesitating a moment the other woman walked purposely toward the altar. There was something different about her, Blythe thought, rising, but she had little time to speculate. Somehow she had to meet the woman.

Her chance came sooner than she expected. To the

side of the altar, Mrs. Selley paused briefly at the bottom of a short flight of wide, worn stone steps. There was a small knot of people there, looking at the effigy of a knight at the top of the stairs or at something else that was beyond Blythe's vision. Confident that Mrs. Selley would climb those stairs, Blythe walked forward and thus was startled when the woman abruptly turned, nearly colliding with her. Blythe realized two things in that moment: She had been caught at her game; and the woman she followed was not Mrs. Selley, but a stranger.

"Oh!" she exclaimed, and stepped back. The woman caught her arm, and of a sudden Blythe recognized her. It was the maid who had earlier accompanied Mrs. Selley. "Excuse me," she said, trying to pull away. "Do I know you?"

"That's just what I was wondering." The woman glowered at her. She was tall and big-boned, dressed in a plain black gown, with the bright bonnet looking absurd on her. Not that Blythe would say so. The woman's grip was hard, and her expression fierce. "You were following us."

Blythe's surprise wasn't completely feigned. "I beg your pardon?"

"I seen you, you know. Behind us, back on Guildhall Street."

Blythe let out her breath. "I rather wondered if you had."

"You admit it, then?"

"Being behind you? Certainly, but not following you—"

"Not me. My mistress. You thought I was her, didn't you, because of the hat?" She grimaced. " 'Twas my idea to wear it. Silly thing, but it served its purpose. You even followed it to the shrine."

Blythe craned her head to see past the woman, briefly diverted. "Is that the shrine?"

"Huh. As if you didn't know. What I want to know is what you were following us for in the first place."

Blythe thought quickly. No good denying it; the maid wouldn't believe her. No good, either, trying to discover where Mrs. Selley had gone. And how was she ever to escape this woman, who continued to hold her arm in a death grip? "I fear your mistress is in danger," she blurted out.

"Danger?" The maid's eyes narrowed.

"No, 'tis true. I fear—what is your name?"

"Nancy."

"Nancy. I fear that there are those who would prove her responsible for her husband's death. The late Mr. Miller, that is."

"Huh. And who would think that?"

Who would? Blythe thought. "Lady Stanton," she improvised wildly.

Nancy drew back, her teeth suddenly bared. "The viscountess! Yes, I'd believe it of her."

"Yes, yes, I can see you're acquainted with the lady," Blythe babbled. The Viscountess Stanton? What had ever made her come up with that name? She'd never heard of the woman—ah. Wait. Hadn't Mrs. West mentioned her? But why, why? "Proper upset she was, all the business she'd done with Mr. Miller, and she wants what's coming to her."

"What's coming to her? Huh! She's the one who owes the money."

" 'Tis not what I've been told."

"No? How do you know so much about this?" Nancy's eyes narrowed. "And how do you know what Lady Stanton is doing?"

Blythe looked down at her hands. "Because she hired me to follow you."

"You!" Nancy suddenly released her arm.

"Yes." Blythe glanced about. "But this is not the place to discuss this. No telling who's listening."

Nancy eyed her for a moment and then nodded. "True. That woman has spies everywhere."

Did she, indeed? Intriguing. Who *was* this Viscountess Stanton? "Then let us go outside and I shall explain."

"You had better," Nancy said, so grimly that Blythe's heart clenched. Oh, yes, she had best invent some suitable tale for the nonsense she'd been spout-

ing. Nancy, hulking large beside her, was not a woman
to be trifled with. How had Blythe ever mistaken her
for the dainty Mrs. Selley?

Sunlight hit Blythe full in the face as the two women
left the cathedral, making her blink. "Along here,"
Nancy said, pulling Blythe into the cathedral yard.
"Not so many people. Now"—with a push from her
meaty hand, she shoved Blythe down to sit on a
bench—"explain yourself."

Blythe looked up at Nancy's stern, uncompromising
face and then quickly away. Look meek, she told herself, folding her hands in her lap. "I am Lady Stanton's companion," she said, and the quaver in her
voice was not feigned.

"Yes, so?"

"I must do what she bids or I will be turned off."

"Huh. I'd think that would be a relief."

"Oh, no!" Blythe looked up, face earnest. "You see,
we are distantly related. My mother was her father's
second cousin twice removed, a Remington, you
know."

"For all I care."

"Yes, well, there weren't so many of us, and now
most are gone. Lady Stanton took me in as her
companion."

"Hard on you," Nancy commented, sitting at last.

"More than you can guess." Much more. "She was
quite upset when Mr. Miller died, and more upset
when the man who killed him escaped." She dared a
glance at Nancy. "Have you heard of that?"

"Who hasn't? Go on. Though I'm not sure I believe
any of this faradiddle."

"Well, you see, she thought he'd come here."

"Why?"

"Well, to . . ." Blythe looked away. "You know. To
see Mrs. Selley."

"Why would he do that?"

"Because he and she were . . . well, you know."

"No. Wait. Are you implying they were lovers?"

Blythe winced. "Yes. Something like that."

"Missish little thing, aren't you?" Nancy sounded

amused. "Well, you're out there. Mrs. Selley wouldn't have nought to do with that Woodley fellow, him being an actor and all. Though I'll allow as to how he's good-looking enough."

More than enough, Blythe thought. "Yes. Well. That is what Lady Stanton told me. But now I can go back and tell her she was wrong, and that Mrs. Selley didn't conspire against her husband. She'll likely turn me off," she added gloomily.

"Wait. What is that you said?" Nancy demanded.

"What? That I'll be turned off?"

"Before that. Are you daring to suggest that Mrs. Selley had something to do with her husband's death?"

Blythe shrugged. In for a penny, in for a pound. Nancy was likely to crush her with those huge hands, at any rate. "It was her knife that was used," she said in a very small voice.

"Not because she was there, I can tell you that! No, she was in the country visiting family. I was with her. And a rude shock it was, to come home and find what we found."

Blythe looked up. "You were with her?"

"Yes, didn't I just say so?"

"Oh, dear." Blythe sank her chin into her hands, not needing to pretend to be vexed. If Nancy was telling the truth, Mrs. Selley could not have killed her husband. "Lady Stanton will not be pleased."

"That's no never mind to me. Now, look." Nancy rose, looming over Blythe. "Just you leave Mrs. Selley alone, do you hear? There's been enough talk. Next you know, someone will say Mr. Selley had something to do with it. And, no, before you say a word"— Nancy glared at her—"he was in London at the time."

"Oh." Blythe sank her chin into her hands again, this time in genuine dejection. She had set out to learn what she could about Mrs. Selley, and so she had. Unfortunately, the information was of no help to Simon. "I shall just have to tell Lady Stanton, then," she said, sighing.

"You do that." Nancy nodded once, emphatically.

"Tell her as how Mrs. Selley is innocent. Poor thing, she's the one who's suffered most because of this. Her and that baby."

Blythe looked up. "Does she have a child?"

"No, not her, poor thing." Nancy's face softened, looking almost sympathetic. "The little boy who now must live with the shame of what his father did."

Blythe frowned. "I'd not heard of a child being involved."

"No, 'tis not commonly known. I know because of working in Mr. Miller's house. 'Tis why Woodley borrowed money, to support him."

Blythe went very still. "To support . . ."

"People like that, what can you expect?" Nancy shrugged and turned. "Mind you, leave Mrs. Selley in peace, now."

"I—this child—who is his father?"

Nancy stared at her as if she were daft. "Weren't you listening? 'Tis Woodley, of course."

Chapter 22

The sun was just sinking behind Canterbury's West Gate when Simon returned to his lodging. It had been a long trip, and fruitless, and yet he felt almost cheerful. Optimistic. As if he were coming home to joy and peace and acceptance, rather than having to face again the fact that the circumstances surrounding him were very dark indeed.

His journey as a merchant traveling to London had turned into the chase of a very wild goose. It seemed at first as if he would never encounter the two men he sought, the Persians who had done business with Miller and might be connected with his death. But he had, finally, at the Crown Inn in Rochester, of all places. What he had never expected was that he might know the two men. What he had never really thought was that they might not be Persian at all, but rather actors he'd met in his early days in the theater.

They were an agreeable pair of rogues, these two, done up with butternut staining their skin and poorly made black wigs tossed upon the table, disclosing their real hair color of sandy brown or fading blond. Acting hadn't paid, they'd explained, passing around a bottle of port with a freeness no true Muslim would ever have shown. Each of them having a flair for accents, and people being so easily fooled, they'd decided to pass themselves off as travelers from far-off lands, selling trinkets for exorbitant sums. Miller! Oh, yes, they remembered him. He'd taken one look at their stock of brass and glass and sent them packing. Most people weren't so knowledgeable, though. Paid well, it did, to be a foreigner. They were content, and their wives, back in London, were glad to see both their money and their backsides when they left. For themselves there were always women fascinated with men from strange lands, with their exotic ways of making love. Oh, and hadn't Woodley run into a spot of bother last year? How had that turned out?

Simon, draining the last of his port, had managed to smile and imply that his arrest and subsequent trial had been mere trifles. He had left the pair with mutual expressions of friendship and congeniality, and only when he was retracing his steps to Canterbury did it hit him. Two days gone, and he'd not learned any more about Miller's death. Time was running short.

Now he was back, with little to show for his efforts. It was looking more and more as if he wouldn't be able to clear his name, which meant that he'd best start thinking of how to leave the country. Not with Blythe, though that thought made him stop dead on the stairs, feeling as if a fist had been driven into his stomach. If he left the country, he would never see Blythe again. Aye, and why should that matter? They were chance-met companions, with only circumstance to keep them together. He'd known that from the beginning. Once this adventure ended, no matter how it ended, they would each go their separate ways. It was the best thing. If that was so, though, why did it feel so wrong?

There was light glowing under the door of Blythe's chamber. So she was not yet abed. He hesitated, hand on the door handle, and then went in. She was sitting across the room near the candle, stitching some article of clothing. At the sight of her, something settled into place within him. He was home.

Blythe looked up from the shift she was mending. Simon was back. She'd heard his voice belowstairs; followed in her mind his every step; bit her lips as he hesitated on the landing. Yet she hoped that her face was calm, her manner composed. It was the hardest bit of acting she'd ever done. "You're back," she said, taking another stitch.

"Aye." Simon sprawled on a chair. "And that's a poor greeting."

Was she supposed to jump up and run to him? Oh, no. She would no longer expose herself in such a way. She had been open with him, honest, about her feelings and her life, and all she had received in return were secrets. It hurt. "Did you have any luck?"

Simon was frowning as he sat back, arms crossed on his chest. "None. Oh, I found our foreign gentlemen, but they weren't what they seemed," he said, and went on to relate to her a tale in which wine and the theater held at least as much importance as Miller's death. "So I fear they had nothing to do with it," he concluded.

"Mmm. Neither, I believe, did Miller's widow."

"No?"

"No. She was visiting family in the country when he died."

"But she walked in—"

"She had just returned." One more stitch, and then she knotted the thread and bit it off. "And there are people who can testify."

"Damn." He leaned back again, frown deepening. "How did you find that out?"

Blythe picked up her mobcap, examined it for signs of damage, and then put it down. Her mending was done. There was nothing more she could use as a shield between her and Simon. "I followed her," she said calmly.

"I should have guessed." Simon's frown remained in place, but other than that he seemed not to react. She could tell, though, from the stiffening of his shoulders, from the look in his eyes, that he was angry. An actor he might be, but she was beginning to learn what was artifice, and what was real. "Bloody hell, Blythe, that was dangerous."

"Why?" She faced him calmly, hands folded, and wondered if he, too, could tell she was acting. "There was little chance she'd know me. We had to discover more about her, Simon."

"Not with the chance of being found out. I don't want to land in prison again."

"I was the one taking the chance," she retorted. "Mayhap what I learned isn't helpful, but there's no need for you to cut up at me."

"Bloody hell," he said again, and rose, stalking to the window. "I don't want you in prison, either, Blythe."

"I'm quite safe," she said, almost but not quite soothed by his concern. For there was the small matter of all she didn't know about him, all he had held back from her. "The woman I spoke with is Mrs. Selley's maid. She is a very . . . forceful person." Blythe contemplated her hands. "She told me something interesting."

Simon didn't turn from the window. "What?"

"She told me about your son."

For a long moment Simon didn't move, and then he let out a long, deep breath. "Damn."

"Would you have told me?"

He turned, an odd look on his face. "Is that what matters to you?"

"Simon, after all we've been through, you could have told me. And pray do not tell me it's not my affair. You've made my life your affair."

He glanced away, his mouth tucked back. "Well, it isn't your affair, Blythe. And as it never came up—"

"Oh, of course. An unimportant thing like a child."

"Damn it, Blythe!" he roared, goaded at last. "Don't you understand? I'm a bastard. Do you think I want my son to bear the same shame I have?"

Her breath caught. "Oh. I didn't think of that."

"No," he said bitterly, turning back to the window. "Because you've no idea what it's like."

"No idea?" she blazed, goaded herself. "No idea what 'tis like to wonder about your parents, whether they wanted you or you were an inconvenience? No idea how hard it is to be without a family, never knowing where you belong or to whom? Oh, yes, Simon, I know it all well. Someone had to give me a home. Someone had to remind me all my life that I was a mistake my parents made. No, no one called me bastard. But they might as well have." She leaned her head back, weary from the outburst and the weight of emotions she hadn't even known she felt. "They made me feel that way."

"I'm sorry," Simon said quietly. "I didn't mean to hurt you."

"No?"

"No. I meant . . ."

"What?" she prompted when he didn't go on.

"To protect myself." His smile was sheepish. "I didn't want you to think less of me."

"Because you have a child?"

"No. Because I didn't marry my child's mother."

Blythe leaned forward, chin resting on her fist. "Yet you borrowed money to support him."

"Bloody hell! Who told you that?"

"Nancy. Mrs. Selley's maid. Was that the money you owed Miller when he died?"

"Yes. I . . . yes." He shrugged and dropped into the chair again. "I was in the devil of a coil, Blythe. I'd always been careful, you know—"

"Careful?"

His face reddened. "Yes, well, careful not to have children."

"Oh." Blythe could feel her cheeks going warm as well, but she didn't look away. "Now I understand."

"What?"

"Nothing. Tell me what happened, Simon. I need to know, and I think you need to tell me."

He looked startled at that. "It's not something I can easily discuss, Blythe."

"I know." Sharing himself with her was hard for him; that she had finally learned, though she didn't know the reason for it. "How old is he?"

Simon took a deep breath and let it out again. "Not quite a year," he said, spreading his hands in a gesture of resignation. "I've never seen him."

"What?"

"I've never seen him." He turned away, and she could see through his shirt that his back muscles were knotted and bunched. "Like my father, who, I'm told, never saw me. A proud Woodley tradition."

"Simon—"

"It's not entirely my fault," he went on, as if she hadn't spoken. "And I didn't abandon him by choice. But nevertheless, I've never seen him."

"That must hurt," she said quietly.

Simon's hands gripped the windowsill. " 'Tis better for him. She's married, you see."

"Oh, Simon—"

"She wasn't when I knew her, if that is what you're thinking."

"No, it isn't at all, Simon."

"She was a strolling player. Like me. You know what life on the road is like, Blythe. We became close. And . . . well, things happened. Bloody hell!" He pounded the sill with his clenched fist. "All the time I was careful, and that one time—I offered to marry her. I don't want you to think I'd've abandoned her."

"I don't think that."

"And I knew she'd need money, or rather, that I would. My thinking was muddled. 'Twas why I went to Miller. To borrow money to set up a home. I would have stayed with her, Blythe. We would have made a family."

"I believe you, Simon."

"And so I offered her marriage."

"And?"

"She laughed in my face."

"What? Why, the nerve of her."

"She'd found herself a protector, she said, someone else who could give her a real home, a settled home, not a strolling player with no past and no future. She was tired of the stage and wanted to settle down. And so she married him, her protector. He is a solicitor and does well, so I understand. And to this day he believes the child is his." He paused. "He may well be."

Blythe rose and went to him, laying her hands on his shoulders. Of all the things he had told her, this last must be the most painful. "I'm sorry," she said, resting her face against his back. "So sorry."

"And yet you stay."

"Yes, why shouldn't I?"

He turned his head, and she could see that his face was twisted into something very like a sneer. For himself, though, not for her. "You know the worst of me now, Blythe. That I'm not a father to my child."

And yet he had been accused of killing a man. Oddly enough, that didn't matter so much anymore. He was a good man, a caring man, in spite of the way they had met, in spite of the crime of which he stood accused. "Do you love him?"

Simon's muscles under her cheek tightened. "Aye," he said after a moment. "I do."

"And do you think he's happy?"

"Lord, I hope so!" He paused. "I've heard he is."

"Then you've done what you can for him. He has parents, Simon," she felt him wince, "and a settled home. You did your best for him."

"I wish I could believe that."

"Try," she said, and, going up on tiptoe, pressed a light, nipping kiss to the back of his neck.

He went very still. So did she, aware suddenly of the warmth between them, and of a new tension that had little to do with the past and everything to do with now. "If you don't move, Blythe, I fear I'll take you to bed."

Heat surged through her, and she kissed his neck again, just a bit harder. "Why is it you never carry through on your threats?"

With one swift motion he spun about, first knocking her off balance and then dragging her close to him. He was hard, hot, male, and his every curve and ridge was impressed upon her body. "Why," he said, voice rough but his eyes alight, "do you keep putting yourself into danger?"

She hooked her arm about his neck, undaunted by his fierceness. "Because you always rescue me."

"Blythe." He crushed her to him. "Not this time.

Don't you see? I've no future, no life to give a family, and if there's a babe—"

"There won't be."

"How can you be sure?"

"I'm a doctor's daughter, Simon." She pulled back to see his face. "Is this what's been bothering you?"

"Of course it has. I'll not bring another bastard into the world. Not a child of mine."

"The timing is wrong, Simon." She smiled at the confusion in his eyes, pressed her finger against his lips. "Trust me in this."

His mouth curled around her finger, drew it in, tugged on it, making her breath catch. "Princess, I trust you with my life," he said huskily.

"And you with mine."

He looked down at her for a long moment, and then, without a word, scooped her up into his arms, holding her high against his chest. Blythe burrowed her head against his shoulder. There would be no going back this time. They both knew it, as he carried her across the room. By the side of the high, narrow bed, piled with darned quilts, he let her down, holding her so that she slid against him. There was no doubt what he wanted. What she wanted, as well, though she knew the signs were more subtle. And motivated differently, perhaps. She loved him. Oh, she loved him, though he could never give her the home, the family she needed so much. But perhaps she had a chance. She would love him as he had never been loved. It might be enough.

Simon's mouth came down on hers, hot, heavy, seeking, and she gave herself up to him. His unshaven cheek rasped against her neck, and she arched her head to allow him access. He groaned when her hand wandered over his chest, but he held her there when she would have pulled back. The taut muscles of his shoulders, the soft fullness of her breast, his undeniable desire for her—all became familiar, dear, in that long, hard embrace. When Simon at last let her up for air, his own breath coming in gasps, Blythe clung to him, boneless, liquid, her body melted and molded

against his. If he were to let her go, she would
surely fall.

He did release her, but only for a moment, and only
to tear off his shirt. "Explore your kingdom, princess,"
he murmured, raising her hand to his chest. She let
her fingers roam at will, shivering at the crisp curls of
hair, fascinated by his brown nipples. She wondered
if his were as sensitive as hers were at the moment,
and if he would ever touch her—*ah.* Her head fell
back as he fondled her breast, thoroughly, intimately,
his thumb rubbing again and again over her nipple. A
feeling too intense to be merely pleasure stabbed
through her, and she clutched at him, feeling again his
muscles bunch in response. Why, she could affect him,
too, just as he did her. Delighted to know that, she
gave him a little push, and to her surprise he fell back
onto the bed. She laughed.

"What the . . . If you think you're getting away with
that, you're wrong," he said. He caught her about the
waist, pulling her down atop him, her legs splayed to
either side and her skirts kilted about her waist.
Laughter left her at the feeling of that most masculine
part of him pressed against her so intimately, and her
eyes grew round. "Ah. Much better."

"Simon—"

"Shhh." He was concentrating on the laces of her
bodice. "Not enough light in here to see what I'm
doing. Hell, is that a knot?"

"Where?"

"Here."

She fumbled at the laces and found that he had
indeed tangled them together. "Just a minute."

"I'd rather not wait that long," he said, and with a
quick twist of his hips flipped her over, in charge
again. "If I had a knife . . ."

"Simon Woodley, you've done enough damage to
my clothes. There, it's undone."

"And about time." His fingers, so frantic a moment
earlier, now leisurely resumed their task, plucking at
the laces, pausing to explore the interesting distrac-
tions of her nipples, and then finally, finally pulling

her bodice free. After that, he made short work of her shift; she was twisted and raised and set down again, his body looming above her, the air cool on her naked breasts. She was defenseless before him, and she didn't care. She reached for him as he reached for her, bringing his face down to hers, their mouths meeting just as his hands found her breasts again. She clutched at him against the almost intolerably pleasant sensations his knowing, supple fingers awoke. No words of love from him, no promises; but then, she hadn't expected any. And if she was at last releasing the dream she'd held to for so long, well, that was her choice. She would deal with the consequences later.

She was soft and warm in his arms, and giving, so giving, offering him her body with such unselfish generosity that Simon couldn't help but respond. It had never been quite like this before. Before he'd always held something of himself back. Not this time, though. As he learned through the touch of fingers and tongue what pleased her, what made her respond, his own need grew stronger. He wanted her with an urgency that stunned him, so rare was it, and yet he didn't want to hurry it. He wanted this evening, this moment, to last, to savor her soft skin and the wine-dark taste of her lips, the warmth and the giving that were so very much a part of her. As she gave to him, he wanted to give to her.

Blythe shifted under him restlessly as he toyed with her nipple. "Easy, princess, easy," he murmured, lowering his head.

"Simon." Her fingers tunneled into his hair as his mouth found her breast at last, at last. "Please . . ."

"What, princess?" He raised his head, his eyes gleaming. "What is it?"

"I don't know!" she wailed. "I just know when you touch me like that, I want—I need—"

"Shhh." He drew her against his chest and rocked her, as if for comfort. "We've waited a long time for this, princess." He felt her nod against his shoulder. "We needn't rush."

No need? When her blood ran hot and pulsing in

her veins? Oh, easy for him to say no need, though the hardness of him against her belied that. This was heaven, and it was torture. The feelings rushing through her were like nothing she'd ever felt, not even that time in the forest, when he had first shown her what pleasure could be. Then he had held himself apart; now he was with her, his hands urgent, compelling, drawing from her feelings she had not known she could feel. She wanted them never to end, and at the same time she wanted to be herself again, safe and sane and not at the mercy of her desires. And he— oh, heavens, he was kissing her breast again, drawing her nipple into his mouth. Someone cried out, and she realized dimly that it was she. Her hands explored restlessly over him, his neck, his shoulders, his back, learning him in a way she'd never expected. This was adventure, she thought, and with that the fear left her. Adventure wasn't comfortable, it wasn't something she could control, but it gave her more than safety and sanity ever could. It was terror and excitement and joy, the sheer joy of being alive.

And so when he began to work at the waistband of her skirts, she helped him, laughing a bit when they both fumbled with the laces of her petticoats. She raised her hips to let him draw down her clothing, lost in feeling and yet sharply aware of every sight and sound and touch, all her senses alive. Some more quick fumbling, and she realized that he had discarded his breeches. He was naked against her, hard and hot and gloriously male. Arms about his shoulders, she rolled onto her back, bringing him with her, his hand on her thigh. And his fingers were moving, teasing and tickling along her hip, her stomach—oh, dear heavens, moving downward. Instinctively she tried to press her legs together, but his knee was there between them, opening her for him. The panic she had felt earlier surged through her again, intense, overwhelming. Then he was touching her, his fingers sliding intimately into her, and the fear was gone. "Yes," she gasped against his shoulder, clinging to him, wrapping her leg around his hips. "Now."

He groaned. She was slick and wet and warm, all for him, all for him. The need pounded within him, in his head, in his groin, in his heart. To take her, to give to her . . . and panic surged through him. He'd never quite felt this way before. "We have all night," he managed to answer.

"No, we don't," she said, and grasped his hips with surprisingly strong hands. Need, desire, a yearning he'd never before felt, all warred with the panic and won. He sank slowly, easily into her welcoming warmth.

Blythe stiffened. For a moment she had been in control, but now things were different, now he was inside her and it felt very strange. Hot and urgent and painful, as she stretched to accommodate him, and felt a sudden, tearing ache. She must have made some sound of protest, for he was murmuring something in her ear, soft, silly words of comfort. Gradually the pain ebbed, making her more aware of the very new sensation of being filled by him, of being complete. When he began to move within her she gasped, first from discomfort, and then from something else altogether. There was an ache, a need, that had her holding to him, moving with him, searching for she knew not what. No time for panic now, as his mouth clamped on hers, fusing them together. No time for fear as her hips rose to meet his, faster, harder. She had given herself into his control, trusting herself to his care as she had never before trusted anyone. When she felt the first faint tingles of response, when her body drove her toward completion, she knew, deep in her soul, that this was something she could share only with him. She shattered into a glorious tumult of joy and pleasure and love, crying out, clinging to him, the other half of her. In giving up herself, she had found herself.

And Simon, who rarely shared this moment with any woman, who held himself back always, gave himself to her completely and utterly, and then was still upon her.

"Mercy," Blythe said, a long time later.

Simon lifted his head. It seemed to take a very great effort. He knew not when he had last felt so depleted, so complete. "I trust you aren't begging?"

"What? Oh." Her arms looped about his neck. "Maybe for more."

"Good Lord, Blythe."

"Well?"

"Give me a moment." He rolled onto his side, pulling her close to him, holding her, cherishing her. Who would ever have thought, when he had abducted her on a London street, that ultimately they would come to this? Aye, and come they had, he thought, and chuckled.

Blythe rose onto her elbow. "That sounded very self-satisfied."

"Not just self." In the darkness, his fingers toyed with her hair, thick and yet softer than he'd imagined. "You, too."

"Hmph. You're disgustingly proud of yourself."

"I think I've reason."

Blythe burrowed her head against his shoulder. She thought he had reason, too, but she wasn't about to tell him so. It would only make him more cocksure, she thought, and laughed out loud.

Simon pulled back, as if to look at her. "Are you laughing at me?"

"No. No. Just . . . laughing." She flipped over onto her belly, raising herself on her elbows, her fingertip tracing the outline of his lips. They felt as swollen as hers, she realized with some delight. "And why shouldn't I?"

"When a woman laughs at a time like this, a man can get concerned."

"Don't be." She reached up to kiss him lightly. "You have absolutely no reason to be."

"Compliments, Blythe?"

"Mmm. Maybe."

"Be careful, madam." His hand swept down her back and came to rest on the soft cheek of her buttock. "My head may swell."

"Or some other part," she sputtered, and dropped

her head to his shoulder, shaking with laughter. Mercy! She'd never been like this before, so open, so free, saying what she thought without fear of ridicule or censure. She liked it.

He pinched her, and she yelped. "Witch," he said, but there was laughter in his voice, too. "Have you no concern for my person?"

"Oh, great concern, sir." She tossed her hair over her shoulder. "I am a doctor's daughter, remember, and if there is any swelling I should attend to it."

"Indeed?"

"Indeed."

"Well, then." With one lithe movement he flipped her onto her back, hovering above her. "Madam doctor, there is a part of me that should be attended to."

Blythe's fingers walked along his shoulder. "Oh, really? Is it uncomfortable?"

"Rather."

"Can you describe the symptoms?"

"I believe it would be best if I showed you," he said, and brought her hand to curl and curve about the part of him that was, indeed, swelling and pulsing. She drew back, but his hand held her there. After a moment she relaxed, her fingers moving, seeking, learning. He groaned, the laughter of only a moment before gone.

"I believe I understand your problem," she said, voice shaky. "That does need care."

"What would you suggest, madam doctor?"

She twined an arm about his neck, a leg about his hip. "Me."

"A fine remedy. But, Blythe." His voice was suddenly serious. "Are you not sore?"

"It doesn't matter." She pushed her hair back, grasped his shoulders, and pulled him down to her. "Lay on, Macduff," she whispered, and he let out a laugh. But he was with her again, hers again, and as his mouth took hers, it began anew, the giving, the taking, the trusting, the love. And it was more glorious than ever she had dreamed.

Chapter 23

Dawn light was stealing into the room when Simon awoke, with such a feeling of well-being that he thought he could go out and defeat all of the king's soldiers. Blythe sprawled across him in sleep, one leg over his, her arm flung upon his chest, her head tucked under his chin, where her hair tickled his nose and mouth. Blythe. Had there ever been such a woman, such a night? Twice they had made love—aye, that was what it was, truly—and twice he had lost himself in her utterly. Twice he had courted disaster.

The shining edges of his elation dimmed just a bit. She claimed special knowledge because of her background, claimed that she wouldn't conceive, but what if she was wrong? He had been careless, inexcusably so, not once, but twice. His babe could be growing within her at this very moment.

Fierce joy filled him, but it was fleeting, replaced by his more familiar concerns and fears. Early in his life he had learned to be careful, defensive. Whether he truly was legitimate, the world had judged him otherwise, and the judgment had been harsh. Never before had he been so open with a woman, so giving, and not just because of the fear of creating a child. A fear he'd forgotten in last night's frenzy, and that was unforgivable.

Blythe stirred, her fingers twitching, her legs shifting restlessly. A moment later she raised her head, blinking sleepily at him. "I thought 'twas an uncommonly comfortable mattress," she said, smiling.

He didn't return the smile. "Good morning."

"And good morning to you." She stretched up for

a sleepy morning kiss, pulling back when he didn't respond. "Am I too heavy for you?"

Immediately his arms came about her. He wanted never to let her go. It was wonderful, and frightening. " 'Tis time we should be up," he said, and shifted under her.

Grumbling a bit, Blythe rolled onto her side of the bed, burying her head in the pillow as he rose. But she could still peek through the fingers she held over her eyes, and she did. Heavens, but he was magnificent, long and lean and taut. And he was hers. "Do we really have to get up yet?"

Simon turned, buttoning his breeches, his hair disordered. "Aye, slugabed. We've plans to make."

"Not yet." She held out her arms, aware she was revealing her body to him, and not caring. "Come back to bed."

"Blythe—"

"Please?"

He hesitated, and then crossed the room. To her surprise, though, he sat on the edge of the bed rather than joining her. Something about his face, something about the set of his mouth and the look in his eyes, chilled her, making her pull the sheet she had earlier disregarded closely about her. "Blythe, I think we have to talk."

"About what?"

He glanced away. "About last night. There may be consequences."

That made her sit up, unreasonably annoyed with him. "There won't be," she said, tucking the sheet under her arms and pushing back her hair. "I told you, the timing is wrong."

"Nevertheless. Things happen."

"And if it did? If we had a child, Simon?" Her voice softened. A child. His child. Family, at last. She watched as he rose again. "Would that really be so terrible?"

"Bloody hell, Blythe, you know why I feel this way!" He wheeled on her. "Last night was a mistake."

"Oh."

"Bloody hell," he said again, dropping back onto the bed. "No, it wasn't, Blythe, and I'm sorry I said so."

Blythe had hunched up, knees to chest, face forward, as if to ease the pain. "But 'tis what you feel."

"Not about you." His finger stroked her cheek, a touch that burned her, but not with passion. "Never about you, princess."

She raised her head. "I want children, Simon."

He returned her gaze steadily. "I can't give them to you."

"I see." She glanced away, biting her lip. If she didn't have children with Simon, then she never would. She could not imagine sharing last night's experience with anyone rather than him. He had been warm, caring, giving—but now his mask was back in place. Very well. She could wear a mask, too. "You're right, of course. Our children would be bastards." She used the word deliberately. "And their father a murderer."

"As you're the doxy of a murderer."

She froze. She couldn't let him see how that hurt. "Very well." She raised her face, calm, still. "We've insulted each other. Shall we leave it at that?"

Simon frowned. Good, she'd confused him. "Blythe, I'm sorry. I didn't mean—"

"I know. Neither did I." But he had, and so had she, if only for a moment. "What happened last night, happened." She swung her legs out of bed, wrapping herself in the sheet. Amazing that just a few hours ago she had been so eager, so willing. How very young she had been. How very old she felt now. "We need to decide what we're to do. It doesn't look as if we'll find a way to clear your name."

"I'm not giving up. Blythe—"

"But what will you do?" She pulled her shift over her head and let it drape around her, affording her some protection at last. "We've looked for any enemies Miller might have had and found no one."

"There must be someone. Bloody hell." He turned

to her. "Blythe, I'm sorry. I never meant to let matters go so far."

"But they did." She gazed at him from across the room. "I can't go home, not yet, and I don't wish to leave the country. I think"—she took a deep breath—" 'twould be best if we parted."

He turned sharply toward her. "We can't."

"Why not?"

"Because." He turned back to the windows, fists jammed into the pockets of his breeches, shoulders knotted. "Ah, hell. You can't go."

"Do you fear I'll tell where you are?"

"No! No. 'Tis not that. I know you won't." He turned back to her, his face softer. "Blythe."

Merciful heavens, the way he was looking at her. His eyes were huge and blazing, his mouth working, the yearning in his face so strong it was almost frightening. He wanted her, and not just physically. In that moment she knew, as surely as she'd ever known anything, that in some way he cared for her. Was it enough? It would have to be, she answered herself. "Yes?" she whispered, her mouth dry, her breath caught, as time stilled, waited, for his answer.

He licked his lips and turned away, shrugging. "Where will you go, then?"

She couldn't answer. Not just yet. Nor could she face him. She spun away, arms wrapped about her waist against the raw pain spreading through her. "I'm—not sure."

"If I can help—"

That wasn't pity in his voice, surely. She couldn't bear it if it was. "I don't know what you could do."

"I ruined your life. I'd like to do something to repair that."

"You can't." Dry-eyed, she stared at the wall, feeling rather than hearing him come up behind her. If he touched her, she thought she might shatter. "Everything's changed," she said, moving away, beyond his reach. "Even if I could get a position as a companion, I doubt I'd want it. There's nothing I can do except . . ."

"What?" he asked.

"I could go on the stage." She turned to him, no longer feeling quite so helpless. Her old life was gone, and Simon would never love her as she loved him. Yet in the past months she'd learned something about herself. She'd learned she could stand on her own. She'd learned she had a talent she'd never before suspected. "Yes. I'll go on the stage."

"Blythe, for God's sake, you'll be caught."

She shook her head. "If I join some small touring company that never goes to London? No. I expect I'll be safe enough. Besides, it's not me they want, Simon. You know that."

"It's not the life for you."

"Why isn't it? Simon, I felt comfortable in the theater. Almost like being home. It's not what I ever imagined for myself," she said, smiling wryly, "but 'tis at least something."

"Bloody hell," he said, and pounded his fist into his hand, startling her. "I wish I'd never laid eyes on you."

Her breath drew inward in a great rush. "Simon!"

"Because," he rattled on, "you wouldn't have this trouble now. You'd still have your position, your reputation. You'd be safe."

"It can't be changed, Simon," she said, absurdly touched.

"I know. I know." He turned to face her. "Will you at least let me escort you to wherever you're going?"

"Aren't you staying here?"

He gestured with his hand. "There's nothing here, Blythe. Not for me. We've both tried and found nothing. And the longer I stay, the more chance that I'll be caught."

"What will you do, then?"

"I'll have to leave the country." He smiled, and she thought it perhaps the worst bit of acting she'd ever seen. "If I can. And if I'm taken—"

"No!"

"You'll be safe." His eyes were steady on hers.

"I've a thought. The Rowleys should be at Dover. Why not join them?"

"Simon, won't they be looking for you in Dover?"

"I'll manage somehow." From across the room he watched her, not smiling now. "Shall we do it, then?"

From across the room, she returned his look. This was the end. Perhaps they'd be together a bit longer, but this, now, was the end of anything between them. "Yes," she said, and accepted the inevitable.

Late that afternoon, a tired-looking cart bearing what appeared to be a rustic farmer and his very pregnant wife drew up in the alley beside the King Theater in Dover. "Stay here," Simon said, swinging down to the ground. "I'll seek out Giles and McNally. If I'm not out quickly, you should go."

Blythe, holding the reins to the old swaybacked nag who was tethered to the cart, nodded. It had been a quiet, tense trip from Canterbury, though they'd met with no mishap. Neither had talked, of the past or of the future. Now that the trip was over, now that their time together was ending, Blythe regretted those lost hours. "Don't go," she said impulsively, holding out her hand.

"There's no danger to me here, princess," he said, and turned, ambling toward the stage door.

"That's not what I meant," she called, but too late. He'd gone inside. Too late to tell him she wished him not to leave her; too late to say she wanted to stay with him. The playbills out front attested to the fact that the Rowley troupe was, indeed, playing here this week. If all went well, Blythe would stay at the theater and Simon would be on his way. And she would never see him again.

The stage door banged open again and Simon came out, followed by Phoebe, her brow furrowed. In spite of her misery, Blythe smiled at the small, familiar figure. "Phoebe—"

"Hush, we must get you inside," Phoebe said, as Blythe rose. "The soldiers were here this morning."

Blythe glanced at Simon in alarm as he helped her

down from the cart. Odd, but even through the padding she used to simulate pregnancy, she fancied she could feel the brand of his touch. "Soldiers? Are they here now?"

"No." Simon took her arm, ushering her into the theater. Instantly smells that were strange yet familiar assailed her nostrils: dust, powder, paint, fresh wood. Her tense shoulders eased. She felt as if she'd come home. "But they're keeping watch on the place. No telling when they'll be back."

A door opened before them in the corridor, and a figure stepped out. "In here," Giles said, gesturing into the room. "Best if you're not seen yet."

Blythe stepped into a room containing a table and several straight chairs. Through the dusty window she could just see the alley beside the theater, and the farm cart. "I won't stay if it'll put you in danger."

"Nonsense, lass." Giles grasped her arms, turning her toward him. "A fine disguise," he said, eyes twinkling. "It should serve you well. You look as if you are really in the straw."

"Then she may stay?" Simon broke in.

Giles's face sobered as he looked past Blythe. "Of course she may, and you, too, lad."

"Thank you, but no." Simon reached for his hat. "I've decided it's best for everyone if I leave the country."

"Rest a minute," Giles commanded, and Simon, giving Blythe a glance, took the chair beside her. "The soldiers seemed to expect you'd be here, lad. How did they know?"

Simon shook his head. "I've no idea, but they've been close behind us all along."

"And of course they'd expect him to go to a port town," Blythe put in, disturbed by the look on Giles's face. Something had happened.

"Mayhap that's it, though they acted as if they had some knowledge. Ian's here, by the by."

"What? Has he left the Woodley troupe?"

"No. He brought news. It's not good." Giles braced

his hands on the table. "Your family is in Maidstone gaol."

"Bloody hell!" Simon jumped to his feet, hands balled into fists. "Who? Why?"

"Your uncle and your aunt, and I'm sorry, but Young Harry, too. Ian and the rest were in, but they were let go."

"Damn."

"But why?" Blythe said. "Because they took us in?" If that was so, then she wouldn't stay; the Rowleys would not wish to risk a similar fate. She'd have to go with Simon, she thought, feeling oddly lightheaded at the prospect.

"No." Simon paced a few feet away. "Or not just that. There's another reason." He glared at Giles. "They want me."

Giles nodded. "About what I figured, too."

"Damn," Simon said again, and let out his breath. "There's nothing for it, then. I'll have to turn myself in."

Chapter 24

Silence rang for a moment in the tiny room, and then Blythe got to her feet. "If that is so, then I am going with you," she announced calmly, slipping her arm through Simon's.

He looked down at her. "Why, princess? To tell them how I abducted you, so I'll be punished?"

"No, silly, they'll likely not believe me now, after all this time. And what more can they do to you than they already plan?"

"You'd like to see me hanged, then?"

"Don't be foolish," she said tersely. She may have said so in the past, but no longer. "They want me, too, for helping you. If it means they'll release your family . . ."

"They may not, you know," Giles said almost gently, and they turned to look at him. "Why should they?"

Simon frowned. "Because it's me they want," he repeated. "Bloody hell, Giles, if I leave the country as if this hasn't happened, what will happen to them? Harry and Bess aren't young any longer, and Henrietta—"

"Think, lad," Giles interrupted. "Do you really believe the authorities will let your family go? They aided in your escape. You'll have made a sacrifice for nothing, not to mention Miss Marden."

"She's not coming with me."

"Yes, I am," Blythe put in.

"And don't forget their sacrifice, what they've been through to free you. Do you wish it to go for naught?"

"They shouldn't have to make such a sacrifice."

Simon stared ahead, face bleak. "It didn't work. They've risked their lives for me, and I'm no safer than I was before. I failed." He looked down at Blythe. "I tried to clear my name, and I failed."

"You did what you could," she said.

"It wasn't enough." He straightened, and though he didn't actually pull away from her, his arm was stiff. "I shall have to return to Maidstone."

"Then I'll come with you."

"No, you won't! I won't take you with me, Blythe."

"No?" She looked up at him and nodded, pulling her arm free. "But what is to stop me from going to the authorities here?"

"Blythe—"

"I'll do it, Simon, I swear I will."

"Bloody hell," Simon said into the silence that followed. "You would, wouldn't you?"

She put up her chin. "I would. You'd have me on your conscience then, too. And don't tell me you don't have a conscience."

"The lass is right," Giles said. "There's naught you can do to help your family, and every chance you'll harm them."

Simon rounded on him. "Am I just to run away, then?"

"I wonder," Phoebe said, so diffidently that she had to repeat herself. "I wonder if that won't help."

Giles's face softened. "Why is that, wife?"

"I may be wrong." She peered up through her lashes. "But if the authorities think Simon's left the country, they'll have no reason to hold Harry and Bess."

"I think that may be so," Blythe agreed slowly. "Simon, they could have taken your family anytime. This is a trick."

He stared at her. "Do you seriously think they'll let my family go if I escape?"

"I think there's a chance." She paused. "But they'll still have reason to hold me."

"I think you've no choice," Giles said, as Simon

continued to stare at Blythe. "For the good of everyone concerned, you have to leave."

"We're all in danger if you stay," Phoebe put in.

Simon briefly closed his eyes. He looked tired, defeated, as he had not in all the weeks of their adventure. "Then I'll have to go." He looked at Blythe. "Will you promise me not to turn yourself in if I do?"

She nodded. "I'll do as we planned. If you'll let me stay?" she appealed to Giles.

"Aye, lass, that you can. You've a good disguise just now, too."

Blythe made a face; she'd hoped to be rid of the cumbersome padding and pillow. "When will you go?"

"I don't know," Simon said. "I'll have to find a boat to take me."

"Let McNally do that," Giles put in. "He might be able to find something without alerting anyone."

"I hope so." Simon glanced about at all of them, his gaze softening as it touched on Blythe. What courage she had, offering herself in his place. He didn't deserve it, not any of it. But if she was safe, if she found some measure of contentment, then he was satisfied. He would have to be. "You look tired, princess."

"I should, being eight months gone," she said, managing a smile.

"Come." Phoebe stepped forward. "We'll find a place for you to rest," she said, and led Blythe out, leaving the two men alone.

There was silence for a moment. "Well," Simon said finally.

"That woman loves you," Giles said at the same time.

"Who? Phoebe?"

"Don't be daft, lad. Blythe, of course."

"She does not."

"Of course she does. Why would she go through this, else?"

"Hell," Simon began to protest, when the door from the corridor opened and McNally stepped in. He nodded at Simon, as if they'd only recently parted.

"I've been to the quay," he said without preamble. "Thought I'd check out the lay of the land, so to speak. There are soldiers there."

"What do you think?" Giles asked.

"I think it may be possible." McNally looked at Simon. "If you don't mind some discomfort."

"I'm well aware I'm not the usual traveler, Joseph," Simon said wryly.

"That you're not. Dangerous cargo, but there's them that'll take you, for a price."

Giles nodded. "When?"

"A few days, perhaps. Dark o' the moon is coming up."

"So?" Simon said.

"Smugglers," McNally explained. "They won't go out when 'tis bright."

"Then we'll keep you hidden until 'tis time," Giles decided.

Simon nodded. "I'm sorry I've brought this upon you, Giles."

"Just don't let it be in vain. McNally, find someplace for him?"

"O' course. Come with me, Master Simon, and we'll fix you up."

"Thank you," Simon said, and followed McNally into the corridor, tired, dispirited. His family was in gaol. He had not cleared his name, and now he would have to flee the country. And Blythe loved him. *Bloody hell.* What was he going to do now?

There was still a play to be performed that evening, no matter what dramatic events might be taking place backstage. Blythe, still well padded, was pressed into service as a seamstress and a dresser, helping the actresses with their changes of costume. The troupe knew her, of course, but anyone from the town wouldn't. Simon, whose face was better known from the posters that had circulated, was a different matter. For his safety and that of the troupe, he stayed hidden in the small room Giles used as an office until it would be safe for him to leave.

Blythe, a cloak draped carefully over her arm, scuttled along the corridor from the dressing room as the interval ended and the cast prepared to take the stage again, giving the closed office door a wistful look. She missed Simon. He was still present, still accessible, but she missed him. And this was just a taste of what life would be like once he was gone. When the time came, would she be able to let him go?

Lips set against the pain of that thought, she scurried into the green room and immediately collided with something solid, yet yielding. "I say!" a voice exclaimed, and she stepped back, startled. As he flailed for balance, the man she had struck brushed against her augmented belly, and a puzzled frown passed over his face. "I say," he said again, regaining some of his poise. "I am sorry."

"No, 'twas my fault." Blythe smiled. A quick glance was enough to tell her that this man was of the gentry. His velvet coat was well cut, and his powdered wig fit well to his head. A sponsor, perhaps, and thus someone to placate. "I fear I wasn't watching where I was going."

"Are you a member of the troupe?" he asked, his eyes again flicking down to her stomach and looking confused. They were nice eyes, she thought, warm and dark, and his smile was friendly.

"I . . . yes, among other things. If you'll excuse me?"

"Of course, of course." The man stepped aside, inclining his head. The action triggered a sense of familiarity within Blythe. She'd seen this man before. Hadn't she? But no, she told herself as she hurried to the stage with the cloak. Where would she have had occasion to meet such a person? Not in the theater in Rochester, or at any place since. Yet there was something about him, about the shape of his face, that was familiar. Probably, she thought, fading back into the wings as the cast returned to the stage, she would never know.

The green room was relatively quiet, with the interval ended and the play proceeding again. Tired from the day's events, Blythe looked longingly at the carved armchair set against the wall like a throne. She knew better than to sit in it, though, not after that incident with Odette in Rochester. Instead, she began setting the room to rights, gathering a wineglass here, replacing a cushion there. At the next interval, and after the play, members of the audience would be coming backstage again.

"My dear, what are you doing?" a voice said, and Blythe looked up to see Katherine, offstage now until she was needed again.

"Straightening up. Someone has to do it." Blythe smiled. "I've missed this."

"I'm glad to see you, too, and in such an interesting condition." Katherine cast a glance down at Blythe's distended stomach. "A good disguise, but you need to work on your walk."

"Oh?"

"Yes, you move much too lightly for someone so far along. And you would never be able to bend to pick things up."

"Oh. Well, as it looks as if I might never be like this in real life—"

"Tut, tut, don't say such things! Your life's hardly begun."

Her life would be over once Simon left. She glanced toward the door, as if he were there, and the memory of her earlier encounter returned. "Katherine, there was a man in here during the interval."

"Yes, so?"

"He was familiar, but I don't know when I've seen him before. He's gentry, that much I could tell, and he had very nice eyes. Rather a weak chin, though." She frowned. "And he was wearing a coat of brown velvet. Well cut, but it made him look sallow."

"Sallow skin and a weak chin. Quite an attractive specimen."

"No, really, he was quite nice."

"And I thought 'twas Simon who interested you."

Blythe drew herself up. That was a subject not to be discussed, not even in jest. "Do you know the man I'm speaking of?"

"Yes, I believe I do. It sounds rather like Stanton."

"Stanton?" Blythe went still. "Stanton?"

"Yes, the Viscount Stanton. What is it, Blythe? You've gone all pale."

"Something I'd forgotten. Who is he? Please, I can't explain just now, but if you could tell me—"

"Very well, but you must promise to explain to me later. He has an estate near here, Moulton Hall. He's quite a dear, really. Usually we don't see him because he's in London—he's quite active in Parliament, you know—but he always stops in to see us when we're in Dover."

"Is he married?"

"Yes. Really, you are making me most curious."

"I know." Blythe quickly grasped her hand. "But you've helped me enormously. Thank you," she said, and all but ran from the green room.

She had to find Simon. No matter that everyone had agreed to ignore his presence. She had to see him. Without stopping to knock, she threw open the office door, and Simon, who had been sitting at the table, jumped to his feet. "What's amiss?" he demanded.

"Nothing. Nothing. 'Tis just—"

"Then why did you burst in that way?" He picked up the chair he'd knocked over in his haste and closed the door. "For a moment I thought 'twas soldiers."

"I'm sorry. Simon, do you know a Viscount Stanton?"

"Who?"

"Or the viscountess?"

"Blythe, what in the world—"

"Do you?"

He leaned against the table, arms crossed on his chest and a small smile on his face. "Stanton. Let's see. In my travels I've met a Thornton, a Stanley—"

"Simon—"

"—but I cannot remember a Stanton." He grinned at her. "Why?"

"Because I think he might know something about Miller's death."

Simon straightened. "What!"

"I'm not sure, of course, but Nancy—Mrs. Miller's

maid, remember—said something about the viscountess having business with Miller. Oh, if I could only remember what it was!"

"Blythe," he said, maddeningly slowly, as she danced from foot to foot, "what could a viscountess have to do with a common tradesman?"

It came to her in a flash. "Money," she said, bracing her hands on the back of a chair. "Miller was a moneylender. Is it possible he lent money to the viscountess?"

"Blythe, for God's sake, are you blaming a peer for Miller's death?"

"No, not him. His wife." Her hand flew to her lips. "No! Of course I'm not saying such a thing, but she was there, Simon. There's a connection."

"I can't imagine what."

"Neither can I," she admitted, leaning against the table next to him. "But I'd like to know."

"Blythe, it doesn't matter."

"No? Have you really given up on clearing your name?"

"Do you think it can be cleared?" he retorted.

"Yes," she said, and looked up at him, lips parted. When she had changed her mind, she didn't know, but of one thing she was certain: Simon had not committed the crime of which he stood convicted. "Yes."

He stared at her. "You believe that."

"Yes."

"You think me innocent."

"With all my heart. Oh, Simon!" She threw herself into his arms. "You couldn't have killed him. I don't know why I didn't see it before."

"Mayhap because I abducted you," he said dryly, though his arms had gone about her.

"Oh, that." She dismissed it with a wave of her hand. "Understandable, really. But Simon, do you know what this means?"

He pulled back to see her face, though his hands were warm, solid, at her back. It seemed like forever since he'd held her. "No. What?"

"You can't leave. You have to clear your name."

He looked at her a moment longer and then pulled back. "It's too late, Blythe," he said quietly, pacing away.

"I don't believe that."

"But it is." He took her hands in his, brought them to his lips. "This means a great deal to me, Blythe, more than you could ever know. But the best thing I can do for everyone now is to leave."

Her hands tingled. She wished he would hold her, but he'd crossed his arms, and she didn't want to throw herself at him again. "And in the meantime?"

"In the meantime, I stay here." He forced a smile. " 'Tis for the best, Blythe."

"Mmm." He had to stay within, hidden; his face was too well-known. But hers wasn't, she thought with sudden excitement. Here in Dover no one knew who she was. "I suppose it is," she agreed. If he was suspicious of her meek answer, Simon didn't show it, and that was just as well. He could not go out and discover what the Stantons had to do with Miller's death. However, Blythe could. And since she would have to do so very soon, she began to make plans.

The first thing Quentin did when he arrived in Dover was register at the Ship Inn. The second was to stroll by the King Theater, idly swinging the gold-topped walking stick that matched so well with his new coat, red velvet with gold lacing at the cuffs. Quite an inspired combination, really, even if the weather was warm for velvet. He had thought of it after studying an army officer's uniform during one of the attempts to take Woodley. It was well worth the time it had taken in London to be made. Honoria would be—probably was—angry about what she would no doubt see as his failure. Really, it was becoming tiresome, the way Woodley managed to elude him. But now he was certain his quarry was near. This time he would not fail.

Quentin smiled thinly, scanning the theater's playbill. The Rowley troupe again, they who'd made a fool of him in Rochester. It was unlikely that Woodley or the woman was with them, but Quentin suspected that everyone in the troupe knew where they were. All he need do now was acquire that information. Pity that Odette had joined a different troupe. She had been useful.

A man emerged from the alley near the theater, and Quentin's smile briefly widened. Ah, Montaigne. Just as Quentin had suspected. When he had had the Woodley troupe arrested he had soon let Montaigne go free in hopes that he would go straight to Woodley. It was time to see if the ploy had worked.

Leisurely crossing the street, he came up behind Ian and poked him in the back with his walking stick. Ian reacted as any man might; he jumped with surprise and then whirled around, his own stick held high, with a blade protruding from the tip. "Who goes there? By God, I'll—Heywood."

Quentin smiled again, faintly, and leaned on his stick. "As you see. Well met, Montaigne."

Ian's eyes narrowed. "What are you doing here?"

"Enjoying the sea air. Walk with me, dear boy," Quentin said, grasping Ian's arm. "Quite bracing, the wind here. There'll be no crossing the Channel today."

Ian gave him a sharp look. "It feels rather like rain," he said, mildly enough.

A worthy adversary. One had to be careful with actors; they could change characters at will. One would almost think Montaigne was indeed just out for a stroll. "I take it, then, that Woodley is still in Dover?"

Ian shrugged. "I don't know where he is."

"Oh, but you do, dear boy. You came to tell him of his family's unfortunate fate."

"You had something to do with that, didn't you?"

"Mayhap. How did Woodley take the news?"

"I don't know. He's not here."

Quentin laughed. "Oh, but I think he is, dear boy, he and the Marden woman. And you are going to tell me where."

"Over my dead body."

"Oh, no, no, no, only if necessary. Otherwise 'tis rather messy."

"What do you want with him, sir?" Ian sounded honestly bewildered. "What has he ever done to you, that you pursue him so?"

"That is my business. Well?" Quentin said crisply. "Will you tell me where he is, or will I have to force you to?"

Ian swung his sword stick back and forth, back and forth, an apparently idle gesture. "And just how do you propose to do that?"

"Why, by telling what I know about you, of course."

"Which is?"

"That you betrayed friend Woodley for money."

Ian glared at him for a moment, and then, to Quentin's surprise, grinned. "Is that all?"

"All? Sir, I'd think it was quite enough. What will your friends in the theater think when they know? You'll not go onstage again."

"You can't say anything without exposing yourself, Heywood." Ian's smile thinned. "Which is exactly the sort of deed I'd expect from you."

Quentin ignored the double entendre, and the insult. "Ah, but I can. Rumor, dear boy. Innuendo. Let me whisper a few words in the right ears, and soon all in the theater will know. Yes, even the great Garrick, and he'll not take you on at Drury Lane, will he?"

Ian shrugged. "I'll take my chances."

"Oh, will you, dear boy?" They were near the quay now, the wind fresh in their faces. "I think not."

"And I think I shall." Ian stepped onto the pier, leaving Quentin no choice but to follow. Curse the sea air; the salt spray would do nothing for his new coat, or for the curl of his wig. Nor did he think Montaigne would be so foolish as to inquire into passage on a ship, not when he was being observed. "Shall we see who is right, then?"

"By all means," Ian said affably. "Though there is one thing you should know."

"Which is?"

"I played the role of priest when Simon was on the scaffold," he said, and, reaching out, pushed at Quentin's shoulder.

Quentin stumbled back, his foot finding only empty air. Cursing and flailing, he fell, splashing into the grease-slicked water of the harbor. For a moment he panicked, striking out with his arms and legs, and then he reached the surface. Air! He gasped with the pleasure of simply breathing again.

On the pier above, Ian looked down, appearing only mildly concerned.

"Montaigne, for the love of God, help me."

"Sorry, dear boy, but I've an appointment." Ian stepped back. "Pity that water ruins velvet," he drawled, and walked away, swinging his stick jauntily. And all Quentin could do was sputter and curse, until someone on one of the boats fished him out. He'd pay, Quentin thought, stomping away down the pier. They'd all pay.

"I still say this is a fool's errand, miss," McNally grumbled, hunching over the reins to the cart. "What you think you'll find out here, I don't know."

Blythe reached up to make sure her bonnet was secure as a gust of wind rocked the cart. It was a clear day, but blustery. Simon would not be crossing to the continent tonight. "Mayhap more about how Miller died."

"Can't think what a viscountess would have to do with that."

"I can't, either," she admitted. " 'Tis a chance, I know, but one I have to take."

McNally straightened as the road curved and a pair of stone pillars came into view. "You don't even know if she'll see you."

"I can only try. Is this Moulton Hall?" Blythe leaned forward, gazing past the gate into a broad, grassy field. "Where is the house?"

"Down a ways, near to the water, I'm told. It's not too late to turn back, miss."

Blythe's stomach clenched. She could turn back,

could forget about this particular masquerade.
McNally disapproved of it, and so did Katherine, who
had helped Blythe with her costume. Simon had no
idea what she was doing, but she had no doubt he'd
disapprove, as well. Yet, if there was any chance she
could learn something to clear his name, she would
take it. "Let's try it, Joseph. The worst that can happen is that we're run off."

McNally turned the cart into the drive. "Well,
there's no gatehouse, so we can get in, at least. 'Tis
what happens at the house that worries me."

"We'll deal with that as it happens. Gracious!" This
as the cart topped a slight rise and the land fell away
before them, revealing a vista of green fields crossed
by stone walls, leading down to the Straits of Dover.
The water was deep green, with frothy whitecaps,
darker where clouds cast their shadows. Blythe could
see, just faintly, the outline of shore far across the
water. "Oh, how lovely. What a beautiful place to
live."

"Damp during storms, I'll wager. Ah. I was right."

"About what?"

"Someone's coming to see what we want."

Blythe looked to where he pointed and saw a man
on horseback crossing a field toward them. "How did
he know we were here?"

"No matter. Can't go back now, miss."

"No. We can't." Blythe straightened, gathering the
elements of her character together within her. She was
Leonora Higglesby, of the Seamen's Benevolent Aid
Society in Dover. Miss Higglesby was a very proper
spinster who dressed only in gray or black and always
wore a cap under her old-fashioned coal-scuttle bonnet. That this also disguised the distinctive blond
streak in Blythe's hair was an added bonus. Miss Higglesby was immersed in good works. She arranged
fresh flowers for her church every week and had something of a tendre for her vicar. She also had absolutely
no sense of humor and was a dedicated missionary for
the causes she took up.

The man pulled up before them. He was middle-aged, grizzled, dressed in shirt and breeches. "Who goes there?" he called.

"Good afternoon, my lord," McNally replied, before Blythe could speak. "Would the viscountess be at home?"

The man frowned. "Who wants to know?"

"Pray excuse my servant, my lord," Blythe said, leaning across McNally. "I am Leonora Higglesby, from the Seamen's Benevolent Aid Society in Dover. I am sure you know of us. No? But that is a surprise, my lord. We help seamen in need, those who are ill or—"

"And you want a donation," the man said.

Blythe pulled her head back. "You are direct, my lord."

"Don't 'milord' me. I'm the steward." He frowned, and then shrugged. "Well, you look harmless enough. Go on to the house. They'll take care of you there."

"Oh, thank you!" Blythe gushed as McNally set the cart in motion again. "May God bless you for your kindness."

"Coming it a bit too brown, aren't you, miss?" McNally muttered.

"Miss Higglesby would be absolutely sincere."

McNally snorted. He didn't hold with her method of becoming a character and had told her so. Still, here they were, advancing along the drive and coming into view of a house. "The big house, I'm thinking."

"Yes." Now that she was here, now that the moment was at hand, Blythe felt her throat tighten and her stomach pitch. Stage fright, of course, but made so much worse by her choice of theater. For Moulton Hall was enormous, a great block of rosy-red brick facing the sea, a fitting home for a nobleman. Yet it had a comfortable look to it as well, she thought, tidy and cared-for. Under other circumstances she might even wish to live here. Now she wished only that this escapade were over.

McNally drew the cart up under a pillared portico of white stucco. No one came to take their horse; no one opened the door in welcome. Gathering her courage, Blythe smiled quickly at McNally and then climbed down from the cart. She took a deep breath as she walked to the door and let the knocker fall. So much was at stake.

The door was opened by a tall gentleman who quite literally looked down his nose at her. "Tradesmen go around the back," he said icily.

"I am not in trade," she said, and handed him a card, a prop from the theater that had dictated her choice of name. "I am Miss Higglesby of the Seamen's Benevolent Aid Society. Might I speak with her ladyship?"

"The viscountess is not receiving today," he said, and began to close the door.

"Oh, please." Blythe stuck her foot between the door and the jamb. "If you will just take my card to her ladyship, God will bless you, I am certain of it."

From around the door the man regarded her suspiciously. "I shall inquire," he said at last, and pushed at the door.

"Oh, please," she said again, wincing as the pressure against her foot increased. " 'Tis so hot here in the sun. Might I just wait inside?"

That same narrow, fish-eyed look. "Will God bless me if I let you in?"

"God will always bless you, sir," she said earnestly; Leonora Higglesby would not know she had just been mocked.

"Very well. I suppose you won't do any harm." He opened the door, and Blythe stepped into a cool, airy entrance hall. "But just you stay there," he warned, and went toward the stairs that rose to the left of the hall.

"Thank you, sir," Blythe called after him as he went up the stairs. "Bless you, sir. And now what?" she muttered, turning about to survey her surroundings. Her first time in a nobleman's house, and likely her last, as well. She might as well see what she could. After all, Miss Higglesby would need to know enough about the nobility to get money from them.

The hall was square and high-ceilinged, with oak

wainscoting and white plaster walls. No carpet covered the wide board floor, and yet everything in the hall spoke of comfort and ease, from the silver candelabra set on a highly polished table, to the red-cushioned window seat on the landing, to the paintings on the wall. She knew little about art, but she suspected that these paintings were likely valuable. One was rather dark, of fruit and wine; another showed a stag being brought down by hunters. Shuddering, she turned away and faced some decidedly cheerier scenes: one of Moulton Hall, against a backdrop of dramatic thunderclouds; and another of the view across the Channel. Someone in the family was an artist, she thought, and turned again.

At first she didn't quite comprehend what she was seeing, but then a shock ran through her. Dazed, as if in a dream, she drifted over to the painting on the opposite wall, resting her fingers on the frame and staring up at it, dumbfounded.

It was a portrait of Simon.

Chapter 25

Simon paced the length of the attic room once more, stopping to look, unseeing, out the grimy window onto an unimpressive view of streets and rooftops. Another lodging in someone else's house. Sometimes it grew tiring, this business of traveling, even when he had been able to come and go as he pleased. Sometimes he wished he had one place to stay, to come to. A home.

Matters were worse now. Since arriving in Dover yesterday, he'd spent most of his time hiding in the office at the theater, until he'd been smuggled last night into this room, which he shared with Ian. He was disguised as an old man again, a somewhat more detailed disguise than the one he'd used in London, but as subject to discovery. Anyone who gave him a close look would realize that he was not as old as he appeared.

The door behind him opened and he turned, grasping the cane that served as both prop and weapon. "Peace, friend," Ian said, closing the door behind me. " 'Tis only me."

Simon lowered the cane. "I didn't hear you come in."

"Then you should be more alert. I made enough noise." Ian rubbed his hands together as he pulled off his coat, slinging it onto the bed. In public there was no one more fastidious; his clothing was always clean and fashionable, his hair faultless, his manners impeccable. In private was another matter. "Damned cold out there. Feels more like autumn than summer."

"No chance of crossing the Channel today, then?"

"No, unless you swim. And 'tis damned cold for that."

"What?" Simon asked, seeing Ian suddenly smile. "What have you been up to now?"

"I could answer that several ways." Ian settled into the comfortable bow-backed chair, fingers steepled. "Arguing with a man about his taste in clothing, teaching him to swim—any number of ways."

Simon waited. From long experience he knew that Ian had a tale to tell and was working up to it as dramatically as possible. "What man?" he asked mildly.

"Quentin Heywood."

"Good God!" Simon stared at him. "He's here?"

"Aye." The laughter had left Ian's eyes, and his mouth was grim. "You'd best sit down, Simon," he said, gesturing toward the bed.

Simon didn't move. "Does he know where I am?"

"No, not yet, but he knows you're here. And I suspect 'tis my fault."

"Why?"

Ian stared at his fingers. " 'Tis possible he followed me."

"Ah." Simon nodded. "So that's why you were set free from gaol. I should have guessed. Why is he chasing me? Do you know?"

"Unfortunately, yes."

"What do you mean?" Simon demanded.

"Have you never wondered, Simon, why Miller was killed when he was?"

"I don't know. Coincidence, I thought. Or . . ."

"Or?"

Simon frowned. "Someone wanted me blamed for the killing. That's occurred to me, though I can't think who."

Ian looked up at him. "Can't you?"

"My God." Simon dropped onto the bed. "You know."

"I suspect."

"Who?"

"Heywood."

"Good God! Why?"

"Why, I don't know. As to the rest . . ."

"Have you known this all along?"

Ian stared at his fingers. "Yes."

"Bloody hell!" Simon jumped to his feet. "I could have been hanged! I spent months in prison and I've been on the run since, not to mention what I've done to Blythe. And all the time, you knew."

"There was no proof," Ian said simply. "Even now I'm not sure."

"Why?" Simon turned from the window. "Why did he do it, and why didn't you tell me?"

"I told you, I don't know his reasons." Ian kept his gaze on his fingers. "The rest is more difficult."

Simon crossed his arms. "I have time."

Ian winced. "Well. They say confession is good for the soul. We shall soon see. Simon." He looked up, his face serious. "Heywood knew you would be at Miller's because I told him."

"And just why did you do such a thing?"

"Gambling debts."

"I beg your pardon?"

"Gambling debts. You may not recall, you were in some difficulties yourself, but I had managed to run up a substantial sum. It had to be paid, of course. A matter of honor."

"Gambling debts. And the price of redeeming them was . . ."

"Information about you."

"I hope you gave fair value for your thirty pieces of silver."

Ian winced again. "I deserve that."

"You do," Simon said grimly. He was so angry, so stunned, that he was numb. Ian, feckless and unthinking, had used people in the past to get himself out of his own messes. This, however, went beyond anything that Simon had ever known.

"If it comforts you, Simon, I've paid for it every day since."

"How?" Simon lashed out. "With your good name? By spending time in prison? By nearly being hanged?"

"Don't shout. You'll be heard."

"I don't give a damn. I—"

"You should. Heywood may very well find out where I lodge."

Simon snatched up his cane. "Damn you. You led him here."

"Actually, I threw him off the quay."

"What?"

"I threw him into the harbor." Ian looked up at him over his fingertips, an affectation Simon had never detected before now. "I stopped to see Giles before coming here. He's finding another place for you."

"Which you, no doubt, will tell to Heywood."

"I have no more gambling debts."

"Bloody hell, Ian, my life is at stake and you make jests?"

"Sorry! Sorry. But I'd no idea it would lead to this. Sit down. Please."

Simon glared at him for a moment. Ian's eyes were pleading. Behind his facile exterior lay a complicated and sensitive man. Sometimes. "Tell me what happened or I'll beat it out of you," he growled, sitting again, though some of his anger had eased. Even now he found it difficult to remain angry with Ian for long.

Ian nodded. "I wouldn't blame you if you did. Yes, I'm getting to it!" He held up his hand as Simon shifted on the bed. "Yes. Well. It started in Canterbury, when we were having that good run at the King Theater. Remember?"

"Yes."

"I met Heywood in the green room. Someone introduced us, I don't know who, and we got to talking. His name wasn't Heywood, by the by. It was Tansy. Well, before you know it, we adjourned to a tavern, where we both had a trifle too much to drink." He frowned. "At least I did."

"So?"

"So I fear I talked rather a lot. He didn't seem particularly interested in you, by the by. He just seemed to enjoy theater gossip. You know the type."

Simon nodded. "I do."

"Well. He came to the green room again a few nights later. Now I think on it, I know why you never met him. You and I weren't in the same plays. Well. He invited me to dine afterwards, and then introduced me to some friends. I had some wine, played some cards . . ." Ian spread his hands. "The rest you can guess."

"You lost."

"Badly. I was actually relieved, you know, when Heywood purchased my markers. He was a friend, he said, he wasn't going to press me for payment. And I said that I was good, else I'd have to go to a money-lender and end up as you did."

"Ah. Now we come to it."

"Yes. He started asking questions about you, Simon, but the impression I had at the time was that his grudge was against Miller."

"Really. Why?"

Ian rubbed at his nose. "I'm afraid I can't remember. Too much wine. In any event, when he asked what you were going to do, I told him, and when."

"And?" Simon said, when Ian paused.

"And that night you were arrested for Miller's murder." Silence fell in the room. "The next day Heywood came to the theater and returned my markers."

"Bloody hell! So you know."

"Oh, yes. I knew. He thanked me for the information, laughed in my face, and left. And all I had for proof were the markers."

"Bloody hell," Simon said again. "Why didn't you tell someone?"

"I did, but Heywood was gone, and no one knew of him, at least not as Tansy. I had no proof," he said. "The magistrate, King's counsel, the gaolers—no one would listen."

"He set it up well." Simon pursed his lips, no longer angry. It was past, and Ian had more than redeemed himself. He had saved Simon from hanging. "Your story was so implausible, people would think you were just trying to protect me."

"Yes." Ian leaned back, his face lined, aged. "I suspect he also managed to have Mrs. Miller walk in at just the right—wrong—time, but I don't know for certain."

"Probably."

"But that's past," Ian said, echoing Simon's earlier thoughts. "The problem is now."

"Yes. How did you come to throw him into the harbor?"

"What? Oh, that." Ian smiled. "We had a disagreement over his coat. Red velvet with gold lacing." He shuddered.

"Ian—"

" 'Tis the truth," Ian said, spreading his hands and looking so wide-eyed innocent that Simon knew he'd just been fed a Banbury tale. No good trying to get the truth from him; once Ian decided to keep a secret, it stayed secret.

"I should beat you for this."

"But you won't. I . . . hush!"

"What?" Simon said, but then he heard it, too, the stairs creaking outside and an odd sound, a squishing sound. As if someone were walking in wet shoes. The two men looked at each other and then, in unspoken agreement, took up posts on either side of the door, Simon with his cane and Ian with his sword stick. The creaking stopped. There was a rustling, as of clothing being adjusted, and then someone pounded on the door.

Blythe stared up at the portrait. The brass plate on the frame identified the subject as the Honorable Geoffrey Vernon, with no other explanation. The likeness to Simon was uncanny, though this close, Blythe could see differences that went beyond the man's clothing, out of date by some twenty years. His eyes were light, hazel, she thought; Simon's were dark. His nose was somewhat thinner than Simon's, his chin somewhat rounder. Not Simon, then, but someone enough like him to be his twin. Who was he?

"Ahem," a voice said behind her, and she turned, to see the butler who had earlier let her into the hall.

"The viscountess regrets that she is not receiving visitors today."

"Who is this?" Blythe demanded, gesturing at the portrait.

The butler looked down his nose at her again. "I believe that is obvious, miss. He is the Honorable Geoffrey Vernon."

"Yes, but who is he?"

"He would have been the fourth viscount," the butler said, and the regret in his face made him look human for the first time.

"Would have been?"

"Yes. He's been gone these many years. Ahem." He straightened, pulling his dignity about himself. "The viscountess will not receive you. You may leave."

"Of course," Blythe murmured, and, with one last look at the mysterious portrait, went to the door. It closed behind her with a solid thud, leaving her standing under the portico, baffled and stunned.

"Miss?" McNally called from the cart. "Are you well?"

Blythe looked up, startled. "Oh! Yes. We'd best leave," she said, her voice lower as she climbed into the cart. "There's something very strange here."

"Problems?"

"No." She stared blankly ahead as McNally drove along the drive. "Joseph, has Simon ever been here?"

He frowned. "Not that I know of, miss."

"Then why . . ."

"What?"

"Nothing." She shook her head. "I must think on this."

McNally cast her a look, but otherwise made no comment, for which she was grateful. Deep in thought about what she had seen, she was unaware that a man on horseback was approaching from the opposite direction, until McNally hissed. "What?" she said, looking up to see the horseman passing them. She went very still. It was Quentin Heywood.

*   *   *

Quentin turned in his saddle, staring back at the old farm cart rumbling on up the hill. The devil, but he could swear that was Blythe Marden in that cart. She looked different—older, heavier—but that meant nothing. She was obviously in disguise. What was she doing here?

He watched the cart for a moment, and then shrugging, turned back, guiding his horse along the drive. A few hours earlier he would have pursued her, but things had changed. He had had enough. He was getting out.

It was a little thing, really, unimportant to most people, but vital to him. A man with his lack of resources and his sense of fashion could not afford to have his fine clothes ruined. So far in this escapade he had lost a pair of boots, some breeches, and an expensive wig. Now his fine new coat of red velvet was gone, ruined beyond repair by the filthy water of Dover harbor. It was too much. He had been running around England doing Honoria's bidding, and for what? Loss and humiliation. It was time for her to pay.

At the house he tossed his reins to a groom and strolled inside, hat tucked carelessly under his arm. The butler bowed, went to announce Quentin's presence to the viscountess, and then returned to lead him up to her boudoir. And all the time Quentin thought of the strange sight he had just seen.

Honoria looked up from the blue velvet chaise longue, where she reclined in apparent relaxation, one arm along the back displaying her lush figure in all its glory. "Well? Have you news?"

"Yes." Quentin set down his hat and sat in one of the spindly velvet and gilt chairs that furnished the room, crossing his legs. "What was the Marden woman doing here?"

"Who?"

"The Marden woman. The one who's been with . . . the actor."

Honoria frowned. "You are talking in puzzles, Quentin. No such person has been here."

"No? I saw her leaving just now."

"Leaving—oh. The charity person."

"What?"

"Someone was here collecting for some charity. I sent her away, of course. But her name wasn't Marden. It was . . . let me see, something absurd. Higglesworth, I think?"

"She was in disguise," Quentin said patiently. "Are you saying you didn't see her?"

"Of course I didn't." Honoria leaned forward, her careful pose forgotten. "Are you seriously telling me the actor's companion came here?"

"Yes."

"Why didn't you stop her?" she demanded, getting to her feet and pacing the room. "Really, Quentin, your incompetence amazes me at times!"

Quentin gazed at her over his folded hands. She was, as always, lovely in an open robe of pale blue silk, her hair tossing magnificently about her shoulders and her body—ah, that body. Strange that he wasn't the least bit moved by her. Strange that he ever had been. "It is for compliments like that that I do what I do," he murmured.

She whirled about, glaring at him. "You think this is funny? A jest? Because I warn you, Quentin—"

"Spare me." He held up a languid hand. "Do you know, Honoria, I think—no, I know I do—I believe I see wrinkles about your eyes?"

Honoria's hands flew to her face, and then back down. "I do not like being insulted, Quentin."

"Pity," he went on, as if she hadn't spoken. "You were a great beauty, but there's a certain"—he tilted his head—"coarseness about you now. Too much paint on your face, I think, my love."

"I am not your love!" she exclaimed, and slapped him open-handed across the face.

Quentin barely flinched, though his cheek stung. "No. You never were, were you."

"You are trying my patience, Quentin. Say what you have to say and then get out."

"This makes me wonder what my reward would have been had I stayed the course. But, my love, I will do as you just requested. In fact, I have come to tell you that very thing. I'm getting out."

"What are you talking about?"

"Just as I said. I will not be a party to your schemes any longer."

Honoria stared at him for a moment, and then threw back her head in a laugh. "You can't be serious! Why, you know I'd expose you in a moment!"

"Would you, my love?"

"Yes. It would be very easy, Quentin, to find someone who would claim to have seen you leaving Miller's. Perhaps if I pay him enough he will say there was blood on your clothes."

"Pity. For then I shall have to tell your husband what I know about Fowler."

She went very still. "Fowler? I don't know what you're talking about."

"Don't you?" He was rather enjoying this, watching her realize that she no longer held the upper hand. "But I think you do. Ethan Fowler, who was steward here, and who stole so much from the estate? Money and other things of value, I believe. And then who came to such a tragic end, drowning in the Channel." He shook his head. "Or do I have the name wrong?"

"He did those things," Honoria said through stiff lips, "though we could never prove it. But what has that to say to anything?"

"Interesting how your cohorts seem to meet unsavory ends," he mused. "I believe one of the objects stolen was a valuable miniature of the first viscount. Something like this."

Honoria jumped forward as he pulled his hand from his coat pocket, opening it to display a miniature painting of a man in Cavalier dress, with hair in ringlets. The painting itself was unremarkable; the frame, however—gold encrusted with pearls and rubies—was not. "Where did you get that?"

"A pretty thing, and valuable. I can understand why you wouldn't wish to part with it." He smiled at her. "I found it in your jewel box, my love. Did you not know it was missing? No? Careless of you." He clucked disapprovingly, shaking his head. "You really should have disposed of it, Honoria. Not left it where anyone could find it."

Honoria was standing transfixed a few feet away, her hand raised as if to snatch the miniature from his hand. "I had that locked up."

"Oh, so you admit it?"

"No! When Fowler took it, I—"

"No, love." He shook his head. "Good try, but no. Because I have it now." He tossed it up in the air, caught it one-handed, and then carefully stowed it away. "I think the viscount would find it interesting, don't you?"

"He wouldn't believe you."

"He might not," he agreed, "but do you want to take that chance? As I recall, he was quite upset about the whole thing. He'd be quite upset with you." He let the silence spin out. "We appear to be at a stalemate."

"Why are you doing this?" she asked, seemingly bewildered. "After all we've been to each other—"

"I was your pawn, nothing more, haring about England and taking all the risks while you sat here in safety, with never a word of thanks from you. And, if it came to it, you would have put the blame on me, would you not? Ah. Don't answer that, my love. I see it in your eyes." He rose. "I was a fool, letting you dictate to me, but I'll be fooled no more. I am out of this affair."

"But—Miller—the actor—"

"I care not about him. He may go to the devil, or he may go to the continent. As I believe I shall do for a time. He is not my concern any longer."

"Quentin!" she wailed as he reached the door. "What about me?"

He paused. Once he had loved her, or had thought he had. More fool he. "I care not," he said, and went out, closing the door very, very quietly behind him.

The knocking came again at the door, where Simon and Ian waited, weapons at the ready. "Ian! Are you in there, man?"

"Giles," Ian said, lowering his walking stick at the same time as Simon and opening the door. "You gave us a scare."

Giles walked in, frowning. "Why?"

"We were just discussing that Woodley here should be moved. He is a dashed uncomfortable person to share quarters with."

Simon smiled. "Uncomfortable, Ian?"

"Yes, unless one likes the imminent threat of being carted off to gaol."

"Heywood is here," Simon explained to Giles. "He and Ian had a conversation."

Giles grimaced. "Well, that's done it. Though where we'll put you, lad, I've no idea. Have you seen McNally?"

"Not today, no."

"Well, no matter. He said something about going up the coast. Possibly something to do with your passage. You know you'll not be going tonight?"

Simon nodded, just as another knock came on the door. The three men stiffened. " 'Tis me," Blythe said, and they relaxed.

Simon opened the door, letting her in. "Well, princess? And what are you doing in that getup?"

"I've news." She put her hand to her heart, and Simon could see that her breath was coming quickly. Dressed all in black, with her hair covered, she looked dowdy, older. "I saw Quentin Heywood not an hour ago."

"Where?" Ian said sharply.

"At . . ." She looked at Simon. "Simon, I need to talk with you."

He frowned. "Is Heywood coming here?"

"No, you're safe enough for now."

"We're moving him elsewhere, anyway, lass," Giles put in.

She paled. "To the continent? So soon?"

"To a safer place," Simon said. "It seems Heywood is acquainted with Ian."

Blythe glanced from him to Ian, who was relaxed, leaning on his stick. "I don't understand."

Simon shrugged. "It matters not. Where did you see Heywood?"

"At Moulton Hall."

"Where?"

"Then you don't know of it?"

"The Stanton estate?" Giles said. "Why were you there?"

"Bloody hell!" Simon put his fists on his hips. "Did you go to see the viscountess?"

"Yes, but she wouldn't see me. Simon, I saw something strange—"

"That was dangerous, Blythe. What do you think you're doing, risking your fool neck like that?"

Blythe straightened, folded her hands, raised her chin. Before his very eyes she had suddenly become someone else. "To save your fool neck, of course."

"I think," Ian said, "I shall go for some ale. Join me, Giles?"

Giles didn't look at him. "Hmm? What?"

"Ale, Giles." Ian took Giles's arm, leading him to the door. "We'll discuss finding you a safe place," he said to Simon. "We won't be above twenty minutes."

Simon nodded as the door closed, leaving him and Blythe alone. "Well?" he said. "Why were you at Moulton Hall?"

"Pray do not take that tone with me, sir," Blythe said, sinking into the chair, her back ramrod straight, her skirts arranged in precise folds and her face dour. "I will not tolerate it."

Simon grinned. "Who are you supposed to be?"

"Leonora Higglesby," she said in a more normal voice, and pulled at her bonnet ribbons. "An insufferable prig, if you must know. I thought if I posed as someone collecting for a charity I might see the viscountess."

"And do what, Blythe? Ask her what her grudge was against Miller?"

"It sounds foolish, I know. But the answer is there, Simon." Her face sobered. "I saw a portrait of a man who could have been your twin."

Chapter 26

Simon took a moment to respond. "I beg your pardon?"

"I thought it was a portrait of you at first, the resemblance was so close. He was Geoffrey Vernon, and he would have been the fourth viscount."

Simon dropped onto the bed. "What are you telling me? That I resemble a lord?"

"Simon, what do you know of your father?"

"Good God." He stared at her. "You don't seriously think . . ."

"I don't know! But this painting could have been you, Simon. *He* could have been you."

"Bloody hell," he said blankly. "I don't understand." He paced to the window. "I don't know who my father was. I told you that, I believe? Uncle Harry is no help. Apparently he never knew, either."

"Your mother never told him?"

"No. But he told me that my parents met here. In Dover."

"Simon! Do you think—"

"No." He turned, frowning. "That I am the illegitimate son of a nobleman, deprived of my inheritance? That kind of thing happens only in plays, Blythe."

"Simon, if you were arrested and hanged for murder, who would benefit?"

"What do you mean?"

"You've said you think someone made you look guilty. That someone had to have a reason. If the viscount is involved . . ."

"But this becomes more fantastic, Blythe! Are you saying he killed Miller just to get me out of the way?"

"I don't know! Oh, I know it sounds ridiculous, but I can't think of another explanation that fits."

"It was the viscountess who had dealings with Miller."

"And who would she get to help her, if not her husband?"

"Quentin Heywood," Simon said slowly. "By God! It fits."

"What?"

"Ian confessed something to me today," he said, and told her the tale of Ian's betrayal and subsequent remorse. "Which is why I need to move to safer quarters," he concluded.

"Ian paid for what he did, Simon," she said softly. "He stood on the gallows with you. He saved your life."

"Aye, and I've forgiven him the earlier mistake. Why was Heywood interested in me, Blythe? Why me and not someone else?"

"He had something to do with Miller's death," she said, slowly. "Then, when you escaped, he tried to recapture you."

"Chasing us across half of England. And now you see him at Moulton Hall."

"Yes. Oh, Simon!" She rose. "You have to leave!"

"I can't," he snapped, realizing at once that he'd known this all along. He had to stay and see it through, whether he cleared his name or ended up on the gallows.

"You have to! I don't understand what is happening, but Simon, don't you see? They know you're here in Dover. 'Tis only a matter of time before they catch you."

"And you, too?"

"Yes. No! That's doesn't matter, Simon."

"It matters to me. I've no desire to see you in prison."

"Simon Woodley, are you saying you're doing this for me?"

"Partly. I'm responsible for you being in this mess."

"Yes, you are, thank you very much, but may I

remind you I stayed with you? And what that's done to my life, traveling with an escaped convict, I don't know."

"But I didn't ask you, did I?" he said, very softly.

"Excuse me?"

"I didn't ask you to stay with me, did I?"

"Not at first, no, but—" She stared at him. "What are you saying, Simon?"

He braced his hands on the back of the chair. "It always comes back to that, doesn't it, that I was accused of a crime? No matter that I'm innocent."

"I know you're innocent. But others don't."

"And you'll never forgive me for that, will you?"

"Don't be silly, Simon. 'Tis not your fault, and it wouldn't keep me from staying with you."

"I'm not asking you to stay with me."

She stared at him. "Simon, what are you saying?"

"I'm saying it's over, princess. That 'tis time you and I went our separate ways."

"Simon—"

"We never did suit each other. You made that clear from the first."

"What are you asking me to do, Simon? To leave?"

He gazed at her, his face a still mask, hiding, he hoped, all his turmoil and pain and despair. Dear God, what would he do without her? He'd come to rely on her common sense, her unexpected humor and resourcefulness during the weeks of their adventure. God help him, he'd come to love her. He stood still, absorbing that knowledge, realizing it was something he'd known for a long time, deep inside himself. He loved her, wanted to be with her, wanted to see her belly swell with his child, as he never had with any other woman. Losing her would be like wrenching out a piece of his very soul, and he would never be whole again. Yet he couldn't stay with her. The issue of his innocence would always be there, a spector between them. It wouldn't have mattered so had he not loved her. But he did.

"Yes, Blythe," he said finally. "I believe that is what I'm asking you. Leave, princess." He made his voice harsh, the quicker to end matters. "Go back to your safe little world where nothing bad ever happens and you don't have to live with the shame of being with a convicted murderer."

Blythe was utterly still, her face pale. "Why are you saying this, Simon?"

He straightened. " 'Tis best for us both." Because she didn't love him. If she did, she would believe in him utterly, and he needed that, needed her faith. All his life he'd been on the outside, the stigma first of his birth and then of his conviction, setting him apart. He would not let that happen with her. "You know it as well as I. And you knew this wasn't forever."

"Yes." She was still pale. Something had come into her face, though, a hardness he'd never seen there before, and her chin was raised. "You're quite right, Simon. The time has come for us to part." She reached for the old bonnet, tying it in place with fingers that trembled just a bit, and turned to the door. "But you are the biggest fool God ever made," she said, and stalked out, pushing her way past Giles, standing in the doorway.

Giles turned to look at her. "What is amiss?" he asked.

"Nothing," Simon said, voice clipped. She was gone. He had asked her to go, but that didn't lessen the pain.

"Nothing?" Giles's eyes narrowed. "What did you say to her?"

"It's not your concern, Giles."

"It is my concern. You have both come to me for help. I believe I've the right to know if you are endangering yourself, and us."

Simon didn't answer right away. "No danger," he said finally. "We had a disagreement."

"Hmm." Giles's glance was suspicious. "Whatever happened, I image you're to blame."

"Me? Why?"

"Everyone knows that girl is head over heels about you. Pack up your things, lad. We've found you a safe place."

Simon stood very still. "What is that you said?"

"We've found another place for you."

"No, before that. About Blythe."

"Don't be daft, lad. Surely you already knew?"

"No." Simon stayed still, fingertips resting lightly on the chair. No, he hadn't known. That Blythe had become fond of him, that she had stayed with him when she didn't have to, those things, yes, he had known. That she felt anything stronger than affection, no. "Are you sure?"

"Ask anyone. Come, gather your things. We've not much time, if Heywood knows where you are."

Nodding, Simon turned away to gather his belongings. His mind was a whirl. Blythe loved him? Impossible. She had pointed out too often how he had ruined her life, implied too often that his past made him unacceptable and that she wanted nothing to do with a strolling player. Hadn't she? Yes, but she had stayed to take care of his wounded leg when she could have returned to London. She had faced danger both in Canterbury and today, and not for herself. For him. *Good God.* The implication was clear. She loved him. And he, being the fool she called him, had sent her away.

He straightened, his mouth grim. No, he'd been right to do that, no matter her feelings. Mayhap he'd been too harsh, but he'd been right. If he couldn't live with her doubting his innocence when he thought she didn't care, how much worse would it be if she did? Whatever grew between them, if anything grew between them, had to come out of mutual respect as well as love. He had to try again to clear his name. No matter what the outcome might be, if he was ever to have hopes of getting Blythe back, he had to try.

He turned, his few belongings tucked into a small parcel, his mind clear at last. "I'm ready," he said, and let Giles lead him out.

Dover was quiet during the night. The local authorities didn't seem any more interested than usual in the Rowley troupe, nor had Heywood been seen. Still,

Simon knew he was risking great danger as he turned his horse onto the coast road heading away from Dover the following morning. McNally had told him that the village near Moulton Hall, where Simon hoped to find answers to some of his questions, was named Barstow. That McNally disapproved showed only in his eyes. There had been a lot of that today, from the other members of the troupe staying in the barn just outside of town, where he had spent the night. They had all evidently heard of his argument with Blythe. They also apparently were on her side. She had become quite popular with the troupe in a short time, which was just as well. If he failed at his task, she'd need a place to stay.

A signpost at a fork in the road pointed toward Barstow and away from the coast. Simon rode on, leaving behind him the scenery of gray-blue sea, roiled by a wind that again made crossing the Channel impossible. He had time enough to seek out information, though he wondered if he'd learn what he wanted. Every place he'd gone seeking answers, he'd encountered more questions instead.

It wasn't inconceivable that his mother had taken up with a nobleman. Oddly enough, that was the only fact in the whole tangled story that didn't bother him. He knew well how the gentry would come to plays to seduce the actresses. He might be related to the Stantons, and the thought of it made his heart pound, his head spin. Family. But if that was so, what was their connection with Miller's death?

Ahead, above the green fields and hedgerows, rose a square Norman church steeple. Simon rode around a bend, and there it was: a tiny village, sleepy and quiet, with only a few people about on its narrow lanes. The church was surprisingly fine, larger than he would have expected, but otherwise the village was indistinguishable from any other in England. Near the church was an ivy-covered stone house he took to be the vicarage. A row of weather-boarded shops lined the High Street, facing houses whitewashed clean under their shingled roofs. Some sheep grazed on the green, which contained a duck pond, and a stream ran across the road. Simon splashed through the stream, stopping in front of the church. If he was going to find any answers, he would have to begin here.

Tethering his horse, he opened the lych-gate and went into the churchyard. Modest slate stones were fringed by daisies and buttercups, while toward the rear of the yard rose a mausoleum, reminiscent of the crypt where he had masqueraded as a ghost. The memory made him smile as he walked across the grass, but the smile faded as he read the name on the mausoleum. It was the Stanton family crypt.

A sudden chill made him rub his arms, though the day was warm. Was his father buried here, or did he live yet, unaware he had a son? If so, Simon would be as big a shock to him as the man would be to Simon, probably an unwelcome one. And there was one way to dispose of this particular unwanted son, Simon thought, his face grim. Turn him over to the authorities.

"Have you come to see my church?" a voice said behind him, and Simon turned to see a very old man, his cheeks rosy and his white hair sparse. His clerical collar proclaimed his identity: the vicar, the person who might be able to give him answers. "Not many people do so anymore—ah!"

"Are you well, sir?" Simon asked, as the man's hand flew to his heart.

"Yes, yes. Now, where did I put those spectacles? Dratted things are never where I need them. Ah." From an inner pocket he withdrew a pair of metal-rimmed spectacles and placed them, somewhat askew, on his nose. "Ah." He peered at Simon. "You are younger than I thought."

Simon smiled, though he had no intention of explaining his disguise as an old man. "Are you the vicar here, Father?"

"Yes, son, I am the Reverend Tulley, and I have been vicar here these thirty years. I was wondering if I'd ever have the chance to see you again."

"I beg your pardon?"

"Yes, yes." Reverend Tulley ambled closer, his pale eyes, though rheumy, surprisingly sharp. "I baptized you, you know."

Simon reached out to grip an outcropping of the mausoleum, feeling suddenly dizzy. "You did?"

"Of course. I—you didn't know? No, you probably wouldn't," he went on to himself. "Not after what happened."

Simon took a deep breath, almost afraid to ask the next question; almost afraid of the answer. "Who am I?" he asked, his voice thin.

"You truly do not know? *Tch, tch.*" The old man shook his head. "Such a shame. But I am pleased to welcome you back, my lord."

Simon's grasp on the mausoleum tightened. "What did you call me?"

"Your title. You are Christopher Simon Edward Vernon, and by rights you are the fourth Viscount Stanton."

Chapter 27

McNally didn't approve of her plans at all, Blythe could see by taking one look at him. He sat hunched over the reins as he drove along the coast road, with Moulton Hall coming up to the right. Bad enough, he'd said, that she'd gone to the hall the first time, but this was folly. Blythe had nodded at his protest, but held firm. The answers were there. She had to seek them.

And why, she didn't know. She'd get no thanks for it. Drat the man. Why had he turned on her as he had? At first she had been numb from his verbal assault, until the tears came. Now she was simply, coldly furious. All that she'd done to help him, and he'd thrown it back in her face. He knew she believed him to be innocent. But . . . didn't he realize? If the questions surrounding him weren't answered, then the remainder of his life, whether short or long, would be clouded.

McNally twisted on the bench and then turned back. "Hmph."

"What?" Blythe asked, momentarily distracted from her thoughts.

"Thought I heard someone behind us."

Blythe turned, but the rises and dips in the road defeated her vision. "Simon, do you think?"

"Him?" McNally made a face. "Not likely."

"You don't seem to think well of him," she said, absurdly annoyed. After all, it was because of Simon that she'd spent the night sleepless, staring up at the darkened ceiling. Because of him, she knew a new kind of pain that caught her under her heart and seemed like it would never relent. Because of him, she was on this road.

McNally glanced at her and then returned his attention to the road, snorting. "You don't have to tell me he's hurt you."

Blythe wrapped her arms about herself, shielding her heart, shielding the pain. "It's not really your concern, Joseph."

"Huh. So say you, when I've been running about all England for the both of you. And when you're putting yourself out for him like this." He looked over at her. "He doesn't know, does he? What you're doing."

She sighed. "No," she admitted, reaching up to tuck back a strand of hair that had come loose from her cap. "I haven't seen him today." She leaned forward, elbows to knees, fists to chin. "He sent me away."

McNally snorted again. "More fool he, when you're in love with him. Don't look at me like that, girl, all surprised. Everyone knows."

Everyone? Oh, dear heavens. "Does it show that much?" she asked in a very small voice.

His face softened. "Aye, to everyone but him, most like. No, I mean it, lass. He's too close to you to see it."

She turned. "Then why did he send me away?"

"For your own good, most like. Because of what he feels for you. Now there you go, staring at me again."

She gripped his arm. "Joseph, what are you saying?"

"Now I've put my foot in it," he muttered. "Only that he loves you, too. And proper mad he'll be, when he finds out where I've brought you."

"He—if he—but it doesn't make any sense! If he loves me, why tell me to leave?"

"For your own safety, lass." He glanced at her. "So you won't spend your life tied to a convicted murderer."

"But he didn't do it."

"Aye. But he has to prove it, doesn't he? Here we are." McNally turned the cart from the road onto the drive. "And he doesn't think he can."

"It doesn't matter."

"I know, but it does to him." He clucked softly as the horse shied at a rustling in the undergrowth nearby. " 'Tis the only reason I let you come here today."

"Let me! This was my idea."

"Mayhap. But 'tis folly, all the same, with what you know about the viscount."

"Maybe he's not here," she said unconvincingly.

"Mayhap. But I'll be glad when we're done and out of here."

She nodded, her stomach clenching. No use denying it. She was frightened: of what might happen in the next few moments; of what she might learn. She might clear Simon. Equally possibly, she might not. She wasn't sure which prospect scared her more. "You really believe he loves me?"

"Aye. Now promise me you'll not ask to speak to the viscountess this time."

"I promise," she said impatiently, for they had discussed her plans already. "When I get inside I'll pretend to be faint, and someone—a maid, I hope—will get me water. And then I'll find out what I can about the Honorable Geoffrey Vernon."

The cart topped a rise, and there it was again, the splendid view of sea and sky. To the right, the chimneys of the house were just visible. "And then get out of there. The viscount'll wonder why someone from some charity is asking after a member of his family."

She smiled faintly. "Even Leonora Higglesby has maidenly feelings. And the Honorable Geoffrey is a handsome man."

There might have been a smile at the corners of McNally's mouth; it was hard to tell. "Be careful, lass," he said, sweeping the cart around the last curve and pulling to a stop under the portico. "Even Miss Higglesby has her weaknesses."

Blythe frowned, but before she could ask what he meant, a groom had come to hold the horse's head, something that hadn't happened in their previous visit. All else was the same, however, from the hollow boom of the massive door knocker crashing down, to the butler looking down his nose at her.

At sight of her, he assumed a martyred expression. "You, again?"

"Yes." She smiled tightly. "After considering it, I have come to the conclusion that it is my duty to try again to spread the word about the plight of distressed seamen." Blythe took a deep breath. "It is an important cause, you realize, with women and their babies being dependent on the good that the society does. I count it—no, I deem it an honor to serve such a noble purpose, even if in such a humble way." She glanced up at the butler and inexpertly batted her lashes. "Please?"

The butler looked as if he had just caught a whiff of fish dead several days; his lips pursed and his cheeks quivered. "Come in, then," he said, his voice shaking, and abruptly turned away, leaving Blythe to follow. "Wait here."

"Thank you. Excuse me." She batted her lashes again. "Might I have something to drink? I find that being in the hot sun and talking as I must about the poor distressed seamen makes me quite thirsty. And when I think of what they suffer, why, I get quite faint—"

"As well you might," the butler interrupted, and Blythe at last managed to put a name to his expression. He was laughing! "I'll have someone bring you some water."

Blythe watched him go, delighted. Why, that had been easy! The butler was completely fooled by her nonsensical pose, and so would anyone else be. She might even persuade him not to tell the viscountess of her presence when he returned with her drink, though that would likely make him suspicious. Unless she asked him for a donation? She nodded. Yes. Leonora would do that kind of thing, she decided.

A footfall made her turn to see a maid in starched black and white, holding a tray, upon which sat a crystal tumbler of water. It looked so inviting that Blythe, who a moment before hadn't cared about a drink except as a prop, was suddenly very thirsty. "Thank you." She took the tumbler from the tray as if being served were something she was accustomed to. "Where is the butler?"

"Mr. Goodfellow?" The maid's voice squeaked. "Dunno. Gone abovestairs, I think. He said as how I was to bring you this water." Her brow puckered. "Did I do right?"

"Exactly right," Blythe said bracingly, sorry for the brusqueness her disguise required. "Do you know of the Seamen's Benevolent Aid Society?"

The maid fidgeted. "Er, no."

"As I thought. Well. We were formed in—"

"I'm sorry, miss, but I must be about my duties," the maid broke in.

"What? Oh. Yes. Quite. And I imagine they are considerable." She let her gaze sweep the hall. "So many paintings. I suppose you have to dust them all?"

"Well, er, yes, miss."

"Hmph. As I thought. That is the house there, is it not?"

The maid glanced at where Blythe pointed. "Yes, that is Moulton Hall. Miss, I really should—"

"And him?" Blythe had turned to the portrait of the Honorable Geoffrey. "Is this the Viscount Stanton?"

"Oh, no, miss," the maid said, sounding shocked. "He's been dead and gone this age."

"Oh? Then is the viscountess his wife?"

"No, miss." The maid stared at her. "He had no wife."

"Pity. And no children."

"The viscount?"

"No, no, this man here." She prodded at the painting. "Did he not have children?"

"No, miss." The maid stared at her, clearly perplexed. "Why?"

Blythe sighed, a heavy sound. "He was quite a handsome man. Not that I usually notice such things, of course, but I couldn't help but see it this time. A pity."

"What?"

"That he had no heirs, of course. I firmly believe in the laws of primogeniture." Now, where had that come from?

"I beg your pardon, miss?"

As well she might, Blythe thought. She had no idea herself what she was talking about. "A nobleman should have a son to inherit. It is as the world was meant to be."

The maid licked her lips, and glanced to the side, as if to assure herself they were alone. "Well, as to that, miss, there are those who say he did."

"Really." Blythe's voice was frosty. "And yet you say he wasn't married."

"Huh. Things like that don't always matter to the gentry."

"Really."

"Really." The maid drew herself up, apparently offended, the last reaction Blythe desired. Leonara Higglesby was not, she reflected, a comfortable person. "I am sorry, miss, but why are you asking all these questions?"

"That is what I would like to know," a musical, amused voice came from behind them. Blythe turned to see a woman poised on the staircase, a beautiful woman, with raven-dark hair dressed without powder, and a gown of shimmering lilac silk. Blythe's stomach clenched. Dear heavens, the viscountess.

She froze, and yet one thought remained clear. She must protect Simon. The best way to do that was to stay in character. "My lady." She dropped into a deep curtsy. "You honor me with your presence. Indeed, I did not expect to see such an august personage as yourself today. Hoped—nay, prayed—but knowing the demands you must have on you—"

"Miss Higglesby. Miss Higglesby!"

Belatedly remembering what her name was supposed to be, Blythe looked up. "Yes, my lady?"

"You do prattle on." The viscountess continued down the stairs, her skirts swinging from side to side. Why, she wasn't much taller than Blythe herself. It was her bearing that made her appear tall, something Blythe would have to remember in future. "I hadn't heard that about you."

Her stomach clenched again. "You have heard of me? Oh, indeed, my lady, I am honored indeed—"

"Yes, yes." She snapped her fingers. "You, there."

The maid straightened. "Yes, my lady?"

"Miss—Higglesby and I will be in the morning room. Pray see to it that we're not disturbed."

The maid curtsied. "Yes, my lady."

"In here, Miss Higglesby." The viscountess swept along ahead, past a bowing footman who opened a door off the hall. They entered a sunlit room, with the windows opening onto the vista of fields and sea and sky. Within, all spoke of quiet, gracious comfort and a long heritage: the pleasantly faded carpet; the soft table, highly polished, but dark with age; even the pair of dueling swords, hanging crossed over the mantelpiece. "Pray be seated."

"Thank you, my lady." Blythe sat down, composing herself, wondering desperately what to say. "I am honored that you deigned to see me today, and all because of the good work the society does—"

"Please." Honoria held up her hand.

"My lady?"

"Spare me that, at least. But would you care, Miss Marden, to tell me why you're really here?"

"I've often wondered what became of you," the Reverend Tulley said after his housekeeper had served them tea and cakes in the study and then departed. "Terrible shame what was done to you, and so I told the old viscount many a time. Not that he would ever listen."

"No," Simon said mechanically, holding the fragile china cup in both hands, as if afraid of dropping it. His mind was awhirl. He had family. He had had a father. He had . . . by God, he had a title! Or should have had. For some reason it had all been taken from him. "Did you know my father?"

"Oh, yes, that I did, that I did. Quite a handful, young Master Geoffrey. You favor him."

"So I've been told."

"And your mother, my son—is she well?"

Simon shook his head and set down the cup untasted. "She died, Reverend, when I was young. My relatives raised me."

"Ah. So that is why you never returned."

"Returned to what?" Simon rose, restless, and began to pace. The study was a good-sized room, but it was dark from the ivy growing over the diamond-paned windows, and so filled with books and papers that it seemed small. Yet everything was clean, and there was a strange sense of order to the various piles. His history, Reverend Tulley had told him—or, rather, the history of southern England that he was writing, particularly in regard to the churches of the area. It was his magnum opus, his life's work, and he fully expected it would still be unfinished when he died. It was all very strange, Simon thought. Taking tea with a country vicar in his home—what else seemed so normal? Yet there was nothing normal about the situation. "I didn't know where to come to, until now."

Reverend Tulley's eyes grew round. "Did you not know who your father was, my son?"

"No. My mother never said."

"Oh dear, oh dear." He shook his head. "That is bad, very bad. To be denied your rightful place . . ."

"Why was I?" Simon interrupted. "Do you know?"

Tulley seemed to consider his answer. "I do," he said after a moment, and looked up, his eyes remarkably sharp. "I fear I don't fare well in the tale, though."

"Why?"

"I let the page in the parish register listing your parents' marriage be destroyed."

Simon sat down, hard. "Why?" he asked, stunned.

"Well." Reverend Tulley made a face. "I was young and, I fear, rather weak. I liked my brandy, you know."

"Oh?" And what had that to say to anything?

"Yes. When I married your parents, I knew there'd be trouble. Your grandfather—a hard man he was, my son, perhaps it is just as well you never knew him—would not be pleased at his son's choice. Not that he ever was." Tulley leaned back, folding his hands. "They never did get along, those two, not from the day Master Geoffrey was born."

"Why not?"

"The viscountess died in childbirth. Very difficult, you see, for the viscount, as it was a love match. He blamed his son. What made matters worse is that they were so much alike."

Simon leaned forward, listening intently. "How?"

"Oh, hardheaded when they had to be, quick thinking, quick to argue, stubborn to the point of being pigheaded. Yet they wanted different things in life. For the old viscount, there was the land. For Master Geoffrey, there was the whole world." He sent Simon a sharp look. "You're like him in that, too, I think, but maybe not elsewise? You strike me as perhaps more subtle than they."

Simon smiled. "I'm an actor."

"Ah. I believe I understand. You've learned other ways of getting what you want. Good. They had some memorable battles, those two." Tulley shook his head. "Worst of all was when your parents married. The old viscount would have none of it, of course. He threatened to cut Master Geoffrey off without a penny. Master Geoffrey said he didn't care, he'd make his own life. We never saw him again here."

"Where did he go?"

"Off someplace with your mother, I don't know where. I do know the old viscount was upset—oh, my, yes, he was. Though he wouldn't admit it. He was angry at his fool son, that was all. Not worried. Not sorry."

"Was he ever sorry?" Simon asked softly.

"I think so, my son. We heard nothing from young Master Geoffrey—"

"Excuse me." Simon held up his hand. "How do you know all this?"

Tulley nodded. "Fair question. Your grandfather and I were by way of being friends. At least, the closest to a friend as he came, and even that went wrong in the end. I told him what he'd done was wrong, but he wouldn't listen." Tulley shook his head. "Then we heard that Master Geoffrey had joined the army."

Simon sat up straight. "What!"

"It was in 1746, my son."

"The year I was born."

"Yes, and the year of Culloden."

The battle that had finally ended all hopes for a Stuart monarchy in England. Simon was beginning to understand. "Oh."

"He fought for the Pretender, I'm afraid, but he did die a hero. He pulled a wounded comrade to safety. You've much to be proud of in your father."

"Mmm." Simon rose and began pacing again. His father, fighting for Bonnie Prince Charlie and dying for a losing cause; his mother, alone and pregnant. "She came back here, didn't she?"

Tulley nodded. "Yes, carrying you, my son. And she went up to the big house." He looked away. "She did not stay. The old viscount cast her out, refused to recognize her, or you. She begged him for your sake, saying you were his heir." He stopped, lifted his shoulders, and then went on. "He said she had no proof and he would not accept you. Grandson or not, his heir was not going to come from a common actress."

"Why did you let him do it?" Simon demanded, wheeling and facing him. "How could you, a man of God, have let him destroy the register?"

Tulley lifted his shoulder again. "Weakness, my son. I liked my brandy in those days, perhaps too much. And the Stantons hold this living."

"I see," Simon said after a moment.

"I would have had no place to go. Oh, I've regretted it bitterly since. I've prayed about it and about you and I've no doubt I'll do my penance for it. Weakness, my son. Just . . . weakness." He looked at his fingers. "But after that day, I never touched another drop, no, not one, and never have I done anything more difficult. But in the end I found my courage again. I realized I'd been most derelict in my duties, one of which was to save the viscount's soul. I never missed a chance after that to remind him about you."

Simon shot him a look. "For all the good that did."

"Oh, I think it did do some good. Toward the end, he would talk about you."

"He would?"

"Yes. He'd mention your age, wonder how you were getting on—he knew you were with a theatrical troupe, and I think that worried him, though he wouldn't admit it."

"My aunt and uncle were as fine a set of parents as anyone could wish," he said sharply.

"No doubt, no doubt. I think, though, at the end your grandfather would have sent for you."

Of all possible outcomes to the story, this was one Simon had not imagined. He stood very still, not breathing. How different his life would have been. "Why didn't he?"

"He died, my son. A sudden apoplexy. It was very fast. The title passed to his cousin."

"The present viscount?"

"No, the present viscount's father. I don't believe he knew of you, my son. Your grandfather kept matters very quiet."

"So the viscount now doesn't know about me."

"No. And I thought it best to leave things be." He looked squarely at Simon. "If I mentioned your existence, there would have been problems over it. I knew you at least had your mother, and she had family. I knew you were taken care of." He paused. "I don't know if I did right or not. But I've thought of you often, my son. Yes, that I have."

Simon nodded, looking out the window onto a garden in dire need of weeding. "You did do the right thing, I think," he said finally.

"How can you say that? I helped take away your birthright."

"You left me with people who loved me. I lacked for nothing, you know." He turned. "Except a father, and my father's name. And if we'd come back here, my mother and me, I wouldn't have been just a bastard. I'd have been Geoffrey Vernon's bastard."

"Harsh words, my son."

"But true. No, I'm not sorry," he said, and as he did so realized he spoke the truth. He didn't regret his upbringing, didn't regret the loss of a title and the power that came with it, tempting though it was. Who would he be, had he become viscount? Not Simon Woodley, but Christopher Vernon. A stranger. Not, however, a man falsely charged with murder.

He frowned and turned. The reverend was a decent man, and apparently unaware of the cloud over Simon's name. With anyone else that would be to the good, but not with this man. Not if Simon wanted the answers to all the questions that plagued him. "There's something I haven't told you about myself," he said.

"Whatever it is, it can't be very serious."

"Oh, but it is," Simon said, and, sitting down, plunged into his tale, telling of his arrest and the subsequent events. Though he tried to keep it short, the telling took some time. He finished by explaining how he had learned of his connection to the Stantons, and the possibility that the viscount was involved in some way.

"His lordship?" Tulley recoiled. "Never!"

Something uncoiled within Simon at the protest, a knot of fear he hadn't known was there. Fear that, for some reason, the family he'd never known wanted rid of him permanently. "You sound quite certain."

"As certain as I can be of any man, yes." Tulley shot him a look. "You've been through a great deal, my son."

"I don't ask you to believe me, but—"

"But I do."

Simon leaned back, his relief complete. It had been a risk to tell his story, but worth it. "Thank you."

"However, I think you are completely wrong in your ideas about Lord Stanton. Completely wrong. He is a good man. There are many around here, and not just his tenants, who owe him a great deal. Not that he sees it that way. He does what he feels he has to do, what is right to do. And honest as the day he was born."

"Well, whoever conceived this plan, if there was a plan, isn't honest. Devious is a better word." Simon stiffened as the old man went still. "You've thought of something, haven't you?"

"In your story, you said you had reason to believe the viscount knew Mr. Miller. Why did you say that?"

Simon frowned. "Actually, the connection is through the viscountess."

"Ah. That explains much."

"What?"

"I did not understand why the viscount would go to a moneylender. But her . . ." His voice was scornful. "That surprises me not at all."

Simon leaned forward. "Why not?"

"She gambles, my son. Excessively. It is a sickness with her, I fear. She is here now, at the hall, but only because the viscount cut off her allowance. Else she'd still be in London. Even here, though, she manages to go through prodigious sums."

"How do you know this?"

"Lord Stanton and I have discussed it a number of times. It is quite a problem to him, as you can imagine."

"Yes." Simon frowned. He had learned a great deal from Tulley, and yet not enough. The rest of the answer was elsewhere. At Moulton Hall.

"Thank you, sir, for your time," Simon said, rising. "I must be on my way."

"Glad I am to see you again." Tulley rested his hand on Simon's shoulder. "Be careful, my son."

"I will be, Reverend."

Outside, Simon mounted his horse and set off for Dover, his head reeling. He had family. He should have a title. And, perhaps someone at Moulton Hall wished him out of the way. He would have to be very careful, indeed.

At the crossroads Simon pulled to the right, to

make way for a rider coming fast along the coast road, in the same direction as he. He wasn't in such a hurry, not with all he had to think about and decide. He nodded absently at the other rider as he galloped past, intent on his own musings. Should he go to Moulton Hall to confront the viscount, or should he choose subtler means?"

"You, there!" a voice called, sharp and clear, and Simon looked up, startled, to see that the other rider had stopped. He was abreast the road, blocking the way, and, with the sun at his back, was an indistinct figure. But there was something familiar about him, about the set of his shoulders, about the way he sat his horse. "Hold up."

Simon pulled to the side again, but not because of this man's order. "Why?"

"Ah." It was a satisfied puff of sound. "As I thought. Simon Woodley, as I live and breathe."

Bloody hell! To be recognized when safety was so near. Simon's horse shied, reflecting his sudden tension. "You must have me confused with someone else."

"Oh, no. I'd know your face anywhere."

The man rode back toward him. Simon turned his horse, and with the sun no longer in his eyes, he could see the man's face. *Bloody hell!* he thought again. It was Quentin Heywood.

Chapter 28

Blythe looked across the morning room at Honoria, sitting straight-backed and composed, as if this were an ordinary social call. Her eyes were alert, interested, her mouth curved in a little smile. Blythe relaxed. Surely this woman couldn't be involved in the events that had complicated Simon's life. "How did you know?" she asked.

Honoria laughed, a brilliant trill of sound. "Oh, my dear, I am not stupid. Although your disguise is clever. I might almost have believed it, if . . ."

"If?"

"If Quentin hadn't recognized you the last time you were here."

Blythe froze. "Quentin? I don't understand."

"Quentin Heywood, my dear. You know quite well who I mean. And a merry chase you've led him." She laughed again. "I was quite, quite angry at first, but he was so upset over his clothes being ruined—it was all quite delicious."

This was madness, Blythe thought. "Then you do know him?"

"Know him?" Honoria reached for a sweetmeat from the silver dish on the table near her. "Would you like a comfit? No? They're quite tasty." She took a bite, closed her eyes, savored it. "Mmm. Yes, you might say I know Quentin. He was my lover."

"Good heavens!"

"Oh, my dear, don't look so shocked! It is a common enough occurrence. And Quentin suited me well."

"It's true, then," Blythe said slowly, trying to fit it

all together. "Mr. Heywood arranged for Simon to be found with Miller's body. And you had a connection with Miller."

"Very good! You're very bright, my dear. But you're not quite there yet. Do go on."

"I can't," Blythe said. "I know that Mr. Heywood has been chasing Simon, and I know he's connected with you, but . . ." She licked lips gone suddenly dry. "Did you have something to do with Miller's death?"

Honoria reached for another sweetmeat. "Not something, my dear. Everything."

"Good heavens!" Blythe stared at her, this attractive, yet ordinary woman, calmly confessing to evil. A few moments ago she had dismissed her suspicions of the viscountess; now they were being confirmed. Masks, she thought. Everyone wore a mask. Which could work to her advantage. She was an actress, was she not? The only problem was, there was no script for her role. She would have to be very, very careful.

Honoria was eyeing her coolly. "You don't appear very shocked," she commented.

"I don't believe I am," Blythe said, finding her role. Of course she was shocked. Somehow, though, it was imperative to hide it. "Now that you say it, I see the clues were there. What I don't understand"—she leaned back, trying to match the other woman's poise—"is why. And how."

Honoria laughed. "The how is simple. I used the proper tool."

"The knife?"

"Really, my dear, do I look that foolish? No. Quentin, of course. He was quite besotted with me at the time, although . . ." Her face darkened. "But that is all by the by. Quentin arranged everything. He learned everything he could about your actor friend, set an appointment with Miller, and then . . ." Her shrug was eloquent. "I believe you know what happened next. All Quentin's doing, and if he dares say otherwise, why, he has no proof, has he?"

But why? And why involve Simon? "Wasn't it a

complicated way to get rid of someone who had lent you money?"

Honoria stared at her. "You don't see it, do you?"

"See what?"

"One day, when I was first married, and my husband, the tedious man, insisted I stay here with him rather than go to London"—she made a face—"I decided to try reading a book to pass the time. And what did I find in it but the Honorable Geoffrey Vernon's marriage lines."

"The Honorable—"

"I destroyed them, of course, and for years didn't think a thing about it. And then, at a play, I saw your actor fellow."

A chill went down Blythe's spine. She knew. "Simon is his son."

"Exactly! I knew I wasn't wrong about you. Very bright, indeed."

Strange woman, this, applauding Blythe's reasoning, as if in pride. "But what has Simon ever done to you?"

"It's not what he's done. 'Tis what he could do. He could take all this"—she waved her hand about the room—"away from us. From me." She glared at Blythe. "My father was a baronet, a weak man, he gambled everything he owned away. We lived hand to mouth, my mother and I, and all I had for a dowry was myself. I was lucky that Stanton married me. But he, the fool, would let your actor friend take it away."

"Are you saying that Simon is legitimate?"

"Of course he is. He should, by rights, be Viscount Stanton."

The last piece fell into place. "And you wanted to stop him."

Honoria inclined her head. "Very good."

Very good? A man had died; Simon had been wrongfully imprisoned; and her own life had been disrupted. Madness. To her own surprise, Blythe began to laugh. "Oh, my lady," she gasped. "Oh, how wrong you are!"

"Simon didn't know. Didn't you realize that? He

didn't know. Oh, my." She took a deep breath, let the laughter come again. Hysteria, she thought with detachment. Dangerous, and yet perhaps it was something she could use. "All that effort, all that danger, and he didn't know!"

"Stop it!" Honoria jumped to her feet, her hands balled into fists. "Stop that laughter at once!"

"I'm sorry." Blythe wiped her streaming eyes. " 'Tis just so funny. All that you did to prevent him finding out, and now he will."

"Oh?" Honoria, standing by the mantel, raised her chin. "And how will he?"

"Really, my dear." Blythe mimicked Honoria's tones as she rose, shoulders back, head high, staying in character. "I shall tell him, of course."

Honoria calmly reached up and pulled down one of the swords that hung on the wall. "No. You won't."

Blythe froze, staring at the sword. Danger, danger. Of course Honoria couldn't let her go, she could see that now. But surely she wouldn't harm Blythe, not here in her own home? "You won't use that," she said, surprised at her calmness.

"But I will. I'm quite good, you know." Honoria flashed the sword several times, enough for Blythe to realize that she did, indeed, know how to handle the weapon. "Really, my dear, did you think I'd let you go?"

"You have to," a masculine voice said, startling them both. Blythe looked over to see that a door she hadn't previously noticed, presumably connecting to the next room, was open, and that a man stood there. The viscount. "Because I won't let you go on with this any longer."

Simon's first impulse was to dig his heels into his horse and set them both flying along the road. He didn't. It would do no good. His horse was an old nag, while Quentin's, though lathered, was obviously of good quality. There would be no escape. "Mr. Heywood, at last," he said coolly, marshaling all his actor's resources. They were all he had for defense.

Quentin inclined his head. "Strange that we meet this way, after the past weeks."

"Strange, indeed." Simon straightened. "What do you do now, Heywood? You've no soldiers behind you."

Quentin gazed at him consideringly. "Do not underestimate me, dear boy. Perhaps I carry a pistol. Perhaps I'll use it and win acclaim for capturing an accused murderer."

"I'll not give up easily."

"Or perhaps I shall go to Dover." He glanced along the road. "Yes. I believe that is what I'll do."

"And do you expect me to come with you?" Simon asked incredulously. "Just like that?"

"You? No." Quentin leaned on the pommel, watching Simon. "Your fate is no longer my concern."

Simon's fingers bit into the reins, and his horse danced a bit in response. "I beg your pardon?"

"I'm getting out. I bear you no ill will, you know," Quentin went on. "I have no personal grudge against you."

"Not personal? When you set me up to be accused of a murder I didn't commit? When you have chased me across half of England? It is very personal to me, sir."

"I suppose it is." He pursed his lips and then nodded. "Ah, well. It's all by the by now."

Rage was building within Simon. "By the by?"

"Oh, yes. Did you not understand me? I'm leaving."

"Leaving?"

"Leaving the country."

"Why?"

"Why?" His laugh was mirthless. "Because if you're not retaken, I'll be charged with the murder. And I've grown rather fond of my neck."

"Who would charge you?" Simon demanded, determined to find the answers to the questions that plagued him. "Who?"

"You don't know yet? No, I can see that you don't. Strange." Quentin leaned back, smiling, and took up the reins. "If you will excuse me—"

"Why is it strange?" Good God, the man wasn't just going to ride away, was he?

"I saw your companion, Miss Marden, at Moulton Hall."

"Oh. That." Simon relaxed a bit. "I know."

"Do you? Oh, no, dear boy, I'm not speaking of yesterday, but of today."

"What?"

"I had a bit of business in this part of the world, and I rode past the hall," he mused, glancing away over the Channel. "I could swear 'twas Miss Marden in an old cart with—who would the old man be?"

"Bloody hell." Simon bit off the words. "I thought she was safe in Dover."

"Well, she isn't, dear boy. Not that it matters to me." Quentin turned his horse. *"Au revoir,"* he said, and began galloping again, toward Dover.

"Bloody hell! Wait!" Simon yelled, standing up in the saddle. Chasing the man would be futile, just as trying to escape would have been. But this was bizarre. He had encountered his enemy—one of his enemies—and yet still he was free.

Frowning, he glared at the dust kicked up by Quentin's horse and then glanced along the road, where Quentin had indicated Moulton Hall was located. It had to be a trap. Did they really think, after dodging all of Quentin's attempts to capture him, that he would ride tamely up to Moulton Hall and let himself be taken? The answers were there, though, he thought, turning his horse. The answers, and Blythe, and that one fact made him uneasy. Because if the viscountess was behind all the events that had changed his life, Blythe might be in danger.

"Bloody hell," he muttered, and slapped the reins. Risk of capture or not, he was going to Moulton Hall.

Tension and silence hung heavy in the morning room at Moulton Hall. The three people within stood transfixed, in tableau. Then Honoria laughed, breaking the spell. "You?" She looked contemptuously at her husband. "Are you going to stop me?"

"If I have to, I—" He stopped abruptly a few paces from the door as Honoria brandished the sword, not at him, but at Blythe. "Honoria," he said quietly. "Put down the sword."

Her smile was almost sweet. "I don't think so."

"I heard everything, you know." He advanced another pace into the room. "I know what you did."

Honoria tossed her hair. "But you won't say a word, will you? Not if it means ruining the precious Stanton name."

"How little you know me." He shook his head, looking past her to Blythe. "Go, while you can."

"Stay!" Honoria ordered immediately, brandishing the sword again.

"Oh, for heaven's sake," Blythe muttered, sitting down abruptly and pulling off her gloves. "If we're to have a fight, at least let's make it a fair one."

Honoria glanced back at the mantel and then turned, smiling. "You wish to have the other sword?"

Blythe had removed her shawl and hat and was reaching down to unfasten her shoes. "Actually, yes."

"Really, miss—who are you?" the viscount asked.

"Blythe Marden. We met once before, my lord," she said, reaching under her skirt to untie her garters and then roll down her stockings. "Though I doubt you remember." For she had been playing a role then, much as she was now. Or was she? The coolness, the confidence she felt weren't completely feigned. She was fighting for all she had come to hold dear. She was fighting for Simon. "Shall we?"

"What?" Honoria stared at her incredulously. "You really wish to duel?"

Blythe rose. She would have liked to roll back her cuffs, but knew they wouldn't stay; she didn't need the distraction in the coming fight. "Yes."

"Ridiculous!"

"Are you afraid?" she asked, using the one taunt that might work.

"Afraid? Of you? Certainly not." Honoria tossed her hair again and then reached up to pull the other sword from the wall, throwing it hilt first across the room. Blythe caught it just before it fell to the floor. "I am classically trained." Honoria held her sword above her head, with her skirts bunched in her hand. She was wearing high-heeled slippers, Blythe noted. Overconfidence, or a simple mistake? "Are you?"

Blythe waved the sword experimentally, testing its weight and flexibility. Stiffer than she was used to, and heavier, but she would manage. She would have to. "No. But it doesn't matter." Gathering her skirts, she raised her sword and stared coolly at the viscountess. *"En garde."*

Simon galloped the last few feet of the drive to Moulton Hall, noting not at all the fine view, the verdant fields, the lush gardens. The portico, so carefully molded by the builder after one in Rome, was merely a convenient place for him to dismount. He cast an eye at the ramshackle farm cart standing near the shallow front stairs; something familiar about that. No groom ran to take his horse; no one appeared to challenge him. Even more oddly, the door was open. Simon began to walk in and then stopped, struck suddenly by the enormity of what he was doing, of what he had lost. This fine house could have been, should have been, his.

Inside, the hall was empty, but he could hear a murmuring of voices to his right, and the sound of metal on metal. Puzzled, expecting at any moment to be questioned, Simon walked toward the sound. He came up short when, after passing under an archway, he saw a collection of people, footmen and maids and the like, grouped around a doorway and gazing into the room. Again there was the sound of metal, and then a woman's voice, imperious, commanding. Someone replied, a voice he knew very well. Bloody hell. "Blythe!"

One of the men in the small knot of people—the butler, by his dress—turned to look at him, frowning, and then took a second look "My lord!" he exclaimed.

"What is happening?" Simon asked tersely, as if he'd the right.

The man gave ground before him. "I—I—my lord!"

"So you said. Oh, bloody—oh, dash it." For he could see into the room now, and the sight was not heartening: Blythe, facing another woman, both with swords drawn. What was she doing?

"Careful!" a man across the room called, as the other woman lunged forward in a flurry of strokes, which Blythe seemed barely to parry. "Those were my grandfather's swords."

The other woman ignored him, but Blythe smiled. "He chose well, sir," she called. "They're well balanced—oh, no, you don't!" Blythe danced backward, away from the sword weaving toward her. The other woman had the advantage of height and reach, but, as Simon remembered, Blythe was light on her feet. He prayed it would be enough.

"Oh, yes, I do," the woman retorted, and lunged, the point of her sword catching Blythe's upper arm and leaving a long, jagged tear in her sleeve. "First blood."

"Oh, lord, Blythe," Simon groaned, and one of the maids looked up at him. As the butler had, she, too, looked again, and nudged the maid next to her, both of them turning to stare at him. Simon ignored them.

Blythe suddenly darted forward, and her blade clashed with the other. For a moment the two women struggled, sword to sword, and then the other woman broke free, spinning about, as Blythe had during her mock battle with him. She came back with the sword held in two hands, poised to strike, her breath coming hard, and once again Blythe had to dance away.

By now, all the servants who had been watching the duel were staring at Simon. He couldn't imagine why. "Who is the other woman?" he asked.

The maids looked at each other. "The one in black? We don't know," a maid said finally, timidly. "She's a missionary of some sort. Sir, are you—"

"Not her," Simon said impatiently. "The other one."

There was silence for a moment. "The viscountess,

sir," the maid said, staring at him, and at that moment there was a crash of glass shattering inside the room.

"My Venetian crystal!" the man standing across the room howled. "Honoria, do have a care!"

"Do you know," the viscountess ground out, all the time pressing Blythe back in a volley of motion nearer and nearer to the wall, "how tired I am of hearing about your Venetian crystal and your grand tour and any of the other things you prose on about? Ha! Got you now."

"No, you don't," Blythe said, and scrambled sideways onto the gold satin sofa. She stumbled, making the spectators gasp, but then righted herself, bouncing easily on the soft cushions, sword held in both hands. Sweat streamed down her face and stained her gown; there was also a darker, more ominous stain at the rip in her sleeve. Terrified though he was for her, Simon thought he'd never seen her look more magnificent.

Honoria laughed, a short, angry sound. "You don't look any too steady," she sneered, circling about with her sword held ready. "Be careful you don't fall."

"Be careful of yourself," Blythe snapped.

"Oh, I will, my dear, I will." And with that, she, too, clambered onto the sofa, hampered by her shoes and full skirts, but bringing her weapon within close reach of Blythe. Both women stood still, swords at the ready, measuring each other. Then, with only a quick glance to the side to betray her intent, Honoria climbed again, first to the arm of the sofa and then to the table behind it, as easily as climbing stairs. She had regained the advantage of height, and in addition was on a steadier surface. Blythe backed away, waved an arm for balance, and regained her footing. She looked, Simon thought, a little shaken.

"Have a care, Honoria!" the viscount called. "That table is Elizabethan!"

"And I've always hated it," Honoria retorted, and, quite deliberately, lowered the point of her sword to scratch an X in the polished oak.

"Can't he stop this?" Simon asked the butler, indicating the viscount with a jerk of his chin.

"There's no stopping her ladyship when she wants something," the butler said dolefully. "I hope your friend can handle herself."

"I hope so, too." Simon's face was taut with tension. Neither of the women had moved, but instead stood facing each other on their precarious perches, eyes locked, breath rasping. Blythe was in trouble. He had to do something.

Blythe chose that moment to lunge forward, an attack that Honoria parried easily, and that left Blythe fighting for balance again. As if time had slowed down, Simon saw it all happen in excruciating detail: saw Blythe's arms flailing; heard the viscountess's hiss of triumph; watched as Honoria pressed forward, the tip of her sword aimed directly at Blythe's heart; and held his breath as Blythe, in a movement of unexpected strength and grace, brought her sword back up in defense and deflected the blow, pushing Honoria back.

This time it was the viscountess who fought for balance, the unyielding polished oak not as forgiving as the upholstered sofa cushions were. Her arms windmilled, her feet shifted, and suddenly her foot shot out from under her. With a shriek she toppled off the table and hit the floor hard, her sword beneath her. And then there was only silence.

Lord Stanton broke through the shock first, rushing across the room to his wife. Over his head Blythe looked at Simon, the first indication she'd given that she knew he was there. Her face was so pale, her eyes so wide and stricken, that he acted from instinct. Breaking free from the group of stunned, murmuring spectators, he rushed across the room to the sofa where Blythe still perched, hand to her mouth. From the corner of his eye he could see something dark and wet seeping out from under the viscountess, who lay very still. *Bloody hell.*

"Is she hurt?" Blythe demanded, voice high and thin. "Is she—"

"I don't know, princess." Simon caught her about

her waist and swung her to the floor, and she clutched at his shoulders.

"I didn't want to hurt anyone," she went on, still in that thin voice. "I just wanted to get free—"

"Honoria!" the viscount's voice broke in. Simon, his hand holding Blythe's head against his chest, looked quickly down. Lord Stanton had turned his wife over. Her eyes were closed, her face pale. The sword sprang upward, swinging back and forth as on a pivot. Its point was embedded in the viscountess's breast.

Simon swallowed hard. "Princess . . ."

"Honoria. Oh, God," the viscount said.

Again Simon looked down, catching the other man's gaze. Brown eyes, much like his own, he noticed detachedly, but the hair was darker. "Is she . . ."

"She's dead," Lord Stanton said, dazed. "She's dead."

Chapter 29

Simon sat on a sofa in another room of the big house—the viscount's study, judging from the huge leather-topped desk and the tall bookcases—holding Blythe close against him. From the hallway outside they could hear muffled sounds—voices, quiet footsteps, a thump of something hitting the paneling. Blythe flinched, and Simon tightened his grip on her. The viscountess was dead, and Quentin Heywood was leaving the country. The people who had so completely disrupted his life were gone. He was free now, free to claim Moulton Hall and all that came with it as his. And yet, all he really wanted was what he held in his arms.

The door opened and the viscount walked in, looking older than he had just a little while ago. Simon asked a question with his eyes; the viscount nodded. "She's gone," he said, crossing the room to splash an amber fluid from a heavy crystal decanter into an equally heavy tumbler. This could be his, Simon thought again.

"I'm sorry." Blythe sat up, brushing at her face and leaving streaks of drying tears. "I really am. I never meant—"

"I know that." Shaking his head, Lord Stanton dropped heavily into a leather wing chair. "What a mess."

Odd way to put it, Simon thought. "Will there be an inquiry?"

"There'll have to be. The way she died . . ." He grimaced, leaving the sentence unfinished. "But I have the highest rank in the neighborhood. Whatever I say will be the end of it."

"I was defending myself," Blythe began.

"I know that." Stanton seemed to see her for the first time. "My apologies to you, for having to go through it."

Blythe shook her head. "I never meant it to end so."

"I know."

"Believe me, sir I'm terribly sorry for your loss."

"Thank you." He leaned his head back, the bones of his face standing out stark and gaunt. "It wasn't a happy marriage. Still . . ." He gazed across the room and then straightened. "I knew she was plotting something. She usually was, but this was different, her and Heywood—"

"You knew about him?" Simon interrupted.

"Oh, yes." Stanton's smile was bitter. "I am not nearly the fool my wife thinks—thought—me. Of course I knew, and about her other men. And the gambling was a problem from the beginning. But never did I think she'd . . . I heard the whole thing."

"Everything?" Blythe said.

"Yes. Everything."

"How?" Simon asked quietly.

"This room connects to the morning room, which she very rarely used, by the by. When I heard her voice I knew there was a reason. So I eavesdropped." He grimaced. "Not a very honorable thing, I admit, but 'tis what I've been reduced to."

"Sometimes life forces us to make choices we wouldn't otherwise make," Blythe said softly.

"I know." Stanton looked at Simon. "Do you know who you are?"

Simon nodded. "Yes. Christopher Vernon."

Blythe looked up. "Christopher?"

"Yes. And my cousin," Stanton said. "The rightful viscount."

"There's no proof," Simon said. "My mother never had her marriage lines."

"It matters not. We both know the truth, and that is enough for me."

Simon nodded again, aware of Blythe staring up at him, aware of the man across the room, who had already lost so much and was prepared to lose more.

All this, Simon thought, a quick glance taking in the ormolu clock on the marble mantel, the mahogany desk, the fine Oriental carpet—all this could be his. "You would give all this up?"

"I would have to." Stanton leaned forward, hands clasped, in his intentness looking somehow familiar to Simon, like someone he knew. Like himself. "It isn't mine."

Simon pursed his lips. Money, the fine estate, the power that came with the title—all was his for the taking. For a brief moment he imagined himself in the role, Lord Stanton of Moulton Hall, and then the image faded. A role was all it would be. "It is, if I give it to you."

Beside him Blythe stiffened in surprise, and Stanton straightened. "What?"

"If this is mine, then I can give it as I wish."

"Moulton Hall?" Stanton said, sounding dazed.

"No. The estate, the title—everything."

"Good God, man, you can't just give up a title! It isn't done."

"Why not?" Simon regarded him. "No one knows who I am."

"I know. Do you think I want to cheat you?"

"But you're not, you know. What do I know about being a viscount?"

"You'd learn."

"Mayhap. And mayhap I wouldn't." Simon, too, leaned forward, releasing Blythe. "I know nothing of farming, of running an estate. Of speaking in Parliament. Of getting along in society." He counted them off on his fingers. "By all I've heard, you're a good man, well liked. You've been raised to this life. I haven't."

"You are Christopher Vernon! The rightful viscount."

"I am Simon Woodley." He spoke quietly at first, his voice gaining strength and conviction. "Simon Woodley, an actor, by God, and glad of it! Christopher Vernon never really existed."

"My God." Stanton was staring at him. "You're serious."

"Yes."

"My God." He sat back, looking dazed. "But what of your family?"

"My family is the Woodley family, and as fine a one as a man could have. As for the rest . . ." His face softened. "I've learned my father didn't abandon me, that he loved my mother enough to marry her. I've learned I'm not a bastard. 'Tis enough."

Stanton was frowning. "You are a very strange man."

"Of course." Simon laughed. "I'm an actor."

Stanton rubbed a hand over his face. "Well. This is a fine mess. If you will not take the title, sir, then who will?"

"Why not you?"

"It isn't mine. Miss Marden, can you not do something to help?"

Blythe, who had been quietly listening, looked up. "Your wife said you are an honorable man."

He grimaced. "Perhaps the only good thing she ever did say about me."

"She was right." Extricating herself from Simon's arms, she stood. "I'm certain you'll do the honorable thing now. If you'll excuse me, I think I'll see how Joseph's doing."

The men rose, Simon resisting the urge to pull her back into his arms. So precious she was to him, and so lost, now that the adventure that had kept them together was over. "I won't be long," he said.

"It matters not." Smiling, she whisked herself out the door.

"If you can do anything," Simon said to Stanton, staring at the closed door, "then restore that woman's good name."

"What of your own?" Stanton asked, sitting down.

Simon shrugged. "As I said, I'm an actor. My reputation matters little."

Stanton leaned forward. "What has happened here today is shocking enough, but I'll not let that stop me from doing what's right. I'll see to it your name is cleared."

Simon's eyes closed briefly. It was really over, then. "Thank you."

"As for Miss Marden . . ." He frowned. "Unfortunately, people will be harder on her than you."

"I know."

"There is something you can do about that."

Simon looked again at the door, and shook his head. "No. There isn't."

McNally had gone through his own ordeal, having been tackled by a groom not long after Blythe had gone inside, presumably to keep him from aiding her in any way. The viscountess had been thorough, Blythe thought, after looking in on Joseph, now resting in the kitchen and regaling the staff with tales of his theatrical career. She then rambled outside. Not thorough enough, though, or perhaps overconfident. With a shudder she remembered the moment when Honoria's heel had slipped out from under her. It was an image that would stay with Blythe forever.

Outside, the sky was as blue as it had been earlier—could it have been only a few hours ago?—the sea as restless, the sun as bright. She blinked, not quite able to reconcile this peaceful scene with all that had happened. It was over. No longer was she on the run, helping an escaped fugitive hide from the law. Her life was again hers to do with as she wished. She wasn't sorry that Simon would be proven innocent, of course not. In a strange way, though, she wished the entire adventure were beginning again.

A footfall made her glance around toward the house, to see Simon striding toward her. Silhouetted against the building behind him he looked strong, confident, in control, a man who had found his place in the world. "Is McNally all right?" he asked as he reached her.

"Yes. Just a bump on the head." They began strolling together, the space between them almost tangible. "All this is yours."

"Good God. Isn't that amazing?"

"Yes." She turned to him. "Simon, you're a viscount."

He shook his head. "I'm not taking the title, Blythe."

"But how can you refuse?"

"It's not who I am." He held out a hand and then pulled it back, that gap still unbridgeable. "Look at me, Blythe! What do I know about being a viscount?"

"I imagine you'd do well enough in Parliament."

"Mayhap, but as for the rest of it? I can't do it. And I won't."

He began walking again, and she joined him. "So what happens now?"

"I've convinced him to keep the title, I think. It's havey-cavey, but since there's no proof of who I am, there should be no trouble. He's not happy about it."

"He's a decent man."

"Aye, that he is. Finally I said I'd hire him as steward." He grinned. "Funny, for all his honor, I think that's when he realized what he was giving up. I told him I couldn't do the job he had, and to think of all the people who would suffer. That did it, I think."

"Then nothing's changed for you."

"I have my name back. That matters. The charges against me will be dropped. And there'll be money."

She looked up, startled. "There will?"

"Aye. Stanton offered to practically beggar himself, but I think we'll reach a fair agreement. Harry and Bess will be taken care of, too. And," he added softly, "my son."

"Of course." She nodded, still reeling from the day's events. "You can give them what you choose."

"They'll have to manage without me, I fear."

"Why? Where will you be?"

He gazed out to sea. "In America."

Her breath drew in sharply. "What?"

" 'Tis something I've thought of for a long time, and now . . . I don't feel comfortable here any longer, Blythe." The wave of his hand seemed to encompass all England. "There'll always be doubt in people's minds about my innocence, no matter what Stanton does. I don't want to live like that. I can't stay."

"But you just found your family!"

"No. I learned I have family. I had a father, and he didn't renounce me. 'Tis enough. And"—he took a deep breath—"my son has a family to care for him. Yes. I think I'll go to the colonies."

"Oh."

"What will you do?"

Blythe's fists tightened. "I shall go home, I suppose."

"Stanton will clear your name, too."

"Kind of him." She spoke in a monotone, staring fiercely out to sea with her eyes open wide, to hold back the tears, to face the truth. Simon didn't want her.

"You'll have a place to go now. It will be as if all this never happened."

Could he really be so blind? "Yes."

"And I'll feel better, knowing you're taken care of."

It was too much. "Oh, you would!" she exclaimed, and shoved at his chest.

It caught him off guard, so that he fell back, sitting with legs splayed before him and hands braced in support, staring up at her in stunned surprise. "What did you do that for?"

"I hate you, Simon Woodley," she said, and flounced away, half running toward the house.

Simon caught up with her with a few long strides, grabbing her upper arm and swinging her around to face him. She found herself against his chest, gazing angrily up at him through the tears that she did not want to shed. He didn't deserve them. "Blythe." He rubbed her cheekbone with his thumb, wiping away the lone tear that had fallen. "Tears? Why, princess?"

"Why? Oh, you stupid, imbecilic—man!"

"Wait." His hand, still on her arm, held her, as she would have run again. "What have I done to deserve this, Blythe?"

She stared up at him. "What have you done!"

"Yes. What have I done to make you so angry? I want only what's best for you."

"Oh, do you."

"Yes, of course."

"And you think the best thing is to send me to live in some village where no one will ever let me forget that I once consorted with an escaped convict, never mind it wasn't my choice, never mind you're innocent?"

"Memories fade, Blythe."

"These won't. Do you think it's best that I never take the stage again?"

"I didn't think you'd want to."

"Well, you're wrong. And, do you think"—she took a great, deep breath—"that what's best for me means being apart from you?"

He stared at her. "What kind of life could I give you?"

"The life I want."

"Hell, princess, I've already told you I won't take the title and that I can't stay here—"

"I'm not asking you to!" She rounded on him, hands on hips. "Why can't you take me with you?" she asked, her voice breaking on the last words, to her horror.

He was very still. "I don't want you," he said finally.

It hurt, enough so that she took a step back. And yet, when she looked up at him, she knew. He was an actor. "You lie."

Blythe—"

"Look at me and tell me you don't love me."

He swallowed. "I don't love you."

"Oh, you actor!" she exclaimed, and threw herself at him. Her arms went about his neck, his about her waist, and his mouth settled on hers with satisfying possessiveness. It was she who finally broke the kiss, pressing up against him, glad, so glad, to be in his arms again. "I knew you couldn't say it."

His lips nibbled along her neck. "But I did."

"Ha."

"Blythe." With a deep breath, he held her away from him. "Do you know what you're doing?"

"I think so, yes."

"You'd come with me?"

She stroked his cheek with the back of her fingers. "Is that really so surprising?"

"I never thought—Blythe, think carefully of what you're doing. Think what you're giving up."

"What? A family that would not stand by me in trouble? Work that suffocates me? I was dying,

Simon." She threw out her arms. "I didn't know it, but until you came along, I was dying."

"Aye. I came along and made a ruin of your life."

"I think that's for me to decide, don't you?"

"Lord! You told me so enough yourself."

"I didn't know any better."

"Blythe, I really believe 'tis best for you to stay here, with people you know."

She gazed at him. How a man could look so hopeful and so despairing all at once, she didn't know. "Only if you can honestly tell me you don't love me."

The silence stretched out. "I can't," he admitted, and held his arms out to her. "Oh, Lord, Blythe. I love you."

She pressed against him, letting the tears she'd earlier held back fall. "I love you. I do! If you make me stay behind, Simon, I will, but I'll never forgive you, never."

"I won't leave you," he said, and caught her lips with his again. It was a very long, very thorough kiss, and when it was over, her lips and body were tingling from his caresses. "But it won't be easy, Blythe. America, from all I've learned, is a savage place."

"What do you plan to do there?"

"Open a theater company, of course. I imagine there's need for them in the cities."

She drew back, taking his hands, and they stretched apart, glorying in the knowledge that they could come back together again as they wished. "That sounds acceptable."

"It won't be easy. We'll have to work to establish ourselves."

"Another adventure, then?"

He looked startled. "You might call it that."

She bridged the distance between them, locking her arms about his neck. "Lay on, MacDuff," she said, and captured his lips again, forever.

Author's Note

When I started this book, I had no idea that Simon was an actor. That was something that he decided himself. Of course, what that meant was that I had to do a good amount of research on topics that were previously unknown to me. It's not the first time this has happened. Because of writing, I now know about 19th century morgues and 18th century prisons, horse breeding and prize fighting, and people's underwear—or the lack thereof. Such are the strange things authors learn.

What this means is that over the years I've had a great deal of help with research. For that reason I'd like to acknowledge the help of Margaret Evans Porter, Barbara Ward, and, as always, the staff of the New Bedford Free Public Library, who never turn a hair when I present them with requests for odd knowledge. I am also grateful to Jennifer Sawyer Fisher, and Meredith Bernstein.

Now I'm on to something I'm familiar with—ships and the sea. In this case, I'm writing about America's whaling history, and two people whose lives are forever changed because they meet each other. This book, with the working title BEYOND THE SEA, will be released by Topaz sometime in 1998.

I'm always glad to hear from my readers, and will answer all letters. Please write to me care of:

New England Chapter/RWA
P.O. Box 1667
Framingham, MA 01701-9998

I'm looking forward to hearing from you!

◆▼ TOPAZ

DANGEROUS DESIRE

☐ **DIAMOND IN THE ROUGH by Suzanne Simmons.** Juliet Jones, New York's richest heiress, could have her pick of suitors. But she was holding out for a treasure of a different kind: a husband who would love her for more than just her money. Lawrence, the eighth Duke of Deakin, needed to wed a wealthy American to save his ancestral estate. Now these two warring opposites are bound together in a marriage of convenience.

(403843—$4.99)

☐ **FALLING STARS by Anita Mills.** In a game of danger and desire where the stakes are shockingly high, the key cards are hidden, and love holds the final startling trump, Kate Winstead must choose between a husband she does not trust and a libertine lord who makes her doubt herself.

(403657—$4.99)

☐ **SWEET AWAKENING by Marjorie Farrell.** Lord Justin Rainsborough dazzled lovely Lady Clare Dysart with his charm and intoxicated her with his passion. Only when she was bound to him in wedlock did she discover his violent side . . . the side of him that led to his violent demise. Lord Giles Whitton, Clare's childhood friend, was the complete opposite of Justin. But it would take a miracle to make her feel anew the sweet heat of desire—a miracle called love.

(404920—$4.99)

Prices slightly higher in Canada

Buy them at your local bookstore or use this convenient coupon for ordering.

PENGUIN USA
P.O. Box 999 — Dept. #17109
Bergenfield, New Jersey 07621

Please send me the books I have checked above.
I am enclosing $_____ (please add $2.00 to cover postage and handling). Send check or money order (no cash or C.O.D.'s) or charge by Mastercard or VISA (with a $15.00 minimum). Prices and numbers are subject to change without notice.

Card #_____ Exp. Date _____
Signature_____
Name_____
Address_____
City _____ State _____ Zip Code _____

For faster service when ordering by credit card call **1-800-253-6476**

Allow a minimum of 4-6 weeks for delivery. This offer is subject to change without notice.

⬥T TOPAZ

Journeys of Passion and Desire

☐ **TOMORROW'S DREAMS by Heather Cullman.** Beautiful singer Penelope Parrish—the darling of the New York stage—never forgot the night her golden life ended. The handsome businessman Seth Tyler, whom she loved beyond all reason, hurled wild accusations at her and walked out of her life. Years later, when Penelope and Seth meet again amid the boisterous uproar of a Denver dance hall, all their repressed passion struggles to break free once more. (406842—$5.50)

☐ **YESTERDAY'S ROSES by Heather Cullman.** Dr. Hallie Gardiner knows something is terribly wrong with the handsome, haunted-looking man in the great San Francisco mansion. The Civil War had wounded Jake "Young Midas" Parrish, just as it had left Serena, his once-beautiful bride, hopelessly lost in her private universe. But when Serena is found mysteriously dead, Hallie finds herself falling in love with Jake who is now a murder suspect. (405749—$4.99)

☐ **LOVE ME TONIGHT by Nan Ryan.** The war had robbed Helen Burke Courtney of her money and her husband. All she had left was her coastal Alabama farm. Captain Kurt Northway of the Union Army might be the answer to her prayers, or a way to get to hell a little faster. She needed a man's help to plant her crops; she didn't know if she could stand to have a damned handsome Yankee do it. (404831—$4.99)

☐ **FIRES OF HEAVEN by Chelley Kitzmiller.** Independence Taylor had not been raised to survive the rigors of the West, but she was determined to mend her relationship with her father—even if it meant journeying across dangerous frontier to the Arizona Territory. But nothing prepared her for the terrifying moment when her wagon train was attacked, and she was carried away from certain death by the mysterious Apache known only as Shatto. (404548—$4.99)

☐ **RAWHIDE AND LACE by Margaret Brownley.** Libby Summerhill couldn't wait to get out of Deadman's Gulch—a lawless mining town filled with gunfights, brawls, and uncivilized mountain men—men like Logan St. John. He knew his town was no place for a woman and the sooner LIbby and her precious baby left for Boston, the better. But how could he bare to lose this spirited woman who melted his heart of stone forever? (404610—$4.99)

*Prices slightly higher in Canada

Buy them at your local bookstore or use this convenient coupon for ordering.

PENGUIN USA
P.O. Box 999 — Dept. #17109
Bergenfield, New Jersey 07621

Please send me the books I have checked above.
I am enclosing $_____ (please add $2.00 to cover postage and handling). Send check or money order (no cash or C.O.D.'s) or charge by Mastercard or VISA (with a $15.00 minimum). Prices and numbers are subject to change without notice.

Card # _____ Exp. Date _____
Signature_____
Name_____
Address_____
City _____ State _____ Zip Code _____

For faster service when ordering by credit card call **1-800-253-6476**

Allow a minimum of 4-6 weeks for delivery. This offer is subject to change without notice.

ROMANTIC TIMES MAGAZINE
*the magazine for romance novels
...and the women who read them!*

♥ **EACH MONTHLY ISSUE**
features over 120
Reviews & Ratings,
saving you time and
money when browsing at
the bookstores!

ALSO INCLUDES...
♥ Fun Readers Section
♥ Author Profiles
♥ News & Gossip

PLUS...

Also Available in
Bookstores & Newsstands!

♥ Interviews with the **Hottest Hunk Cover Models** in
romance like Fabio, Michael O'Hearn, & many more!

♥ **Order a SAMPLE COPY Now!** ♥
COST: $2.00 (includes postage & handling)
CALL 1-800-989-8816*
*800 Number for credit card orders only
Visa • MC • AMEX • Discover Accepted!

♥ **BY MAIL:** Make check payable to: **Romantic Times
Magazine**, 55 Bergen Street, Brooklyn, NY 11201
♥ **PHONE:** 718-237-1097   ♥ **FAX:** 718-624-4231

♥ **E-MAIL:** RTmag1@aol.com

VISIT OUR WEBSITE: http://www.rt-online.com